Can't Leave Him Alone

A Novel

MickiMichelle

Moqa Books

This book contains adult content and is not intended for readers under the age of 18 years old.

Moqa Books
www.mickimichelle.com
Moqa Books
P. O. Box 352
Amite, Louisiana 70422

Can't Leave Him Alone

Book Cover by Perry Bennett of Vivid Images, Baton Rouge, Louisiana

Printed in the United States of America

ISBN: 978-0-9828746-0-8

Book formatted by Rukyyah for Erotic Ink Publishing

Dedication

To the piece of me who left much too soon but whose memories
will forever reign in my heart

My loving sister, Neicee

1

My First Love

*A*rriving home after a three-day business trip, I sat inside my car for a minute trying to figure out what my husband could possibly be up to.

He called not more than ten minutes ago to tell me that he was still at work, working hard as he usually does. I didn't reveal that I was on my way home, as I wanted it to be a surprise. I wasn't due back until tomorrow but I couldn't tolerate being away from my family another day so I cut it short and headed home.

As I pulled into my garage, I noticed that Todd's truck was parked in its usual spot. He has never taken up racing cars so I guess it had to be some kind of miracle that allowed him to make it home from downtown in ten minutes.

Maybe the surprise was really for me. I thought.

He always did special things for me. I wouldn't put it past him if he had some type of welcome home celebration planned for us. The three-day separation was just as hard on him as it was on me. So, I'd said all that wasn't done would have to wait. I missed my boo.

I got out of the car in search of my man; strutted up to the kitchen door, turned my key in the lock and slid into the kitchen; kicked off my sandals and left them on the floor.

"Baby, are you here?" I called out to my husband of eight years.

I didn't get a reply so I moved into the family room in search of my sexy chocolate lover.

At this point, I wasn't sure if he somehow knew that I was on my way home and wanted to play a game with me or not. It really would have been easy for him to call my assistant to check my agenda for the day. So I stood for a moment and let my mind whirl around aimlessly. I know I was thinking too hard, but I just couldn't help it. I was excited and just glad to be home.

I came to the conclusion that Todd wanted to play his usual games and I was all for it, so I quietly strolled to every room inside the house. Even tiptoed up the stairs in search of the most handsome man I've every known.

I couldn't find him anywhere in the house, so the thought of getting some 'good welcome home, moan as loud as you'd like while the kids are at school loving' went out the window.

I gave up on thinking about Todd. I guess he'd ridden in to work with his best friend Trent this morning, so to get my mind off him, I moved upstairs to my bedroom, took a warm shower, wrapped in a short white terry robe, and then went back downstairs to catch Oprah and relax. I would have a surprise for him as soon as he walked through the door.

After a few minutes of watching my favorite talk show, it dawned on me that Todd's job allows him to work from home on several project, and that he'd probably said he was working down in his office in the basement.

I got up from the sofa with a big smile and started down to the basement to go get my boo. The basement was the only other place he could be in the house, so he had to be there.

As I reached the basement door, I could hear Anthony Hamilton's voice moving throughout the large room. My favorite love songs played just for me.

Easing the door open to where I could see inside, I whispered in my soft kitten voice that I reserved only for my

man. I smiled as his name slid from my eager tongue. That
name alone placed a grin on my face that stretched wider than
the state of Texas. He was just that special to me.

He'd proven a long time ago to possess traits that no other
man I knew had ever possessed. He was a dynamic man who
was not only good to me but to his children and everyone
around him.

I was ready and willing for the creativity that he had in store
today. I grinned and released my robe to the floor and lightly
took to the steps in search of my sweetheart.

As I gently stepped into the basement, I moved over to the
awful wall that divided the room. "Todd baby." I purred
seductively.

I awaited the sound of his masculinity, but didn't get a reply
so I decided to quietly peek around the wall.

As my head slowly rounded the wall, in my sexy voice, I
began to release his name from my tongue again.

"Todd baby." I called out.

As my eyes focused in on my boo, I immediately felt a tingle
of warmth consume my desperate body. I blinked one good
time, refocused, and saw my life, as I'd known it for so many
years. Instantly, my mind traveled to the loving marriage I
shared with Todd.

Our marriage was storybook. My life was an absolute
fairytale in my eyesight, and my husband's love was all I ever
needed to survive in the world. As the soft music played,
thoughts like these flooded my mind.

In rhythm with the smooth sounds of the music, I could see
the beauty that covered the face that was robbing my husband of
his strength; his sanity. There was a lustful and death defining
grip of passion covering the part of him that I'd grown to love,
worship, and claim as mine for the last eight years. Everyone
dressed in their birthday suits; even me. But I wasn't invited to
their party.

As time seemingly stood still, I listened to the breaking glass of a crushed heart; that being my own. I listened to the love of my life speak words of passion to a woman who was not me. The shock that pierced my soul wouldn't allow me to move a muscle, speak a sound, or cry a tear. So still I stood; weakened by the events that were unfolding. Hurt refused to release my feet, but took hold of my arms. Held my body close.

Astonishment and shock could never describe what I felt. Couldn't force myself to catch a breath. Everything was caught up in one big knot in the middle of my chest. Words had escaped me. Tongue twisted in confusion, mimicking the actions of my head.

Of all the times my girlfriends and I talked about what we'd do at times like these, I couldn't do any of that I'd said. Nothing; absolutely nothing.

Still trying to catch a breath, I felt the anger of an anxiety attack approaching my trembling body. The onset forced me to slowly back up in an attempt to move up the stairs. I needed air. Still not believing what I'd just witnessed.

I made it up the stairs pretty quickly, scooping my robe up off the floor and wrapping it around my shivering body. As soon as I made it into the kitchen, gravity took my body down to bless the hard tile on the kitchen floor.

Breathing heavily, heart beating profusely, I tried my best to breathe normally. Tried calming myself, but the downpour of tears consumed me.

The tears washed away the physical sadness that had overcome my beauty, only to replace it with a show of heart-wrenching agony and pain. I didn't have the ability to calm myself. I quickly lost sight of reality. Had lost sight of life just that fast.

As I lay on my kitchen floor, I couldn't see past the starving whore down in my basement who was feeding off my husband's sugar coated body like her life depended on it.

Though I loved him dearly, I'd never gone to that extent of loving him. And that thought alone sent a wallow of guilt my way. Made me feel less than who I knew I was.

The horrific images continued to vividly dance in my mind. As I tried calming myself, there was nothing I could do to erase those images.

I wanted to scream and tear up something, but I needed to calm down and breathe so my heart rate could slow down.

I took some deep breaths, tried to focus on my two boys. I thought about what their lives would be like without me if I died right on my kitchen floor. That thought gave me another breath of life and told me to pull it together.

As I lay on the floor staring at the ceiling for what seemed like days, but in reality only a few minutes, I tried meditating to regain control of my breathing.

What did I do to deserve this? I asked myself.

I've only been faithful, loving, and by my husband's side every single day since we've been together.

Back in the day before I met Todd I was a little on the wild side, but every since we'd been together, my attitude and ways had changed. I was a good wife and mother.

Why was this happening to me? I quizzed again. *I know I don't deserve this.* I continued telling myself this, in some way trying to convince myself.

Deep down I knew I didn't deserve it. I knew it wasn't my fault. *Or was it? Maybe I shouldn't have left town for so long. Did I have to stay gone three days? Maybe he missed me too much.* I just couldn't think straight.

Then a little voice in my head that sounded like my Aunt Mae began to speak to me. *"You're not the one breaking your marriage vows baby. Get yourself up off of that floor and pull yourself together. You've got to handle this like a woman and crying won't get you anywhere. And besides, this is your house, what the hell are you running from?"*

I wiped my tears with the end of my robe and sat up on the hard tile.

"You're right." I said out loud before I knew it. "He can't do this to me."

I took a few deep breaths in an attempt to regain composure and shake the anxiety. After a few more minutes, I raised up from the floor with strength I didn't realize I could muster and a different perspective.

I found the strength to go upstairs to throw on some old jeans and a T-shirt.

After dressing I came back down to my car, opened the trunk, got my gun, checked the clip, and stuck it in the back waistband of my jeans. I went back inside and headed down the stairs to the basement. For some reason, my little steel friend gave me the confidence I needed to handle the situation.

I walked boldly into Todd's office in the basement. The music was still playing, so my presence again went unheard. Not that anyone was trying to hear anything other than their own sounds of passion.

Besides, Todd was in no hurry. He had all day. He wasn't expecting me back until tomorrow morning. I guess it was my bad for trying to surprise him by arriving today; thought he missed me as much as I missed him.

I still cried though. Couldn't help it. Tears fell but at least I was breathing normally.

I followed the same path as before and strutted boldly around the wall in search of the two fools who obviously didn't value life. But for some odd reason, no one was there.

I looked around to see the door to the bathroom open so I eased over to the bathroom to take a peak in.

His back was to the door. She was seated on the sink with her eyes shut tight. Todd was in front of her giving it to her real good.

Sadly, I watched in awe. But yet the sight was unbelievable and quite disgusting.

He was so busy that he never saw me standing in the open door way. Nor had she opened her eyes to notice me.

Not that I really wanted to, but I watched while my heart continued to crumble into a million pieces. For some reason I couldn't turn away.

After another minute, he began saying that his final destination was near, so I figured it was as good a time as any to speak.

I wiped my face with my shirt, and uttered a simple, "Why?"

What I'd planned to say just wouldn't come out. Emotions had taken over again. My heart was wide open for this man.

He didn't hear me nor did she. His grunts and her moans were too loud. He was in a rage handling his business like he always did.

I felt weak.

It just wasn't a good feeling to watch your husband bang a bitch, let alone in *your* house.

"Why Todd?" I managed to mumble while closing my eyes to hide the shame.

"Oh! I love you!" He yelled out in satisfaction. Still never taking notice to me.

What...did he say love?

"Todd!" I screamed to the top of my lungs. For some reason that got me moving.

He abruptly turned around, took hold of himself, stumbled back, and clumsily knocked her into the sink.

He was so stunned and busted that he didn't know which way to turn. His first thought was to slam the door.

My husband slammed the damn door in my face.

My first instinct was to beat on the door, kick it in, or just shoot straight through it.

I took two deep breaths to calm myself and remove at least the last thought from my mind.

Through the door, I could hear her saying, "I thought you said she was out of town."

Her voice was the only one I could hear.

"I need to get outta here. I need my clothes." She spoke again.

"Todd, open the door." I knocked and yelled.

There was complete silence. No one said a word. Or at least *I* couldn't hear them.

"You're busted, so come on out and face the music." I added.

"What are you gonna do?" I heard her whispering. "I gotta get home to my baby. I don't have time for this."

"Shut up!" He lashed out.

"No, you shut up. You said you was getting a divorce anyway, so what you scared of?"

"Would you just be quiet?" He tried his best at whispering. "I'll handle this."

"Well, we can't stay in here forever. Just let me leave. I can handle my own."

Did she say, handle her own? I thought.

"You're not trying to jump bad in my house are you missy?" I said through the door.

I vaguely heard Todd saying to her, "I told you to shut up!"

I interjected into their little lover's quarrel.

"Todd let her out of the bathroom. And bring your sorry behind on out too. I've already seen everything. This is stupid."

I waited, but no one emerged. So I waited some more.

While trying my best to stop the tears from flowing, I began to get pissed at the whole pitiful situation. The poise and politeness that I possessed was on its way out the window. The profanity that I'd left behind way back in the day wanted to spew out of my trembling mouth. I was trying to refrain and stay within my character but they were getting on my nerves. The whole little scenario was unreal. I still couldn't believe it was happening.

Silence was all I heard.

"You know what?" I said. "Stay in there. I'm gonna call your sisters and tell them what's going on. Put them on speakerphone so they can hear how dumb and no good you are. Then, I'll call the CEO of your company, your supervisor, coworkers, friends, pastor, police, and fire department and tell them you're stuck in the bathroom and I can't get you out. Maybe one of them will come over here to pull you and your ho out of there. I'mma give you three minutes before I start calling."

I sat down in a chair at his desk and turned that darn annoying CD player off. I was prepared to sit and wait until the both of them exited the bathroom.

After about two minutes, I heard, "Go ahead! It's on you."

Guess he didn't care anymore. He was caught, and she was disposable at this point.

I heard the door unlocking.

She came out running to her clothes. Hands over her breasts and front trying to hide herself from me.

"Too late honey, I've seen it all." I smirked.

"Oh God!" Todd yelled.

He was sitting on the toilet with his face buried in his hands.

"That's right boo, you can't lie out of this one." I threw out to him.

Homegirl dressed in about five seconds flat.

Todd slowly emerged from the bathroom. He stood looking at me like a damn fool.

"How am I gonna get home?" She said in a squeaky immature voice turning to Todd.

She looked no more than twenty-one. Couldn't be too much older than that.

Todd looked up at her as if he wanted to spit on her. Then shamefully looked at me.

"How the hell should I know?"

I'm looking at him like, "good answer", because I was about to show him my gun.

She put her hands on her hips. "Oh! It's like that?"

"What you want me to do Jasmine, I can't take you home?"

Jasmine. I thought. *So this ho's name is Jasmine.* Now I know she's young. I wanna whip Jasmine's ass in a million different ways. But I knew it was him I needed to deal with.

So many times women blame only the other woman not even placing blame on the man. It was evident he'd told some lies, like most men do. But somehow I thought my husband was different. This whole scenario was lower than low. Having sex in *my* house. I felt like shooting both of 'em.

"I can't walk all the way across the river." She screamed.

I'd really had enough of her disrespect in my house, so I interjected.

"Look." I calmly said. "You'd better be glad that you're getting out of my house alive. I catch you having sex my husband in *my* house and you stand here and ask him to take you home. Little girl you better hit that door running." I said nonchalantly.

She turned to me. "I'm sorry. I didn't mean to disrespect you. He told me you were out of town or I wouldn'ta never came to your house."

"You shouldn't have come to my home regardless. It really didn't matter if I was out of town or not. Did you not know that he was married?"

"Well, he said yall were getting a divorce."

"Well he lied! And I'm gonna tell you this one last time. I want you out of my house now! I don't care how you get home, but my husband won't be taking you."

She turned her back to me and focused her attention on Todd. "So I guess I gotta leave walking?" She shook her head. "Give me my key Todd." She said with her palm held out.

I moved between them. "Wait a minute, what key?"

"My house key." She said boldly. "Give me my key you lying bastard." She said with much attitude.

Now he's a lying bastard? I thought to myself. *When this silly heffa knew very well that he was married. Guess she figured as long as he was lying to me all was good.*

Todd never said a word. Just looked at her like he could break her neck.

This whole little episode was getting more ridiculous by the second.

He had her house key. Which only meant he had *been* coming and going. Which meant he had *been* screwing her.

She was too bold and I was tired of the both of 'em. This called for me to lay my good character to the side for a second.

"I'll tell you what. Todd, you gotta go too. Take this triflin' ho and go wherever you wanna go with her, but both of you get the hell outta my face! And yall betta do it quick!" I screamed.

My nerves were too bad. I felt the old me resurfacing. And I didn't like that feeling. No tellin' what I might do.

She stepped up and started to explain with that ghetto attitude. I was tired and she just wasn't getting my point. I was trying my best to handle the situation with some sense. Trying to be as rational as possible. I could see myself dragging her all over the floor. But I was trying not to go there.

Nevertheless she continued running her mouth, "I'm not no ho. Todd lied to me. I didn't know you were…"

"It really doesn't matter. Just please be quiet and leave my house." I interjected. "This is between my husband and I. I didn't ask you anything." I said running overheated.

"I'm just saying. He said yall were getting a div…"

Bam.

I quickly cut her short of her next words. I punched her right in the mouth that she wanted to put into overtime. I'd hit her twice before she and I knew it. Hit her so hard that I popped her lip.

Todd never moved.

Lord knows I'd been trying to suppress that. But I had to show her whose house she was in.

"I said shut up! Now get out!" I pointed her toward the stairs.

Poor girl ran up the stairs and out of the basement. Heard the kitchen door slam.

I really felt sorry for her but I didn't have time for that. I turned to look at Todd. "You too playa. What are you waiting for?"

"Krisha, let's just talk."

"Oh! So now you wanna talk? This whole time you had your woman talking for you. She's gone and now you wanna talk? Why couldn't you talk when she was in here? Get out of my face Todd, you disgust me!" I lashed out.

"Krisha, please just let me explain."

"Explain what? I saw everything I need to know. It's nothing you can say to explain that. From now on, you don't have anything left to say to me."

"Krisha! You don't mean that." He begged.

"That was low down. You brought your woman into our home. I'll never forget this, Todd. You can go to hell!" I screamed like crazy.

"I know I'm wrong, but let's talk." He said desperately.

"We don't have anything to talk about. Go with her. You can have her. I don't care anymore."

I was starting to blaze every time he opened his mouth. I had discovered a new Todd Taylor. A liar and a cheater.

"I won't leave you to go with her baby. I don't love her."

"That's what the hell you said! And you left me the first time you touched her, so just go!"

"Just listen please." He begged.

I ignored all his attempts to convince me of his lies.

"I'm gonna count to five, and if you're not dressed and out of my house, I'm gonna try my best to blow your nasty little shit starter clean off your filthy body."

I pulled the gun from the waist of my pants and pointed it toward his most prize possession. When he saw that I meant business, he bolted from the basement pulling his pants on and quickly grabbing his shoes and shirt while running up the stairs.

Soon after, I heard the kitchen door close.

I walked up the stairs from the basement to check my house.

Looking into the garage, his car was gone. Both of them had gone. Don't know where, but away from me was a good thing.

I plopped down on the couch in the living room. Mind swirling about 400 miles per minute.

What just happened here? I asked myself.

After about thirty minutes of staring into the ceiling trying to find the right answers, reality began to set in.

My husband was gone. For the first time in eight years, my baby was gone. And I had just issued him over to his river rat whore.

I locked my door and slowly dragged myself up the stairs to my bedroom. Pulled myself together enough to call my mother to ask if she'd get the boys from aftercare for me. I couldn't see myself driving, and I was pretty sure Todd wouldn't get them after all that had happened here today. He wasn't crazy enough to bring his grimy ass back here so soon.

I needed to submerge myself in a tub of near hot water. I needed to relax. Needed to relieve some of the stress that had welcomed itself into my life.

I started the water in the tub and began to slowly undress in the bathroom taking a good look at myself in the mirror. I didn't like the reflection that was staring back at me. Already I looked as if I'd cried a thousand tears.

I sat on the side of the tub and threw my feet in the water first. Remained there for a while thinking about the direction my life would take without Todd being in it. I had never dreamt of, or planned on going down this road. I had no clue as to how I'd go on without my lifeline.

I slid into the tub and allowed the warm water to surround my body as I sank deeper and deeper, along with my grief.

I heard the phone ringing, but decided to ignore it. I didn't care to speak with anyone at this point. Not even my mother or children. I just wanted to be alone. And, alone I sat.

I lay back in my tub and allowed the tears to take refuge in the water. I daydreamed about our first meeting, our first date, our first kiss, the first time we made love, our wedding day, and the births of our children. All of the important moments in our lives.

I thought about how Todd's presence in my life had changed me and allowed me to be more open to and receptive of the love that was being offered to me. He broke that hard shell I was in and tore down the wall that surrounded my heart. Gave me a new attitude. Made me a different person.

The phone continued to ring interrupting my thoughts. I took a peek at the caller ID on the receiver, and just as I'd thought, it was Todd's cell number. I turned the ringer off on the phone, and sank a little deeper.

My mother agreed to watch my kids for a couple days until I got myself together. I must admit; I was a wreck. I couldn't eat, and when I tried it came right back up. I couldn't think straight. I couldn't sleep. I had no strength. I didn't want to do anything, nor did I want to exist.

Todd's infidelity hit me like a Mack truck slamming into a wall traveling 600 miles per hour. Blindsided me and completely knocked me off my feet. I never saw any of it coming. I can see if I'd suspected something or knew he was a sneaky son-of-a-bitch. But I had no clue. And that hurt like hell.

They say hindsight is 20/20 vision. Thinking back to the unanswered calls to his cell, working late, and youth group meetings. Those were all times when he was probably with her, and if nothing else, that chat session that I'd discovered on his computer a month ago may just tell the tale.

If he had a key to her house, he evidently was visiting quite often. Maybe even paying for it.

I loved and trusted Todd so much until I never thought my husband would cheat on me, especially not in our home. The whole thing is so hard to believe and it was literally making me sick every time I thought about it.

Despite all the hurt he's caused, I long for him. I love him so much. His touches, his kisses, strong arms around me, just his overall presence would do; I just needed to see his face to keep me sane. I want him so much until my head starts to pound every time I think about him and the whole situation. I really feel as if I'm losing my mind.

He has always been my world and my life has always revolved around him. He means so much to me.

I've always considered myself an intelligent, strong, independent woman, but my husband has always been my weakness. He was the first man to ever truly love me and show me love.

Not only that, he's a handsome, successful, and sexy black man that any woman would die to have by her side. And on top of that he's pretty well off financially. So I know women are probably throwing themselves at him for that reason alone. But, I can honestly say I'd never really thought about that. He never gave me a reason to worry or be jealous, always made me feel like I was number one, and has always given me the uttermost respect in and out of public. So I had no reason but to trust him completely. I've always felt honored to have him in my life. And as I've been given time to really think about it, that's most likely the problem. I believe I love Todd Taylor more than I really love myself.

2

Never Keeping Secrets

Though being with Todd is what I really want, I know that I can't deal with him right now. I have refused his calls for four weeks. He's called everyday, all day and night. He's left messages, sent roses and gifts, letters, emails, texts. You name it he's done it; all in an attempt to win my heart and beg for my forgiveness. But all I can hear is him saying how he loved her. Words I thought were only meant for me.

I love him so much, but at the same time, I hate his triflin' ass!

Nevertheless, Mia thought it was high time I got a breath of fresh air. I'd been caged up inside my house crying my eyes out for four whole weeks. Without even trying, I'd lost ten pounds. And that wasn't good. I was already small to begin with.

"Come on girl lets go!" Mia rang.

Mia was my best friend and definitely my rock. I loved her for always being there for me.

She came over to help Carmen, my kids' nanny, with the boys and she also helped me with my business since I'd been out. If it weren't for Mia, Carmen, and my mother, I wouldn't have made it through.

However, she kept insisting that I go out tonight with her. Since the ordeal with Todd, I just didn't possess the energy or enthusiasm to do anything with myself.

But somehow she convinced me that I needed to get out. So after taking a long hot bath, I felt better about going.

Since I couldn't fit most of my clothes anymore, Mia brought me something to wear. She laid out everything for me to dress. I allowed her to do my hair, slipped into the sexy, tight fitting, black strapless dress that she'd brought and put on a pair of cute black sandals with a four-inch heel. As we exited the door of my house, I promised I'd leave my sorrow behind; at least for tonight.

We had a magnificent dinner at Sullivan's, and then decided on going to a mellow R & B lounge tucked away downtown as I didn't want to be around too much hype.

We drank a little and talked a lot, just like old times. Never too much of any one thing.

I must say I was really enjoying my night. For a few hours, I was able to forget all about Todd Taylor.

Mia and I both had been declining advances all night. She was as beautiful as ever. She wore a black dress similar to mine, but with a wide belt that showed her nice and trim waist. She liked her clothes to really complement her body.

She was about 5'9", 130 lbs., a fair complexion, light brown eyes, long black hair that reached just below her shoulder blades, a perfect set of white teeth, a small waist and big behind. People often mistaken her for Melyssa Ford, in which I could agree there was a slight resemblance.

She took pride in choosing the right clothes to show off her perfect shape that seemed to attract a flock of men everywhere she went.

She adored all the attention her body gave her. But her body wasn't what made her who she was. She was very intelligent, hardworking and darn good at what she did for a living.

Mia was a high profile CPA. Her clientele consisted of Louisiana's elite. Mostly pro athletes and business owners. She was always in the company of high profilers. Mia knew everybody and everybody knew her. She had access to every event that took place in the city as well as inside and outside the state. My girl had it going on.

Mia wasn't the only one who could turn a few heads though. I knew I was banging in my black dress also. Mia had done well with the dress selection and it was doing an excellent job at accentuating my curves without revealing my weight loss secret. I could even see the plumpness in my butt through the thin mesh of the tight fitting dress.

We both had nice assets that were devastatingly irresistible to the eyes. I was blessed in the backside department, but I knew Mia definitely had me beat. I wore a perfect supply of breasts, waist, and hips on my small frame. I'd like to say my body was flawless. Like I ordered the packages and put them all together myself.

But, the last few weeks I hadn't looked pretty. I knew I wasn't busted. I've been told I look a lot like that R & B singer's wife that's an actress, Paula Patton. Just a tad bit darker and more exotic; and in a way I guess I kinda do.

It didn't matter because vanity was not my thing. Especially not at the present time. I haven't felt sexy. Didn't feel special. But all the attention I was getting tonight, I must say was flattering. Made me feel alive again. But a man wasn't what I was looking for. I just wanted the one I had.

At this time, being with my husband wasn't an option. Though I didn't have the man I loved, I had my girl who would always be close to my heart.

Mia always looked out for me like she looked out for herself. She was my heart and would offer me hers; had my back at all costs. It had been that way since we were little.

We grew up together, went to college and graduated together, and presently lived only a few minutes away from one another.

During our day we were two forces to be reckoned with though. We were basically good girls and minded our own, but we *did* have to get it in every now and then for those who thought we were push over mama's babies.

The worst thing we did growing up and at the beginning of college was brawl with a few females. We were consistent with the haters fo' sho, but she always had my back and I definitely had hers.

When I fell in love with Todd, my whole outlook on things changed. My focus was totally on loving him. But no matter who goes and comes in my life, Mia will always be my girl. I love that girl like a sister.

After we'd had the best time of our lives, Mia offered me her place for the night. I accepted. Didn't want to go home alone anyway. I was still a little hyped up, so home was not where I wanted to be.

When we reached her condo, we chatted a few minutes and before I knew it, I'd crashed on the sofa. Didn't even realize I'd gone to sleep until the ringing of my cell phone awakened me.

After wiping the sleep from my eyes, I searched for my phone all over the place before realizing it was in my bag. Before I could get the phone out of my nice LV bag that Todd had surprised me with for my birthday, it had stopped ringing and rang two more times already.

When I finally pulled it out, I looked at the caller ID to reveal Todd's cell number.

I hadn't spoken with him since the day he and his ho left my house. I'd packed his clothes and left them outside and asked Mia to tell him where they were. I also had all the locks changed on the house to assure he wouldn't try anything stupid; like gaining entry.

He'd called everyday, but I didn't have anything to say to him, so I never answered his calls. He'd called my mother several times crying about how he missed and loved us, telling her to relay the message. He also apologized to my mother and begged her forgiveness. Told her he wanted to see his kids. So I'd drop them off to her and he would pick them up from there.

I hated getting her involved, but I didn't care to see his sorry behind.

However, considering it all, I decided to answer his call for once to see what he wanted at five o'clock on a Saturday morning.

I jumped right in.

"What do you want Todd?"

"Where are you?" He said in a low tone.

"What?"

The nerve of him to be asking me that.

"Where are you?" He repeated.

"What business is it of yours?"

"I'm still your husband. I care about you."

"I can't believe you."

"Why won't you answer my calls? I just wanna know if you're alright." He said.

"You already know I'm fine."

"I'd like to hear it from you."

"Whatever, look…" I said before he cut me off. He knew I was about to hang up the phone.

"Can I at least come to the house to see my boys? I can't bring them back to where I'm staying. It's kinda crowded there and they don't have room to play."

"You have money. Get a new place. And don't even think about coming to my house."

"Did you forget that it's *my* house too?"

"I'm not in the mood for this."

"Where are you?"

There was that question again. He was really getting on my nerves.

"How do you know I'm not at home?"

"I just know." He replied.

"Are you spying me?" I asked getting furious.

"No. Are you with someone?"

"And if I were?"

Silence. He got extremely quiet.

"Don't do this to me Krisha? I can't take that." He whimpered.

"But I can huh? I'm expected to just take it from you and be fine with it."

"Krisha, I can't live without you. I love you so much. I've been hurting like hell. You don't know how sorry I am." He was talking fast.

"Yes I do." I said sarcastically.

"Baby, what can I do to fix this? Whatever you want, I'll do. But we need to sit down and talk. We need…"

I hung up the phone.

He called two more times. I let my voicemail catch the calls before I turned my phone off completely. Turned over to let sleep take over but the tears beat it to me. Cried myself to sleep.

After a couple hours, I awakened to my eyes lids half stuck together.

I managed to make my way down the hall to the bathroom without running smack dab into the wall.

I grabbed a towel from the closet, bent over the sink then splashed lukewarm water over my face to revive myself and free my eyes from captivity.

I noticed that Mia was still in bed, so I approached her bedroom door and knocked to see if I could come in.

"I'm up boo." She said through the door.

"Thanks for allowing me to stay last night Mia."

"You mean morning right."

"Yeah, morning." I said in light chuckle.

"Krish, come over here. Let's talk." She patted the bed in the spot next to her where she wanted me to sit.

I walked over to her like a child about to be chastised by her mother.

"Sure." I said climbing into her bed.

Mia continued.

"I overheard your conversation with Todd this morning."

"I'm sorry. I was hoping the phone didn't wake you."

"No problem, I understand. It's just that it's been more than a month and you haven't actually talked to him. Maybe you should consider sitting down and having a constructive conversation with him. You deserve some answers. And not only that, your kids deserve much more than they're getting right now."

"I know we need to talk, but Mia you just don't know what I saw and how my heart hurts behind it all. The best way I feel I can handle the situation right now is by avoiding it."

"But you have to find closure to this. Avoiding it is not gonna change anything and it sure as hell won't solve the problem."

"I know you're right."

"Do you still love him Krisha?"

"I don't know what I feel."

"You should know if you love your husband. You've been with him for so long, that should count for something."

"I do love him." I confessed. "But I'm just confused. I hate him for what he's done. All these years, I was completely faithful. I should have listened to Aunt Mae. She always said no matter how good they seem, they all got some shit with 'em."

We shared a laughed.

"Aunt Mae is a mess."

"Yeah she is."

"Just talk to him. I'm not saying take him back, because honestly, I don't know if I would. But, your marriage and family, your future depends on it…Promise me you'll talk to him."

"I guess I'll talk to the bastard…But all I can see is him sexing that girl in our home. I haven't been in that basement since that day. How am I supposed to forget that?"

"I feel ya boo. That was foul, no good, and down right disrespectful. Just give the dog a chance to explain himself."

We laughed.

"Thanks for everything Mia." I hugged my friend and kissed her cheek. "Gotta go."

I left her condo headed for the Jacuzzi tub at my place. I needed a long, hot bath. The tub had become one of my best friends. That's where my release took place.

When I arrived home, I made a dash for my bathroom. Didn't stop until my body was totally submerged in a tub filled with water as hot as I could stand it.

I soaked, thought, dozed and reminisced for a good hour.

As I sat staring at the wall, a great feeling of courage swept over me. I decided that today would be the day I faced my husband. I would demand honesty, learn of his transgressions, open closed doors, and close doors to our past. What was done was done. I couldn't change it now if I wanted to. I had to move on.

After finally exiting the Jacuzzi, I dressed in a lime tank dress and slipper socks. I didn't bother putting on shoes because my intentions were to sprawl out on my couch and finish reading a novel I'd started two days ago.

The boys were still with my mother and I wasn't trying to go get them. So the day was all mine.

But first I needed to put my cell on charge so I wouldn't have to move off the couch for nothing.

I searched around my bedroom for my phone but couldn't seem to put my hands on it. I looked through my purse and all over the house before I realized it was inside my car. So, I bounced out to the garage to go get it.

When I got outside, to my surprise, Todd's car was parked in the driveway. I could see him sitting in the car staring at the house. Now I was thinking that maybe my rushing inside the house to the Jacuzzi and not taking time to close the garage door wasn't such a good idea.

Trying to seem unfazed by his presence, I ignored him and went on to open the door to my car. I was hoping I could get in my car and back inside the house before he would see me.

Even though I'd just decided earlier to face Todd, I'd changed my mind the minute I saw him. The sight of him just pissed me off.

After retrieving my phone, I rose up out of the car and he was in my face. That fast.

"Krish, can I talk to you?" He said dryly.

"I asked you to stay away from me." I said as I moved to walk away.

He halted my stride by gently taking my arm. "I took a chance baby. I just want to talk."

He was gentle with his words.

For a few seconds, I stood and stared him down thinking how much I hated him. But then, as I looked at his handsome, but pitiful face, I saw pain all over it. It hurt me just seeing him like that.

All of his naturally beautiful features were still there, but he was a complete mess. It was obvious that he had neglected shaving a few days, he needed a hair cut something bad, had thrown on anything to wear, looked like his body was stank, and hadn't slept in weeks. I smiled at his appearance.

Good! It's eating him alive! I thought.

"Todd, I've told you, it's not much you can say. It's cut and dry. You had sex with her. I saw you having sex with her and you've messed up your family in the process."

Stepping in closer to me. "Krish, please baby. I can't live without you and my family in my life. I know I'm the stupidest man alive. I messed up big time, I know. I replay the whole thing over and over in my head every night wishing I wouldn't have been so foolish. Hating myself for putting you through this..."

"Wishing you wouldn't have gotten caught." I said cutting him off.

I stepped back to slam my car door close.

"No, baby that's not what I'm saying."

"Todd, tell me something. If I hadn't walked in on you, would you still be with her?"

"No." He looked down at his feet.

"You're so full of it! Can't even look at me and answer that." I spat. "I would have never in a million years believed that you would have done something like that." I said walking away from him.

"Krish, I can't stop saying I'm sorry." He threw out.

"Then save it, please."

"Please baby. I can't stay with Trent much longer. I need you."

I stopped in my tracks and turned to look at him. "You needed Jasmine too. Why don't you go to her?"

"I don't want her. I told you I messed up." He begged.

"You're right you did. Now you don't want her. But as long as you had me, you wanted her." I shook my head. Turned my back to him and hurried toward the door to my house.

Upon entering the kitchen, I turned around to slam the door.

He stood blocking the doorway, "Can I please come in?" He asked with his head hung down.

Silence.

I didn't say anything to the pitiful shame that blocked my doorway. I couldn't muster any nice words. So I let the door be. I guess an unspoken invitation.

I continued on into the living room, took my shoes off and sat my purse on the end table next to where I sat on the couch. I was packing, so I had to keep my purse close. I didn't know what was going to happen next. I loved him, but I wasn't about to let him hurt me. Not in his character, but he was desperate. You just never know.

Todd closed the door and moved into the living room behind me like a nice little puppy.

"Can I sit down?" He asked.

"Todd sit ya stupid ass down." I said calmly. The pitiful act was getting on my nerves.

"I deserve that. You're right I am stupid. The dumbest man I know to do what I did. I don't even know if I'm even worthy of you." Todd said.

"If you don't know just ask me, I'll tell you." I snapped.

Todd sat on the couch next to me. He turned to look in my face as I stared straight ahead trying to prevent looking at him. He took my hand in his.

"Krish, just listen to me. I want to come clean…. I want my family back. I'll tell you whatever you want to know or do whatever it takes to make that happen. We can fix this."

"I don't need fixing, you do playa." I said sarcastically.

"Yeah, I do." And I am willing to go to marriage counseling or family counseling."

"You're not going to drag my boys into your mess. They didn't ask for this."

Todd kissed the back of my hand and held it to his face. As tears formed in his eyes, he said, "Krish, baby, please just let me make it up to you. I'll show you that this will never happen again. My heart is breaking. I can't eat, I can't sleep, I can't go to work, I can't think straight. I can't and I won't live without you in my life. I made a mistake. Please."

A tear escaped his right eye, traveled down his cheek then disappeared under his chin.

His tears brought out my tears and the tremble in my voice.

"I'm hurting Todd. You betrayed me in the worst way. I've loved you more than I've loved myself. How could you be with someone else? How could you do this to me? I said softly. "Wasn't I enough? Was I not a good wife? A good friend? What?" I cried.

He eased closer. Holding my hand in his.

"It had nothing to do with you. I've been pleased with you since the day we met. A man couldn't ask for a better woman. It was me being a fool. Believe me it had nothing to do with you."

"I don't need this. I'm exhausted and I can't do anymore. We can't have a marriage like this."

He reached out to me with strong arms pulling me close. Both arms surrounding my body. Softly laid my head on his chest.

"We can have a marriage just like we used to. As long as we still love each other. Don't turn me away." He cried.

He slid off the sofa and onto the floor on his knees to face me. Still holding my hand, he caught my eyes. Made me look at him.

At this point, the tears were pouring from his eyes. Looking into his painful, sleep deprived eyes, my heart softened. The tears became plentiful. He laid his head on my thighs. His embraced tightened. We both cried.

I didn't want to, but I gently caressed his beautifully round head, something in me just made me do it. We didn't say anything for a long while. The cries that were caught in our throats delayed our speech.

I wiped my tears with the back of my hand. "How long Todd?" I spoke softly.

Raising his head from my lap, he pierced my eyes.

"How long has it been going on?" I asked again.

Turning his head away from me so he wouldn't look into my face.

"Baby, I don't …" He stuttered.

"Please tell me the truth." I whispered. "That's all I'm asking for."

He paused as if he were thinking for a minute. His embrace tightened.

"About a month before." He managed to get out.

"A month, huh. Must have been something special keeping you there a whole month, then you bringing her here." I said.

"Just stupid."

"She mentioned you telling her you were getting a divorce that day."

"I admit I lied. I was never in a million years gonna divorce you."

With tears still freshly falling and with a frown, I said, "You're a liar and a cheater. So how can I believe anything that you're saying now? I really don't believe you. I thought you wanted to come clean?"

"I am being honest. I'm pouring my heart out to you Krisha."

His facial expression was convincing but he wouldn't look me straight in the eyes. I knew better.

"Get the hell out of here." I spat angrily. "You're not pouring anything out."

I was emotional, and I knew if he couldn't look me in my eyes he was lying.

I tried getting up from the sofa to put him to steppin'. He was still kneeling on the floor with his head lying across my thighs.

"Get up and get out. Until you start being honest, don't come back!"

"I am being honest."

He held onto my waist.

"Todd, let me go and get out!" I screamed.

I tried to stand; however, the grasp on my body closed in tighter every time I attempted movement. He was pressing his weight down onto my legs.

"I can't take this anymore." I cried and begged.

"I can't go Krisha. If I let you go, I know I'll lose you." He began hard down crying.

"I just don't understand why you never considered the consequences for your actions before. You thought I'd stay with you, if I found out. Are you telling me you think I'm *that* stupid?"

"No baby." He cried.

"Just leave me alone. You disgust me. Guess you thought you were that good that you'd never get caught, huh? How long have you *really* been doing this? Move!" I screamed as I pushed at his upper body. He was truly a disgusting liar.

"I can't let you go. I'll never let you go."

With his face buried deep into my thigh, he continued crying and repeating, "I'm sorry...I love you...I can't let you go."

All of that meant absolutely nothing to me. But in reality I guess the fool meant that he wouldn't let me go because he held me with a death grip without bulging.

I twisted and turned, pulled and pushed, wiggled and fought to remove his arms from around my waist so that I could get up from the sofa. But, the more I struggled and cried, the more he pushed his body farther and farther into me. Hindering any movement.

"I love you too much to let you walk out of my life Krisha. I'll never do that; I'll die first." He said through tears.

"You really don't understand how heavy my heart is. I don't know if I can ever get past this."

"We can get through this. Just give me another chance. I'll never keep secrets from you again. I need you baby."

He planted a kiss where his head had rested.

"Todd please." I resisted.

"You're always going to be my wife. Always, no matter what."

The sensations of his warm breath on my warm skin sent tingles all over my body. I looked down to see that my dress had risen above my thighs.

Tender kisses caressed my skin. Soft lips moved to rest between my thin thighs.

"Please leave. Don't..."

The passion I felt for him wouldn't allow me to finish the protest. The charismatic movements that were pulling me deep into a web of satisfaction took me aback. I felt myself drifting.

He buried his head deeper and massaged my waist with his strong hands. Soft tongue quickly began searching my triangle while strong hands continued caressing my lower back. Making my body more at ease and receptive of his quiet pleasures.

I protested by struggling to push him away.

His teeth grazed my skin as he tugged at my bikini. Attempting to move them out of the way to make room for his exploration.

I continued with the shallow protests that fell on deaf ears.

"Please…Todd."

"I miss you. I need you." He managed to muffle out.

Oh God! I said to myself as my head fell back against the sofa.

I couldn't stop it. There was this automatic reaction to the magical tongue with the magnificent skills belonging to the man with the dynamic sex appeal and charm sent straight from hell just for my demise.

The feelings being created stirred at my soul causing me to close my eyes.

My body so warm, so good. Stimulation so intense. I could feel my body pouring out its own juices around the warmth of his awaiting mouth. I didn't want him sexually. Not now, not ever. My mind tried to convince me of this. My body told me differently.

Locking his arms around my thighs. Strong arms gently moved my body toward the edge of the couch and closer to his love spell. Removing one arm from around my waist, talented fingers peeled my bikini aside to reveal a ridiculous throbbing.

The wetness from his eagerness sent his tongue sliding up and down the length of my engorgement. The shivers from the intensity almost sent me into submissiveness. His tongue circled me, moved like a melody. Seductive and sweet.

Getting frustrated with the cloth that insisted on hiding my secret, he removed his arms from around my waist and ripped my bikini at the seat. Making a very large opening for his pleasure.

While staring down at my body, he caressed me. Moved thick fingers across my opening. His lips covered me with soft kisses.

"You're beautiful." He said looking up at me with love, lust, or whatever, in his eyes. It didn't matter.

He dipped his head a little lower until his tongue met flesh again. Stroked the length of my womanhood. Before I knew it, he was inside of me. Telling me he loved me as he made love to me with his strength.

"Please." I offered a faint protest.

Though my protests were very shallow, my breathing was heavy. The more I protested the more intense his pleasure became. I was being ravished, nice and slow.

There was absolutely no fight left. I was overcome.

The desire to feel loved; to be with the man I loved, out weighed the hatred I felt for what he'd done to us. When I managed to open my eyes, I saw the man I loved loving me wholeheartedly. With tears still falling as he expertly tantalized my soul, mentally and physically, I closed my eyes and cried some more.

3

I Can't Let Go

"*D*amn bae you look lovely this evening."

"Thanks honey." I said.

"Uh…you sure you wanna go out, because we can go right back up those stairs?"

"No. You owe me a good time tonight."

"Don't hurt a man to try." Todd said with a smile.

Three and a half hours later we had eaten dinner, taken a riverboat ride and was sitting out on the riverbank having a nice and much needed conversation. This was the type evening I liked spending with my husband. Just the two of us spending a little quality time together. Nothing elaborate. Just simple and nice.

Things were almost back to normal with us. I must say we'd been doing really well. I found it in my heart to forgive Todd for what he'd done. It took a lot of praying and counseling, but our love for each other out weighed whatever he thought he felt for Jasmine. I decided that the love we'd shared over the years and our family was worth more than some two-dollar trick.

Tonight I wanted to show Todd the nice little R&B spot Mia and I had gone to downtown. He enjoyed listening to R & B; therefore, I knew it would be something he would enjoy. So, after we left the river we stopped over to pay visit to one of Todd's coworkers and his wife who were hosting a party at their home, then we went to the club. Before going inside, I could tell that the club was not like it was on the night Mia and I went. The parking lot to the club and the one across the street was packed with nothing but expensive rides; BMW, Benz, Bentley, Cadillac, and Range Rover you name it, they were all there.

Before entering the club I could tell that the crowd was much larger than before. Though the building was a rather large one, every inch of the place contained a body. I guess since it was a Saturday night all the ballas came out. And where there are ballas, or wannabe ballas, there are money hungry women trying to come up.

By 11:00 pm we were inside and getting our drinks on. We danced a few songs but for the most part we were chilling at a table. Todd and I acted as if we were new in a relationship. All booed up. He was all hands and kisses.

As the alcohol started working on me, which usually didn't take much since I was never a heavy drinker, my body became glued to his. After slow dancing two songs straight, we took to our seats. He ordered more drinks. I sipped, he drank, and we listened to Keyshia Cole sing *I Shoulda Cheated*.

Uh, perfect song. I thought.

I eyed Todd as I sang along with the song. At times over the last two months, that song was my testimony. Yes, indeed!

"Gotta go to the restroom, bae. Will you excuse me for a minute?" Todd said while getting up from the table and giving me a peck on the lips.

"Sure, go ahead."

I watched him as he walked to the back of the club toward the restroom until he vanished into the crowd. I thought to myself, *my baby is still as sexy as the first day I laid eyes on him.* He was thirty and still fine; athletic build and all.

While he was gone, I sipped on my drink and listened to the DJ play another slow song. When *Step* by R. Kelly came blaring through the speakers, I was ready to hit the dance floor.

Where's my partner? I thought.

I'd just realized that Todd hadn't returned from the restroom. I was dancing around in my seat. *Man, I hate to miss this dance.* I thought.

Out of the corner of my eye, I could see an attractive guy staring at me from the bar. I'd noticed him all night watching me, but I tried to play it off and act as if I didn't see him looking. I guess he'd been watching me long enough to realize that Todd had been gone a good while. Guess he thought I was alone for the rest of the night, so he made his move. I could see him coming, and before I could take a deep breath, he was standing in front of me.

"Hello beautiful." He said in a deep masculine voice that was loud over the music.

Brotha looked even better up close. Very muscular build, smooth skin, low cut, about 6'3" at least, cute smile, and yes indeed, handsome. I could tell he was used to having top-notch women, especially if he was bold enough to approach me.

"Hi." I replied.

"I see you like that cut, would you like to dance?"

"I would love to dance; however, I don't think my husband would agree with me dancing with you."

"Husband huh?"

I showed him my ring.

Smiling, he said "Congratulate dude for me. Tell him he's one lucky man."

I smiled.

He raised his glass as he turned to walk away.

Just when I thought he was leaving, he quickly turned around and said, "You look like a lady who takes real good care of her body, so if you would like a full body massage and a day of pampering, stop by and check me out, on the house for you Ms. Lovely."

He pulled out his card.

"Thanks, but no thanks." I shot him down.

He smiled, laid the card on the table, and then walked away.

I picked the card up so it wouldn't be there when Todd returned.

Reading the card, I found that brotha man owned the spa he'd invited me to. That is, if his name was Brian he did. And has two other locations within the area. I slipped the card inside my purse knowing it would get flushed as soon as I got to the bathroom. Speaking of flushed, what was taking Todd so long in the restroom? This was the second song being played since he'd left.

I left the table to go check on Todd. I thought maybe the line was long to the restroom. When I made it to the restroom there was no line, so I guessed he was inside. So, I went inside the ladies room to get rid of Mr. Hershey's card. When I came out, I asked a guy coming out if there was anyone left in the men's restroom. He said no. So, I turned to walk back into the club scanning from corner to corner, front to back. "Where in the world did he go?" I thought. I began walking to the front of the building when someone tapped me on the shoulder. I turned around; it was Todd.

As I turned, I bumped into a sista, or a sista bumped into me, whichever it was I almost tumbled over on my stilettos. She looked as if she was in a hurry to get outside. Someone had definitely pissed her off. She almost took me out without even saying 'excuse me.'

"Oh! Excuse me." I humbly said.

"Uh huh." I heard her say with much attitude.

I sucked it up and focused on my husband.

"Baby, that's my jam lets dance." He took me around the waist pulling me toward the dance floor. I stopped him by standing still and refusing to walk a step further.

"And where have you been?"

"Over at John and Kevin's table talking to them for a few. I saw them on my way out of the restroom. They started talking about work. Can you believe that? I almost didn't get away. When I saw you looking around, I told them I had to go."

"Really?" Was all I had to offer. I wasn't asking for the drawn out excuses. I was just saying.

"Yes." Kissing me on the lips. "There they are right over there." Pointing to the corner in the far back.

They caught Todd pointing, so I waved, they waved back.

"Whatever." I said with attitude. Every since we got back together, he feels the need to explain every little thing in detail to me. Damn. He makes me think he's hiding something else. "Let's dance this song, then I want to go home."

"Fine with me." Pulling me onto the dance floor.

Todd and I ended up dancing to two more songs. We ended it on *Slow Jam* by Usher and Monica. That song really got me in the mood. I was ready to go home and make some more music. I guess Todd was ready too because after the song ended he grabbed my hand and led me out the door without saying a word.

When we reached the parking lot, our car didn't look the same as we'd left it. Something looked strange.

I looked down and saw that the front driver's side tire was flat.

"I knew I should have checked that tire earlier today." Todd said angrily.

"What happened?"

"I rolled over some broken glass today leaving work. I was hoping it didn't puncture the tire."

"Well, looks like it did."

Taking off his shirt. "Here, hold my shirt baby. I gotta change this freakin' tire at 1 o'clock in the damn morning!"

He was fuming.

He had gotten just as turned on as I had and was ready to get home to make something happen, but instead we were stuck outside of a club with a flat tire that would take too long for my patience to fix.

Nonetheless, I had to wait. By the time he finished, I was no longer in the mood to be bothered. I just wanted to sleep.

When we opened the door to our home, the microwave clock read 2:35 am. I sat on the couch, took my shoes off and before I knew it, I was out.

4

Bigger and Better

*T*odd and I were moving on with our lives in a positive direction. We were doing well and making new changes for our future together.

We'd discussed a new home. I'd told him that I couldn't bear going into his office in the basement since his little fiasco down there. And every since that day, I have not set foot back down there. And I meant I wasn't. So my baby did what he was supposed to do in providing a comfortable home for his children and me.

"Todd are you sure you want to build a house because buying an existing one is fine with me." I asked.

"Baby, look, I know you've always wanted to design and build your own home. I'm in the position now where I can give you and the kids whatever your hearts desire, so why not? Is that still what you want?"

"Are you serious?" I said with excitement. "Yes indeed. I can't wait to get started."

"The contractor says after today's meeting, he can start securing permits as early as tomorrow."

"It's going to be nice living outside of the city. I was getting tired of the traffic anyway."

Pulling me close to his hard body he said, "Anything for you." He planted a kiss on my lips while running his big hands over my backside.

I savored the moment and kissed him back. Letting him feel my tongue.

"I gotta tell Mia...I'll be back baby." I said abruptly pulling away from Todd.

I kissed his cheek and turned in search of my keys and purse.

After locating them on the kitchen table, I dashed toward the door and headed for my car.

"What about our meeting with the contractor?"

"You can handle that right? I don't really need to be there this time."

"Go ahead and have fun." Todd shook his head. "I'll tie things up with the contractor and pick up the kids."

"Love ya, see ya later."

I blew him a kiss as I hurriedly exited the door.

I was so happy with Todd being back in my life, I felt like I'd died and gone to heaven.

I felt the need for girl talk with Mia; needed to share my excitement with someone. I was so pumped that I forgot to call to see if she was home. I bumped my radio as I rushed over to holla at my girl.

When I arrived at Mia's condo, I realized it was only a little after four in the evening and Mia probably hadn't made it home from work yet.

"Oh well." I thought. "I'm here, I may as well see if she's in."

I walked up to Mia's condo, knocked on the door and called out my friend's name.

"Mia. Are you here girl?" I screamed.

I didn't get an answer so I knocked again.

"Girl open up I have some good news for you." I screamed through the door. I knew that would get her butt to the door.

"I'm coming." She screamed from the other side.

Opening the door, she looked puzzled.

"Hey. What's got you screaming, girl?" She said in a pant.

I leaned in to kiss her cheek and give her a tender hug. She hugged me back, but stood in the doorway unmoved.

"I just wanted to talk and tell you my good news."

It was then I noticed that she was gripping her robe.

I looked her up and down and it dawned on me that my girl was not alone.

I smiled. She blushed. She knew what I was thinking.

"My bad. Didn't mean to impose." I whispered.

"You know I always got time for you."

"I just wanted to share my news about the house. It can wait. Go handle your business." We grinned at each other.

"Congratulations." Mia gave me a hug. "Maybe this can be like a new beginning." She said in my ear.

"That's what I'm counting on." I said with a smile.

"You deserve it."

"Thanks. I'll call you later." I turned to walk away from the door.

I stopped and turned around to face Mia who was still standing in the doorway grinning from ear to ear.

"On second thought, you call me when you can." I told her.

"Girl, I might hit you up tomorrow. I think this will be an all-nighter."

Leaning in and whispering, "Is it all that?" I asked.

Looking over her shoulder, then moving closer to me. "Don't you see the smile on my face."

"Oooo la la! Call me girl. Call me with details."

"You know it. See ya!" Mia threw out before closing the door.

I smiled as I walked away. It was good to see my friend happy and enjoying life. She deserved it.

She's a good girl who's been in a few bad relationships in the past. But I can say this; she doesn't let anything get her down too long. She may stumble, but she gets up, and keeps moving on to the next adventure.

Getting a new man is nothing to Mia. Once a man starts acting a fool or she finds out that he's not who she wants to be with, she moves on to the next.

Mia was engaged a couple times. She was even married for a short time after graduating from college. She married a guy that she'd dated her last year of college. He was four years older than Mia, more experienced and full of himself.

The marriage lasted about eighteen months. She found that Trent, Todd's boy, really was the no good, lying, three timing bastard that all the other women said he was. Mia was blinded by the lavished lifestyle that the now, Dr. Trent Jacobs lived at that time. Dr. as in PhD. Trent is dean of the Chemistry department at our alumni university, but then he was in grad school working on his doctoral degree. He came from a wealthy family, so he was already a balla before he started making his own money. In the daytime, they both were career professionals who had it going on, and at night they were partiers and movers. They knew how to have fun. Mia just didn't know exactly how much fun Trent was having without her. But she moved on, and is doing quite well. If you didn't know it already, nobody would ever guess. Though that was several years ago, Mia still wants no part at marriage right now. She enjoys her life just the way it is.

I strolled to my car thinking about what Mia was probably putting that man through up there. If I could be like Mia and not give a care; talk about a new beginning. I would probably be thousands of miles away from here by now. But me, I gotta have a big ole' weak heart. One that keeps me trapped in some BS.

I hadn't talked to Kyra in a couple days, so I thought about going by to talk to her.

Kyra was my girl too. Mia and I met her when we were freshmen in college, she was one of our suitemates, and we'd been going strong every since.

She always had drama going on with her and her no good man, Eric. I loved Kyra like a sister, but sometimes I had to question her sanity when it came to men. Hearing her complain about their drama got tiring at times. You just didn't want to hear about the same crap over and over, especially if she wasn't willing to do anything about her situation.

Her baby daddy lives off of her, does nothing for their child together or his other children. Brotha won't even clean the house or watch the baby while Kyra's at work. The killing part about it is that he has the nerve to be cheating. That I just didn't understand. But that was my friend and I loved her nonetheless.

I dialed her number, took a chance on her being home. Just my luck her man answered the phone.

"What up?"

"Hi Eric is Kyra in?" I said holding in a big sigh.

"Nah, she at work."

"Could you please have her call Krisha when she gets in?" I asked as politely as I could get it.

"Fo' sho boo." He said.

"Thanks."

I hung up the phone and shook my head. That was so sad. But if she likes it, hey, I love it. Who was I to tell her anything?

Since my girls were all tied up, I drove over to my mother's house to share my excitement with her. We talked for a long time before we took a ride to Baskin-Robbins to get a double scoop of vanilla ice cream on an original cone just like old times.

I missed spending time with my mother, just the two of us. I was a big baby and I knew it, and my momma was my heart.

After a short four months, my new house was completed. The contractor finished it in record time as promised. My business was booming and Todd had started his own engineering firm. He was very excited about his new venture and was already doing quite well. We were happier now and more financially stable than ever before.

He had reclaimed his place as a part of my soul. I sacrificed what I knew in my mind for what I felt in my heart. I loved him more now than could ever be explained; more than anyone would ever care to understand. That love allowed me to forgive, to be accepting of his faults. The years, the good times, and the growth we shared together. I couldn't forget those times and I definitely couldn't throw them away.

Todd's little affair no longer threatened our marriage. I was fine, living life to the fullest, and my children were happy. This made me a very blessed woman. We had truly found a new beginning.

5

I Run This Town

*W*hile sitting in my office between appointments talking to Cheryl, my assistant, the phone rang.

Cheryl sang into the receiver, "Taylor Mortgage, how may I help you?"

There was a gentle pause, then "Hold please." I heard her say. "Mrs. T, you have a call on line three."

"Thanks, Cheryl. I'll take it in my office."

Sitting down at my desk, I happily picked up the receiver, "Krisha Taylor, may I help you?" I sang.

"Mrs. Taylor, how are you this morning?"

"Fine. Thank you."

"Mrs. Taylor, this is Gerard Stevens from the city council's office. I wanted to tell you that you have been chosen to receive the Most Outstanding Community Leader Award from the city."

"I...I didn't know I was a candidate for an award."

"The city council nominates individuals for this award and the members of the community vote on the recipient. You were chosen hands down."

"I'm honored, but I don't know why or how..."

"Due to the positive images that you portray in the community as well as the city, your leadership abilities, your business support to various organizations, and the help that you and your business gives to a vast majority of citizens throughout the city so that they may own homes and prosperous businesses."

"Thank you Mr. Stevens." I said still stunned.

"No, thank you Mrs. Taylor for being an asset to our city. There will be an awards ceremony on Friday night at 7:00 pm at the Radiance Center. Can you make the event?"

"Yes sir I will be there." I said happily.

"Please be prepared to make a short acceptance speech, three minutes or less."

"I can most definitely do that."

"We'll see you then."

"Thanks again Mr. Stevens."

I rushed into Cheryl's office to tell her the news. Cheryl was just as excited as I was; however she said she wasn't surprised.

I was gleaming from the news all morning. I couldn't wait to tell Todd my good news.

Todd and I met for lunch at Jack's Café.

I knew Todd would share in my enthusiasm. He was always supportive and stood by me no matter what.

We ate and talked about Friday night. I talked about my speech and our attire because our clothes had to be on point. This was truly an honor and I planned to look the part.

After lunch I followed him back to his office to pick up some business documents to take to our attorney, Craig Meadows. Craig was the best attorney the area had to offer. He was a high profile attorney and knew his stuff. We'd worked with Craig since we started our first business.

However, instead of getting the papers and leaving, I went into Todd's office and ended up talking to him more about the award. I knew I was rambling too much about the award, but my baby could feel my excitement and never said a word.

Instead he eased his way over to where I was sitting on the sofa and stole a kiss while I talked.

"Congratulations baby." He said as his lips brushed against mine.

He threw me off in mid-sentence. I couldn't help but respond. I'd missed his lips the past couple weeks.

I realized that it *had* been a while since we'd actually kissed and held each other. Partially due to the demands of our businesses, we didn't have a lot of energy left for anything else. So needless to say, I was melting right there on the couch in my husband's office.

The kiss was long and soft. My tongue was taken captive and my body was responding at a rate of speed that had me afraid of myself.

"Todd, I have to go back to work and so do you." I said in a moan.

"I'm working."

Though my body was telling me yes, my mind said no mam! Not in his office. I was a dare devil at times but I wasn't crazy.

His secretary was on the other side of the door. And I was a moaner and a talker, so I knew she'd be first to witness the intensity of what was taking place on the other side of the door. There was absolutely no way I could keep quiet, so I objected again.

"We can finish this at home." I said in a heavy pant.

Todd's advances abruptly stopped. He got up and walked over toward the door, opened the door and walked out closing it behind him.

So, I sat up and straightened my clothes. Prepared myself to make a clean get away.

While Todd spoke with his secretary, I began buttoning my top.

I heard him say, "I'll see you tomorrow", in that deep sexy voice of his.

I tried to get to the door before he came back, but before I could get the door open, he was back.

"Where do you think you're going?"

"Todd I told you I have to go back to work."

I pulled him to me giving him a peck on the lips.

"Naw boo, you're the boss. You don't have to do nothing."

"I have a meeting at three."

I was trying to think of every excuse to get out of there.

"It's only one. We have an hour and a half at least."

"Yeah, but I still have other things to do at the office. Cheryl is expecting me back."

"That's another thing. We need to hire some more people. Business is good and you're way too busy these days."

"I agree. I was thinking that myself."

"Let's advertise for the positions ASAP, but as for right now, I'm in the mood for you."

"Oh my, how aggressive you are today." I grinned as his lips went for my neck.

"You ain't seen nothing yet girl." He smiled mischievously.

"Who else is here?" I grinned.

He plastered a bigger grin on his face.

"Everybody's gone, and the doors are locked."

"All that for some lovin' you can get at home."

"Yes, you got a problem with that?" He flirted.

I stepped back and looked at him. Then stepped to him and wrapped my arms around his neck as my chest fell into his.

"Hell no baby, I ain't got nothing to say 'bout that." I smiled.

"Damn girl." Was all I heard him say before taking his stance behind me.

He'd started this, now I was gonna make sure I finished it.

6

Silent Whispers

On the Monday after an outstanding awards reception, Mia came over to my office to invite me to lunch, chat, and basically waste time until lunch.

Something was bothering me that I hadn't mentioned to anyone, so I thought it was time I shared it with my friend.

I told Cheryl to hold all my calls and I closed the door to my office so Mia and I could talk in confidence. We got comfortable on the couch in my office.

"Mia, I've been getting these crazy phone calls all week long."

"What kind of calls?"

"Well, someone has been calling the office asking for me, then when I get on the phone they hold the phone and then just hang up. Its like they're trying to say something, but they just hang up instead."

"Really? What you think that's about."

"I don't know. I assumed it was business related since it had only happened at work.

But last night the same thing happened at home."

"Don't you have caller ID."

"At home, but not at the office."

"Didn't you see who it was last night?"

"No, It only showed UNAVAILABLE."

"Well, isn't that something. What good is it to have that mess if people can still block their identities?"

"Now, that's what I'm saying."

"I don't know girl but sounds like you may have a secret admirer."

"Yeah, right. If anyone knows me good enough to call my house and office, they know damn well I have a man."

"And your point? You know that means nothing to some men. That only means they can be as discrete as they want to be. They like that."

"I don't need or want an admirer. But, I wish whoever it is will stop playing on my phones."

"What did Todd say?"

"I haven't told him. I didn't think it was much until it happened last night at home. Maybe I should tell him."

"I think you should. And watch your back girl, there are some crazy people out there these days."

"Fo sho'."

"Now hurry up and let's go I'm starving."

We made it to Kero's Grill around 12:15 pm for lunch and the crowd was thick.

"Guess we'll be here a while."

"I'm in no hurry. I don't have any more appointments today. Every since I hired the new loan officer, I can breathe a little."

"That's one good thing about being the boss."

"Not all the time, Mia. If you don't follow some of your own rules and maintain a degree of professionalism your business doesn't have much of a chance at prospering."

"As you always say, 'you gotta do what's right to stay on top'."

"You got that right."

As that was said, the waiter took our orders. Then quickly returned with our drinks.

"Krish, look at all these fine brothas up in here by themselves for lunch."

"Girl please they're probably waiting on their girlfriends or going home to them."

"I mean there's two fine chocolate ones at the bar, one in the corner and another behind you. This must be my lucky day."

Mia was seriously surveying the scene.

"Girl, don't you have a man."

"*A* man?…*A* man?…Girl be for real. You know I don't have time for one brotha all up in my grill everyday." Mia chimed.

"You need to stop. You know you aren't getting any younger."

"I'm not trying to get old too fast either."

We laughed.

"I feel ya, have fun while you can."

"Girl, I'm just tripping. I know I still got it going on. I can pimp these fools just as hard as they will try to pimp me." Mia said laughing.

"You gotta wanna settle down one day."

"Yeah, one day, but not *this* day. I'll be back…gotta potty."

Mia quickly pushed her chair back, got up from the table and strutted toward the restroom. Putting on a show for all spectators. She knew damn well she didn't have to use the restroom. She wanted to turn heads. Switching and swaying that big booty in those tight pants.

"That girl is a mess." I said and laughed to myself.

A tall, brown skinned brotha with a pretty smile who sat two tables over kept sneaking peeks at me when his girl wasn't looking. I smiled and waved. He upped his head and smiled a cute hello. As soon as he did, his girl slapped his arm and scolded him for the disrespect. She glared at me through squinted eyes.

I don't want him. I thought. *You can have 'em chic.*

Always good to know I can still attract 'em though. But it sure wouldn't be his triflin' behind. Openly cheesing up in my face right in front his girl. I just wonder if my man does the same thing when I'm not looking.

Mia returned smiling. "Did you see that?"

"No, see what?"

"That cutie over there approach me when I was coming from the restroom."

"No, which one?"

"Him over at the table by the window with those two white men." She pointed them out.

He caught us looking and smiled our way.

"Oooowee girl. That thick hunk of chocolate is all I need for my late night cravings." Mia said.

"Damn he's cute, *and* wearing a suit. What did he say?"

"Said he'd been watching us every since we came in...blah, blah, blah. Then said he wanted to get to know me and asked for my name and number."

"Did you give it to him?"

"Now what kinda crazy ass question is that? ...Helllll, yeah!"

"Mia you are a trip. Brotha don't know what he's in for."

"Got that right."

We laughed and sipped our drinks.

"Here you are pretty ladies." The waiter sang as he delivered our lunch.

We both thanked the waiter and proceeded to dig in. Not much was spoken until we were done with our lunches.

"Krish, let's make a date for Saturday."

"To do what?"

"I would like to see Tyler Perry's stage play called *Meet the Browns*." Then you know...I figured we'd do the usual, get our party on."

"You are wild girl. But that sounds good. Are you inviting Kyra?"

"I guess. I'll check with her but she took her man back the other night so you know she's got issues."

"She just has one issue. One tall, broke and ugly issue." I said.

We cracked up.

"Sho' ya right!" Mia belted.

"Let's go girl."

"Let's ride cousin."

Before leaving the restaurant, Mia smiled and waved goodbye to her next victim as she sashayed her big tail out the door.

After dropping Mia off at work, I called my office to inform my assistant that I was going to a couple of meetings. I advised that I would not be back in the office.

My appointments took the rest of the evening to complete. Then I stopped by the mall to pick up a couple of things before going home.

7

No Pain, No Gain

*W*hen I arrived home, Todd and the boys were already there and he was preparing dinner.

"Thank goodness." I thought. My feet were killing me in the heels I had on. I just wanted to take a long hot bath and relax.

"Thanks baby." I gave Todd a kiss on the cheek.

"Just doing my thing. I don't mind."

"I'm going up to bathe. I'll be back down shortly."

I ran up the stairs, stopped in my boys' room to say hello, and then moved on to my bedroom. I started the water in the tub then went into my closet to undress when the phone rang. I answered on the second ring.

"Hello." I chimed into the receiver to a deaf ear. "Hello." Still no one spoke.

Click.

I hung up the phone. Those stupid calls were happening again.

I bathed, dressed, looked over homework, and joined my family for dinner.

The phone rang twice while we were eating dinner. I answered the phone in the kitchen to silence. Another unavailable call.

I thought about what Mia said and began to get nervous, so I decided to tell Todd what was going on.

"It's probably the wrong number." He said nonchalantly.

"No you don't understand. If it were the wrong number, then why wouldn't they ask for someone, so I can tell them they have the wrong number? I don't think that's it at all. I'm calling the phone company tomorrow to see what can be done. If someone is calling my office *and* my home, the call is definitely no mistake and gotta be for me."

"Well, you know that beautiful face of yours is all over the city on billboards. I'd hate to think that you have a stalker."

"I know. I'm gonna have to start packing my nine again."

"I got you." Was all Todd offered.

I started clearing the table of dinner dishes and cleaning the kitchen.

"It's better to be safe than sorry." I said.

"Fo' sho." He added. Then said, "Baby, if you don't mind, I'm going to go play a few games of pool with Trent and Brad over at the daiquiri shop."

"Okay. Go ahead and thanks again for dinner."

I walked over to him, threw my arms around his neck and gave him a kiss. He wrapped his arms around my waist and kissed me back.

"I love taking care of you guys." He said softly.

"I love you."

"Love you too sweetheart. Are you sure you'll be okay?"

"I'm good, go ahead. Have fun. I'll probably be in bed when you return. If I'm asleep wake me up please. I got something for you."

"I bet you do." Todd said gripping my butt with his big hands. "Maybe I shouldn't go at all."

"No you go on. I'll be here when you get back. Promise."

He gave me another kiss before going out the kitchen door.

As soon as he left the house, the phone rang again. I looked at the Caller ID box and it showed UNAVAILABLE again. I ignored the call. The phone rang three more times in the next half hour from whoever the UNAVAILABLE caller was. I ignored all three calls. I knew the outcome of each, so I said to hell with it. I wasn't going to let that phone ruin my night.

I read to my kids. Kissed them goodnight and returned to my bedroom to finish reading the novel that I'd been trying to complete for the last two weeks. I refused to put the book down before finishing it so I stayed up until around 12:30 am. The time surprised me. I didn't realize it had gotten so late and Todd still wasn't back.

Oh well, I told him to wake me. I thought. So, I let the sandman take over. I was out before I knew it.

The clock read 2:45 am as I reached over to the night stand to retrieve my ringing phone. I looked to the other side of the bed to find that it remained empty. I immediately snatched the phone up.

"Hello." I almost screamed in the receiver.

"I'm trying to reach Mrs. Taylor."

"This is she." I was talking fast.

"Mrs. Taylor, this is nurse Jonathan Davis over at Community Medical Hospital. We have a Todd Taylor here at the hospital. Is he your husband?"

"Yes, is there something wrong?"

"He was in an accident tonight."

"Oh my God. Is everything alright? Where is he?" I screamed.

"Please calm down Mrs. Taylor. He'll be okay, but you need to come down to the hospital."

"I'll be right there." I hung up the phone.

I gathered my thoughts to make sure I wasn't dreaming. Called Carmen to see if she could rush over to be with the kids. Carmen said she'd be here in ten minutes, so I jumped up out of the bed and started scrambling for clothes.

Talking to myself as I ran around the room getting dressed. "What happened Todd? Baby, hold on I'll be there."

I began to cry for the unknown.

"Lord please don't let anything happen to my husband." I prayed. "I don't know what I'd do without him."

Carmen got there in no time. When she arrived, I was waiting at the kitchen table. I dashed out the door promising to call her as soon as I got more information.

The usual twenty minutes drive took about ten minutes for me.

"Where were you that you were brought to Community Medical which is across town, when you were to be seven minutes away shooting pool?" I questioned Todd in my mind.

I was a nervous wreck when I reached the hospital. From the information desk, I was directed to the third floor. When I got up there, I was sent to room 3012 where a nurse said the doctor was waiting.

Nervously, but anxiously, I walked to the room. The doctor and a nurse were there.

"Are you Mrs. Taylor?" The doctor asked as I entered.

"Yes, I am." I suddenly became even more nervous. "What happened? Is he okay?"

Seeing Todd lay there helpless brought tears to my eyes.

"Mrs. Taylor, your husband was in a car accident. He was ejected from the vehicle…"

"Oh God no." I said softly fearing the worst was yet to come.

"He's sleeping from the pain medication. He was in and out of consciousness when he was first brought in, but he's been asleep for about thirty minutes now."

"Do you know what happened?"

"Police say his car flipped about five times before stopping. You'll have to get more details from the officers."

"Is he going to be okay?"

"He hit his head during the accident. His head is swollen and cut. That's the reason for the bandages around his head. He has a fractured hip. Other than that he's a lucky man. There was no internal bleeding and no signs of serious head injury. However, we would like to keep him for a couple of days. It's gonna take him a while to heal."

"Sure doctor, do whatever you need to do."

I stood over Todd and took his hand in mine. He was totally out. Not knowing I was there with him.

"Mrs. Taylor officers are waiting in the lobby to see if they could speak to Mr. Taylor when he awakens. You may want to speak with them to find out more about the accident and whereabouts of the vehicle."

"Thank you doctor. I'll do that."

"Here, I'll walk you out to show you where the officers are."

"Will he be okay alone doctor?"

"The nurse will stay with him until you return. He'll be fine."

Doctor Henson and I walked into the lobby where he directed me to a detective with the Sheriff's Office. I extended my hand to the deputy.

"Hello, I'm Mrs. Taylor. I believe you have some information regarding my husband's accident."

The officer reached out to take my hand in his. "Oh! Yes, I'm very familiar with you Mrs. Taylor, glad to finally meet you. I'm Detective Jones with the Pearl Parish Sheriff's Department."

"Thank you. Nice to meet you Detective. Can you tell me what happened?"

"Would you like some coffee?"

"No thank you."

"Well, it seems that your husband hit a guard rail while traveling south on I-10 and flipped the car over. From the tire marks, it looks like the car probably flipped about five times before resting in a ditch off the interstate."

"He was traveling southbound on I-10; the accident occurred around 2:15 am."

"Still, I'm trying to figure out why he'd be going south on the interstate at that time when he was supposed to be only a few minutes from our home."

"I can't tell you that, but I can tell you that the vehicle is a total loss."

At the moment, I realized I was driving Todd's truck and he indeed had taken my car. My brand new, two month old, black BMW 550. I'd wanted that car for a long time, so when Todd's business took off he went out and bought it for me as a surprise.

"What's important officer is that my husband is okay."

"The car is at the wrecker yard on 29th street so you might want to retrieve your belongings and call your insurance company. By the way, here's your insurance card back. I needed it for my report.

"Thank you. Thank you for everything officer."

"I hope your husband has a successful recovery. He and his passenger were very lucky."

Passenger. Did he say passenger? I thought.

"Thank you...but there was no passenger." I said confidently.

Looking down at his report. He began flipping through the pages.

"Aw, yes there definitely was a passenger."

My mind immediately raced back to my conversation with the nurse who'd phoned my house. I recalled him using the word "they". I stood there thinking.

"Officer can you tell me who the other passenger was? I'd like to check on him too, being that he was hurt in my vehicle."

"Well, the other passenger miraculously wasn't hurt very badly. They refused medical attention and quickly left the scene before we could even get a name. We turned our backs to tend to your husband and she was gone."

"She?"

The expression on my face must have told the officer that he'd said enough. He was now eager to leave.

"If you need a copy of the accident report, you can come by the station tomorrow after one pm and pick up a copy. I'll have one waiting for you."

"Thank you for everything Detective Jones. I'll do just that."

"Goodnight Mrs. Taylor."

I took a seat in the lobby for a few minutes. My mind was still on the detective's words. My mind started telling me that he must have been mistaken in thinking whoever this *she* was, was a passenger in *my* car.

If the person left that fast, he probably didn't get a good look at them. Then again, why did this person leave the scene so fast? If so, who was she? I had no idea, but I was sure gonna find out. My head began to ache profusely. I let it ride for the moment and went back to the room to be with my husband.

I stayed with him the entire time. I took care of the car and all insurance business from the hospital room. Being that his hip was fractured, he couldn't move his lower body. I had to bathe him, dress him, and even wipe his behind. I loved Todd and I didn't mind taking care of him. But only one thing bothered me. *She.*

Two days later Dr. Henson released Todd from the hospital. Todd came home on crutches. The kids were glad to see him and I was glad to finally be at my own home to sleep in my own bed.

Carmen had stayed with the kids and sent them to school the entire time. I owed Carmen my life. She was a good woman. That's why I had no problem with compensating her well.

Todd was mostly silent on the way home as he was in the hospital. Guess he was thinking about the accident.

Later that night after the kids had gone to bed and I was getting into bed, he said, "I'm sorry Krisha."

His apology caught me off guard.

"For what baby?" I asked.

"I know how bad you loved that car."

"I can always get another car honey?" I rolled over to him and kissed his lips for reassurance. "As long as I have you, I don't need a car."

"Yeah, but it was for you. I don't know why I didn't take my own vehicle that night."

"Stop Todd. I don't care about that car as much as I care about my husband."

"I'm also sorry for getting you up that time of the morning to come see about me. I didn't mean to scare you like that. I should have been home anyway."

"Well, baby we live and we learn. There was nothing wrong with you going out to shoot pool. You always play pool with the guys."

"I know but it was late. I should have had my behind at home at 1 am with my wife and children.

"Todd, don't beat yourself up over it, okay."

"And, if I remember correctly you wanted me to wake you up for a lil something, that night?"

"Yeah, I did. But I stayed up reading a book and managed to knock myself out. I don't think I would have felt up to it anyway."

"You would have if I were home earlier."

"Stop it Todd. You're acting as if something else is bothering you about that night. Is there something else you want to tell me about the accident?"

"No...no baby. Why you say that?"

"I keep telling you that saying I shoulda, I coulda is not gonna change anything. All that's important to me is that you're okay."

"Thanks baby. That's why I love you so much. You're like no other. What did I do to deserve a woman like you?"

"What did you do? You know exactly what you did." I sashayed across the room.

I laughed.

"Come on now girl don't start that now. It was hard enough watching you get dressed over there. You know I'm broke down for a while."

I climbed in the bed next to my boo and caressed his chest while we talked.

"Now you know if I wanted some that bad I would take it. You can't move, but I can."

Jokingly pushing me away. "Girl, don't you come over here hurtin' my hip. Do you know how bad that hurts?"

Laughing and leaning in to kiss him.

"Okay, fine." I covered my mouth with his and took in his tongue between my lips. Gently suckled on it.

Smiling as he attempted to catch his breath, Todd said, "Yeah, you're right. You know you got that any time."

We both kinda laughed and caressed each other.

"Now go your hot butt to sleep." Gave me a good slap on my bumps.

I blushed.

I kissed my boo. Told him good night and was out like a light.

After a week, I finally went to get my belongings from my banged up car. This would be the first time I saw the car after Todd's accident. It was horrible. I'm surprised he got out of that car alive. The car was smashed at every angle. There wasn't a part of the car that wasn't dented. The top of the car was completely smashed in. I looked at the car and thanked God for his life. I wanted to get my things and hurry away from there.

I quickly filled Todd's Escalade with some boxes of old files that I'd brought home from my office that had miraculously remained in tact in the trunk. After that I retrieved everything from the glove compartment inside the car and checked the car for miscellaneous items. On the back floor, I noticed something sparkling gold laying on top the floor mat. It was a single gold key. The key was not labeled but it seemed to be a house door key. Wasn't mine. Must have come from Todd's keys while the car was tumbling. I picked up the key and put it in my pocket.

On the way home, I ran a few errands for Todd and myself. I went to check on Mia and bring her a few things she needed. She'd been in bed sick with a virus, flu, or some illness for a week. I hadn't seen her since we went out the night before Todd's accident.

After that I went to pick up Todd's meds from the drug store. I had gotten back in the truck and was backing out the parking lot when a car pulled behind me and blocked me in. I sat there and looked in my mirror as I watched a tall, attractive, brown skinned woman approach the driver's side window of the truck. The tint was so dark she couldn't see inside. She stood there at the window until I rolled the window down. She seemed surprised and confused.

She said, "Oh! Sorry I thought you were someone else." She smiled. I smiled. She walked away.

It dawned on me that Todd's personalized license plate reads TAYLOR1 and mine reads TAYLOR2; therefore, our vehicles are easily recognizable by anyone who knows us.

She blocked me in so she had to have read the plate.

Oh! Yes she knew exactly who she was looking for. I thought.

I hopped out of the truck and rushed back to her car where she was just getting in. She looked up saw me coming and hurried to start the car.

"Excuse me." I tapped on the passenger side window. She rolled the window down

I don't know what led me, but it just came out.

I dug into my pocket, got the key out that I'd found in my car. I held it up.

"Is this your key?"

"What?"

"Is this your key?"

"Miss, I've mistaken you for my friend. I don't know you, so how can that be my key?"

"I think you do know me."

"I'm sorry, I don't."

"Is your friend's last name Taylor?"

"What? I'm afraid not."

"Then why'd you think I was your friend? I know you read my license plate."

"Excuse me, but I gotta go."

"You thought I was Todd didn't you?"

"Todd who? I don't know what you're talking about."

"Oh! I think you do."

"You're crazy."

"I'll show you crazy."

She rolled the window up in my face and burned rubber out of the parking lot.

I jumped in the truck and hurried home.

When I arrived home Todd was playing video games with the boys. I kissed all three of my boys and continued in the kitchen to cook dinner.

"Hey bae, where are you going?" I heard Todd call out.

"I'm about to start dinner."

"Why don't you sit down a minute and come chill with us?"

"I think I'd better go ahead and start dinner now while I feel up to it."

"Ok then. Well I'll help you."

"Baby, that's not necessary. Just continue playing with the boys."

"Are you sure? Cause I can wobble in there and help you. After my therapy session this morning, my hip feels pretty good."

"No, you just take it easy. Don't get excited too fast. I'll handle this, I'll call you when dinner is ready."

"Okay babe, whatever you want. Now come over here sweet thang and give me a kiss."

I walked over to the couch where Todd was sitting and leaned down to kiss him on the cheek.

"What? I know you're not trippin'. That's all a broke down brotha can get is a kiss on the cheek?"

"Well you said a kiss. You didn't say where."

Taking hold of my arm and pulling me down on his lap.

"Come here girl. You know I don't play that."

"Todd slid his arm around my waist and planted a kiss on my lips."

I really wasn't feeling him after what had just gone down at the store's parking lot. I just wanted to go cook dinner and have a long, hot bath, and maybe get out of this house for a little socializing later on. Besides it was a Friday night and I was too tired of being cooped up. It wasn't me that was hurt.

"What's wrong, Krish?"

"Nothing."

Todd moved his hand from around my waist to begin caressing my thigh.

I whispered. "Todd stop. The boys are right there."

"So. They're not paying any attention to us. They're all into that game."

And they were. When they played that video game. I don't know how, but they couldn't hear nor see anything else.

"I have to go cook dinner anyway."

"Okay, just one more kiss."

This time I kissed him back, so he'd leave me alone and let me go. Things were running through my mind and I needed to be alone to think.

"You're acting shady and I want to know why."

"I am not acting shady. I'm okay."

"No, something's wrong with you. After all these years I know when something's bothering my wife."

"Todd, I…"

He cut me off before I could finish. Began caressing my thighs again making his way to my crotch.

"I think I know what's bothering you."

"What? I told you…"

"I know it's been a few weeks and you're frustrated. Like I said, after therapy today, I feel pretty good. My hip doesn't hurt that bad anymore."

Grinning and nibbling at my bottom lip while expert hands roamed my body.

"I'mma relieve you of that frustration later on. So you go ahead and cook dinner and get ready for me. I'll put the boys to bed, have it ready, just like I like it."

He was now feeling my breasts through my shirt and making circles on my back with the other hand.

This man made me feel so good, even when I didn't want to.

I couldn't resist kissing him back. I'd forgotten all about the parking lot incident, and more importantly forgot that we were on the family room couch with the kids in the room. Mesmerized, sexually deprived, just plain old hot, whatever. I was feeling it. It had been a good three weeks since Todd and I had made love. I'm not one to complain about anything, especially in his condition. I didn't want to hurt his manhood because he couldn't perform. Besides a lot had been going on and I'd been extremely busy handling my business and Todd's business, waiting on him hand and foot, so all of that kinda took my mind off of my need to be loved. Now more than ever, I realized that I really needed it. The kids calling Todd's name helped us out of our trance.

"Daddy, its your turn. Daddy…come on."

"Okay son, I'm coming."

Pulling myself away, "Go ahead Todd. Let me go ahead and start dinner. Things are getting too hot in here." I smiled.

He smiled deviously. "Not as hot as its gonna get later."

"Whatever, you better be able to back some of that talking up." I threw out.

"You know how I do it."

Yeah, I knew exactly how he did it. That's why I went in the kitchen and cooked the fastest dinner ever. As soon as I took the chicken out the oven, the phone rang. I yelled to Todd that I'd answer the phone.

"Hello." I said.

There was silence on the phone.

"Hello?" I said again.

I could hear what sounded like cars passing by. Then the phone went dead.

The phone calls had started once more. As I set the table, I thought. *This is definitely something personal. The calls are not for Todd, they are meant for me. Whoever this was calling my office and home, they definitely wanted me.*

The boys talked continuously during dinner about friends, video games, and everything they could think of. I had to tell them to stop talking so much and finish eating. I had dome business to take care of. They must have been really starving because both of them had a second helping of everything. I thought they'd never finish dinner.

"The boys and I will clean the kitchen baby. You can go on up."

"Are you sure?"

"Yes, we got this. You've done enough. Go relax."

"Thanks honey. Thanks babies." I practically ran up the stairs to my bedroom. I know I soaked in my tub for at least an hour. I'd taken a nap and everything before getting out. When I dressed, I went to kiss my boys before going to bed. Todd was just turning their light off and they were already in bed. I kissed my babies and told them good night. Thought I'd read at least a chapter of the novel I'd been working on for a while.

Todd finished in the shower, but due to his injury he was moving a little slow. The phone rang as soon as I opened my book. I'd already decided earlier that If I got another anonymous phone call, I was gonna let them have it. So I grabbed the phone without looking at caller ID. With a huge attitude, I screamed into the receiver,

"Hello!"

"Hey girl what's up?" Mia chimed.

"Oh! Hi Mia."

"Boy you sound happy to hear from me." She said sarcastically.

"I thought you were another crank call."

"You still getting those?"

"Well, they'd stopped for a couple of weeks. But today, they started back."

"So, did you contact the phone company?"

"No, not yet. The caller ID shows unavailable, but I think this is something personal."

"Why?"

"I think someone is trying to tell me something."

"I'm confused Krish. I don't understand what you're saying."

"I don't know yet either Mia, but my gut tells me this has something to do with Todd."

"Don't jump to conclusions girlfriend."

"I'm not jumping to anything. I said I don't know yet but some things are beginning to seem a little strange."

"Well, if it's a chic you know we can handle that."

"I know I can handle that, but I don't know if I can handle what she may have to say."

"Like I said don't go assuming anything and getting your panties in a bunch. Call the phone company or police or something. This could be some sick maniac. You gotta be careful Krish."

"I know Mia. I know."

"Well, I was calling to see if you wanna get together tomorrow evening to go shopping or something. I haven't seen you in a couple of weeks.

"That sounds good. Let me just see if I can get away and I'll let you know."

"Okay, call me tomorrow girl."

"I will. Good night Mia."

No sooner than I hung up the phone. The phone rang again.

I guessed Mia had forgotten to tell me something. So I grabbed the phone off the receiver without looking at the ID.

I was so sure it was Mia. I answered without thinking, "What up girl?

There was silence on the other end. Extreme quietness.

"Hello?" I said again.

Still no response.

"Look, whatever you wanna say, be adult and say it. Other than that, don't call my house anymore."

I quickly hung up.

Todd stepped out of the bathroom drying himself with the towel as he walked into the bedroom.

"Who was that calling so much baby?"

"Oh! That was Mia. She called to invite me out tomorrow evening."

"Are you going?"

"I don't know. I told her I'd call her back. I wanted to make sure you and the boys would be okay first."

"Well, you go right ahead. We'll be fine. I'm doing much better. Besides, you deserve time with your girls. You've been by my side every day since I had the accident. You need to get out and enjoy yourself."

"Are you sure?"

"Go have fun baby. I don't mind at all."

8

Never Too Much

*W*e decided against going out so Mia, Kyra, and I had a nice time just chilling at Mia's Place.

Mia had sprain her arm while trying to play tennis with Derric a few days ago, so she wasn't trynna go out all bandaged up anyway. Said it cramped her insatiable style.

So we made our own drinks, listened to some music and talked all night. Before I knew it, it was nearing eleven pm so I figured I'd better get home.

On nights like tonight, I envied Mia for being single with no attachments and Kyra for being single with the exception of having one child. The both could basically do exactly as they wanted without having anyone to answer to.

Mia wasn't searching for a Mr. Right, just having fun. Kyra had just gotten rid of Mr. Wrong, so neither of them gave a damn about a man in particular. Me, on the other hand, had a beautiful family. I had a man who I'd been with for the last ten years. Now some women would envy me, but the way I really felt inside tonight was nothing to be envied.

I didn't share my thoughts with my girls, but Mia knew there was something wrong with me because she knew about the phone calls. My body was tired. Although I thought I was in the partying mood at first, I really wasn't. That was why I suggested staying in, in the first place.

It was now after eleven and I'd decided it was time to go home.

Then, Mia *had* to pop in my girl, Keyshia Cole's CD. After I heard "Love" blaring through the speakers, the next thing I knew I was reminiscing about my issues and found myself shedding tears.

I knew in my heart he was cheating again, but at this point, I had no proof.

Why does life have to be so unfair? I thought.

I have always been the most faithful, loving, and supportive wife to him. *Why wasn't that enough anymore?* I couldn't figure it out. Our sex life was and has always been outstanding. We seemed to please each other well, or was I the only one pleased?

I lay on Mia's floor and cried baby tears, just thinking.

I hadn't said anything to them, so I guess they thought I was losing my mind or something being sprawled on the floor like that. I couldn't begin to explain to them what I was feeling. I'm sure they'd think I was stupid crying like that because I was only assuming.

Then, the only thing that could make me feel worse tonight was hearing my once special song, "I Can't Let Go" by Anthony Hamilton. I guessed that as the night grew older, Mia decided to slow the mood and play the slow jams.

My head began to ache as the music warmed my heart. The only thing I could see was Todd having sex with Jasmine in the basement with that song blasting. It used to be *our* song, but I would turn the radio off every time I'd heard it since then. Now, there it was, coming through Mia's speakers.

Lying on my stomach with my face to the floor, my depression went unnoticed. After a minute of reminiscing, I couldn't help but turn over and cry out. And it didn't help that I'd been drinking. That only made me feel worse.

Mia rushed over to me. Kyra kneeled down with surprise and concern on her face.

Kyra spoke first, "Krish, what on earth is wrong?"

I covered my face. I felt so stupid to be lying here acting like a lovesick teenager.

Mia joined in, "Krisha, what's up girl, what's going on?"

Kyra picked my head up off the floor and put it onto her lap as she sat on the floor. She wiped the tears from my face with her hand and moved the hair from my face.

"What is it Krish?" Mia asked with more concern.

"Please turn that song off."

Mia got up to honor my request. I'd never told my girls every detail of the day I walked in on Todd and Jasmine. I was too embarrassed. I know some people would judge me, saying I was stupid to take him back. So, other than what Todd and I told the marriage counselor, I'd kept it all in. I did share some of the details with Mia but I didn't tell her everything. I didn't even tell my mother everything. Now I was faced with the memory of his affair through this song, and the possibility that it could be happening again. I was sure tonight was a sign. I felt sick.

Kyra continued to stroke the side of my face and my shoulder as my head rested in her lap. Mia had gotten a wet towel and was lying on the floor beside me wiping my face looking puzzled. Neither of them asked what was wrong again. I guess they figured I'd speak when I was ready. They were just being supportive of me. Just being my girls.

I truly loved them. They were like the sisters I never had.

I turned over and looked up at the ceiling. Decided to just let it out; thought maybe I'd feel better. I stared at the ceiling and told my friends everything about Todd's affair leading up to the phone calls and my suspicions.

Kyra continued to hold me while Mia wiped my tears as I described every detail to them. I'd thought this was behind me, but I guess for some reason it seems to be rearing its ugly head again and aiming for my heart taking my mind along with it.

"Oh My Gosh Krish." Kyra said. "You should have told us, you know we would have been there for you."

"I know. But I just couldn't. I was ashamed and embarrassed to even go into details to anyone. It took a lot for me to try to block that out of my mind and find it in my heart to forgive him. That was the hardest thing I'd ever done in my life."

"Other than the phone calls, why do you think he's at it again?"

"His demeanor at times. The details of his accident, the female who was supposedly in the car at the time of the accident among other things. I know the police wouldn't make a mistake like that."

"Yeah, I would be suspicious too, but until you get some more evidence don't beat yourself up. You don't need that." Kyra said.

"I know. I'm just tired and the drinks...I'm sorry."

"Who are you apologizing to and why?" Mia said as if she was getting upset. "You have every right to feel like you do. I hate to say it, but nine times out of ten your intuition is probably right. Don't dismiss what you feel so fast. Look, all three of us know you don't take anything lying down. So you're entitled to times like these."

"Thanks. I love you both so much."

I hugged both my friends. I loved them both very much. Mia was my boo. She was my heart. I would feel for her and no doubt she did the same for me. We all had much love and respect one another and we showed it. That's not something everybody can say about their friends.

After talking some more, I finally pulled myself up off the floor around 12:35 am and went home to my family. Tonight was a weak point in my life, but I did feel a little better. But lets bet one thing, there wouldn't be too many more nights like tonight. Some reason I feel I have the strength I need, thanks to my girls.

Two months after Todd's accident he had healed fine and was back to normal. Our lives were getting back to pre-accident status. He went out and purchased me another car. This time he bought me a brand new black BMW 760Li. Guess he figured a bigger, more expensive car would excuse him wrecking the other. I was way beyond the car thing, but for some reason he couldn't stop saying he was sorry.

9

Ho, Ho, Ho

The holiday was a time where I really enjoyed being with my family. Todd, the boys, and I had a wonderful Thanksgiving dinner at our home. My mother was out of town with her friend this year, so we were unable to share with her.

For Christmas we invited our families to be with us at our house. My family wasn't big, just my mom, aunt Mae, Mia and Kyra. Todd's family was much bigger than mine, but being that they were in Virginia, I hardly even knew anyone other than his immediate family. Todd's two sisters and their families arrived the day before Christmas Eve. Over the years Todd's sister Cicily and I had gotten close and would talk on the phone weekly. When we visited Virginia, she and I would always hang out and shop. However, his youngest sister, April and I could never see eye to eye. I think maybe because she was the youngest child and always felt like I stole her big brother away. Well, for the most part I loved his family and they loved me. My mother and Aunt Mae joined us on Christmas Eve for the gift exchange.

Our day was filled with laughter and love. The families blended very well. We were having a blast before Todd decided that he needed to go take care of something at the office. He made this announcement to everyone as we were gathered in the family room tearing open gifts and then quickly went for the kitchen door. I quickly went behind him into the garage.

"Todd, its 6:00 pm, on Christmas Eve and you're going to the office?" I asked in astonishment.

"Bae, its not gonna take long. You won't even know I'm gone."

"I already know you're going, so yes, I'll know you're gone."

"Krisha, I'll be right back, promise."

"What on earth are you going in for?"

"Well, I need to retrieve some papers for a client to sign on a deal tonight."

"Tonight? Why didn't you meet with your client on yesterday before you closed the office for the holidays?"

"He's an out of town client and he just arrived in town today to be with relatives for the holidays, so I need to get this done because he'll be gone day after Christmas."

"Well, I guess that makes sense, but I'm gonna miss you. You should be here with the rest of the family."

"I know baby. I hate this as much as you. But, I'll be back shortly, I promise."

Pulling me close and kissing my lips.

"Okay, be careful."

"I will. See ya later, boo."

Todd got into his truck and drove off.

I went back inside to entertain the family. I was already missing my husband's presence. I have always felt that family and friends should be close during holidays. As I entered the kitchen from the garage, the phone rang. I answered only to confirm that the phone calls had started again. After two months, here they were coming in once again. And as usual, they quickly hung up when I answered.

It was now around 9:30, my mother and Aunt had gone home, and Todd's family members were downstairs drinking hot chocolate and playing with the kids. I decided to come up and shower as the day's events had taken a toll on mind, body and me.

I was about to step into the shower when the phone rang. I stepped back into the bedroom to answer.

"Hello." I chimed into the receiver.

Silence was on the other end.

"Look, I told you once if you can't say whatever it is to be said, don't call me anymore."

"You need to come get your man." Someone with an obviously disguised voice said.

"Excuse me?"

"Come get your man bitch."

"Bitch? And who are you?"

I always knew this crazy ass calling me had to be a female. I just knew it.

"516 Essence Avenue."

Click. She hung up.

I didn't have to think about who was at this address. I already knew. I knew that office crap was a bunch of bull. I thought about it long and hard first. I thought about all the risks. *What if I was being set up to be raped or kidnapped?* I thought.

This person had finally spoken after all these months. I felt like I had to follow-up. Besides, other than phone calls no one had ever tried to harm me in any way. That's why I always believed that it was someone who just wanted to simply tell me something.

I politely dressed again and went downstairs to inform my relatives that I'd be leaving for a little while. I made up something crazy. I was so vexed I don't even know the lie I told them. I asked Cicily if it was okay to use her rental car as she was parked behind me in the garage. Also, I needed another vehicle besides my own.

But before I left the house, I dialed Todd's cell. He answered on the first ring.

"Hey boo. It's getting late. I was just checking on you."

"I'm sorry baby. This little meeting is taking longer than I expected. I'm going to be at least another hour or so."

"Oh, that's okay baby, I was just about to shower and turn in. I'm really tired."

"How'd everyone like the gifts we gave them?"

"They loved them. Your brother-in-law especially liked the Rolex you bought him."

"I figured he would."

"Well, I'll be in bed when you get here, so you be careful."

"I will. Love you."

"Love you too, bye."

I forgot my peacemaker, so I had to run back upstairs to my closet to get it. By this time, everyone was so into watching "Meet the Browns". They were laughing so hard; they never noticed me leave.

When I got into the car, the first thing I did was call Mia's cell. She was with her new man, Derric, and I hated to interrupt, but I had to let someone know where I was going.

Mia asked if I needed her help. I told her I'd call if I did. I promised to be careful and struck out to see what was at 516 Essence Avenue.

Before going on my journey, I drove to Todd's office to see if his car was there. I couldn't find it anywhere. Now, I was really afraid of what I'd find.

After driving for thirty minutes, I finally located the two-story stucco home in Crestwood Subdivision. But not before calling Mia again to ask her to find the address on MapQuest. I left the house so fast, I never even thought of that. There was a white E class Mercedes Benz in the driveway and nicely kept lawn. It was a new and very swank neighborhood. As I drove by for the second time, a light in the bottom half of the house was on while it was dark throughout the top half. I drove around the block and parked my car. I needed some time to think. First of all, I asked myself, *what the hell are you doing out of your home on Christmas Eve in an unknown neighborhood, looking for God knows what?* Then, I thought of my kids and how this was definitely a dangerous risk that I was taking. I thought of a lot of things, but none of them detoured me into going home. After all these months of anonymous calls, I had to see what the calls were about. Then, I thought about Todd's strange departure to "go do business". I sat and thought about how players play the game. I'd never been a true player but I wasn't stupid either. Gut told me that Todd had to be there. Though his car wasn't there, that was all part of the game. I drove back through the subdivision and thoroughly checked out all the cars that lined streets.

I still didn't see any sign of Todd and his vehicle. Giving up on the mystery, I headed out of the neighborhood. Before I could reach the main street to exit, something told me to make a right down another street that was about three blocks away from the residence.

Four blocks down in the cul de sac in front of two vacant lots I spotted a black Escalade SUV. As I drove down the side of the truck slowly, I was praying the license plate didn't read Taylor1. I almost stopped and backed up the car so I wouldn't see the license plate. I wasn't sure if I really wanted to see it or not. In my heart I knew whom the truck belonged to. The tires and rims had already given a good indication.

And at that end of the street, it was very dark as it contained several vacant lots. As I passed the truck I refused to look. I drove right by without looking at the plate. I rode around the cul de sac and came up behind the Escalade. As my lights hit the truck, the plate was easily visible and the word TAYLOR1 stood out like a sore thumb. My heart sank.

I stopped alongside of the back of the truck just for the hell of it. For some reason, still in disbelief.

I still didn't want to believe it was his truck. So to prove it to myself, I took out my keys and hit the unlock button on my key remote. Sure enough, the interior and exterior lights came on. I sat there for a few minutes to gather my thoughts. I thought of every excuse in the world for my husband to be on the other side of town with his vehicle parked in front of vacant lots of property. I wanted to believe the guy that he was meeting for the business deal was staying over here or something. I knew better.

As I sat, as always, I thought about our children, our families back at the house and how much I loved him. I called Mia who was now at her apartment, to advise of my whereabouts and fill her in on my findings. Mia tried to convince me not to go to that house, but I told her I had to go see if my husband was in there. I'd come this far and there was no need in turning back now. Mia told me she was on her way to make sure I didn't do anything I'd regret. I told her I wouldn't, but I knew Mia, and I knew she would be coming soon.

I parked a few houses down from 516 and exited the car. I left my purse in the car like I'd promised Mia. When I made it there, there were more lights on inside than before.

I walked up to the house where I could hear Christmas carols playing and nervously rang the doorbell. I guess the music drowned out the doorbell because no one answered so I rang the doorbell again. I could hear footsteps coming down the stairs.

"Who is it?"

I didn't know what to say, so I didn't say anything.

I guess the person on the other side couldn't hear over the music so they took a chance on opening the door. When the door was opened the woman acted as if she'd seen a ghost then changed her expression that fast.

"Yes, may I help you?" She said trying to hide her attitude.

To my surprise this was the smart bitch from the parking lot the day I was driving Todd's truck. *I'll just be damned.*

I'm sure she knew who I was, but she wasn't trying to let on.

We stood in the doorway eye to eye. I didn't have time for the BS so I jumped right in. I knew what was up. And I started to get quite upset.

"Where is he?" I said boldly.

"Excuse me?"

"I don't have time to play games with you so ask him to come out."

"Honey, you must be crazy. Who are…?"

I cut her off.

"Didn't you approach my truck a few months ago at the drug store with this same dumbfounded act?"

"You must have me confused."

"Don't play with me. I never forget a face." I threw out.

"Whoever you are, you need to get …"

Calming down a little. I softened my tone and cut her off.

"Look. I didn't come here for this. I was told that my husband was here and I came for him. It hasn't much to do with you right now."

"There's nobody…"

Before she could finish, a child came down the stairs and stared at me in the doorway.

"Mommy, daddy wants to know who's at the door."

The child was playing with a baby doll, combing her hair as she spoke.

The little girl was absolutely adorable. Beautiful with big hazel eyes.

My heart weakened at the sight of her.

I saw the eyes that I'd seen many times before. The same eyes I bore twice. The same eyes I fell in love with.

She followed my gaze. Knew exactly what I knew.

Nervously she tried slamming the door.

I stuck my foot in the doorway to prevent it from closing.

"Where is he?" I threw out.

"Look, Ms…" She paused and turned to speak to her daughter. "Destiny, go to your room please."

The child did as she was told. Ran back up the stairs.

I stood there stunned staring up the stairs behind the little girl. I didn't need anyone to tell me anything else. The child could have been mistaken as my own.

"All I want you to do is tell my husband I said come down. It's up to him as to whether he's gonna come or not."

I looked back over my shoulder to see Mia's car pulling to the curb.

"Get out of my doorway or I'm calling the police." She threw out.

"I don't think you want to do that." I hissed. "Tell you what, go ahead and call. I'm gonna wait and make sure they search your house because I think you got something that belongs to me."

She glared at me as if she could take my head off. She saw I wasn't giving up. To my surprise she turned and walked up the stairs.

I looked back at Mia who was in the car bobbing her head to music. I'm sure she was getting herself pumped up off some gangsta rap. I wasn't really looking forward to that kinda drama but if something jumped off, I was ready to handle mine. I just wanted my husband.

After a few short minutes, she came back downstairs with looks that could kill.

"He's not coming down so you might as well leave." She said proudly.

"What the hell do you mean he's not coming down?"

Reality really set in. The no good bastard was really there. I was so stunned that I took a step backwards almost falling.

She caught me slipping.

When I stumbled, she said, "I'll make sure I save some for you. Now get the hell off my porch!" She quickly threw out and slammed the door so hard the windows shook.

I felt so cheap and out done. Now there was my husband up in this woman's house and I couldn't do a thing about it.

The longer I sat outside that house in Mia's car, the madder I got. Mia offered to take me home, but I couldn't leave. I waited three hours outside that house. He never came out. I called his cell phone numerous times, but he refused to answer.

I cried and I called. Called and cried. I let the phone rang until the voicemail picked up and I left a message every time.

Around 1:00 a.m., he surprisingly answered the phone.

"Why not just be a man about it and come on out? We've been through this before, right?" I said calmly.

"Baby what are you talking about?"

"Don't insult my intelligence Todd. I'm tired and ready to go home and you're coming with me."

"Where are you? What's wrong with you? I'm just finishing my meeting. I'll be home in a few." He threw all of that out in one breath.

"It took you all this time to come up with that?" I shook my head. "Okay fine, just stay in there then."

I quickly disconnected.

I turned to Mia. "Can you believe he's still lying? Still claiming to be with a client. I can't believe he's playing me like this."

Mia just listened.

"Drive me down the block please." I asked Mia.

I had a plan for him.

I got into his truck and went home.

What a way to begin Christmas day.

I managed to enjoy sharing Christmas with our families and friends. We ate Christmas dinner, exchanged more gifts, and socialized all day. Everything was beautiful and the day turned out really nice. I was very appreciative of our families being close this year. Made me feel like there were people who really loved me. If it hadn't been for the ordeal that occurred last night, everything would have been perfect.

Todd had come home around two thirty a.m. I was in bed without any idea of how he got there. I was so mad that I'd initially sat outside in the cold waiting for him. I wanted to make sure I saw how he got there. I sat outside with no coat, just steam coming from every crack and crevice on my body. I didn't care. I just wanted to mess somebody up real bad. I finally said forget it and brought my crazy behind in my house.

He'd climbed into bed and turned his back to me. We hadn't spoken since the last phone call I made to him last night. Now tell me if that's guilt or not?

I left his gifts under the tree and he put mine on the bed in our bedroom. I didn't feel like faking so I didn't bother opening them. Guilt was eating his black ass alive, and I could tell he was trying to figure out where my head was.

I was waiting until our home was free of family members, and the holidays were over because I didn't want to ruin Christmas for my children. I know if I had mentioned anything at that time, all hell would have broken loose between the families, with April heading it off. So, though it was eating me up, I kept quiet.

It was two days after Christmas, everyone had gone home, and my children were at my mother's for a couple days. I was left to face my issues head on.

Todd had been avoiding me all day once we were alone. So around four in the evening, I decided to break the silence.

"Is she yours?" I said while walking into the family room where he was sitting on the couch watching TV.

He looked up at me with the saddest puppy dog eyes. The same eyes I saw on that child; but didn't utter a sound.

His silence told me his truth. Now, heartache was wrenching at my insides once again.

"Why, Todd?" I asked with a tremble in my voice and on the brink of tears.

He didn't offer an answer. Continued to watch the television.

"Don't just sit there like you don't hear me! I deserve to know what's going on with you!" I screamed.

After a few moments of silence and me staring upside his head, he decided to say something. The pissed off, mess this fool up tears had started to fall.

"I never wanted to hurt you."

"Then why do you keep doing it?" I trembled as I cried.

"I didn't know how to tell you."

"Tell me what?"

I wanted him to say it. Wanted him to admit it to me out of his own mouth.

Silence.

"What didn't you know how to tell me?"

I stood before him with my hands settled on my hips.

"I...ummm." He hesitated.

"Talk to me." I urged sitting next to him on the sofa.

"...I love you so much."

"You've got a hell of a way of showing it."

"I can't do this Krisha...I can't do this to us." He stared at the ceiling.

"Just tell me the truth. That's all I ask."

"You don't understand. It's so hard. I don't wanna hurt you."

"You're hurting me now, so why not just get it all out, so I can hurt all at once."

"I can never lose you."

"What do you mean Todd? Would your actions reflect losing me? Just tell me the truth. Don't go jumping to conclusions without me knowing what I'm facing."

"Krisha, I would lay down and die for you."

He was beating around the bush. And I truly didn't wanna hear the crap he was spittin'. He shoulda been an actor. I knew this guilt trip. I already knew.

"You're screwing her aren't you?" I threw out there.

"No, that's not what I'm trying to say, it's not like that."

"Then, how is it? That child is yours, isn't she? ... She's the spitting image of you and April."

Silence.

"Be a man about it. I'm gonna do what I wanna do regardless."

His hands covered his face as if to block out his indiscretions. But I saw right through to them. I already knew in my heart. Just wanted him to say it.

"I'm sorry baby . . . I'm *so* sorry baby."

As he confessed, he looked at me with teary eyes drenching in sorrow.

I stood hurt but stern and correct. My heart had already hit the floor. I just needed to know the details now.

"How old is she?"

"Umm...she's...she's three."

"Three huh... so you were with her mother when you were with Jasmine?" I shook my head in disbelief. "You weren't just having one affair, but you were having two? I can't believe this."

He slid down on the floor onto his knees to face me. Took my hands in his.

This was his game. He knew how to do this very well. I thought as I shook my head.

"Baby, I was so stupid. I never...."

Cutting him off.

"So, you've been lying to me for the past three years?" I searched his face for an answer. *Why did this little scenario seem so familiar?* I asked myself.

"I haven't been lying. I just couldn't find the right way to tell you about my child."

"How do you know she's yours?"

I asked this stupid question searching for some hope. Anybody that knew Todd could look at the little girl and tell she was his. But, hey, I had to ask.

"She is."

"Are you still sleeping with her mother?"

"No."

"I don't believe you."

"That's the God's honest truth, baby. You're my wife, I only want you."

Now I'm wondering what kind of fool does he really think I am? He's dabbled with two different women's bodies that I know of right now, and now he wants me to believe it's all about me. Unbelievable!

"Todd, you've kept this secret for three years. You left your family on Christmas Eve to go see your mistress and child and play Santa because you knew you couldn't get away on Christmas day. This is unbelievable. Somebody wake me up because I'm having a nightmare!" I screamed.

"This has been the most difficult thing I've ever dealt with in my life. I just didn't know how to tell you. I knew you would leave me and I know I won't last without you."

"Todd, please. You're so selfish. That's what you say to me now. You were keeping that woman quiet somehow. I know women and with some, nothing pleases them more than the wife finding out. They try to mess up your house so they can get the man full time."

When I said that I thought about the phone calls. She was the one who called me. Then tried to play stupid at her door. That fueled me even more to think that the heffa played me.

"Its not what you think. Sometimes women are interested in things other than sex or a relationship."

"So you've been taking from us, giving to her? Is it about money?" I don't know what angered me more. The thought of his sexual relationship with her or him taking care of her.

"Is that how she got that Benz in her driveway and that nice house in that immaculate neighborhood? Did you do all that Todd? Are those gifts from you?"

"It's not like that Krisha."

Ignoring him and jumping up from the sofa. "So she got it like that? She's that good huh?"

"It's complicated baby."

"Complicated?"

I was livid.

"Todd, I've given you too much. I don't need this anymore. I've been here before remember? And it's obvious that you have a problem with being a married man. Maybe that's not what you really want anymore. I don't know. But, I'm not gonna wait around and suffer until you decide which side of the fence you wanna be on. You can't do both."

"I know what I want Krisha. There's nothing in this world more important to me than you and my family. Nothing and nobody else matters baby. I just made a mistake."

He was crying and so was I.

"You made a mistake the first time. The second time is never a mistake. And you say that like it's something minor."

"You don't understand. It was all my first time."

"It really doesn't make a difference anyway now does it? I just want you to do exactly what you wanna do and I'll do the same." I threw that out quickly. "Until we find a way to settle this, I'll be cordial to you for our kids sake. But as far as us, you've cut me too deep this time and I don't think I can forgive you; therefore, there's no need for us to continue in this marriage."

My heart skipped a beat. Head began to pound. All at the same time. I didn't mean it, but I said it. I felt it. But I didn't want it. I had to sit down on the couch to remain stable.

"You don't mean that. You're deciding that too soon."

"I've had three days to think about this. It's the severity of the offense that's the deciding factor here. I love you more than I could ever tell you. You are my life." I stroked his face with my free hand. He still held the other. "I thought I'd never get over the first incident, but I found it in my heart to forgive you and learned to trust you again. You took advantage of me Todd and I don't deserve that, nor will I accept it."

He got up off the floor and sat next to me on the couch, wiping his face with the end of his shirt.

"You're my soul mate and I can't imagine my life without you in it. This is old Krisha."

He hesitated a long while before speaking. After a deep sigh, he continued.

"A couple years ago I wasn't only seeing Jasmine, but I was seeing this other girl too. I admit I was wrong. I wanted it all, you and them. At the time, I felt like marriage was tying me down. When you found out about Jasmine, I thought I'd die. And, I would have died if I'd lost you. My relationship with Destiny's mother didn't stop for a minute. You didn't know about her, so I felt like I was in the clear. When you didn't take me back for weeks, I was with her. I tried several times to leave her alone, but I was always drawn back to her since you wouldn't even talk to me. When you finally took me back, I left her alone for good, but she was already pregnant. I think she tried to trap me into staying with her. So, for almost three years, the only thing I was thinking about was you finding out about my child and the relationship I had with her mother. I just didn't want you to know. I wasn't man enough to tell you that. I know I've hurt you, but I never, ever meant for this to happen…Please just bare with me baby. I can fix this. I need you…please…don't leave me Krisha…I can't live without you." He begged and pleaded.

He was sobbing his eyes out. I'd heard all he'd said, but I pulled from it what I wanted, and that was the truth.

"So you've been sleeping with her for the last three years out of love for me, so I wouldn't find out about your child?" I wanted this to sound just as crazy to him as it did to me.

"Baby, no…" He embraced me.

I pushed him back and jumped up from the sofa. He followed. I stood in the middle of the room. He reached for me. I pulled back.

"Don't touch me." I screamed.

"Please don't push me away. It's been three years baby. Three years. I love *you*."

"You don't hurt the people you love. Have I ever hurt you like this? Have I ever expressed my love for you like this?" I yelled out.

"I know you've been a good woman…"

"I hate you Todd! I hate you!" I screamed through tears.

On impulse, I rushed at him. Struck his face. Wanted to let him feel what I felt. Only my pain stretched from the top of my head to the soles of my feet, inside and out.

He jumped back and looked at me with astonishment.

I gave him blow after blow to the face and chest.

"I hate you! Why would you do this to us?" I cried.

The erratic behavior that I'd tried so hard to contain insisted on making its debut.

My connections were coming so fast to the side of his face and chest that, he backed into a chair and fell over with me falling on top.

He tried grabbing my arms to stop me from hitting him. We began rolling around on the floor, mainly him trying to stop the blows. I ended up pinned under Todd with him whispering in my ear, "I'm sorry. I'll always love you."

At the moment, sorry didn't mean shit to me. Yeah, he was sorry alright, but not like he meant it.

I was tired, out of breath, and forced to lie underneath him. His body weight wouldn't allow me to move. So I remained still. Heart beating profusely. On it's way out of my chest.

As I cried, he professed his undying love for me. Begging like the dog he was surprisingly turning out to be.

We lay on the floor, him on top of me, without moving or speaking; just a whole lot of crying. After about 10 minutes, I became as composed as possible and regained my strength.

"Get the hell off me!"

Todd looked down into my eyes. He didn't want to move, but his good sense told him to give up. He reluctantly rolled off me.

I got up, searched the room for my keys and purse and left the house. Slamming the door behind me.

That was five days ago. I haven't been home in five whole days. My mom agreed to keep my children and I've been with

Mia, snuggled up next to her in her bed, crying my eyes out. I said I'd never be at this point again, but life's full of surprises.

Over the first few days, I beat myself up pretty bad. Blaming myself for the things Todd had done. Asking myself how could I have changed anything. How could I have pleased him more that he wouldn't have had to turn to another woman, or other women for that matter?

Then, I had a revelation. Something made me realized that there was absolutely nothing I could have done to make my husband be faithful to me. I did everything I was supposed to do as a wife and mother and a bit more. I began to recognize that the heart is so vulnerable to love that sometimes when we're faced with issues that are so clear, we are yet blind. And I was blind. There were plenty of signs that I chose to ignore. I was faithful to him, so I figured he would be faithful to me. The rules of the game are to treat others how you want to be treated. But not everyone plays the game fairly. I've been hurt beyond repair. Not one but two times in my marriage. I just didn't know how much more I could take.

I love my husband. I love him so much until my chest hurts with the immediate thought of him being with someone else. Another one of life's lessons staring me in the face.

I asked myself the ultimate question: *How could he do this and expect me to happily stay with him?* I can't believe that some men expect women to stay with them and live happily ever after, especially after they deliver some devastating BS to you.

They protest their love for you, but will go after a piece of ass if they don't think you'll find out. *Why? Why isn't what's at home good enough? Risk takers?* Is it safe to say that men love taking risks? That they're born gamblers?

I'd decided that I didn't want to fight anymore. Many women would say, "don't go handing your man over to another woman, fight for your man."

The way I saw it, if I truly had his heart, that wouldn't be necessary. I'd rather just let it go. I didn't need the drama. I love him, but I was willing to let him go.

I knew I couldn't continue to live my life one episode after the next. I'd overcome one obstacle, and another one came hitting a little harder than the last. I needed happiness too. I desperately needed to get my life back to the way it was before I began loving Todd, or at least to the way I felt in the beginning. Situations like this aren't meant to make you happy. The devil comes to steal, kill, and destroy. And this is of the devil.

Todd will always be my first love and unconditional lover, but loving someone doesn't always make you happy. Sometimes, it can be the downfall of your life.

Love tends to change demeanors, break characters, and will come in and cause a whole 360-degree turn. And that can be for the good or the bad.

I recognized that as ladies we must hold our own. We must never let a man and his drama change who we are. Stick to what's in the heart and transform them before you let them get to you.

Mama always said, "where there is something good, there's always something better."

10

First name Drama, Last name Taylor

"What are you pretty ladies having tonight?" The bartender at Club LA sang.

Mia, Kyra, and I knew we were too much for two eyes to handle. We were on point and nobody could tell us any differently. When we walked into the club, I know all eyes were on us. We figured we'd go into Club LA for drinks before going home.

We'd just sat down at the bar when the bartender asked us what we were drinking. I was sure my drink would be Hpnotiq because I wanted to be hypnotized.

It had been three months since I found out about Todd's child. I'd stayed between Mia's and my mother's for two whole months before coming back to my house. We'd been living under the same roof for a month now and I had not said two words to him. He was dealing with his issues, I assume. I didn't know what he was doing because I didn't ask. I'd just got up enough nerve on yesterday to go see an attorney about divorce. That's the reason I wanted to be hypnotized tonight. Maybe I'll forget all about Todd and his crap.

We were very casual. I wore a pair of tight low rider True Religion jeans, black tank accented with a bronze belt around the waist and a pair of bronze open toe high heel sandals. Kyra wore similar low rider jeans that fit just as tight. But Mia's fast behind, had to have on the tightest fitting black pencil skirt I'd ever seen. She just has to show off her butt at all times. Anyway, tonight was all about having a good time.

"Excuse me beautiful, can I buy you a drink?"

I turned a little to check out the body that went with the sexy voice.

Yes indeed. I sang to myself.

The body most definitely went with the voice. Tall, black, athletic, and sexy. For some reason, I seem to attract the sexiest men.

His denims were nice and baggy, not hanging off the butt but nice. Crisp white polo shirt with a small gold chain, a cross pendant around his neck, and a pair of black leather boots of some sort.

He wore a low fade, small diamond in his right ear, pearly whites and sexy smile. Brotha looked young, but there was a sense of maturity about him. And I always seemed to attract young men too. Most told me I didn't look a day over 21. Guess that was good in a way. He wasn't as appealing as Todd at first glance, but what the hell, nobody will ever compare to my boo.

Hpnotiq led the night. My friends were both occupied, so I decided to let my hair down. After conversing with lil youngin', turned out he was twenty-three years old and played some kind of sport, so he claimed. I'd forgotten soon after he told me.

We shared a few drinks and danced a bit. While we were chillin' at the table having an interesting conversation, he was approached by a very upset young lady, who out of nowhere decided her drink looked better all over his face. I quickly excused myself from the situation and moved back over to the bar. He took his problems outside and never even looked back to see where I'd gone. Now, I was shaking my head.

Everybody's a playa. Single and married men alike. This is not something I wanted to get used to.

The girls and I had a few more drinks, some laughs and around 12:30 am we turned in.

Since Todd and I had been going through our little funk, my girls were really supportive of me. We had been spending more time together than usual. They were trying to help me keep my mind occupied.

So the next day, Kyra and I decided to meet at the coffee shop at Books Galore. I needed to pick up some books to read to relax, so we decided this would be the perfect spot to sit, sip, and chat.

I'd paid for my books and had read a few lines of one before Kyra arrived. She walked through the door looking like a supermodel. She had the height, the beauty, and the little bitty body. My friend was really pretty today.

I waved my hand to signal for her.

"What's up chic?" She rang as she approached.

We greeted each other with a hug and a kiss on the cheek.

"Are you tired from last night?" Kyra smiled as she sat across from me at the table.

"Yes, indeed. That's why I hate hanging out with you guys on a work night. Yall always wear me out."

"Well, get used to it. You've been cooped up in the house too long."

"What do you mean? I've always hung out with you guys. You're the one always M.I.A."

"You know, you just might be right."

"I know I'm right. Especially when you had that triflin' dud in your house."

"Those days are long gone boo. And it's my time now."

"I noticed the last few months you've seemed more relaxed."

"I feel like a big weight was lifted when I finally put Eric to stepping. I feel free girl." She smiled.

"I'm glad you finally made that move. Sometimes it takes us a while to come to our senses."

"Girl, ain't that the truth. Women are so vulnerable to some good sex and a pack of lies. We always fall for that bull. And it seems like they always come together, huh?"

We laughed to signal that the truth had been spoken.

"You know little boys who want to play little boy games got that game down packed and they know just what kind of drama to bring. We all are different and we tolerate different things. They feel us out first to see what kind of crap they can get away with."

"Yeah, you right. Eric knew I was a hard worker and I was gonna provide for my daughter, so he used that to his advantage to sit on his butt all day."

"Exactly. And Todd knew I loved and trusted him to the fullest and basically never questioned his whereabouts or intentions. That gave him the okay to fool around. I loved him so much that I forgave him the first time, so I guess he thought it was all good."

"Do you still love him Krisha?"

"You know Kyra I can sit here and easily pretend that I don't, but the truth is I do love him. He's been a part of my life for so long until it's hard to not love him. But at the same time, it's not strong enough to make me stay with him. I don't think I'm in love anymore. There's a big difference in loving someone and being in love with them. He's hurt me too bad and I will never look at him the same again."

"I feel ya. I just hate so much that this happened to you and your family. It's not fair to you Krisha."

"Thank you. You of all people know I could have cheated on Todd a long time ago, if that's what I wanted. But I loved that man too much to even go there."

"You did right, so don't go second-guessing your decision to be faithful. A man is nothing to get. All of them have drama; one way or the other."

"Sho' ya right." I chimed. Giving each other a high five in laughter.

"But, I'm not worried about finding anyone right now. I'm gonna make myself happy first. After all the drama I've gone through, I may *never* want another man."

Kyra gave me a "girl please" look.

"Now you can go tell that to somebody else."

I had to laugh.

"Girl, you know I'm tripping. I just got caught up running my mouth."

We laughed harder.

"Let's order or we'll be sitting here all day."

"You paying right?"

"What?" You 'bout one freeloading heffa."

"Every chance I get."

I had to laugh at my friend and her antics.

Kyra and I chatted it up for an hour or so, and then I headed on home to tackle my issues.

As soon as I entered the door to my home, I faced Todd glaring all up in my face.

"Krisha can we sit down and talk about this divorce that you ordered?"

He stood in front of me.

"What about it?"

I walked around him to get him out of my face. If I did decide to pay any attention to him, then this would be our first conversation in about two months.

"I don't agree with it."

"Really? Well I don't agree with you being the father of some sideline ho's baby either. Nor the fact that you've been cheating on me for three years. But I sure can't do anything about that, can I?" I calmly spat.

"I told you I am not sleeping with her."

"What difference does it make? The damage is already done now. We've been living a lie for three whole years."

"No we haven't. Just give me a chance. I can make this right."

"Todd you don't want to be married. You just don't want to face the fact that you've lost and you're the blame. And most importantly, you don't want me with anyone else."

"I want to be with you. I'm begging you not to do this, but if this is what you really want, then go for it. I'm tired of beating myself up. I can't apologize anymore to you so just go ahead and do what you want to do."

He turned his back to me.

"Excuse me?" I gave a hard stare to the back of his head.

He turned around glaring at me with something that looked like anger on his twisted face.

"You heard me. Get your divorce. You'll find a man to treat you like crap and take you through hell. Then you'll be happy. When you start getting hand put on you don't come crying to me. Nobody's gonna treat you as good as me."

I didn't know what to address first. I was so amazed at what he'd just said and the whole attitude that was copped.

"Good? So you treat me so good? How is sending my blood pressure up treating me good? How is making babies and getting caught with your tramp in my house good? And now everything is my fault right?"

"I'm not saying all that. I'm saying, I'm not perfect but I'm trying to make it right. I'm a man Krisha, and I'm not begging no more."

"I never asked you to beg in the first place!" I proceeded to go up the stairs to my bedroom. "Just sign the divorce papers and leave me the hell alone!" I threw back at him.

When I reached my bedroom, I slammed the door.

I lay across my bed feeling like I carried the weight of the world on my shoulders. My mind was so full of unanswered questions and confusion until I felt like I would never be able to think straight again.

A million drums went off in my head. I didn't even want to move to get something to relieve the pain. I began to feel sorry for myself again. The tears welled up in my eyes but I held them back. Thought about the things Todd said and wondered if there was any truth to them. I'm definitely not thinking about hooking up with anybody right now or in the near future, but I wondered if when it happens would I indeed get someone who's abusive or someone who's carrying a lot more baggage than I could handle. I've got to think of my children. Everything I do has to be in their best interest.

My cell phone began to chime as I finally raised up to get something to soothe my aching head. I slid over to the nightstand to grab my phone. Caller ID revealed that Todd's sister was calling but I wasn't up for conversation, so I let it roll over to my voicemail.

I went into the bathroom to get a couple of Tylenol PM's from the medicine cabinet. Grabbed a cup of bathroom water to wash them down, climbed back into bed and covered my head with the comforter. I just wanted to sleep my troubles away. Before this, my life seemed so complete. My heart was so happy. I thought I had everything on lock.

As I slept, I saw myself as a little girl with a smile as wide as a rainbow. I saw myself as a teenager. I was sitting with my two friends outside my mother's house on an old swing talking and laughing; doing what teenagers did best. Then I saw my children and my mother outside playing around in her front yard. I then saw Mia and I laughing, talking, and carrying on as usual on a casual day. At every stage of my life, I was as happy as a kid in a candy store. All smiles. There was no crying, no sadness, no stress, no anxiety attacks, and no Todd. Todd was not in the scenarios at all. I wondered what that meant for my future. Was that a sign that we were never destined to be together forever? Were we divorced in my dream? Was he dead? Why wasn't he there? I wasn't sure what to make of it. I'm sure if he were dead, I wouldn't have looked so happy. Ya think?

It seems like I slept and thought at the same time. I didn't realize how tired my body was. I needed rest. Physically, mentally, and emotionally. My body ached along with my head. Though, I think my body ached for the source of my drama also. Feelings that I've tried to suppress due to the situation. But having a husband like mine, that was simply hard to do. I couldn't remember the last time I had been touched by him. I know it was at least three long months ago. But I pushed those thoughts and feelings way back in my mind. I had to deal with the matters at hand and get my life straight. If life wasn't so damn confusing, I'd be straight right now, but instead I'm torn. Torn between what my mind is telling me to do and what my heart is singing. Not to mention the crap my body whispers to me every now and then.

I knew way deep down I didn't want a divorce, but I couldn't imagine living with a liar and a cheater the rest of my life. I'd probably be in worst shape staying with him because the things Todd has done is enough to send a weak woman into a mental institution. Good thing mama always taught me to be strong and to hold my own. She would always say "It's a good thing to have a man who loves you and takes care of you, but you've gotta make a way for yourself. A man will be here today and gone tomorrow. And where will that leave you?"

Being that my mother was a single mother most of her life, she instilled the strength of a woman in me on a daily basis. We did everything around the house a man could do. Basically, we had no choice. If she didn't have money to pay someone, we did the job ourselves.

When my mother graduated from high school, she started cleaning houses to provide for herself. She soon realized that that wasn't for her. She went to college obtained a bachelors degree in education and became an elementary school teacher. She then went back to school to obtain Masters and Doctoral degrees. She has been Dean of the Department of Education at a nearby university for the past 15 years. My mother taught me a lot about being a strong, independent, educated woman; however, she never taught me about the trials of relationships. Some things I just had to learn from others or experience on my own.

No one had ever told me about loving a man. No one ever said that it hurts like hell to be hurt like hell by someone you love more than anything else in the world. No one ever said that you can love someone with all your being, but harsh reality tells you that they don't have to love you back.

While I slept, I dreamt a thousand dreams and cried a million tears. In my final dream, I remember finally seeing Todd. He was at a far distance. I could vaguely see his face, but I'd know my boo anywhere. He was screaming my name and reaching for me. He was being pulled back by and unknown force. With outstretched arms, we tried to connect, but the force kept us apart. No matter how hard I tried to get to him, I couldn't find enough strength to reach him. It was like something was riding me and wouldn't allow me to be free. Todd kept screaming my name and repeating, "I love you" until whatever was pulling at him, finally succeeded. He was forced to go somewhere he definitely did not want to go. The force had more control and over took his body. As he was being dragged away, I lost sight of him, but I still heard his cries for me.

I frantically woke up out of my dream crying my eyes out. My heart was pounding and I was a nervous wreck.

I could still hear Todd confessing his love for me. It sounded so real. I lay there with my face in the pillow crying and scared to move or look around the dark room.

As I was coming back to reality, I felt a gentle, soothing hand, smoothing my back and a voice telling me it was okay. I could feel the warm, sweet breath in my ear, which sent chills all over my body. I turned to my side and slowly raised my head from the pillow, tears clouding my vision. The most beautiful eyes I'd ever seen were watching me as I lay while sitting on the bed next to me caressing my back and whispering in my ear. At the sight of him, I became internally elated. My dream was only a dream and my baby was still right here. My arms surrounded him in a tight hug around his waist as I rested my head on his thighs.

He spoke softly. Much different than earlier.

"Don't do this Krisha. I know it's not what you really want."

I knew he was talking about the divorce but I didn't reply.

"I'm so sorry for hurting you. I just don't know what else to say or do short of killing myself."

"Please, don't say that, you don't know what I just went through."

"Huh?"

"Never mind. All that matters is that you're here."

"I'm here and I ain't going nowhere. All you gotta do is let me back into your heart baby. I promise I'll make things right. Allow me that chance. I'll never hurt you again."

"I never wanted to be without you, but this thing is no good for me Todd. I don't know if I can get over this. We've built a lovely family together and that was our dream since our days in college. But you've gone out and made another family somewhere else. You don't know how that makes me feel."

"I know. That's why I could never bring myself to tell you. I was afraid of losing you and our family. You guys are my life."

"You should have told me. You should have talked to me then. That's what loving and respecting someone entails. I know you did wrong, but you should have found a way to talk to me and somehow make it right. I shouldn't have found out like I did."

"This is killing me Krisha. It hurts to see you hurting and crying like this. If I could take it all back I would. I'd never intentionally hurt you. We were apart and I just messed up baby."

"Have I ever done anything to deserve this? Anything that gave you any doubt about my love for you?"

"You don't deserve this. Not at all. And I'm beginning to think I don't deserve you."

"I don't know how to be a different wife to you. Why would you even cross that line? Unprotected sex? It's not like we were apart for months, it was only a few weeks."

"I can't explain why I've done the things I've done. I can sit here and give you a million excuses, but I can't give you one good reason. But rest assure, nothing was meant to intentionally hurt you."

I gathered my knees and crammed into a tight fetal position resting my head on his lap.

There was an awkward silence that lingered between us.

I shifted in his lap. Pulled my legs closer to my body. I wanted to be held.

"I love you." I said hugging my knees.

"And I love you." He bent to softly kiss my forehead.

"This is tearing at my heart." I spoke softly.

"I'm so sorry."

He kissed my cheek and allowed his lips to stay.

He whispered as his lips grazed my cheek. "Give me your pain and I'll hurt for you. I'm about to burst open I hurt so bad."

"Try about three times worse than that. You can have this."

He removed his face from mine and leaned back on his elbows on the bed. Sighed heavily. Caressed my shoulders. A heavy sigh again.

"My relationship with her mother lasted a short minute. When I left her alone, six months later she called to say she was pregnant. I didn't believe the baby was mine, especially since she waited six months to tell me she was pregnant, so I had no contact with her until the child was born. When she called to say the baby was born, I went over to the hospital and got a DNA test while they both were still there. When I got there and looked at her, I already knew I'd messed up. I instantly knew she was mine. She looked just like April as a baby. I ordered the test anyway which later confirmed that I was 99.99% her father. Despite what I told you before or anything you may have heard, this is the God's honest truth. I've been running ragged all this time trying to support her and continue my life with you so you wouldn't know."

He took a deep breath and continued.

"Her mother was supposed to be moving out to California, so I figured I wouldn't have to tell you, that it would work itself out. Being so stupid, I should have known that being honest was the only way through this. But this was hard for me Krisha. I'm being honest and I hope it means something. Either way, I need to get this out in the open. I see how you're hurting and it's not fair to you. I know you deserve to know the truth. The truth may not make you feel any better, but now you know. I haven't touched her mother since way before she was born and I have no desire to be with her. I was just being stupid. Let temptation overtake my mind. Plus I didn't think you were gonna ever take me back the way that incident went down. I love only you. You're the only woman I want and no one will ever take your place. I mean that Krisha. You gotta believe that."

He leaned down to kiss my cheek close to my ear. In a whisper and a slight nibble, his words caressed my spirit. Told me just what I wanted to hear. "I'll never let you go. No matter what. I'll never let you go."

I didn't know what to say. There were no words for your husband's truth to his infidelities. At least no nice words. There was nothing that could be spoken that would change anything that had already taken place. I was helpless, speechless. I lost myself in tears.

The more I told myself that I could handle this, and the more I tried to convince myself that I no longer desired to be married, the more love I felt for him.

My heart ached and I couldn't make it stop. Emotions consumed me and I found myself losing control. I quickly lost the ability to think straight. My head found a tremendous pain that shook my cranium with a lethal force.

Should I stay or should I go? That question turned cartwheels in my head. I just didn't know.

Wiping my tears with the back of his hand, he continued to console my depleted spirit while attempting to mend a broken heart.

"I don't ever want you to cry again on my account."

Those words sank me a little deeper.

I began a heart-wrenching sob that took me back to the front of my troubles.

Oh. My. God. This man has done this to me once again! I screamed to myself.

Even though it had been three months since my first discovery, the wound was still fresh. And here I was on another discovery. This was no doubt unbelievable.

Todd lifted my head, slid down on the bed and scooped me into his arms, cradling me like a little child.

"Baby, please just stop crying." He pleaded. "I know this is a shock to you. We can work through it. Stop all the tears."

He leaned down and kissed the tears from my face. Caressed my lips with his. Held me tight. Rocked me back and forth as he planted tender kisses over my lips and face, over and over again while whispering forgiveness in my ears.

In the back of my mind, I thought it was funny how when everything hits the fan, how sorry and compassionate a person can be. But when they're out doing the dirt, they don't think about you or the consequences. Not once.

Todd showed love to the length of my body by allowing his fingers to gently massage my skin. Tried to relieve me of the stress that he knowingly had caused.

His hand slid under my top as he massaged me from my shoulders down to the small curve in my back.

Large hands so good on my bare flesh that I was blinded by what was yet to come.

With one hand, my top was unbuttoned and sliding to the floor before I could even part my lips in protest.

"Let me take care of you." He whispered.

The masculinity in his voice soothed me. I found it hard to resist him.

My bra had hit the floor right behind my top and I found myself in a painful daze while succumbing to the haze of sincerity that lingered over me.

He moved like a pro. He was a pro. Not missing stroke one.

My bottoms mingled in the pile at the side of the bed as I lay as I'd come into this world so many years ago.

Sliding me off his body, onto the bed, and then onto my stomach, expert hands took to my delicate skin once again.

I realized how smooth he'd just pulled off undressing me and thought about how he probably did the same to others. I tried to dismiss the thought, but it stayed as the tears freely fell.

Todd reached over to the nightstand drawer and retrieved a bottle of massage oil.

Before I knew it, his hands were working magic all over the back of my body in a rhythm that could not be stopped.

The massage was much needed. My muscles were tense and I was at the maximum stress level. The strength in his hands had me drifting back to sleep.

My mind had told me a long time ago to stop him from replacing his hands with his lips, but my body wouldn't allow a sound above a moan.

He was my lover. And I couldn't do a damn thing about it.

There was no need in stopping him. He was down to my cheeks and loving them like his life depended on it. Down to my feet, my toes. I was steaming.

I was in love.

My body was on fire beyond salvation. I was giving in.

"Turn over baby." He whispered.

I slowly obliged by moving my body until I was positioned on my back. Never breaking contact with the breathtakingly beautiful eyes that stole my heart in my youth.

The love that was shown to my body was nothing less than pleasurable.

I pleaded for mercy but my cries went unheard. He ignored my protests until all desires were met.

After endlessly tantalizing my upper body, he obliged by moving down over my navel in pursuit of my most prized possession.

The warmth of his breath traveling my skin had me slowly losing it. But it was also what I needed to save myself from the drama that I knew would come.

I grasped his head between both hands in an attempt to halt the advances that would cause my life destruction then let out a cry of desperation.

My eyes penetrated his.

"Do you really want me to stop?" He asked softly.

"I don't know." I sighed heavily as my heart raced. "...Uh, just let me catch my breath."

I held my chest.

My nerves were really bad from all the stress so I had to take it easy. Anxiety attacks seemed to like me for some reason.

I wasn't sure if I wanted it. But I released the grasp, which indicated to him that I was ready for him.

I couldn't determine if it was the wet touches from his tongue or soft peck of the lips that sent me into full submission.

Light kisses entirely covered me. Soft and slow. Sent shivers throughout my body.

Experienced fingers that I knew so well opened me up like a flower. Lustful eyes adorn my beauty. Fingers intensely searched my body. Drenched in passion. Loving me like a blessing. Softly and magnificently bringing me to a terrific hallelujah.

My mind was a mess. Soul uneasy. Spirit was burdened. But my body was peaceful.

I was totally out of my mind, and I knew it. At this point it wasn't him who was unbelievable, it was me.

Knowing and doing are just two different things.

I ignored everything and rode that wave for a few minutes until that wave of ecstasy escaped me. He stayed in position until I found that wave again. Rode it with a smile of satisfaction.

I was opening myself up for another broken heart. I knew it. I knew it all. My mind had told me that much. But my heart wasn't listening. My body said "ta hell wit it." I loved him. That's all I knew. I think I loved him more than I truly loved myself.

As Todd moved up over my body, he captured my love struck gaze. I knew what he wanted.

"Where are the kids?" I mumbled while looking deeply into mesmerizing eyes.

"Asleep."

"Asleep?"

Astonished I looked over at the clock on the nightstand. It was 12:25 am.

I had no idea I'd been in bed that long. I'd missed dinner and everything. I thought.

"I came to check on you since you'd been up here so long. When I got up here you were crying in your sleep. I guess you were having a bad dream. Figured it was probably about this mess I've made."

I didn't answer. I just looked at him.

"That broke my heart." He continued. "But don't worry baby, you'll only shed tears of satisfaction from this point on."

My heart wanted to believe him. My mind told me, don't believe the hype. My body at that point didn't give a damn. But mama always told me, always follow your first mind.

Todd pushed my legs back and opened them wide. Entered me with ease. Slid all of his manhood inside. Then back out again. He wore an expression of hurt. But I knew it was far from pain that he was feeling.

He caused a friction that ignited a wet and furious flame before sliding into me once again. Began making love to me in slow, long strokes, which was tantalizing and too good to be true. Talk about good lovin'. He was better than good.

Slow and easy action allowed me time to become even more aroused. I loved it when he took his time and made love to me. Making love always brought out the tears. I was exasperated from all the stress and strain, but now I was melting inside. That wall that I had up around my heart was suddenly being torn down; brick by brick.

He knew making love to him would have a profound affect on me, as well as my decision to be with him. That's why he always resorted to sex to mend my heart.

Nevertheless, we made slow sweet love for at least an hour. Shed more tears and made heartfelt promises to one another. I was touched. I was open. I was loving this man with all my heart, soul, and everything I had and desired. I gave him myself as if it would be the last time we'd be together. We held each other tight. Shared a thousand kisses, gazes, whispers, and stares. I was so passionate for him. I loved him about a hundred degrees more.

After the tears dried, we experimented a little more. Sex with Todd wasn't just good. Sex with him was my motivation for life on earth. We moved mountains and made music only we could hear.

Todd knew that he had some making up to do. He didn't want a divorce and knew exactly how to make me change my mind. I could be mad at him forever, as long as he didn't remind me of his beautifully talented skills. Once that happened, emotions would take over, and I'd be in love all over again.

I realized that I didn't need to just get over him to move on with my life. I needed to get over his love jones and that spell he seems to cast over me we're entangled somewhere between love and lust. At this point, I couldn't spell divorce if you paid me ten million dollars so I took him for a ride that was sure to affect him for eternity. That's just how passionate about him I was.

After a stellar performance, I stayed into place and we drifted off to sleep.

11

Never Can Say Goodbye

We'd made amends once again and my eyes couldn't see anything but Todd Taylor. He was loving me like our days were growing short. Worshipped the ground I walked on.

"So you can't go to Virginia with me because...?"

"Baby, I have a convention here to attend on Thursday and Friday, plus my assistant is out on vacation this week."

"Krish you are the owner of the company not an employee. You can take a week to be with your family if you wanted to."

"If it weren't for the convention I could, but I have to be there. I have to make a presentation."

"I think there's another reason you want me to go without you."

"And what would that be?"

"I think you already know." He eyed me suspiciously.

"Look, I'm sick of your accusations. If you have something to say, say it, otherwise leave it alone."

"All I'm saying is, any other time you'd be more than happy to go visit my family."

"I would love to visit with them now, but this weekend is just not good for me."

"Yeah whatever."

Walking out of the room and slamming the door.

I plopped down on my bed.

This has got to stop! I said to myself.

Every since I decided to give him yet another chance and drop the divorce he'd been acting like he can't trust *me*. Now, I definitely had my reasons not to trust him. I guess he thought I'd mess up in retaliation for his wrong doings. If he only knew, that was the farthest from my mind. I was too crazy in love with his sneaky ass.

Six months had passed and I still had not accepted his child. I know it wasn't the child's fault, but I couldn't help what I felt. I refused to let him tell the boys, but he did manage to tell his sisters. Surprisingly, some of his family members, including his messy sister, April, knew of his little secret all the way in Virginia. And here I am sitting right here in Louisiana and had no clue. I guess that was why she was looking at me sideways during Christmas last year. Her and Todd took rides together and would often be tucked away somewhere talking. I'm sure he took her to see his child. I knew it was something behind those satisfied looks she was giving me.

Todd interrupted my thoughts. "Are you gonna take us to the airport tomorrow?"

"Of course bae. You know I gotta see my boys off."

"Gladly, I'm sure." He said accusingly.

"Todd don't start."

"I'm not gonna start." Pulling me to his body. "You just be careful here by yourself."

"I'll be fine. If I get scared, I'll call Mia over."

"If you get scared, call me. I'll be back on the first available flight."

Taking his face into my hands. I planted a kiss on those sexy lips.

"Aww, my hero." I smiled.

"You got that right."

He pulled me closer placing a big wet kiss on my lips. He knew I hated wet kisses so he held me tighter so I couldn't get away. Kept planting big, wet, sloppy kisses all over my face.

I began fighting him off and squirming to get out of his arms when he started licking the side of my face.

I started laughing so hard; I could barely get the words out.

"Todd, stop that's nasty!" I struggled.

The more I fought him I couldn't get out of that grip.

"Stop fighting and I'll stop licking you."

"Stop lickin' me and I'll stop fightin'."

He thought it was hilarious and continued licking my entire face.

"Okay, I give up. I'll stop. Just stop slobbering on me."

Laughing really hard at the disgust, he finally stopped.

"Now, nobody's gonna want you while I'm gone with my scent on you."

I picked up the nearest shoe and started chasing him through the house. He thought it was so funny when he locked me out of the bedroom.

"I'm gonna get you Todd. You're so nasty…Open this door!" I screamed.

"Promise you won't hit me."

"Okay, I promise." I threw out playfully.

As soon as he opened the door, I jumped on him using his chest for a punching bag. He was laughing so hard that he couldn't get me off of him. I had him penned to the floor when I heard the phone ring.

I got up off him breathing heavily to answer the phone.

"Now sucker!" I threw out.

"I love it when you're feisty." He confessed with a smile.

I rolled my eyes and continue to the phone.

"Hello." I happily sang into the receiver almost out of breath.

"Um, hello…I was trying to reach Todd." A very soft female voice replied with urgency in her voice. One I didn't recognize.

I held the phone for a couple of seconds. No one spoke.

"May I ask who's calling?"

I wanted to know. You just don't call another woman's house for her husband and not announce your identity.

"I need to speak with Todd." She said with intensity.

No Mr. Taylor, just Todd. I'm thinking like, *what's really up with this chic?*

"And I need to know who's calling him." I said with attitude to let this woman know whose house she was calling.

"Put him on the phone." Was what I got forcefully in return.

"Excuse me?"

"I'm trying to give you a little respect, don't make it hard for yourself honey."

"You're calling my house asking for my husband, won't tell me your name, talking slick, and you're giving me respect? Something's wrong here sista."

"No bitch you're wrong. You're lucky I…"

Todd snatched the phone from me.

Whoever that heffa was just called me a bitch. Now I'll be. I thought.

"Who the hell is this calling my house disrespecting my wife playing on the phone?" He yelled into the receiver.

Then his facial expression changed dramatically. He listened.

"What…where…how?" He paused in silence "I'll be right there." He screamed before slamming the phone down.

Todd began nervously rubbing his head while refraining from making eye contact with me. So, I knew it was BS time. The fun was over.

"What's wrong Todd and who was that?"

"It's Destiny. A car hit her. She's in the hospital."

"Oh goodness. Is she okay?"

I felt an overwhelming concern.

"I don't really know. I didn't get that much information. I need to get down to the hospital."

I sat on the bed and watched as he scrambled to get his shoes on and find his keys.

"Who was the person that called?"

"Her mother."

"What's her name?" I knew the heffa's face but to this day he hadn't mentioned her name.

"Why is that important Krish?"

I threw him a haunted look.

He hesitated.

"Sydnee." He threw back.

"Sydnee what?"

"What difference does it make?"

"I wanna know the names of the people I'm dealing with now. This woman can call my house; know my name and everything else about me. What's wrong with me knowing who she is?"

He couldn't say anything. He shouldn't say anything.

"It's Davison."

"Thank you." I replied agitated.

I was getting mad all over again. *Why do I put up with this?*

He got dressed in five minutes flat. Stepped to me with open arms.

"I'll be back as soon as I can baby." Gave me a kiss on the lips and held me for a few minutes.

"I'm sorry about that on the phone. I'll let her know that she was wrong and I don't tolerate or appreciate the disrespect."

"I know she's upset, but please check her before I do."

He kissed me again and rushed out of the room then out of the house.

I had more than one reason for asking that home wrecking hussy's name. For one, I was gonna make sure that I check her for calling my house acting a fool. And secondly, I wanted to check out this hospital story so I needed to know who to ask for.

I got a telephone directory and started calling hospitals. Every hospital in town I called had no Destiny Davison. I lay across the bed and flipped on the TV to check out Lifetime. I thought about the real life drama that's often depicted in some of the movies. That's when something told me to switch the last name.

I called back to three of the four hospitals in town asking for Destiny Taylor. When all were negative, I started to fume. As I dialed the last number I was sure his baby momma had lied and someone was gonna pay.

When the receptionist confirmed that there was a Destiny Taylor at the hospital who had been brought in through emergency an hour ago, I nearly dropped the phone. Guess that sneaky son-of-a-bitch forgot to mention he put the child in his last name. Now, I gotta rehash it all one more time.

Around ten pm, Todd still hadn't made it home, nor had he called. He'd been gone for the last seven hours without a word. I wanted to know how the child was. I did have a heart. I wasn't mad at the little girl. It was her momma and daddy that I had problems with. So, I picked up the phone and dialed Todd's cell.

"Hello." A soft, feminine voice sang through the cell phone.

Instantly, I thought maybe I'd dialed the wrong number, so I reluctantly said, "Umm...I'm sorry I must have dialed you by mistake."

"Who do you want to speak to?"

"I was trying to reach my husband."

"Oh, you want Todd." She chuckled. "Well, he can't talk right now." She quickly and proudly threw out.

"And why not?"

"He's busy." She calmly said.

"Who is this?" I asked with a serious attitude.

"You know damn well who this is."

It was then that I recognized the voice from earlier. She was smooth with her words.

"Just give my husband *his* phone."

"I said *he's* busy."

"Then let him tell me that. I said still trying to remain composed. "Why are you trippin' anyway? I've been nothing but respectful to you and your child considering the circumstances."

"You weren't when you came beating on my door all times of the night acting bully. And then you wanna talk noise earlier."

"That's because my husband was in your crib boo, and you were calling my home for *my* husband!"

"You know what? You've kept my baby's father away from her long enough. I'm tired of playing games with you and Todd."

"What's that's suppose to mean?"

"Oh! You *will* see bitch."

"You call me one more bitch and I'll make sure I make you pay for it. Now, I'm trying to be patient and talk to you like a sensible adult. And I don't have to do that being as though you're the ho that slept with *my* husband, you're on *my* husband's phone, and …just put Todd on the phone!"

I was tired of talking to her. I didn't have to say one word to the whore and here I was listening to her while on my man's cell talking crazy.

"He's asleep."

"Asleep? Asleep my behind. Wake him up! Where is he? Is he still at the hospital?"

I was allowing this girl to play with me. The hood was trying its best to come up out of me. I couldn't let her control me.

"No step-mommy." She said sarcastically. "Thank God my baby's okay. Just bruised and scared. I'm at home and her daddy's still here with her."

For some reason, I couldn't even say anything behind that. I know how he is with his kids. He loves them to death. I guess this little girl was no different. Had it been one of our boys he would sleep in the bed holding them until they were sound asleep. I know his heart when it comes to children, his children. I just didn't know his heart when it came to the twisted heffa on the other side of the phone.

"Rest assure, I'll send him home after I finish with him."

She really didn't know who she was playin' with this time around. If I really came out the closet, I was going to jail. And I definitely didn't want that. I thought.

Still trying to keep it together, I said, "Now why you wanna go there heffa? But you know what. Let me tell you something and this is the last time I'll have this little talk with you baby girl. I told him months ago, if he wanted you he could have you. Gave him his walking papers and all. Unless you're blind you can see clearly that he's still here, with his family, his children and his wife. Which is *me*! So it's obvious that he don't want yo' ass. If you're still giving him your tired body then shame on you, you're more ignorant than I thought. And I don't argue with tricks over *my* husband. So kill the drama and stop playing wit me before I really get mad. And believe me you don't want that to happen."

"Ignorant huh? I'm glad *you* think so. He may hold on to you, but once he got a little bit of me, ain't no letting this go. Three years strong. Don't let him fool you."

Click. She hung up in my face.

I know her behind was laughing and really feeling satisfied, but I was ready to bring it to her. Forget suppressing my hood roots. Baby girl needs to see who I really am. She needs a good ole' fashioned country ass whupping.

I dialed back, but she'd turned the phone off. I wanted so badly to drive over there and put my foot in that trick's tail. But my husband was at *her* house, so I wasn't going over there disrespecting myself. I wouldn't give her the pleasure. Not again. I'll see her though.

I dialed three more times before I said, "forget it".

I took a long, hot bath to relieve the frustration.

After climbing into bed with a book, I called Mia to give her the low down on what had transpired today.

In disbelief, Mia said, "Krisha you don't have to deal with that crap. You're too good to him."

She spoke words that I already knew a long time ago. My heart just wouldn't let me give up yet. After talking to Mia for another hour, I decided to put my book aside and turn in. It was after midnight, and I was tired. I went to check on the boys first, then rushed back to my bed and hopped under the covers. I couldn't fall asleep, so I clicked on the TV to BET to check out some videos. By that time, I heard the door closing downstairs, then familiar footsteps on the stairs.

When Todd walked into the bedroom, I wanted to unleash all my frustrations from that phone call onto him. But I realized that wouldn't be fair. He didn't make her do what she did. So I watched him walk in without saying a word.

"Hey bae, why are you still up?" He said seeing me propped up in bed.

Oooooo I can't trust his ass! I thought. I wanted to scream in his face.

Instead I said, "Couldn't sleep."

"Sorry I didn't call you but time passed so fast, then I fell asleep and everything."

"Yeah, I know."

"What do you mean, *you know*?"

"I called you and your whore answered your phone."

"She's not my *whore* Krisha; but what happened…She answered my cell?"

"Yeah, she said you were busy. Then she said you were asleep and wouldn't give you the phone."

"Now she's gone too far. I'm gonna have to tell her about this."

He was upset or good at faking. I couldn't even tell.

"Where were you?"

"At the hospital."

"So you were asleep at the hospital?" I drilled.

"Yeah baby. They took forever in there."

"Todd, what's going on? I trusted you when you said you weren't still sleeping with her."

"I'm not."

"She seems to think differently."

"I don't know what she thinks, but I'm gonna set her straight. Matter-of-fact, I'm gonna call her right now."

He rushed to the phone by the bed and dialed her number. I noticed how he picked up the phone and dialed the number without hesitation. It was evident that the number was deeply embedded in his long-term memory. He never noticed his actions.

Men are so stupid. I thought. I shook my head in disgust.

"Why the hell did you answer my phone?" He yelled into the receiver.

I couldn't hear what she was saying, but he was laying it on her from his end.

"Don't you ever play with my wife like that. My wife has never done anything to you. So why are you trippin'?" He listened for a second. "Just take care of my child and don't worry about what's going on over here."

He hung up the phone satisfied, I guess.

"Are you okay baby?" He asked.

"I'm fine."

He'd satisfied himself by calling her and checking her, but I gotta satisfy myself too. I can't wait until he leaves because this ain't over. But, I decided to change the subject for the night. He was getting on my nerves.

"Are you still going to Virginia in the morning?"

"Yes of course, why wouldn't I?"

"I thought since your child was hurt you may change your mind."

"She's gonna be fine. The car came within inches of actually hitting her. She just has a broken arm and few scrapes and bruises. I'll call to check on her while I'm gone."

Reading the expression on my face. Todd sat down beside me on the bed. He leaned down to give me a peck on the lips.

"Krish. I never intended for you to deal with no baby momma BS. I'm sorry for all of this."

I rolled my eyes, turned my back to him, and shut my eyes tight. Without saying another word, he went to shower.

When he returned, I was drifting off to sleep. He got into bed; curled in behind me and whispered into my ear, "Don't worry about nothing. You're the only one I could ever love. You got my heart."

His words spoke a different meaning in my mind. My mind told me that he meant to say, "Yeah, I hit her, but I don't love her."

I know in my heart he slept with her. *At the hospital my brown behind.* I thought.

I started to call back to see when the child was released. But that would have opened a whole new book of drama. I let it ride. There are some things better left uncovered.

I lay there and consumed myself in a load of thoughts. *He's going to Virginia for a whole week and he turned his back to me. That in and of itself is something to clown about. Plus, its after midnight and he decided he needed to get her on the phone to prove something to me. And if he was as dog tired as he claimed to be, he would have showered in the morning, especially since we weren't having relations! I don't think I like this feeling. Matter-of-fact, I know I don't like this crap. This bastard gon' make me cut him.*

Frustration and discomfort made me shift around in the bed. Regardless of what I was feeling and thinking at the time, I blindly fell asleep in his arms.

12

Owner of a Lonely Heart

The next morning I put my three babies on a plane bound for Virginia. Then I went to work to see what was poppin'. I started to get at his baby momma, but I decided against it. She wanted to be me, so forget it. That thought right there brought a smile to my face.

Instead I focused on my marriage. I decided that Todd and I would go on a weekend getaway when he returned since I couldn't go with him to visit his family. Besides, we needed the time together.

Our relationship had been strained for months. I'm hanging in there, but I just don't like the situation that he's put me in. I can't stand it. Playing second sometimes when I've always been first. I never thought in a million years that I, being a married woman, would be caught up in baby momma drama with my *husband*.

My day at work was pretty much useless. All I did was think about Todd and my marriage. The more I thought the worse I felt.

After I left the office around 5:30 pm, I stopped off at my mothers to catch up with her. We hadn't sat and talked for a while. I wanted to immediately go in there and pour all my troubles at her feet, but I just couldn't. I didn't want to burden her with my problems. But, me knowing my mother and she knowing her daughter, I should have known that she would easily read my face for my thoughts.

"Would you like something to eat baby?" She asked in her usual soft motherly tone laced with concern.

"No thanks ma, I'm not hungry right now."

She sat down across from me at the kitchen table. Looked into my face, then turned away.

"Well, I've got to eat baby. It's time for me to take my medicines."

"Go on ma, I'm okay."

My mother began eating her dinner. I began reading the newspaper as we chatted. We talked about the kids, work, and the latest news.

Then out of nowhere, while looking down into her plate my mother said, "Krisha, you are the only one responsible for making yourself happy."

At first I didn't respond. *She knows me too well.* I thought.

"Why would you say that ma?"

She looked up directly into my eyes. Didn't bother replying. She knew that I knew what she was saying.

Trying to play it off, I asked again. "What do you mean momma?"

"I don't see that sparkle in your eyes anymore. Something has taken that away."

"I'm okay."

"I'm not asking you if you're okay. I see that, but are you happy with your life right now? I know you and Todd have been through a few things, but you can't count on him to make you happy. That's your responsibility. Todd will be Todd. He's gonna please himself and give you what he wants you to have. You've got to look out for yourself."

"I know he loves me mama."

Why am I defending that? I thought. I don't know why I felt the need to try to prove that to my mother. *Why did I even say that?* The tears automatically welled up in my eyes. The more intense her stare got, the more I struggled to hold those tears inside.

"Yes, he does love you baby. I believe he loves you almost as much as I do. But sometimes men think about themselves and what they want without considering the consequences. They worry about those after the dirt has been done. And those things definitely won't make you happy. Therefore, as I said, you have to do what it takes for you to be happy. They're not always thinking in your best interest, husband or not."

I couldn't hold them any longer. Tears soaked my face. My mother reached across the table to take my hand.

"Be the strong woman that I've always taught you to be at all times. Never compromise who you are or what you stand for baby. Don't ever let your love for him allow you to become naïve. I know how men can be, especially *your* husband."

My mother handed me a box of tissue. I wiped the tears from my face only to make room for more.

I poured my heart out. I told my mother of my husband's indiscretions. I told her about all I'd been dealing with these past months. I told her about his first affair and how I'd caught him in the act. I finally let go. For some reason, she didn't seem surprised.

She took me by the hand and led me to the couch in the living room. She sat next to me and wiped my face with the tissues, then held me in her arms. Cradled me like I was two years old again.

"Baby, I know you think he's your universe, but you've got to stop being so passive and stop thinking with your heart. That's gonna lead you to downfall in the long run. What happened to that feisty little Krisha that had a mean streak in her? Who was a tough lil cookie and would fight at the drop of a dime. I'm not telling you to pick those negatives ways up again because you're a grown woman with a great professional career. But when it comes to Todd, use your head to think. You've got to be tough.

Put on some armor. I need to see the strength in you. God gave you immaculate intelligence and strength to be a beautiful black woman. Use it in all aspects of life, and in all that you do; don't stop with your marriage. I'm not telling you what to do with your marriage, that's for you to decide. I'm just giving you a little advice on how to handle a smooth criminal like Todd. And baby, I've been around the block in my day, and I must say, he's one of the best. You'll never know the things he's done until it knocks you off your feet with little room for recovery."

Those last words shocked the blaze out of me.

Was she trying to tell me something specific? Did she know something I didn't know? I worried.

Of course she did. She was my mother. She sees all but says nothing. She would never say anything that she knew would tear my world apart. She would only give it to me in her wise and encouraging words. Just as she'd done tonight.

On the drive home, I played tonight's conversation with my mother over and over again in my head. I took in everything she said. But I tried like hell to pull out something that indicated Todd was screwing up again. I wondered why the victim is always the last to know that they're the victim.

I called myself a sharp, sassy, smart girl who has her business together, but in reality I didn't have a clue. I realized that I needed to find myself and come out of this lovesick, sex driven shell that I was in. It consumed me. I know I gotta get real with this and handle it before it handles me. I try so hard to be as nice as I can be and not unleash the ugly side that lies inside. But sometimes nice don't cut it.

When I found Todd, I found true love. My life has been consumed with nothing less than love every since. Love filled me from head to toe, inside and out. I learned to suppress the hate and hurt that I once carried as a child. Hatred from not being loved by my father. Those things kept me within a circle.

A circle filled with frustration and aggression. I knew I had to leave the confines of the circle in order to be happy. I just let it go. So I allowed myself to step outside to love and be loved. I learned to deal with people on a different level. I think I let too much of the old me go though.

I'd become soft, too giving, too loving, and too accepting. I walked a new walked, and talked a new talk. Once my mentality and views of life changed, my personality blossomed and my demeanor came naturally. I guess that's really who I am. Who I am inside has not and will not ever change. I am who I am at heart. I love with everything I have and I respect who I'm with. I guess that's what makes me vulnerable also.

I can have some stuff with me if I chose to; I guess everyone could. Guess I needed to "chose to" and put my game face on so I can handle the issues of my relationship with my husband like a real woman. Crying like a little girl ain't gon' get it. My mom was right. It is time to let a little bit of the old me resurface to get things under control. I need to bring out a little bit of that girl who grew up in the hood. She needs to show her face for a minute.

Yep. I'm from what they call the hood in the South. Really, just an underprivileged area ridden with drugs and petty crime. A lot of people don't know that. I grew up there until I was twelve years old. When my mother finished obtaining all of her degrees and got on her feet, we moved out. But all the learning had already taken place for me. That was where my heart and soul was. That was where my best friend was.

I met Mia when I was five years old in the projects. We'd been kicking it every since.

While driving I'd thought of all kinds of things to do and say to Todd. I had everything figured up in my head until the phone rang.

"Hello". I sang into the receiver.

"Hey baby."

"I was just thinking about you."

"I miss you."

"I miss you too."

"Well, I decided to call you before going to bed. The boys are already asleep. Sorry we didn't call earlier."

"That's okay, I was visiting with my mother anyway."

"Guess you're not bored without us then?"

"I wouldn't say that."

"Truth is, I couldn't sleep. I feel so alone without you. I wish you were here."

"I wish I were there too, but you left me." I whined.

"I should have waited until you got free to come with us."

"It's not your fault."

"It's my fault that I'm laying here with you on my mind."

"Are you sure its me on your mind?"

"Yeah, who else would it be?"

"You don't want me to answer that do you?"

"You can answer all you want, but you are the only woman I love. I don't give a damn what she told you. I made a mistake. My lovin' is for you and you only."

"Now it's all for me? She already knows more about you than I'm comfortable with."

I was quickly getting aggravated.

"Why do you want to go there baby? I just wanted to hear your voice to feel closer to you. I love you Krisha. Why don't you believe me anymore?"

"I do believe you, but I don't trust your baby momma. She's a conniving ho and I see I'm gonna have to get her mind right."

"Leave it alone. Don't stoop to her level."

"I can handle me. You just hurry and bring yourself home to me."

I tried changing the conversation around. I wasn't going to let this control me.

"I was so tired physically and mentally after Destiny's accident that I didn't make love to you. But I'm really regretting that right now."

"If you say so?"

"Girl, you just don't know." He laughed. "This is gonna be a long week. I feel like coming home early."

"Todd, don't be silly. It'll be all the better when you make it back."

"Fo' sho lil mama, believe that." He said trying to mimic the Louisiana dialect.

We laughed at his attempt.

"I love you baby." I admitted.

"You know you're my girl…yo sexy self."

I blushed. "Enough already."

"Alright…goodnight love."

"Good night."

He hung up.

I smiled and proceeded to climb out of my car and move into my house to find rest. My heart felt good.

All the noise I conjured up in my mind was thrown out the window when my baby called.

Imagining life without Todd was hard. How could I ever leave him? It took a lifetime to find this life and I can't imagine throwing it all away on some two-bit sideline whore.

13

Dear Mama

*A*s I dreamt while I slept, I thought I heard a ringing in my ear.

I jumped up and looked over at the phone on the table. It wasn't ringing, but I did notice the light blinking on my cell phone that was sitting on the table.

I picked up my cell to see that I had two text messages. The first message was from Mia at 12:20 am, which was about twenty minutes ago. It read, "Where are you? Call me please!"

If Mia called twice this late, she had some serious drama for me. I thought.

I happily dialed her number. Anticipating the usual good shit she was about to deliver.

She answered on the first ring.

"Mia, are you okay?"

"Not really."

"Where are you?"

"Outside."

"Outside where?"

"Your driveway."

"Why?" I sat up in the bed. What's wrong?"

Her cry was her reply. I became frantic.

"I'm on my way Mia, okay. Just sit right there."

I hung up. Threw on some sweats, T-shirt, and shoes and rushed out the door.

I didn't wait for her to get herself together to tell me what was wrong, so I had no clue as to what was going on.

The ten-second walk to the end of my driveway took about five seconds.

Approaching Mia's car, I could see what looked like a small light on in her car, so I hurriedly moved closer. I could hear sobbing through the closed windows of the car. I knew my best friend's cry anywhere, so I ran over the rest of the way.

Mia was in the driver's side seat with the seat laid all the way back, balled up crying her eyes out. I swung the door open and tried to force her to sit up.

"Mia...baby, what is it?" Worry lined my face.

She didn't want to sit up, so I had to tug on her to get her into my arms. All the while asking for the source of the tears.

An answer did not come. But in my arms, I could clearly see the redness that intensely covered her eyes.

"Mia, what on earth is?"

The pain was evident. So intense that it had an effect on me.

I began to cry for the unknown. Whatever it was, it was eating my best friend alive.

I was sitting in the driver's seat along with Mia, holding her, when she said between sobs, "She's gone."

"What? Who...gone where?"

"She's gone Krish. She's gone."

She began to get hysterical as she tried to talk. I held her tighter. I cried just because something was hurting my friend.

"Who? Baby, who?"

The look in her eyes as I studied her face told me. But I prayed to be wrong.

Despair started to hit me immediately. In a whisper I asked, "Gone where Mia?"

I looked deep into her eyes for an answer.

"No, Mia." Is all I remember saying.

When I woke up, I was on my couch with a cold towel on my forehead and Mia sitting next to me. Kyra was standing in the middle of the room talking on the telephone. *Could I have been dreaming? What's going on?*

Took me a few minutes to gather my senses.

When I looked over to see my mother's pastor talking to my aunt the reality of what Mia had tried to deliver set in. I lay there with my eyes closed taking in the conversations that were going on inside the room.

Turned out my mother had passed away from a massive heart attack around 11:30 pm. Since Todd was away, my aunt figured Mia was the best person to break the news to me. Looking at her, one would think she needed me more than I needed her. Her love for my mother was tremendous. Mia had been in our lives for as long as I could remember. My mother was like a second mother to her.

I felt as if I was trying to get up off the couch, but I wasn't really sure. I was weak. It was like the earth was spinning on its axis at an alarming rate right before my eyes.

I felt sick. I wanted to scream. I opened my mouth, but not a word ever escaped my tongue.

I felt cold. I felt lonely. I felt a horrific pain. One that I was sure would never go away.

The tears came. They fell. I squirmed. Brought attention to myself. Everyone noticed. Mia was first to my side. Curled up like a baby, Mia lifted my head to her lap, and stroked my face, wiping away the tears. I sobbed uncontrollably. I screamed. Realization had set in along with an uncontrollable grief. I couldn't help my actions. I didn't care to. I lost it. What else was I to do? She was my life. She was all that I had left. An absent father. Who else would be there? Who else *could* be there? Who else is there to care? I missed her already. I wanted to hear her voice. If I could just call her to hear her voice one more time. How can I live without her?

A part of me was gone. The other part was missing. How was I to be whole? How was I to live without my mother?

With these thoughts running through my mind, I broke all the way down. I couldn't control the way my grief was displayed. It was as if something or someone was in control of my body, my emotions. I wanted this to be another bad dream. I was a little girl again. I wanted my momma.

I couldn't breathe. My sight was gone. I couldn't feel. I wasn't me. I heard voices not sure of the source. I felt hate. I heard remorse. They say she's gone. I can't feel. God please don't let this nightmare be real. Can't live without her, she's always been right here. Always a step behind me to catch me if I'd fall. Never a need to fear Momma always had the answers; she was my right hand. She was my strength. She helped me see; helped me stand. She helped me be the woman I am.

Then, I saw no colors, only saw black. The comfort of the darkness where I rested scared to look back. Through the darkness I looked for her, tried to find her face. Too dark to see in this ole empty place. Then, there was a light almost at the end of the tunnel. I tried to get there, I knew it was Momma. I ran through the darkness, I found the place. I longed to see my momma's beautiful face. And there she was, dressed in a white gown, with jewels at her feet wearing a crown. "Be still baby, calm to a rest. I love you more than anything, but God knows best. I'll be okay; I'm in his hands now. Take care of yourself and my babies for life is only a test. I reached out to her. The light began to fade. "Momma!" I screamed. "Please don't go...I love you so much don't leave me here alone! Her smiling face was fading away. There was nothing I could do. I kept trying to reach her but she vanished out of view. I heard a voice telling me to hold on. Heard a familiar voice telling me they were home. I still could not see as darkness prevailed. I began to let my body and mind succumb to the darkness and the hold it had on me. I stopped the struggle. Everything went black. I don't remember a thing from that point on. I was free.

I cried. I slept. I slept, I cried. For three days to eat, to get dressed, I tried. I couldn't bare the thought, of my mother being gone. So I lay there trying to sleep off and on. Todd and Mia bathe me, tried to feed me, combed my hair, dressed me. For three whole days while my heart withered away. I cried; they talked. Understanding not one word, I saw the motion of lips. I was there in body. The rest of me was gone.

Todd, Mia, and Aunt Mae had made all arrangements. My mother was to be buried four days after her death. Todd had gone to the airport to get the boys. He'd left them in Virginia when he suddenly left on the night of momma's death.

As I lay in my bed staring at the wall, I wondered why I couldn't be there for her. I'd just left her about two hours before. Why didn't I stay a while longer? If I'd only stayed the night with her like my first mind had told me, I would have been there for her. I had no reason not to stay. My family was out of town, so I had no excuses. Why didn't I just listen to myself?

I began to think about our last words, our last conversation. She'd told me to stand strong and don't allow my love to make me naïve. "Be the woman I always taught you to be", she'd said. I could do that. For her I would try.

I remember them getting me dressed for the funeral. I remember the church. I remember sitting down with my family. I remember crying the entire time. I remember Todd ushering me to say goodbye. I remember her peaceful face. Her solemn smile. Trying to make myself believe that she was in a better place. My world went black. I could see no more. Back to the place I'd gone before. My breath was gone with no more in store. I lost the events of the rest of that day. My next recollection wasn't until two days later. I awakened to Todd at my side.

"Krisha, I'm getting you out of this house today." I heard Todd say as he stood by my bedside with a glass of water and a bottle of pills in hand. He sat on the side of the bed where I laid in a ball on my side.

"You're getting dressed today baby." He said with a stern but caring expression.

He opened up the bottle of meds and poured one small white pill into his hand. Then gave me a hard look.

"You know what? I'm not even giving you this today because you're getting up. You're gonna be alright." He kissed my cheek.

I looked at him but didn't speak.

"I'll be right back with your breakfast."

Todd got up and left the room. There was a soft knock at the door. The door swung back open and in walked supermodel Kyra with the biggest smile plastered across her face.

"Hey baby. How are you today?"

She strolled over to the bed, bent down to place a light kiss on my cheek. Sat on the bed next to me and stroked my face.

"Todd's gonna feed you the breakfast I made for you and then we're going to get you up today. Is that okay with you?" She said softly.

My thought was, *No. I don't have the strength or desire to leave this room.*

"And don't you try to fight it either. You need a breath of fresh air."

I remained in the ball on my side. I managed to look Kyra in her eyes. She was there to help me. I loved her for that. But she'd better get the hell out of my room. I wasn't moving.

She continued to encourage me while massaging my arm. Todd entered with a breakfast tray. His smile widened when he saw me. I really can't understand why, I just felt ugly.

"Are you hungry beautiful?"

He gave the tray to Kyra while he helped me sit up against the headboard, propping my back with several pillows.

"Todd, I'm gonna go clean the kitchen. If you need me holla."

"Thanks Kyra I got this. You go ahead."

Kyra left the room and Todd sat next to me on the bed.

"Come on baby. You have to eat something today."

He picked up a spoon of grits and proceeded to feed me. I stared at him with my mouth shut tight like he was crazy for thinking I was going to eat that.

He tried for the next ten minutes to get me to eat. I refused to open my mouth. I just wasn't hungry. I had no desire to eat or do anything. He even tried to squeeze my mouth open, to no avail. The looks I gave him told him that he was beating a dead horse.

His face was laced with concern.

"Krisha, you gotta snap out of this. I don't know what else to do. You won't eat. You haven't eaten a thing since before we lost your mother."

Little did he know, I hadn't eaten the day before that either, tripping over him and his drama. I thought.

"You won't dress yourself or leave the room. You don't talk." He took my hand in his. "How can I help you baby?" He kissed the back of my hand. "It's been a week and you've been in a vegetative state every since. I'm sure you've lost weight. You've only taken small sips of water for Mia in the last few days. You haven't ingested more than twenty ounces in seven days."

I looked into his eyes. There was genuine concern. There was love for me. Concern for my well-being. But he just didn't understand how bad it hurts. Or maybe he does? I don't know. If I can't share my meals and my days with my mother, there's no use.

It had been she and I for so long. How could I live without her? I didn't want to. How would each day take shape? I had no clue. Tears slipped from the corners of my eyes. I couldn't stop them. I didn't try.

There was a soft knock at the door then the door opened.

"Morning Todd. How is she?"

"She's the same. Still won't eat. I just don't know what else to do."

"I got her Todd. I brought the boys back. They're downstairs with Kyra."

"Were they too much for you last night?"

"Oh no. You know I enjoy my nephews staying with me. We had a blast."

"Thanks a lot Mia. I appreciate everything you've done."

"No thanks needed. This is family. You know I'd do anything for her." Looking over at me with a smile.

I was lucky to have Mia and Kyra. They were two a girl could call friends and mean it.

"Did you get some rest?" Mia asked Todd.

"Yeah, actually I did."

"Good, you needed it. I know this one has been tough." Pointing her finger at me.

"That's my boo though. I've been there so I know what she's feeling." Todd kissed my cheek and wiped my face before leaving the room.

Mia stood over me in the bed. "Hey baby." She bent down to kiss my cheek. "How's it going girl?" She threw out the rhetorical question. "This is your day." She continued.

She let out a sigh and grabbed the bowl of still warm grits from the tray.

"C'mon boo let's do this today."

I stared at her to see if she had all her senses too. *Why don't they just leave me alone?* I thought.

After a few seconds of holding the spoon to my mouth, I remained tight-lipped refusing to take in an ounce of food. Mia stared at me. She looked into my eyes as if she was looking for answers. Lines of frustration formed her forehead. A single tear fell from her left eye. There was total silence in the room. She held her gaze directly into my eyes. Then a tear left her right eye. She embraced my neck.

"I can't lose you too Krisha." She said in almost a whisper.

I looked at my best friend and saw her love for me. At that moment, I realized that she really did love me. My tears began to flow heavily. Her sincerity was making me cry.

"C'mon baby, it'll be okay." Mia said wiping my tears and caressing my back.

After a few silent moments, Mia said, "Just try Krisha…Please." She held the spoon back up to my mouth.

I slowly shook my head.

Through tears she begged. "Please…Its…Its been so long." Mia stammered.

I tried to open my mouth. But not to eat.

I succeeded. "Just let me go too."

Mia hung her head. She put the spoon back in the bowl. Sat it on the nightstand.

"I can't do that." She cried out. Looking at me through tear filled eyes.

I blindly stared.

She placed the breakfast tray on the floor. Moved up on the bed, threw her arms around my upper body pulling me in tightly.

"You're all I have Krisha." She cried with her face muzzled into my head. "If I lose you, who will *I* have?"

"I…I…can't…I want my…I…" I tried to say.

She hugged me tighter. I couldn't get my words out. My chest hurt so badly.

"Shh..shh. You're okay." She rubbed the back of my head as I cried into her shoulder.

I lost control.

"Is she really gone? Did she leave me?" I screamed.

"Yeah baby, its true." She said as we rocked back and forth.

"I don't…I don't." I stammered. Words caught up in cries.

"Get it out baby. Let it all go." We rocked.

"I can't live without her…I can't….just let me go too." I screamed. My emotions had taken over. I poured it all out to her.

"I can't do that Krisha." Mia cried. "I'll never do that."

She climbed all the way in bed with me, lay with me, and took me in her arms. We held onto each other as we cried. I buried my face in her chest.

Todd burst into the room.

"What happened Mia?"

I heard a frantic Todd ask.

"It's going to be fine."

Was all Mia said to him.

He stood in the doorway watching us cry and rock each other. One consoling the other. She was the only one who truly understood me. She felt what I felt. She knew what was in my heart. She was my heart.

We stayed that way for a few minutes before anyone spoke again. She wiped her tears with her hand. My tears with the same hand.

"I can't live without you. Nobody knows me like you. Nobody loves me like you. I need you…you've got to get better. Promise you'll eat."

I looked at her then closed my eyes.

Nobody said anything. My head pulled to her breasts. I hugged her tighter. I thanked God for her. I just felt so alone.

"I love you." I said.

"I love you too."

"Help me."

"I will."

We rocked.

Mia reached to the nightstand to retrieve the now cold breakfast.

She got up from the bed.

"I'll be right back, okay."

She dashed out of the room in search of nourishment for my deprived body. Within seconds, she came back with a bowl of hot chicken noodle soup.

She sat on the bed next to me.

"Let's try this again." She smiled and said.

She held the spoon to my mouth. As I stared into her eyes, I slowly opened my mouth.

"Thank you sweetheart. Thank you so much." She kissed my forehead.

She gave me another spoonful. I sipped some orange juice.

"That's it." She said with a smile.

Before I knew it, Mia had fed me half the bowl. She and I both were crying our eyes out the whole time.

She put the bowl down on the nightstand.

"Come here girl." She embraced me as we continued to shed tears. "Get it all out. You gotta let her go Krisha. You gotta get on with your life."

I weakly said, "I don't know if I can."

"You can. You gotta do it for the boys. They need you just like you needed your mother."

"How?"

"Live on the beautiful memories. She taught you so much, never forget any of it. Live like the woman she taught you to be. But don't let her death stop you. She wouldn't want it that way."

I thought about our last conversation. I thought about the message she sent me right after her death.

I gotta get up and fight. I can't lie down and let it all wither away. I said in my heart.

"I'll try."

Mia got back into bed with me.

She held me and we cried some more.

We'd been like that for about thirty minutes or more before the door to my bedroom flung open.

"Hey momma." A little voice said.

I looked up to see two smiling faces entering my bedroom.
I smiled back.

"How are you doing today mom?" Rang the most articulate, Malik.

They both walked over to give me a quick kiss on the cheek.

"Momma's okay baby." I weakly replied.

"Momma, would you like to go with us to the park today?" TJ said.

"I don't know baby."

"Aw, come on Ma. We haven't been anywhere together in a while."

"I…don't."

Cutting me off. "She's coming guys." Mia said.

"Are you gonna come too Tee Mia?"

"Sure baby, if you'd like, we can all go."

"Let me go see if Tee Kyra wants to go with us too. She can bring Paige."

Mia looked surprised. "Is Tee Kyra still here?"

"Yes, she's talking to Daddy."

"Oh, I didn't see her when I went down. Could you guys please tell her to come up?" Mia asked.

"Okay Tee Mia." Malik answered.

TJ had already run down the stairs.

"Love you mom." Malik said giving me a hug.

"Love you baby."

After eating and seeing my babies, I began to regain my strength to live. I know it was nothing but my momma who sent my reasons for living in at the perfect time. She was sending me a message to live.

Mia went into the bathroom. I then heard the water running in the Jacuzzi tub.

While she was in there, Kyra came into the bedroom. She noticed the almost empty bowl of soup.

"You ate! Thank God. Mia, how in the world did you do that?" Pointing at the food tray.

"Me and my girl have a connection. No one else will be able to understand."

Shrugging her shoulders. "Whatever is fine with me. As long as she ate something."

"Kyra can you get her something to wear out of the closet?"

"Oh, she's getting dressed too?"

"She sure is." Mia rang.

I stared at the two of them.

I had eaten, but I didn't say anything about taking a bath. I thought. Mia must have read my mind.

She put her hands on her hips and looked at me.

"What? Don't look at me like that. You gotta wash that monkey. Todd ain't gonna want that thang smelling like that."

For the first time in days, I managed to laugh. We all laughed. Mia's mission was accomplished. My girl was good.

The next few weeks were so very hard for me, but I survived somehow. On days when I didn't think I would, I did. I prayed alot and thought about what my mother would have wanted.

Things did not get near normal for me until about six months later. Then, I was able to deal with her death with opened eyes. I finally realized that nothing in my power could have prevented God's will from being done. As with all His works, there was a reason behind His doings. God took her for a reason, and that was something that I was just going to have to understand.

I saw her every night in my dreams and every night she gave me messages of love and wisdom. I realized wisdom beyond your years is the absolute best kind of knowledge. This wisdom is rare to some and not always accepted, but I welcomed it and appreciated it. Over the months, my mother, even though she no longer walked the earth, was right by my side. If it weren't for her, life for me would have been down right ugly.

Todd had been very supportive and loving throughout my ordeal. He was so patient and understanding and catered to my every wish and need. The drama that plagued our relationship before seemed to have gone away. He was there for me. I didn't even hear anything else from or about his baby momma. Somehow, our marriage seemed to have strengthened after the death of my mother.

But when the BS started, I knew things were back to normal for me.

"Krisha, there's something I want to talk to you about." He reluctantly said.

I walked into the family room with a tall glass of strawberry lemonade and popcorn and plopped down on the couch.

"Okay, what is it?"

The kids were also in the room watching cartoons and eating popcorn. So, Todd suggested we sit out on the patio. I got up off the couch and he trailed me out onto the well-lit patio.

"You don't look right, what is it?" I asked. Staring at the frightful expression on his face.

"Well, it's just that I'm trying to find the best words to use so I won't come across wrong."

"Todd just sit down and tell me. After what I just went through a few months ago, I feel like I can handle anything."

Sitting next to me, Todd took my hand in his.

"Baby, I don't want you to get the wrong idea or read more into this than what it is. I just wanted to keep it honest with you and be upfront."

Growing impatient because I knew he was gonna say something stupid, I said, "Just tell me baby."

"Well, Sydnee and Destiny are finally moving to California."

"Is that good or bad?"

"It's kind of both."

"What do you mean 'kind of both'?"

"Of course, I'll miss Destiny. I don't really prefer my child being half way across the country. But as for Sydnee, I don't care where she goes."

Rolling my eyes, I said, "Umph, so what is this about?"

"Sydnee is moving but she wants me to move her there and support not only Destiny, but her for six months until she gets on her feet."

I let out a little chuckle. "Support her, huh?" I was calm.

"She has her eye on a condo in L.A. She wants me to pay her utilities and car note as well as the lease and Destiny's daycare expenses."

"For six months? That heffa has really lost her mind." I spat.

"She says if I don't help her, she'll bring lawyers and the court system into it. She already went to see how much she could get from me."

"How did she have access to your income information? How does this woman have so much information about you?"

"I don't know, but she claims she'll sue the both of us for child support and that amount can be ridiculous if she drags you into it; with both the businesses and all."

"What does she do anyway?"

"Uhmm, well, she's between jobs right now."

He was evasive.

"When she *is* working what does she do?

"She's in the entertainment industry."

"Entertainment? Who does she entertain?"

"She's an exotic dancer."

"As in stripper?"

"No, she's a dancer."

"Whatever. She's a stripper and you know it. So is that how she lives so lavishly."

He didn't try to respond.

"You mean you slept with a stripper, planted a seed, then came home and had sex with me like it was no big deal."

I was getting upset at the scenario that played in my head.

"It wasn't like that."

"How else could it be? You put me at risk for whatever she had or *has*."

"Past tense Krisha."

"Yeah whatever... And for what? Only to dig yourself into a deep black hole with no bottom."

I looked all up side his head. I wanted to go off on him!

We sat in silence.

In one minute I'd thought of a thousand ways to mess him up real good.

My good glass of lemonade had turned sour, so I finally got up from my chair and proceeded to walk back inside the house to ditch the glass.

Before retreating back inside, I turned around and said to him, "Look, let this tramp know she don't wanna mess with me. You handle your business the best way you see fit. I'm gonna stay out of it. But let me make this clear, I better not be dragged into this and my kids better not want for a damn thang. So you do whatever you have to do!"

"Krisha, I just wanted to be upfront with you. I'm trying to do this right this time."

"And I'm glad you are, but I don't need this. This is your problem not mine. I didn't sleep with her and I damn sure didn't give you permission to. So you handle it."

I love that man's dirty drawers, but "stupid" is the only word I could find to describe Todd Taylor.

I'd chosen to forget about the situation that was going on before my mother's death. I was hurting too bad to dwell on the dumb. I realized that life is indeed too short, so I decided to forgive and forget. My deciding to forget did not erase the situation. Looks like the baby momma saga continues.

I'm learning more and more about my husband everyday though. I never in a million years would have believed my husband would have had sex with a trick who got naked and showed her ass for a living. You gotta draw the line somewhere.

Todd was always the type who held high standards and believed in honesty and faithfulness. *When did he decide to compromise all that? The girl's sex game can't be that good, or is it the head game that had him hanging by the balls? Was my husband really that weak for women?*

It's evident that he goes for the cream of the crop in the looks department. I'd only seen her twice and I can be woman enough to admit that she's a pretty girl with a nice body, but hell so am I. Times ten if you ask me. But she clearly defines "jump off".

I just don't know what's going on with Todd. I was seeing a side of him that I honestly never knew existed. I thought about the words of my mother, "smooth criminal". A perfect way to describe my man.

14

Let's Get It On

Mia

Derric pulled me close to his body. Lips to my ear.

"Having fun baby?" He asked as his sexy lips nibbled my earlobe at the same time.

Derric's younger brother, Aaron, who was a ball player for the Louisiana Hurricanes was having a party across the river at Level 10.

Level 10 was an upscale club usually frequented by the ballas and stackers. Where everybody who was somebody took their party.

We were all up in there having the time of our lives.

"Yeah baby this party is off the chain. And stop that please." I said looking up into my sweetheart's handsome face.

He smiled and kissed my lips. Soft and quick.

"Come on, let's dance. This my jam." I said pulling at Derric.

We slid onto the dance floor as the DJ mixed it up real good. So good that he decided to go back to Juvie's "Back that Thang Up".

In Louisiana while in the club, that song is the female national anthem. Every female in the club was backing it up, throwing it, dropping it, popping in, rolling it; hind parts going left and right. Females were pulling their skirts up halfway their thighs, spreading their legs and bending the knees a little, getting into the stance that every girl in "The Boot" knows how to do. Then looking back at their tails and going for it. Ya just gotta know how to make your butt pop and roll if you're from "The Boot".

That was so funny to see.

Although I wasn't throwing ass, I had a good time dancing and laughing my tail off.

I wish my girls were up in here with me. I know we would have had a blast together. I thought.

After that song I was tired and it was just too crowded on the dance floor. I really didn't like sweating when I danced, so leaving the dancing to the amateurs and hos who wanted to be seen was what I intended to do.

I'd lost Derric after the first song, so I looked around the club for him. Spotted him at the bar talking to his brother so I walked over to them and asked him to order me a drink.

As I stood at the bar chatting with Derric and his brother, I checked out everything going on in the club. I was nosey as hell and I knew it, but I didn't care. I wanted to see what jump offs the pro ballers were taking home with them tonight.

As my eyes roamed the entire club, they suddenly stopped at the front entrance. My mouth dropped in amazement.

No this mothaf…. I cut my thought short and shook my head instead.

Todd was being led in by a pretty young thang. Tall, tan chic with long wavy black hair and a nice rack leading the way.

"Here's your drink bae." Derric called my attention back to him.

"Thanks…Hey I'm gonna catch a table over there in the corner." I said with a smile.

"I'll be over in a minute bae."

He gave me a quick kiss.

I took my drink and got out of dodge. I wanted to be the one seeing what was going on so I backed into a corner with a good view of Todd's table.

There were so many people in the club that it wasn't likely that he would notice me unless I was right in his face.

His little surprise entrance had ruined *my* party. So now I had to play P.I. and might just have to act a fool on my girl's behalf.

Todd ordered drinks as he and his date sat facing the dance floor. I watched his ass close for about twenty minutes. Chilled for a few more minutes as I watched my friend's husband slow dance with whomever the woman was, palming her buns and kissing her like he owned the heffa.

My blood was boiling now; all in the name of love for my sister.

I don't get in Krisha's business like that, but this scene was just down right ridiculous. I'd told Krisha about not checking up on his lying, sneaky ass.

I had no idea who the woman was but she and Todd seemed mighty familiar and she had a lot of friends. Someone was always stopping by the table talking to her. And because she was inside the club, at this party, probably meant she was somebody Aaron knew.

I thoroughly checked her out as all women do. She was attractive and up on the latest fashions. Her style was on point and the shoe game was sick. Todd really knew how to pick 'em. He loved beautiful women. Guess he tries to keep high standards in the looks department, but most definitely she had nothing on my sis.

As soon as that thought left my mind, another one popped in.

I'm gonna fix this clown tonight. I thought.

I pulled out my camera phone and walked over toward the dance floor where they were belly rubbing. The crowd was so thick and it was dark so he couldn't see me coming. Besides he was all into ole girl and the music that he never looked up.

I snapped two pictures with my phone. I thought the flash would get me caught but he didn't notice at all.

I hated doing it, but I sent the pictures with a text to Krisha's phone. It was now after one a.m. I know she was probably asleep, but she'll hear the phone beeping indicating a message. I didn't want Derrick to see what I was doing so I'd sent him away from the table assuring him I was okay.

After about five minutes, I got up and went outside the club so I could hear because I knew she'd call back. I didn't want Derrick to see me on my phone this time of the morning. That would be a cause for questioning and I wasn't for it.

I waited outside about five minutes, but Krish didn't call. She must have been sleeping hard so I decided I'd get with her first thing in the morning. I had the evidence so I was good.

After standing outside talking to familiar faces for about ten more minutes, I went back inside. This time I went to the bar and stood by the man who claimed to love me beyond all measures. He pulled me down onto his lap and I could feel his excitement.

"What's all that for?" I asked with a smile.

"For you sexy. Did I tell you how lovely you look tonight?"

"Yeah, but you can tell me again." I blushed.

He slid his hand between my legs. Caressed me through my pants, then whispered in my ear, "Aint nobody in here got nothin' on you baby. You one fine, edible bitch."

I twisted my body to look him in the eyes ready to pop that lip.

He was amused. I wasn't.

"That's not funny. Don't play with me Derric. You know I don't get down like that. I'm sensitive to the 'bitches'."

"You know I'm playing girl." He said pulling me into a tighter embrace. "Now give me a kiss."

I leaned my head back to feel his insatiable lips. He was absolutely stimulating.

I rose up from the strong thighs that held my weight so well to stand in front of him. Giving me full access of his sweet lips. I threw my arms around his neck. He felt my bottom. We connected. Tongue so cool and sweet from the liquor. My blood began to boil.

"Bad Bitch" by Webbie flooded the room. The DJ was on it again. I felt the urge to sway my hips to the music and sing along with Webbie and Trina. I felt sexy.

"That's my stuff." I said moving to the music.

"Now I can't call you a bitch, but you claiming to be a "bad bitch". How does that go baby?"

"It's the principle fool, don't get it twisted."

While twirling around to the music, I caught a glimpse of the front entrance. To my surprise, the "baddest bitches" were standing at the front entrance looking like a million bucks. Immediately a smile swept across my face.

I kissed Derric. "I'll be right back baby."

I had to go see my friends in, so I rushed over to the entrance.

Instead of her calling me back, she was on her way. Now that's my girl.

"Where is he?" Krisha angrily rang out as soon as she saw me.

I motioned to where Todd was sitting.

His date wasn't with him, but I looked around and spotted her on the dance floor getting her groove on without Mr. Lover Man.

"Let's go over here." I suggested pointing to an empty table toward the corner.

"No, I wanna go over there." She pointed in Todd's direction.

"Krisha come with me."

I took her hand leading her to the bar.

I told Derric my girls were in the building and we were catching a table. He was cool with it. I'm sure he wanted to mingle anyway. So I led Kyra and Krisha to the table.

"Sit here and check it out first. I want you to see and decide for yourself. Don't just go off what I said and saw." I said as we posted up around the table.

"I've seen enough already. He's up in here which means he lied about his whereabouts."

"No, you haven't. She's dancing. She's not even by him. You gotta see them together and decide for yourself what's going on. My interpretation may be different than yours."

"I trust you."

"Just chill girl...By the way, where are the boys?"

"Aunt Mae."

"Cool."

Krisha chilled much better than I thought she would.

She sat in that chair and watched her husband sit with the unknown female at his table. They danced, he bought drinks, and they cuddled.

Krisha sat there longer than I ever could have. She made a sudden dash to the restroom. I think she went in there to hide her emotions. I know her all too well.

When she came back, she was in full beast mode. I could tell she was ready to do what she came to do.

When she sat down, she studied the dance floor. Todd and his guest were slow dancing to Musiq's "Love". As everyone else on the floor, they were being really affectionate.

Kyra was quiet and observant the whole time. We all were.

"I wanna dance." Krisha said out of the blue.

So, the three of us hit the floor. As soon as we did, we had three dance partners come from nowhere. I had motioned for

Derric to follow me, so the brothas had to back off me, but my girls had 'em all over them.

The dance floor was so packed Todd never saw Krisha coming. His date was really showing affection. She was all over him.

Krisha danced up behind him and began caressing his back and feeling his cheeks as he danced. We were cracking up.

A few seconds later Todd turned around and almost fell over. His jaws dropped, eyes bucked, I'm sure he was peeing his pants. But who knows, he was caught in the act before, so this was nothing to him.

Todd played it off by dancing with Krisha.

Krisha never missed a beat. She turned to dance with the guy behind her, but Todd never turned back around to Miss Thang.

When Krisha turned around and got all up on Todd, put her arms around his neck and tongue kissed him, the girl tapped Todd on the shoulder several times but Krisha wouldn't let him turn around.

She came around to the side of them, tried getting between them but nothing was working in her favor. She was saying something but we couldn't hear her over the music.

Krisha calmly let Todd go and turned to dance with the other guy. Todd's friend took him by the hand and pulled at him until he reluctantly left the dance floor.

After the song was over, we took a seat at the bar. Guys began to walk up to the three of us for conversation offering to buy us drinks. Krisha was occupied with trying to get rid of one when two guys walked up to Kyra and me.

"Anybody ever told you that you look like Melyssa Ford?" He spoke close to my ear.

I gave him a quick answer that meant leave me the hell alone. "Yeah."

He smiled all up in my face showing the glistening gold that covered his top row.

Are you serious? I thought.

"May I ask your name?"

"Yeah."

He waited a few seconds then his smile faded. Stared me down and backed up. "I hear ya beautiful, I hear ya." He walked away.

Krisha had gotten rid of one guy and there was another up in her face. Todd watched her the whole time. From looks, I could tell his date didn't like that.

My girl sat at the bar with her legs crossed sipping on an apple martini without a care in the world.

Next thing I knew Todd was on the other side of me and in her face. He looked up at me and I bobbed my head to the music. He knew I'd have my girl's back at all costs.

I couldn't hear what he was saying when he did talk. For the most part, he just hovered over her looking stupid. Trying to claim his territory.

Kyra tapped my arm then pointed. Todd's friend was making her way over to the bar. She quickly brushed through the crowd almost knocking people over. Stood in front of Todd, planted her palms on his chest and looked up in his face like he was her own personal savior.

Krisha sat calmly. I moved behind her and got in her ear.

"You straight?"

She nodded her head.

I took my place behind her while Kyra sat to the right of her.

I was ear hustling hard. I could hear perfectly clear now.

"Todd what are you doing baby? Who is this bitch?" The girl said extending her voice over the music with no shame.

Krisha smirked and turned to look at Kyra and me. She pointed to Miss Thang. As if to say "you hear this?" Kyra and I both smiled.

"Just chill okay." He told her.

"Chill? No you chill. I want to know what's going on."

"Can you please just go sit down?" He snapped.

He was busted and aggravated. I could feel his frustration.

"Hell no! You're over here in this bitch's face and you talk about go sit down. You're my date. When I do, you're going too."

"Look, you don't know enough about her to be going there so please kill the drama."

Krisha looked at us again and held up two fingers. That meant strike two. One mo' "bitch" and ole' girl was out.

"So you're defending her? Who is this?"

Todd gave her a mean stare but didn't answer.

I shook my head in disgust. His triflin' behind wouldn't even say Krisha was his wife. This was a mess.

"Remember you came here with me and you're leaving with me." She said with her hands on her hips.

She was aggravated. All she knew was that her man was flipping her off for some unknown chic.

"Look, I'll leave with who I damn well please. Now go sit down!" He snapped.

She got all up in his face. "Don't try to play me like that. I knew you was no good...you can have this bitch." She got bold. Pointing her finger at Krisha. "If you want this bi..."

Bam!

Krisha jabbed her; cut her words off. A nice one straight to the face as quick as lightening. Nobody really saw her do it. Just popped the girl.

"You hit me bitch!" She screamed as she turned to look at Krisha in disbelief.

Bam!

Another quick one. Caught off guard. Krisha's hands are too fast.

"You don't know me like that." Was all Krisha said. And leaned back in her chair.

The girl was now holding her mouth where that last jab was delivered.

"You don't know me either." She threw out.

Then she decided to try to get at Krish.

Todd was pulling the girl, but Krisha was sitting in the chair at the bar calm, cool, and collective. Like she hadn't done a thing. She picked up her drink and started sipping again. Completely unfazed by ole girl acting a fool.

"Todd let me go!"

Miss Thang was bucking and wanted to show her true colors.

There was no way in hell Todd was gonna let her go. Guess he somewhat cared about Miss Thang because he knew his wife was gonna get in dat ass if he did, and he knew if she didn't, we would.

"No. Go ahead and leave." Todd had her by the arm.

"You let her hit me and won't let me go?" She looked at him in amazement. "That's messed up."

"Just leave Cassie." He threw out.

"I ain't going nowhere without you."

I shook my head. Poor girl had it bad. It was obvious he hadn't just met her.

Todd knew what he had to do to get her out of the club without a bigger scene. He had to give the woman what she wanted.

She continued yelling and trying to get at Krisha until Todd grabbed her arm to force her outside.

"It ain't over, best believe that." She yelled back at Krisha.

Todd was walking fast. Had her by the waist forcefully walking her toward the exit door, then outside the club.

Kyra spoke first. "Let's go Krish."

With a defeated look on her face Krish said, "You're right, let's go. I've seen all I needed to see."

Her husband had just left with his mistress. What else was she to do? But it wasn't like this was the first time.

I finally went to tell Derric what was going on and that I was gonna see Krish home.

Told him I'd meet him back at his house when I got to my car. He kissed me and asked that I call him when I reached Krisha's.

As we were walking out, Todd came back in. He ran over to Krisha trying to take her arm but she snatched away.

"Let me explain." He begged.

"No need to."

"It's not what you think."

"I think you could have told your whore that I was your wife, but you didn't. Maybe I wouldn't have had to disrespect myself had you done that. But obviously you didn't want her to know."

"It's not like that."

"'I'll tell you what, you'd better make it home within the next thirty minutes or don't come at all."

"Krisha, I'm not in my car."

"I don't care how you get home, but it better not be with her. Walk if you have to."

She was steamed and hurt. And I don't blame her. She had every right to be. But once again, she needed to see this. She needed to see him for who he really is.

It was a fifteen-minute drive from across the river. Kyra had to stop to get gas when we made it back into the city.

It was now about one o'clock in the am and we decided to stop at Waffles n Wings to get something to eat. I was starving and Krisha looked exhausted, but she agreed to come along for the conversation. We got onto the interstate and headed to Waffles- n-Wings to get our grub on.

15

You Can Take the Girl Out Of the Hood...

Krisha

I didn't want to eat but I didn't want to go home either. So I agreed to tag along with my friends. The parking lot at the waffle joint was filled to the max. We found a parking space toward the back of the restaurant, parked the truck, and sat there chatting and hoping this wouldn't take all morning.

As we were about to exit Kyra's Yukon, I noticed a Rover slip into a space about three cars away.

"Mia, I think that car was following us."

"Yeah. I saw that car at the gas station back there."

"You strapped?"

"You know it. You?"

"Fo sho."

"Let's hope we don't have to go there. I need to get home to my babies. I should have never left home in the first place. I don't have time for no ho tripping over my husband. But I'll bring it to her if that's what she wants."

"That ain't what she want. Sista don't know the consequences." Said a confident Mia.

"You think it's her?" Kyra asked.

"Probably. She said it wasn't over."

"C'mon. Let's go inside." Kyra suggested. We exited the truck strapped and ready for things to pop off. We didn't want it but we had to be prepared. People are crazy as hell these days.

We ordered, ate, and got out of the restaurant a little after three. By this time, the large crowd had gone, but there was still a full house.

Small groups of people were still conversing out in the parking lot when we made it to our vehicle. The first face I saw hanging on the driver's side window of a black Range Rover was Miss Thang from the club. She looked at us and ended her conversation with the person at her window.

"She got it on her mind Krish." Mia said noticing what I'd just seen.

"I'm sure. But I don't feel like this right now. I'm ready to go home. The way I feel right now she can have him."

"It ain't even about Todd right now." Kyra added watching the Range Rover.

"I know you, and you know damn well you don't mean that." Mia told me.

"What's that supposed to mean?"

We talked as we strolled over to Kyra's truck.

I noticed that we were being stared down. They were staring so hard their eyes alone had probably whipped our tails a million different ways.

When Mia and I got into the truck, Kyra had already started her engine and was talking on her cell phone.

My cell started ringing.

It appeared to be my home number so I ignored it.

Todd was home and ringing my phone. He was home and his woman was here, so I know she didn't take him. Probably called his baby mama. Who knows?

"I think we have some admirers." Kyra said looking into her rearview mirror as we pulled onto the street.

"Why do women have to be so freakin' stupid?" Mia screamed.

"There's no telling what kind of lies Todd has told her." I added.

Looking in her rearview mirror, "They need to fall back." Kyra mumbled.

They were riding us pretty hard.

This little scenario brought back memories. Back in the day, Mia and I used to ride four girls deep everywhere we went. We had two sidekicks, TaKeila and Yasmine. We all had each other's back. If something went down, we were all game.

TaKeila's promiscuous ways that she'd acquired from fooling around with older men, started to catch up with her and she took to having babies for unknown baby daddies. After child number two at the age of 17, she broke away from us.

Mia and I went to college, and Yasmine decided to go to modeling school, which was the beginning of her career. She got a big break and was swept up into the world of fashion and glamour. Neither Mia nor I have heard from her in over five years now, but I have seen her in a few ads and heard mention of her on the blogs.

Kyra hooked up with Mia and I in the second semester of our freshman year in college. She was 'bout it too. We shared a lot of the same ways and loved each other then as much as we do now. We were and still are as thick as thieves.

We didn't bother anybody. We were all just out to have fun. But we had enemies for no reason other than we were on and we knew it.

Mama tried, but she couldn't keep me out the hood. I was there every chance I got.

My mother had made a good life for me, but taking me out of the environment that I'd lived in since conception, was crazy to me at the time. I couldn't understand her logic on that.

I considered the hood my home and my friends were there. She had moved me out of the hood, but could never take the hood out of me. However, as I grew I learned to suppress my acquired street ways. I learned to value more than what was in front of me.

As I got older, I began to want a good life. I wanted to emulate my mother. So I let all those crazy and wild ways go and focused on my future. I decided to allow my intelligence to lead me. In doing that, I became what I'd like to think of as an educated and sophisticated lady with a heart as big as Texas. This way was more beneficial. I saw longevity. I saw blessings.

But nobody should ever get it twisted, I know how to handle mine if need be. I am not a weak woman at all. It's just that damn husband of mine that's got me messed up.

I decided for Kyra to take me on home even though we were being tailed. I wasn't too keen on these chicks knowing where I lived, but after the way things went down tonight, she'd find out anyway. That's just how little girls did it.

As I approached my house, I could see all the lights were out and the garage door was down which meant Todd was definitely home because I'd left lights on.

The car had ridden our bumper with bright light on the whole ten minutes drive to my house. My nerves were super bad and Kyra was pissed. So pissed that she abruptly stopped the truck in my driveway, jumped out, and headed to the back of her truck where the SUV had halted.

"Yall got a problem?" Kyra rang out.

"Here we go." Mia said. "Let's check these little girls right quick so we can go to bed."

With the quickness we were all out of Kyra's truck when the windows came down in the Rover.

"Bitch, I told you it wasn't over." The girl from the club rang out to me.

I looked at Mia. She held up one finger.

This girl just didn't get it. I thought.

"Look." Kyra said angrily. "Go home. We ain't trippin'."

"Yo' girl shoulda thought about that before she touched my face."

"You should have thought about it before you started messing with her husband." Mia said.

"Well, if she was doing him right maybe I wouldn't have to."

I looked at Mia and held up two fingers. She didn't say the "b" word but she cut me low with the lame comeback. One more strike before I lost my cool. So, being the rational person that I am, I decided to reason with her.

"Look, whoever you are. Todd is my husband and this is our home. I don't know what he told you, but you have been played boo boo. And I would appreciate it if you'd get off my property." I said matter-of-factly.

"See that's where you're wrong. Todd is my man and has been for twelve whole months. He's only with you for the kids. And just so you know, this is soon to be my house. So ho you can go pack right now."

They all roared in laughter when she made the last statement.

I personally didn't think it was funny.

"Is that what he told you?" I asked with a grin.

She just didn't know she'd fallen right into my trap. I wanted her dumb butt at my house so I could tap that ass; and it would be justified for her rolling up on my property threatening me.

"That's what I know." She rang out.

"Then you're more twisted than you look homegirl." I snapped back.

"Twisted? No you didn't go there." She threw her head back in laughter. "You're with a man who's with me *every* night. Now who's twisted, *Bitch?*"

She put a serious emphasis on the "B" word. To me that meant she meant that. She smirked at me as if she'd said something brand new.

"You know what? I tried to..."

"No, Krish." Mia said cutting me off. "Forget the talking. You know that ain't the way it's done. Time's up on this trick."

Mia reached through the side window and grabbed the girl by her hair. Dragged her from the car kicking and screaming. When she hit the ground, Mia let her go at my feet.

"Now deal with her. And you'd better mess her up good."

And she already knew those were my intentions. I don't do anything unless I do it right.

Her friends had jumped out of the car and were trying to get to me. But Mia and Kyra stopped them short.

I allowed whomever the lil heffa was to get up off the ground before I tore another hole into her prissy behind.

Everything was happening so fast. Next thing I knew Todd had come out and was trying to pry me off of her.

"What are you doing at my house?" I heard Todd ask during the scuffle.

He was saying a whole lot of crap I wasn't listening to.

"Krisha. Just stop. Let her go."

I had her pinned down and was choking her blue.

It was questionable as to why females wanted to try me. My good girl image definitely has alot of people fooled.

Kyra and Mia were handling their business with the other two. Todd was running from us to them screaming trying to make it all stop. Guess he thought I'd kill his little girlfriend.

"Let her go Krisha." He kept saying. But I wasn't listening.

Then suddenly I felt a horrific sting across the side of my face.

"Damn!" I yelled.

The sting burned like a ball of fire had fallen on me.

What happened?

Everything was happening so fast I couldn't tell. Then in another swift movement, before I could recoup from the sting, I was on my rear.

I sat on the ground in disbelief.

Then came the apology.

What tha…? In all the years we'd been married, this man had never laid a hand on me. And now tonight he wanna go and hit me? One, in front of five other people; two, in defense of his side whore.

Mia and Kyra had long since put the other two back in the car, but they hopped out of the car to help Todd with their friend. She was almost passed out.

I didn't realize I was choking her *that* hard. My body was throbbing from the fall to the ground but I rose up like a soldier to dust myself off a little.

Mia came rushing over to me.

"Did that bastard just smack you? Was I seeing things? Please tell me I was?" Mia huffed as she watched me sternly.

I didn't say anything. They both had seen it. I was still in shock. Mia and Kyra looked at me and at the same time we charged his ass.

He threw us around like we were men but it was no use. Guess he'd forgotten whom he was dealing with. I couldn't believe things were going down like this. This was my husband that we were beating the crap out of. Served him right for hittin' me like that. He knew I didn't play that. But after I saw blood, I had to call them off him. I didn't want him killed or badly hurt. I did love him. I just hated him at the moment.

We were all huffing and puffing, talking noise and trying to catch our breath at the same time. Todd swore he was gonna whip our asses one by one. Especially Mia's.

He has never been a threat to a woman, but Mia had really fueled his anger when she busted his head with the butt of the gun. Todd wasn't stupid though. He went to sit his butt down somewhere.

"Come on Krisha lets go inside. Forget this whole little scenario. They deserve one another." Mia took me by the arm to lead me to the house.

"No, Mia. They both gonna pay for this." I tried to get back at him. "I didn't ask for this." I yelled.

I was so mad. Just wanted to mess up the whole world.

"Just leave 'em alone Krish, they got their issue." Kyra said pulling my other arm leading me to the house.

I looked back as they were trying to put Miss Thang in the car. She began to release her dinner. I got kinda scared.

Looking over at this girl, whoever she was, Todd had the nerve to say, "See Krisha you didn't have to do all that."

I stopped my stride.

"And I didn't ask them to follow me to my house. They got what they deserved!" I yelled.

"Are you losing your mind? You coulda killed her." He threw back at me.

I couldn't believe he'd asked me that. Was he trying to flip this on *me*?

"No, I think you've lost yours. You think I'mma let you and anyone else do this to me. Seems you got it twisted over the years. That bitch got dealt with, now live with it!" I spat in a dangerous fury.

I was fuming beyond control. Hot and wanted some more so I ran up to him again for talking to me crazy.

"How the hell you gon' defend your ho over your wife?" I spat.

"I'm not defending her. I just…"

One of the girls yelled from the car. "And don't bring your monkey ass back over her crib!"

Up until that point ole girl was in the back seat with her head laid back in the seat. They were attempting to back out of the driveway to leave. She rose up and glared at me. Gave me a cold stare. Our eyes locked for a minute. The way I saw it was she was trying to tell me something with her eyes and I was definitely saying some shit to her with mine.

Next thing I saw was shiny chrome. And it was being raised to the window. I couldn't move. My feet were stuck in place. I heard Todd and Mia screaming. Next thing I heard were gunshots. I heard ringing in my ears. Then everything went black.

Faintly, I heard sirens. Heard people talking. I opened my eyes to my best friends sitting next to me in an ambulance where I was stretched out with tubes running from my arms.

I tried to get up but Mia pushed me back down.

"Mia, what happened?

"Just lie down Krisha."

"Did she shoot me?"

They looked at me, surprised that I remembered.

"No, she didn't. You just passed out."

"Where's Todd?"

They looked at each other then back at me.

"Just rest Krish we'll talk about it later."

"No, I want to know now. Where is he?"

"He's sort of not here."

"What do you mean *sort of?*

"He left." Kyra mumbled.

"He left me here?"

"Well, yeah."

"Where is he?"

"He left with her."

"What?" I screamed in disbelief. "You're kidding right?"

"I wish I were."

Trying to get up from the stretcher, I pulled at the tubes stuck to my arms.

"Get this off me." I yelled.

I could hear the ambulance attendants outside of the ambulance talking.

"Wait, Krisha don't take that off. They need to make sure you're okay."

"I'm okay. Let me get up."

"Are you sure?"

"I'm sure I'm not going to the hospital. Now move!"

16

...But You Can't Take the Hood Out of the Girl

*I*t was just one thing after the next. *When was it all going to end?* I thought.

It had been three days and still no word from Todd. His car was in the garage, clothes in the closet, office was closed. I had no idea where he was or who this woman was he supposedly left our home with. He could have at least called his kids. They were asking for him every other minute.

I hadn't had much sleep since the night the drama went down in my driveway. I'm beginning to look at things differently now. I probably should have handled things better.

Did I really have to whip the girl like that? I ask myself that question over and over. Maybe I should have just let it go and come on inside my house to deal with my husband.

I have tried very hard over the years to be nice and sweet, to be understanding and loving, to show trust, and to handle all things in an intelligent professional, ladylike manner. However, it seems as though that was no longer working with Todd. For some reason our relationship was at a different level than a few years ago. And I could no longer be the sweet and passive Krisha. Seems like I gotta act a fool to get some respect. But when and why did it come to this? Things had gone entirely too far.

His so-called women didn't respect me. Guess they thought of me as soft because of my demeanor and the way I live too. And I'm sure Todd had a lot to do with their interpretation of me also. Funny thing is the heffas know me and I don't know anything about them. So I believe that tail stomping ole' girl got was justified. But why do I feel so bad? Seems like I won the fight but lost the battle. I got shot at and the bitch *still* got my husband. Come to think of it, that might be cause for another butt whipping.

I called everyone who knew Todd, to no avail. No one had seen or heard from him or so they said. Even Trent claimed to not have heard from him, which was unbelievable because they talked everyday.

I got desperate so I called his sister April in Virginia. If anyone knew where he was, April did. Though miles apart, they were as thick as thieves. I dialed her number.

The phone rang several times.

Just as I was about to hang up she answered, "Hello?"

"Hello, April. How are you?"

"I'm fine thank you."

"April this is Krisha."

"I know your voice Krisha. How are my nephews?"

"They're great, thanks. I'll tell them you asked about them...Ummm, I was calling to see if you'd heard anything from Todd."

"Why? What's up?"

"Well, we've been experiencing some problems and he left and I haven't heard from him since."

"Really?"

"Yes."

"Well, Krisha, I don't want to get involved in your business."

"April, I'm not asking you to get involved. I'm just trying to see if he's okay. I haven't spoken to him in three days."

"Whose fault is that?"

There was a numbing pause.

"Excuse me?" I said.

Now I'm thinking, *okay here we go.* I knew she was putting on.

"I heard about what you and your girls did to him."

"And what was that?"

"I think you know better than me."

"All I wanted to know was if my husband was alive. It's obvious that you or someone has spoken with him so I think I got my answer. If you speak to him again please tell him that his kids are asking for him."

"Krish, I told you I didn't want to get into your business, but since you insist. Don't try to sound all concerned for him now. You and your girls were wrong for hurting him like that. Do you know he has two black eyes and a knot on his head as big as his knee cap because of you?"

"Did he tell you everything that happened?"

"Yes he did."

"Yeah right. I'm sure he did. April, remember there are always two sides to every story."

"For whatever reason, my brother loves you Krisha. You gotta stop being so damn jealous."

"What...Jealous?"

"Yes, and insecure. If he's there with you why the hell you worried about the other hos that wanna be with him. He can't help who he is. I mean look at him. There will always be women chasing after him. But they don't mean nothing to him."

"Are you serious little girl?" I asked in disbelief. "He's sleeping with those women. It's called respect. It's called honoring your marriage vows. And what he's doing is called adultery. That'll get you a first class ticket to hell you know." I said sarcastically but pissed.

"I'll tell you what. You'd better be glad that I wasn't there that night."

"And what is that supposed to mean?"

"I think you know. Things wouldn't have gone down like that."

"So what are you trying to say? Please don't tell me you got something for me too? I've got enough issues."

She was quiet. Maybe pondering what I'd said.

"And I thought you didn't want to get in our business."

"Both of you put me in it."

"April, get all the facts before you get into something you can't handle."

"I'm just saying that was messed up Krisha. My brother looks a horrible sight. And he's hurting because he didn't think you would do that to him. And I can handle mine, trust.

"Okay, April. You've made your point. Just tell him to call his kids."

I eagerly hung up and fuming from every crack and crevice in my body. I was relieved that he was okay, but pissed that he'd gone and told only his side of the story to his family, making me look like the bad guy.

It was now obvious that he was in Virginia but *how the hell did he get there with his wallet and everything here at home?* I pondered that question.

That sister of his, April, probably drove eighteen hours to come get her 'do no wrong, oh! so loving brother'. Or I wouldn't put it past that crazy girl, Cassie. She may have even taken him. Who knows? Who cares?

Seven whole days had passed and I had not seen or spoken to Todd. I thought maybe he'd at least call home during the week. But, the week was gone without him even speaking to his children.

I was confused and found it hard to find rest. I wanted to call every family member in Virginia that I knew, but I didn't want to seem desperate, especially since he'd showed no concern about me.

I refused to call April again because I knew where that would lead, so instead, I decided to suck it up and call Cicily.

I dialed the 'all but familiar number' to my favorite sister-in-law, she answered on the first ring.

"Hi Cicily."

"Hey Krisha, how are you?"

I sighed heavily before speaking. "Okay I guess."

"Yeah, I know." My sister-in-law tenderly said.

Silence filled the phone.

"Is he there Cicily?"

"You haven't spoken to him?" Her voiced laced with concern.

"No."

She let out a long sigh, followed by silence.

"I'll make sure he calls you Krisha."

"Cicily, it's not what it looks like. I never intended to hurt him like that."

"Krish, it's okay. You don't have to explain anything to me. We've talked before and you know I know my brother; better yet, I know men. It's never how they say it is."

"But April thinks...."

Cutting me off. "We all know April don't we. Todd is an angel to her. She'll defend him at all costs. Besides, she's still young, she doesn't know anything about relationships yet."

"How did he get there Cicily?"

"Krish, you know I love you so I'm not gonna get in yall's business. I'll have him call you."

"Thank you."

"Take care girl and kiss my babies for me."

I thought long and hard about my relationship with Todd. *Is it worth saving? Is it worth fighting for?* I asked myself. These were questions that needed answers in which I had not a clue.

Physical altercations over a man have never been how I operated. I never saw the sense in fighting over a man because if he were truly mine then that would not be necessary. And for the record, I never had to. Every guy I'd ever claimed as mine was just that. But now I was starting to compromise what I believed in.

I hate Todd so much for what he's done to our relationship, but at the same time, my heart aches for him. I've been in this place before so I'm all too familiar with the pain associated with rejection.

I simply wanted my husband. Was that too much to ask?

Within the next few hours, I'd left the boys with Kyra and was boarding a late flight to Virginia.

She and Mia tried hard to convince me not to go and I almost listened, but my love for my husband wouldn't let me stay in Louisiana while he was hurting in Virginia. They tried to tell me to just give him time to heal and allow him to come home on his own. I was determined to let him know that I could forgive him, if he would only forgive me. I wanted him to know that I was willing to start over and put all of the recent drama behind us.

I arrived in Virginia at eleven p.m., picked up the car that I'd reserved, and got a hotel room at Embassy Suites.

Once in the suite, I called Mia and Kyra to let them know that I'd made it safely. Mia insisted that she come be with me, but I declined her offer. Her presence would only make things worse. So, I assured her I'd be okay.

After speaking with my friends, I showered and lay down for much needed rest. I really hadn't slept or eaten all week so my body and soul was exhausted. I figured I'd gather enough strength to face my husband in the morning.

The next morning I opened my eyes around nine-thirty a.m. to my cell phone ringing. It wasn't a distinct ring so I had no idea who was on the other end. I reached over in the bed next to me and grabbed my phone. The caller ID revealed a 757 area code. It took a few minutes for me to recognize that it was April's home number.

"Yes?" I groggily sang into the phone, ready to battle with April if need be.

"Krish."

My heart lit up at the sound of the masculine voice.

"Yes."

"Krish, it's me."

I knew who it was. I could recognize that voice dead or alive.

There was a gentle pause on the line.

"How are you?" I asked.

"Okay. What about yourself?" He replied.

"Nothing without you sweetheart." I confessed.

"Krish, I'm sorry for not calling you sooner."

"I'm sorry too baby. I was just so angry and you hitting me shocked the hell out of me and angered my friends. You know how they are."

"It was impulse. I didn't mean to, but you were really enraged baby."

"I was hurt Todd. The whole situation hurt. I didn't ask for that drama. I'm tired of feeling like that."

"I know you are. That's why I'm calling you."

"What is it?"

"This week has given me the time I needed to think about my life. I don't know what's wrong with me. I've got everything a man could want, but I keep messing it up. I don't want to hurt you anymore."

"We can work it out baby. Just come on home. The boys are going crazy asking for you. Besides, there's nothing we haven't been able to get through before."

"You know what? That's exactly it. You keep forgiving me and I keep messing up. We get over it because you get past it, but my conscious haunts me. I felt like jumping off a bridge the other night. I didn't know what else to do but leave. Baby, I can't stand seeing you cry. I hate knowing that you're hurting. But there's something in me that won't allow me to stop living this life right now."

"What are you saying Todd?"

"I'm trying to say the hardest thing I have ever had to say and one day I know I'll regret it."

My heart began an uncontrollable beat. I felt faint but managed to sit upright on the bed.

"I can't hurt you anymore. I refuse to. They say if you truly love something, you'll let it go. I love you too much to put you through this humiliation. You're not a street woman Krisha. Fighting…naw, uh unh…that's ridiculous. I'm sorry I led that to you. You're a respectable woman who refuse to let anyone compromise what you stand for. Your image is very important so why let me and my lifestyle bring you down? I won't allow it. So as much as it hurts me, I'd rather let you go."

"Let me go?" I said in astonishment.

"Krisha, it's for the best. I can't give you the commitment that you need or deserve right now."

"You can if you tried. I need you."

I held my chest with one hand, the cell phone with the other.

"No you don't. You may want me, but I'm no good for you right now and you know that. You just don't want to let go. You were gonna divorce me a few months ago had I not begged like crazy."

"I don't know if I would have actually gone through with it. I love you too much."

"I love you too. That's why I gotta do this."

"So are you saying that you're not coming back to Louisiana?"

"I've considered moving back to Virginia."

"You're just gonna leave your children?"

"You know I love them. I'll be there for them no matter what I decide."

"How, when you'll be several hours away?"

"It's nothing for me to get to them. You know that."

"No Todd! I don't want this."

"Krisha, it's for the best."

"What's the real reason you're doing this? Are you still mad about the fight? I'm sorry we hurt you baby, but you hurt me. I'll make it up to you. Just please don't leave me. Don't walk out on our family." I begged through tears.

"I'm not just *walking out* Krish. I'll be there. I'll give you whatever you need and want. You're always gonna be my first and only love baby."

"I don't need your money or material things. I just want the man I married back. I need the old Todd to come back into my life."

"I can't be the old Todd right now. I've tried and I can't."

"What is it? Tell me what I'm doing wrong. I can learn to satisfy you if I'm not doing the job right anymore."

"Have I ever indicated that you weren't satisfying me? See what I'm saying? You wanna bend for me. You shouldn't have to do that."

By this time, I was crying loudly over the phone, sobbing with no shame. There was silence on the line. Thought I even heard him sniffle too.

"Todd, you hurt me time and time again and I forgave you and took you back. Now all of a sudden you want to leave *me*? Wow! I can't believe this. Why didn't you just let me go when I tried to leave? I would have healed by now."

"Then I would have been defeated."

"So you're happy knowing that I'm the one defeated?"

"No, but sad to say it's a male ego thing, I guess."

"I'm glad that you're being honest, but I don't believe you right now."

This conversation was amazing. I didn't know what else to say to him. It seemed his mind was made up. He simply didn't desire to be my husband anymore.

Silence.

"What did you say?"

"Nothing, I didn't say anything."

I thought I'd heard him whispering something.

"I love you Todd."

"I know you do."

He was talking, but didn't sound too remorseful. I didn't detect too much sadness in *his* voice. And here I was about to stroke out.

"So you're at April's?"

"Yeah."

"So what am I to do now?"

"Take care of my children. I'll be home in a couple of days and we'll talk more. Okay? Love you."

He quickly hung up the phone.

I felt like my world that I'd just gotten back was ending all over again. I lay in bed and cried and prayed for an hour. Then I cried some more. I asked God, *why me?* What had I done to deserve this type hurt in my life? First my mother, now my cheating husband.

As I cried, I picked up the phone to call his sister Cicily. When she answered the phone, she knew it was me. All I could do was cry. She already knew.

"Krisha, I'm so sorry baby."

While she talked, I cried.

"I know it hurts. I wanted him to be a man and tell you himself. He was trying to find a way out of talking to you."

"I love him Cicily." I sniffled out.

"Of course you do. I know he loves you too. He's just caught up in his own selfish BS right now. He's really doing this for you."

"How?" I sniffled.

"Krisha, at the rate he's going, he's only gonna hurt you more if he didn't do this. He's my brother, but he's no good for you right now. Believe me when I tell you that."

"Cicily, he's my husband and we can work this out. He doesn't have to leave his family. I forgave him in the past and we moved on."

"Men ain't nothing like women. We have a forgiving heart, especially when it comes to those we love."

"I can't take it Cicily. I don't know if I can live without him and my mother at the same time. I feel like my whole world is coming down around me."

"Krisha, don't say that. You have two boys to care for. Live for them. Don't worry about my dog-ass brother, his day will come."

I cried more. I cried so hard I could barely catch my breath. I began to hyperventilate. I felt sick.

Cicily held the phone through it all.

"I love him." I choked out again.

Cicily talked me through it, reassured me, sympathizing with me.

"I know baby. Try to pull yourself together. I know."

After a long silence and wait until I regained composure, Cicily began to console me again.

"Krisha, where are you? Somebody needs to be with you."

"I'm in Virginia."

"What? Where?" She asked in amazement and concern.

"At the Embassy Suites."

"Does Todd know?"

"No. I didn't have a chance to tell him."

"Where are you right now?"

"I'm still here. But I think I'm about to go to April's."

"Krisha, I don't think that's a good idea."

"I gotta see him. I gotta make him understand that we can overcome this."

"Just stay where you are. I'll come get you. You're too upset to drive."

"I gotta go Cicily."

I'd managed to get up and began throwing on some clothes.

"Aww, Krisha. I'll meet you there." Cicily hung up the phone.

I hung up and wiped the tears from my eyes.

I was in the rental car and on my way within seconds. The hotel was only about ten minutes away from April's condo.

When I arrived at April's, I pulled myself together and sauntered out of the car. I marched up to the door in search of my man. Cicily wasn't there yet, but she was sure to come. She's always been a good friend and I genuinely loved her for that.

I knocked on the door. No one came.

I knocked harder.

After a couple of seconds, the door flew open.

April, on the other side, glared at me through hell red eyes.

I could just separate her head from the rest of her evil behind. I thought.

"Hello April." I said instead.

She offered a dry hello.

"Where's Todd?"

"Who wants to know?"

"Don't play games April."

She rolled her eyes and sighed.

I'd come in peace and this little girl was making me mad.

"Can you tell Todd I'm here?"

She left the door open and went to the back of her condo.

I let myself in and closed the door behind me. She was treating me like a total stranger. This is my husband and my sister-in-law. We'd slept in April's spare bedroom plenty of times, so why was I reduced to sitting on the couch waiting on Todd like this was our first date?

I think not.

I got up and walked toward the back of her condo. She was just walking away from the guest bedroom door as I approached.

"He's coming." She said as if for me to go sit down and wait.

I moved past her like I didn't even hear her.

"I said he's coming out!" She screamed with much attitude.

I reached out to touch the doorknob.

She slapped my hand.

I looked at her straight in her eyes.

"Lil' girl, you don't wanna mess with me right now."

April was twenty-three but was always Todd's baby sister. I could see myself tearing her to pieces right now. She was family. I couldn't unleash this anger on her. It just wouldn't be right. So I refrained from going off.

She backed her smart-mouth butt up though. She knew what was up.

I quickly opened the door to the bedroom to find Todd with his back to me putting his pants on while Miss Thang, better known as Cassie, lay in bed uncovered, as naked as the day she was born. No shame. Then again why would she be, she gets naked for a living. Boy, Todd sure could pick 'em.

Startled, he turned around almost falling over trying to get his other leg in his pants.

"Krisha, wh…what are you doing here?"

Either he was shocked to see me, or good at faking. Maybe April didn't tell him it was me.

Still stunned at the sight, I remained silent.

While April was behind me explaining to Todd how I'd just walked on back, Miss Thang lay there, still not trying to cover herself, with a smirk on her face.

"Baby, what are you doing here?" He repeated while finding a shirt to slide over his head.

After taking everything in, I spoke.

"So, is this the reason you're leaving your family?" I pointed to Cassie who'd slightly pulled a sheet up to her naked body.

"Krisha, I already told you…"

I cut him off.

"Told me what? What Todd? That you would rather be laid up halfway across the country somewhere between this nasty bitch's legs?"

"Halfway across…this is my home."

He didn't bother responding to the other comment. I shook my head at that alone. He knew that trick was trifling.

"Your home is in Louisiana with me."

Cicily came running in the room and took my hand. "C'mon Krisha."

"No, Cicily. Let me get this off my chest."

Then, April had to say something. "Don't be acting a fool in my house if you know what's good for you."

"Good for me?" I snapped and turned around to face her so fast my head almost flew off. I stepped toward her. "Tell me what's good for me April!" I spat with venom.

Todd jumped between us. "Chill out April."

Good call. He knew what the deal was. He didn't want his sister to be slid across her own floor. And she, like a good puppy, rolled her eyes and walked out of the room. The poor girl was so misguided.

"Krisha, I told you I'd be home to talk."

"Talk about what? I knew there was something that was influencing your decision for leaving us. Any other time you'd be all in my behind when you messed up. You think since I whipped your butt that's justification for you walking away! It's okay now, huh Todd?" I shot out.

"I didn't say that."

"You didn't have to. I know you… But you know what. I don't care which way you look at it, you did this, not me!"

"I already admitted that to you."

"I came here to ask you to forgive me for the senseless fight. I felt that if I could forgive you numerous times, you could forgive me for that. I was willing to put all the crap that happened that night with this whore behind us."

"I know you didn't call me no whore." Cassie jumped in, rising from the bed.

I gave her a stare that was deadly. "Did I stutter?" I was heated to a point of boiling over. "I swear, Todd, you better tell that bitch to shut up or I'mma finish what I started or she gonna finish me. One or the other."

My good senses told me not to hit her between the eyes for firing that gun the other night.

Todd looked at her, gave her the eye to shut up. He knew I didn't play. I just wasn't in the playing mood. I was raw and on a new path of rawness.

"And put some clothes on yo' nasty ass!" I added.

I was bold. I'd stopped crying and felt like 'Super Woman' or somebody with some serious powers. Nobody could mess with me. Not this day. I was ready to whip everybody's ass up in that place if they jumped stupid. Even Cicily. And she hadn't done one thing to me.

"Krisha, just leave em' be baby. It's not worth getting upset over." Cicily said.

Todd looked at her strangely. "What do you mean not worth it? She's talking about our marriage."

"Well, it's obvious Todd that you no longer have a marriage." Focusing on Cassie lying there like a queen. "Isn't that what you told her?" Cicily stared him down.

"Not in so many words."

I butted in. "What? How many words did you need to say 'get lost Krisha'? Now you wanna have it both ways, Todd? Is that it? You're having second thoughts or something? Make up your simple mind!"

"No, I'm not saying that. We just need to talk alone."

"Whatever you said to me this morning you obviously said in front of her so why can't you talk now? Is it Cicily you're ashamed in front of? Or were you trying to impress your whore?"

He didn't answer. Silence was truth. Cicily was like his mother and that was his new piece. He needed his butt *whupped*.

Cicily said, "Look baby, I'm gonna love you regardless. You're my brother, but I don't agree with what you're doing to your wife and family. You handle your business. I'm going in here with April."

"Cicily I'm outta here too. This is trash, and trash makes me sick!"

I turned to exit the room.

"Krisha, wait." He yelled behind me.

I turned to look at his pitiful face.

"Todd, I don't care to be in the same room with you and your woman any longer. If the situation were reversed I don't think you would either. Now leave me alone. I'm outta here."

I turned to walk away again, but he grabbed my hand.

"I know." He said looking at his feet as he held my hand in his.

I tried to push the anger aside for a minute. I needed to let him know something before I left. So I stood toe to toe with him.

"As hurt as I am, I'm not ashamed to say that I still love you. You're still my husband. I never knew that loving you would bring me so much heartache. It was so good for us until I never imagined it ever coming to an end, especially not like this.

I've been all I know how to be for you. I've given you everything a man could ask for. What else you needed, I don't know. I hope you find what you're looking for, but best bet you will never find it in these paper-chasing jump offs that wanna have yo' baby and screw you for every dollar you're worth. It can't be happiness and stability you want because that's what you had. You chose to throw it away. Just take care of your children, that's all I ask. And don't worry about me bothering you, I've seen everything with my own two eyes and you've been very clear today. I'm officially done."

I finished as tears swelled my eyes, but I'd be damned if I let them fall. Not in front of him and his tramp. I hugged him tightly. I wanted to kiss his lips, but I knew his 'get a woman' tactics and what he'd probably been doing with them so I kissed his cheek instead.

Cassie had fully covered up and was sitting on the bed sucking her teeth. I walked over to her where she was sitting. She flinched as I stepped to her. I looked her straight in the eyes.

"You may think you've won, but best believe boo, what goes around comes around."

I didn't have much to say to her. Naturally I didn't like her because she was with my man, but he was the problem. Men tell so many lies until some women just don't know the real story. I can't say she didn't know because she knew very well that he was married. But I still blamed him for everything. She's just another young and ignorant girl that he'll use until he gets tired.

I turned and strutted out of the room. I knew this thing would change eventually because despite all that he did, he couldn't stand the thought of me being with someone else.

I hated the thought of knowingly leaving my man behind lying between another woman's legs. That is hard when you know, and can't do a damn thing about it.

I caught the next flight out. Cried all the way home. Guess folks on the plane thought someone had died.

Mia picked me up from the airport and dropped me at home where I slept until the next day.

That next evening I went to Kyra's house to get my children. Through tears, I ran everything down to Mia and Kyra. Their hearts went out to me.

"It may be best Krisha." Kyra said.

"May be? It *is* best." Mia screamed. "That scum is of no earthly good."

"Little did I know. But I see it now...took me to go to Virginia to see it." I replied sadly.

"I wanna whip his tail again." Mia said pacing across the floor.

"Shh! You'll wake the kids." Kyra said.

"Sorry. But I wouldn't get so upset if I thought you deserved this."

"He knows I don't. When all the fun is over, his conscious will eat him alive."

"He'll come crawling back before it's over."

"You know the funny thing?" I said.

"What?"

"When I saw him with her like that, I didn't cry at all. I wanted to. It hurt, but I didn't even cry."

"Probably because you wanted to whip some ass." Mia said pacing.

"Yeah, maybe so, but I just had a different feeling that came over me when I was leaving that room. I became very rational, said what I had to say then left."

Mia sang, "The sign of a new beginning."

17

After the Pain

*A*fter another three days, Todd was brought home by Trent. He waltzed in with no shame around eight o'clock last night.

I'd packed all his clothes and personal belongings from our bedroom and sat the bags in the guest bedroom. He slept in the guestroom with no problem. Didn't trying coming in our bedroom at all.

The only reason I let him stay when he came was because my boys were all over him. It was obvious they didn't want him to leave. He didn't try. I didn't force him.

The next morning he came downstairs as I was going outside to put the boys on the bus for school.

When I got back inside, he was at the kitchen table drinking coffee and reading the paper.

"Excuse me? You stayed with the kids last night. I ain't trying to break bread with you this morning."

He had some nerve. Acting like nothing at all had gone down.

He looked up at me from the paper as I stood leaning against the counter. "I can't eat breakfast in my own home?"

I shook my head. Todd Taylor was absolutely amazing.

"To prevent all of these games, you can have your house. I'll buy another one. You promised it to your little love mistress anyway."

"I didn't say you had to do that. I built this for you and the kids."

"Well don't play with me then."

Silence.

I didn't say anything and neither did he. The tension in the room was dreadful.

After a few deep breaths, he decided to break the silence.

"Look Krisha, I'm sorry for the whole ordeal with Cassie."

"I'd appreciate it if you don't mention her name in my house. And, keep ya' tired sorries to yourself. Sorry don't mean a damn thing to you and you know it."

"I mean every word I say to you baby."

I was tired of hearing him talk. His presence was so unwanted. So I headed out of the kitchen and toward the stairs. Needed to get to my bedroom to get dressed for work.

After reaching my bedroom, I retreated to the bathroom where I showered, shaved, and lotioned my body before returning into my bedroom to dress.

As I moved back into the room, Todd was sitting on the edge of the bed with his face in his hands.

"Why are you in here?" I said with the stereotypical attitude of the angry black woman that society so quickly attributes to us.

"We need to talk."

"There's nothing else to say Todd."

"I need for you to understand me."

"Understand what? I already know that you're a lying, cheating son-of-a-bitch who screws around with anything moving. Thanks. I know that now."

"Krisha, come here."

"I'm not coming near you. And you need to leave."

I commenced to getting dressed. Turned my back to him and bent over to slide my thong on. Took a glance back at him and could see that he was hypnotized by my sexiness. I did that on purpose. He was so transparent. I grinned at the results.

I jumped back to my attitude. "Leave or get out of my bedroom while I'm getting dressed. Whatever you need to say, say to my attorney."

He got up off the bed and walked towards me. Approached me from the back. Pulled me into his arms and embraced me tightly.

I squirmed around in his arms; tried to break his hold.

"Let me go and get out Todd!"

"I love you girl." He buried his face in my neck, squeezing me with a good bit of his man strength.

"Fuck you!" I spat.

"You serious?"

He wanted to play. I wasn't in the mood. I was angry. Very angry.

"You wish."

"You don't want me no more?"

He playfully bit at my neck as I dodged his advances.

"No! And stop!" I screamed while wiggling around to free myself from his grip.

"That's not what you said the other day."

"That was the other day."

"You'll always be mine. You know that huh?" He kissed behind my ear.

He obviously thought this was a game. My life was a game to him.

"Oooh!" I began laughing. "Now I get it. You wanna lay claim to me and my body right? Think someone else gon' get it while you're gone. Get out!"

I was mean with a very foul mouth these days, but I didn't care. This man was unbelievable and I was a bag of emotions because of him.

"This is mine." His hand crept between my legs. Cupping a handful of my chocolate mound. "And this right here…" He pressed his hard-on right into the crack of my half naked behind. "…is all she knows. And we gon' keep it like that."

He planted a kiss on my bare shoulder.

"Are you smokin' something?" I tried turning to look at him. "When you decided to let me go, you told me to be with whom I pleased. That means in every way."

"I would never say that." He kissed my neck softly.

I moved out of his reach.

"Remember Todd, you don't want me. You want Cassie. So I can do whatever I want."

He held me. Man strength growing tighter. Moved his head closer to my ear and whispered, "Krisha, don't make me hurt you girl. You know I'd never say that."

I was shocked at his words and the grip he had on my body. Something told me he meant what he'd just said.

"Is that a threat?" I asked.

He didn't answer. Just loosened his grip, turned me around, and looked into my eyes.

Those eyes. Lord those eyes! I said to myself.

Next thing I knew his lips were on mine.

Lips pleasurable. Hands even better.

I was vulnerable. He was all I knew.

I didn't care to show my vulnerability though. I wouldn't give him the pleasure.

"I don't want you Todd."

"I think you do."

He held my head between both strong hands. Took my tongue between his lips. Hindered my speech.

"I'm still your husband. Let me make love to you." He whispered.

"I don't think that's a good idea considering you were just up in Cassie the other day." I panted.

"This is therapeutic." He spoke softly with a grin.

"For me or you?"

He didn't answer. Instead his magical hands had my thong around my thighs before I could tell.

He proceeded to get down on his knees.

And my knees proceeded to give.

"I don't want this." I struggled.

"Yes, you do."

After removing my thong with his teeth, his face settled at my crotch.

With one leg over his shoulder, I was fighting to stay up on the other one.

He kissed me hard. Massaged me slowly. Softly made love to me. Something inside me was melting. And he was getting the results. My knees were weakening. He knew how to get me. I couldn't resist him. I tried but I just couldn't.

Todd arose from the floor after taking me to a foreign yet familiar place. He was successful at moving my almost lifeless body over to the bed. I was mesmerized by his gentleness.

He stripped down to the bare brown, kneeled on the bed, and then settled in an all too familiar spot between my soft caramel thighs. I spread them wide. Gave him a good view of what he was attempting to give up to Cassie.

Todd was good. In a matter of five minutes, I went from hating him to opening up my world to him again.

I slid my hands down over my wetness; closed my eyes and stirred myself up another hundred degrees while he watched.

Releasing a gasp of approval, he uttered, "You're incredible."

A smile creased the corners of my lips. Something that had become unfamiliar to my face.

I opened my eyes to see a spell bound gaze glued to where he wanted to be.

"Let me taste you." He requested as he leaned down to take my fingers into his mouth. Took the taste of me from my fingers. Cleansed them of my flavor.

I arched my back as the softness of his mouth surrounded each finger. Couldn't believe what that was doing to me.

He shifted his body between my legs. Made my knees touch my chest. Positioned himself to enter my queendom.

"Wait. Condom." I said softly in a heavy pant.

"Why?"

I gave him a deranged look. He knew why. I *was* a little weak behind him, but I wasn't totally stupid.

He didn't object to protecting us. He simply reached over to the nightstand drawer and pulled out a magnum condom. Slid it on, then slid inside me and began his quest to long stroking me into speaking another language.

I was raining sweetness. So much that he found it hard to stay inside me with the condom.

I hated using those slippery life jackets, but they were best for the situation I was in.

His loving was mesmerizing. I thought. *So good.*

From wall to wall, he touched my inner soul. The deeper the penetration, the more he'd grow. Motion slow and easy.

He knew how I liked it. He knew I loved being extra. Making love on a slow grind always sent me over the edge.

I just wanted a release. I needed to get on with my life.

I was never disappointed with him. He always broke me off proper. And I made sure I did the same. Showed him real good, over and over, what he was gonna be missing.

After an hour and a half of intense lovemaking, he went for rain jacket number three. His desire was to please me into late afternoon, but I had to end it for the sake of my ailing heart.

"What's wrong baby? Please don't make me stop."

He was surprised and disappointed. But reality was beginning to set in again.

"It's time for you to go Todd. When you leave, don't come back."

He looked at me with a frown. "What you mean *don't* come back? My children are here."

"I mean this bedroom. Your business will be at the door for you whenever you come. You have no reason being upstairs and especially in my bedroom."

"C'mon Krisha..."

Cutting him off.

"This is how you want it. So you got it."

I attempted to get up. He restrained me with one arm and leg across my body.

I couldn't believe I was actually dismissing him. I guess some things will force you to come to your senses.

He lay across me staring into my face. Trying to see inside my head. Maybe wondering if it were all worth it.

"I need to say something first. I know you don't want to hear I'm sorry anymore so I won't say it, but I want you to know that my intentions have always been good toward you. You're my heart. If I hurt you, I hurt myself. That's why I felt I couldn't lie to you any longer or hurt you anymore. Respect me for being honest."

"I respect you for being honest. But you don't understand the pain that follows your honesty. You're on the giving end not the receiving end."

"Believe the words I tell you."

"That's hard to do considering your record."

"I can understand you feeling like that but listen to me. I don't want to leave you, but honestly Krisha I just don't know if I want to be married right now. Staying is only going to force you to live in misery. And I know you. I probably won't live to see my next birthday."

"What makes you feel like this all of a sudden Todd?"

"It wasn't all of a sudden. I've felt like this for a few years. I didn't act on it until my affair with Jasmine. And you saw what happened then. I got caught. I'm not used to cheating. I get caught every time. I'm not gonna keep subjecting you to that. I love you too much."

"If you loved and respected me, you wouldn't have done any of it. You would have told me this before it all started."

"True in a way, but I do love you. No one can ever convince me otherwise."

"Then why'd you hit me for that girl. You've never hit me before."

"Krisha you were gonna kill her. I didn't want my wife catching a charge over me."

"You wanted to hurt me over her and you know it."

"Hell no. I was just trying to save the both of you. To tell you the truth, she got what she deserved for rollin' up here like that."

"Are you talkin' slick about your new boo?" I was being sarcastic but that was eating me up.

"Never my boo. You gon' always be my boo."

"It's so strange that I'm having this conversation with you. I can't believe I'm openly talking about it. But I'm gonna really try to at least be friends."

"Don't ever stop loving me Krish."

"I could never."

"Don't give up on me. Give me some time baby."

"I'm not waiting on you if that's what you're asking. I can't let you go out and mess around with every woman you see, then when you're old, worn out and deep in debt come crawling back to me sick and ailing."

"I didn't say wait. Just continue loving me."

Todd took my face in his hands and kissed me. Took his time and kissed me slow. Caressed every inch of my mouth with his tongue. Between kisses he whispered to my heart, "My first love. I love you babe."

"I love you too." I said.

Heartfelt. He meant it. I believed him.

Lock gazes. Intertwined fingers. We smiled. For a long moment, we admired each other's beauty. Never wanting the moment to end.

"Can I love you again?" He whispered between kisses to my earlobe.

I didn't answer.

He repeated it until I could no longer resist his warm breath in my ear and fingers searching my lower area.

Between gasps, I decided to take back what I'd said before.

I smiled.

He returned a cuter smile. The man was too good.

He got up from the bed and headed to the bathroom.

Came back with a wet towel. Wiped me down good.

"Now." He admired my body. "She's ready for me again."

All I can say is A-mazing! Todd and myself included.

What started out at the foot of the bed, ended up with me backed against the headboard begging for mercy. He was a maniac.

After I could take no more, my body went into what I like to call a toxic shock. Todd Taylor was definitely toxic.

My body convulsed erratically. When I finally came down from my high, I hurt from my back down to my pelvis. Spasms had hit me and I couldn't move a muscle. Despite the sweet pain I was in, I begged for more. I needed him.

Todd lay back on the pillow. Massaged my back. "Next time boo, next time."

I reached for him.

He lightly spanked my hand. Moved out of my reach.

"Next time."

Unbelievable. I thought.

Here I was begging for him like a crack head needin' a hit. And here he was refusing to give it to me. Another attempt to keep me hanging on to his balls.

This man has got too much game. I thought.

Instead of getting upset at his refusal to love me senseless, I elected to allow him to snuggle up behind me as we drifted off to sleep.

I woke up to his cell phone ringing. The time told me it was 1:10 pm.

We'd slept all morning and into the afternoon. He was snoring hard, which was unusual unless he was dog-tired or drunk.

Guess he was dog-tired because he'd put in some work this morning, and knowing him all last night too.

He didn't hear his phone so I searched his pants to answer it.

"Hello." I sang into the phone.

"Who the hell is this?" The caller threw out.

Terrible attitude. But I knew whom it belonged to. I'd never forget that voice for as long as I lived.

"Mrs. Taylor. May I help you?" I cheerfully said with calmness.

"Where's Todd?"

"Right here. Why?" I was being smart.

"He's supposed to be at work. I've been calling him all day."

"Oh well, try him back later. He's busy." I smiled as I clicked the phone off.

I turned the phone on vibrate then dialed Carmen to ask her to pick up the boys for me.

After speaking to Carmen, I quickly drifted back off into La La Land with all the other fools and dummies. Sleep took over as I lay next to the source of all my heartache.

This was going to be harder than I'd imagined.

Again, I thanked God for Carmen. If I didn't have her I'd be up a creek without a paddle. Carmen cooked dinner, fed the boys, and put them to bed while Todd and I stayed locked away in my bedroom all day and half the night. I got up a couple of times to help with homework and kiss them goodnight, but for the most part I was good for nothing. He'd taken my strength early, and for the most part I just didn't want to leave his side.

Around nine thirty p.m., I awakened to Todd kissing my face.

I smiled as I rolled over on my back.

"I gotta go baby." He said looking down into my eyes.

I searched his face for an explanation, and found it in his hand.

He held his cell phone in one hand, my hand with the other. He'd already gotten dressed and was sitting next to me on the bed.

He stroked the side of my face as he spoke.

"Don't forget what I told you today."

I looked into his eyes; longed for him to stay with me; longed for him to hold me in his arms all-night; longed for him to love me like he used to. I wanted him to stay with me forever. Pride wouldn't let me ask. Things had changed.

As if he read my mind, "What?" He asked as he kissed my forehead.

"Why are you choosing her over me?"

"If you mean Cassie, I'm not choosing her over you."

"What can she give you that I can't?"

Silence.

"It hurts to know you fell for someone like her rather than somebody who could at least compare to me."

He looked at me a few seconds, then he said, "No one can compare to you."

"Then why?"

He didn't answer. Guess he didn't have a good one, so he got up and walked away.

I bawled like a fool until falling asleep.

For the next few months, Todd visited the boys everyday and stayed in my bedroom at least three to four times a week. He was happy with the way things were. I wasn't. But I accepted it. I was playing myself and I knew it. I was now the other woman.

Sometimes he stayed the entire night; sometimes he would get up and leave. But every time, he went right back to her.

He had already laid it down to me as to what he wanted so I had no reason to complain. He loved me. He just didn't want to be faithful to me. He still wanted me. He just wanted half the women in Louisiana too. He was in and out so no other man would claim what he felt was his. He still had all his belongings in the house, with the exception of some clothes. We still went out together on occasions; with the kids or sometimes just the two of us. He still received his mail at the house and continued to pay all of the household bills. I still took care of all the business affairs for him and he consulted with me for business decisions.

However, I was still battling with inner-self trying to break free from the hold he had on my heart, mind, and body. Regardless of how ugly it got, I always found a way to forgive him, or at least look past whatever it was, just to keep at least one hand on him. It seemed like I loved him even more once I was sharing him.

My girls tried to convince me that the whole situation was BS and a down right insult to me as a woman who was still his wife.

I would swear I was leaving Todd for good. I would agree with them at the moment but would fall right back under his spell once we were together. If any woman who had a man that said all the right things at the right time, did all the things you liked, how you liked it done, never missed a beat with the kids, and took care of *all* your wants and needs, would definitely understand where I'm coming from. The kinda brotha who always keeps your hopes up high, even though you know deep down that he only lies to get what he wants, lies so that the relationship can remain the same. We know they're lies, but we latch onto that one ounce of hope that just maybe he'll live up to what he's saying and commit to the things his actions speak when he's blessing your body with mind controlling sexual satisfaction.

On that note, Todd's bedroom skills had improved dramatically since we'd been separated. Or maybe its just that I'm that much more stupid and open for him. Sex with him is the one thing that keeps me blinded, or just not ready to let go. His marvelous sexcapades and insatiable fetish was already completely off the chain, but he was on a level of his own now. Guess he'd been learning a few tricks from those triflin' women. But, nonetheless, I was still with him, so I guess I was just as triflin' as them.

I knew deep down I couldn't keep this thing up with Todd. I was wearing myself out. I'd never been second to anyone and the feeling of that had lowered my self-esteem drastically.

The respect I had for myself had been compromised for a man who wore the title of my *husband*. The man that I promised to love for better or for worse until death. I always planned on holding up my end of the bargain. *But what can you do when two people are not on the same page? What can you do?*

Hearing him say "I love you" just didn't fit the bill anymore. It was time for me to wake up and pull Mr. Johnson out my ass, because I was gettin' screwed every single day. I realized that the relationship was over a long time ago. We just had an arrangement. The only thing he had interest in was keeping a smile on my face and controlling my life by sexing me into a coma.

I'm coming around though. Sometimes it takes some of us a little longer to see the bigger picture when you're on the inside looking out. But when you're on the outside looking in, things are so clear.

Seeing things the way Mia saw them months ago, would have kept me from experiencing some of the drama that I went through. But it was my business. My life. And I had to see this man for who he really was through my own two eyes. But as the bible says, "what's done in darkness shall come to the light."

18

Why Her?

"*H*ere." Mia said as she threw a bag at me as I sat back on my couch.

"What's this?"

"Something to cheer you up. Hot off the press."

I quickly tore open the bag.

I stared at the newly purchased music CD of one of my favorite artists.

"My girl's new CD." I said with a smile. "Thanks Mia. Did you listen to it already?"

"Please. Don't trip. You know B my girl."

"Whatever."

Rolling her eyes.

"Anyway, Krish, how about going to Atlanta with me and Derric this weekend?"

"What are you guys going to Atlanta for?"

"Derrick's going for business. I'm just tagging along. I figured while he's doing his thang, we could be doing our thang."

"You know I don't like being the third wheel."

"Don't sound stupid. How many times over the years has it been you, me, and Todd?"

"You know I'm not you. You just don't care."

"Well, we want you to go. We both agreed it would be good for you to get away for awhile."

"I guess it would be nice. But I'll have to get back with you on that."

"You need to get out of this big house sometimes. We haven't been out in months."

"Yeah, look what happened last time we were out together."

"Technically, we didn't go out together; we ended up together."

"However you wanna put it. It ended in drama."

"So are you saying you're scared to go out with me now?"

"Girl please. I'm just saying I haven't been up to it lately."

"Does it have anything to do with your good for nothing, ought to be by now ex-husband?"

"Nope."

"Yeah right. You been grieving for months while he's out stirring around in more tail than Paula Dean stirring up flap jacks."

I gave her a mean look.

She added, "You know it's the truth and you know I'mma tell you the truth."

Sitting by me on the couch pulling me close to her, she said, "Come on sis'. Snap out of the trance he has you in. This is so not you. He's told you how it's going to be from now on. You've got to face it and move on."

"I am facing it Mia. I just can't...."

Cutting me off. "Stop saying *can't*. Don't use his name and *can't* in the same sentence again, unless you're saying you can't stand his ass."

"I'm just saying it's hard not being with the man you've been with all your adult life when you never asked for any of this. You can't just cut your feelings off over night."

"Over night? Krisha it's been months."

"It's only been five, and you just don't understand Mia. I love him."

"I understand alright. You're still sleeping with him, aren't you?"

"What makes you think that?"

"You."

"Why?"

"Because you would have said 'hell no' if you weren't."

I didn't offer anything else. Mia sat with her face in her hands for a few minutes. She looked up at me with fire in her eyes. "You know he's gonna be the death of you?"

"Mia, stop. He really loves me. It's hard for others to understand."

"He is going to kill you!" She screamed. "If not one way then the other!"

"Why would you say something like that Mia?"

"In some way, form, or fashion, he's going to kill you with the bullshit he's putting you through because you refuse to let go. He's told you out of his own mouth that he does not want to be married anymore. You know you can't take too much of that crap. Those anxiety attacks will turn into a heart attack. If he doesn't give you AIDS or something from his poor taste in women and his filthy lifestyle, he's gonna kill you with his bare hands. He only wants to hold onto you and keep banging your brains out because he doesn't want anyone else to have you. The longer you let this go on, that man is always gonna feel like he owns you and when someone else moves in his spot, he's gonna snap. He won't be able to take it. Find a way to let him go."

"Mia, I know Todd."

"What?" Mia screamed lividly.

She jumped up from the couch, walked around the living room with her hands on her hips then got all up in my face.

"So did you know he was gonna leave you?" She yelled.

"No." I said without looking at her.

"Did you know he was gonna start fucking with hos, and all up in ya house, in case you forgot?" She yelled.

"No."

"You fly all the way across the nation for his dingy ass, and he tells you to kick rocks because he's laid up with his bitch in *your* sister-in-law's pad. Did you know your *husband* was gonna do that Krisha?"

I just looked at her.

"Answer me gotdammit. Don't get quiet now!" She stared at me and screamed.

"No Mia." I said calmly.

"Then don't tell me you know that bastard!" She paced. "I don't know if you know anything anymore. What's your name bitch? Bet you don't know that either!"

I sat staring at her. I didn't know what to say. So I just stared at her.

She managed to calm down a little as she paced the floor.

"Think about what your mother would say about this. Pray and ask for guidance, but somehow you've got to move on with your life."

"Why did you mention my mama, Mia?" I said through teary eyes and a cracking voice.

She looked at me and regained control of her emotions.

"I'm sorry, but something has got to make you think."

I was crying real crocodile tears by this time. She was telling the truth. I just didn't want to accept it.

Hugging me, she said, "Let him go Krisha, because if he kills you, I'll kill him."

And I knew she was telling the truth. She meant every word that she'd just said and it was no way my best friend would be sitting in jail behind my pitiful tail.

She held me for a few until I got myself together. Then I stretched out on the couch to let what she'd said absorb into what was left of my brain.

Mia popped in a movie and stretched out on the other sofa while I lay there consumed in thoughts.

After about an hour, I raised up to take a walk outside to the mailbox while Mia went to raid the fridge.

Not that I was anticipating it, but I was due to receive a check from my mother's retirement that was to come today or tomorrow. It really didn't matter to me because it was going directly into a trust fund for my two boys. I'm sure she would have wanted them to have it.

I sorted my mail from Todd's and found the retirement check, along with a host of bills.

"Bills, bills, bills," I whispered to myself. I plopped down on the sofa, checked out Oprah and decided to see who I was gonna pay out of Todd's account over the phone.

Maybe this will occupy my time for a while so I won't have to think about my life. I thought.

"Isn't it time for the kids to come home." Mia asked entering the family room munching on something.

"Yeah, Carmen's gonna get them today. Today is ice cream day. Can you please hand me my purse so I can get Todd's debit card to pay some bills right quick?"

Mia looked at me and rolled her eyes while shaking her head. She picked my purse up from the table and tossed it to me.

"Mia!" I said in reaction to her throwing my purse at me. "Why you gotta be so mean?"

"Girl pay dem damn bills!" She said annoyed. "At least you're still smart enough to be using his money; so you do have half a brain."

"Whatever Mia."

I commenced to doing my business and ignored my BFF.

I decided to pay my electricity bill, car note, and cell phone bill over the phone, in that order. I knew if I didn't pay them now while I was looking at them, I was sure to forget later.

When I opened my cell phone bill and saw the amount owed, I was like, "Wow!"

There was no way my bill should have been $940 for one month. I never go over my minutes. I thought.

"There has got to be some mistake. My bill is outrageously high this month."

"They'll get you. You better call 'em." Mia said smacking on chocolate chip cookies.

"I don't know where these numbers came from. I didn't call these numbers. There's only a couple I recognize. And look at the times, this is ridiculous."

"Are you sure it's yours." Mia asked.

I thought about what she'd said. "You know what Mia? You have a point."

I found the first page of the bill. Looked at the name on the front. *Todd Taylor.* I'd torn it open so fast that I hadn't noticed that the bill was his.

"You're right, it's Todd's. That explains all those numbers then."

Looking back at the pages with all the phone numbers. "But wait." I said.

"What?"

"Something doesn't add up."

"What is it?"

"They must have combined our bills or something."

"Why?"

"Because I see calls to Kyra's house and cell on here."

"Kyra? Are you sure?"

"Yes. You know I know her numbers back and forth."

"Let me see."

Mia came over to where I was sitting.

"Here, you take that page. I'll look at these. See how many calls there are to her." We looked over the calls for a few minutes.

"I got twenty on this one, front and back." Mia said.

"I'm counting twenty-six on these."

"Krish, this is for one month right?"

"Yeah, I guess so. I know I haven't been calling Kyra at three o'clock in the morning. Look through that stack of mail again for me Mia to see if I have a bill in there."

She quickly got up to retrieve the mail from the table.

"Here it is. Somehow it got stuck to the back of this Black Treasures Book Club bill."

"Let me see that."

Mia handed me the envelope.

I tore it open with the quickness. I was eager to figure out the cell phone dilemma.

And just as I thought, the amount owed was $95.00 as usual. Everything looked fine on my statement. All calls I could account for.

After both of us sat looking at the bill and thinking for a couple minutes, we were both thinking the same, but Mia spoke first, "Krisha, what the hell is Todd calling Kyra for that much?"

"That's what I wanna know. Girl, look at this one 6:35 a.m., 3:00 p.m., another at 11:40 p.m., and 1:15 a.m. And this one was two weeks ago on the 23rd. He was here until about 1:00 am. I remember because that's the night he took the boys to the basketball game and they got in late on a school night. Mia, what is this?"

"I don't know. I hope it ain't what I'm thinking."

"He never mentioned he'd been conversing with Kyra. I talk to him everyday."

"Something is foul Krish."

"Let's not jump to conclusions."

We pondered a minute. Mia jumped up off the floor. "That sneaky bitch!"

"What?"

"She needs her ass whipped for this."

"Don't be crazy Mia."

"How do you explain the calls Krish? Stop being so damn naïve."

"She's our best friend."

"She has the goods between her legs doesn't she? That's what yo' husband likes. He don't give a damn."

"He wouldn't stoop that low."

"So you say, but I say differently. A dog is a dog, it don't matter who his bitch is."

"That's low Mia."

"Well, he's low and she is too if they've been fooling around behind your back."

"Kyra loves me Mia and I refuse to believe that. Conversations can be about anything."

"There's only one way to find out. I ain't trying to tell you nothing. You find out what's going on for yourself."

"I definitely will. Better sooner than later."

Picking up the phone, I dialed Kyra's home, to no avail, then placed a call to her cell phone. She picked up on the first ring.

"Hey boo, what's up?" I chimed.

"Hey Krish."

"I got something for you, so why don't you stop by later."

"Something for me? Oh! I feel so special."

"I want you to see something girl."

"Okay. I'm leaving work now, so I'll come right over before I pick up Paige."

"Okay good." I said before hanging up the phone.

While Mia proceeded to watch her movie, I continued to dissect Todd's bill while we waited for Kyra to arrive.

About twenty-five minutes later, the doorbell rang. Mia got up to answer the door. I remained in my seat, still pondering whether I should even mention the calls to my girl.

Kyra walked in all jolly, being her usual self.

"Hey you guys." She said with a big smile.

Her smile was perfect. She was so pretty. She looked like Angelina Jolie's darker skin twin sister. She greeted both of us with a kiss on the cheek.

"Hey, girl. How was your day?" I asked.

"It was fine. Just tired. Then, I gotta drive all the way out to Central to get Paige, then to Southern Lakes."

"I'm sorry I haven't been to your new house yet Kyra. I've been going through a lot lately."

"Yeah, I know girl. That's okay though. Paige and I will be there whenever you feel like coming."

"Thanks."

Mia sat quietly across from us looking bored.

"What's wrong Mia?" Kyra said.

"Nothing. Just thinking about Derrick."

"Whatever. You can't do without Derrick for a few hours?"

"Nope."

"I think she's finally been touched by the love bug." Kyra teased.

"No, I don't think so. I just really like the man."

"It's been what, a year since you've been going out with Derrick? Is that a record or what?"

"For your information, it's been exactly eleven months, three weeks, and four days."

"Yep, that's a record," Kyra and I said in unison.

We all shared a laugh.

I almost felt bad about what I was about to ask her. But she's like my sister. She'll be alright.

Before I could speak, Kyra chimed in, "So, what you got for me?" She said anxiously.

Mia's cell phone began sounding off its distinct tone for Derrick. She stepped into the kitchen to answer it.

"I got something to show you, but first I need to ask you something."

"Shoot. I'm all ears."

"Have you been in touch with Todd lately?"

"No, why do you ask?" She answered with a calm smile.

"Well I have my reasons to believe that you and Todd have been doing alot of conversing."

"*Alot* of conversing? What do you mean *alot* of conversing?"

Ignoring her question. I asked, "What is it that you and Todd have to talk about?"

"I see Todd in passing every blue moon Krisha."

"Do you talk to him?"

"Not really. Just a quick hi and bye. Sometimes he'll ask about Paige."

"That's it?"

"Yeah, that's it. Why are you asking me this Krish?"

I could detect the attitude approaching.

"I told you, I have my reasons for asking."

"Just what are you trying to say?"

"I'm not trying to say anything. I'm just asking."

"Krisha, you're trippin'. You need to let Todd's no good ass go because he got you going off big time."

"I'm not trippin'. If I got something to ask, you know I'll ask before I bite my tongue."

"I helped you beat some ass behind Todd, including his, and you step to yo' girl like I'm one of his street chicks."

Lines formed in her forehead. She was getting upset.

"Calm down Kyra. Let's not get carried away."

Jumping up from the sofa clearly upset, she had a lot on her mind.

That little red devil was trying to get in my ear, but for her sake I had to control my emotions.

"I'm getting carried away? I can't believe you Krisha. I'm trying to figure out what the fuck yo' point is!" She yelled.

Okay, now she'd started the profanity, which takes this conversation to another level. I thought.

Mia rushed into the room closing her cell.

I sat on my couch and just looked at her guilty butt. She would never be so defensive if she weren't. I've known Kyra since we were eighteen years old. I just hope I'm wrong. But now my thermostat was headed to hot.

"Kyra, just sit down. Chill out. Krisha's not coming at you like that. Why are you screaming?" Mia got in.

"Nope. I'm not sitting down. I gotta go!" She started toward the door.

I walked behind her.

"So you say you haven't spoken to Todd at all?"

"I'm not answering that no more."

"Tell me this. Why all the phone calls then?"

"What phone calls?" She snapped as she turned to face me.

"Why is he calling your house and cell all throughout the day and night, and you calling him the same?"

I held the bill in her face. She looked at it for a few seconds, made out that it was an AC&C Wireless bill, looked back at me and said, "That's yo' triflin' ass husband. Go ask him."

Her response caught me by surprise. Cut me right through to my heart.

"I'm asking you, Ky. I want to hear it from you." I said gently.

"You're asking the wrong one." She snapped.

"What's that supposed to mean?"

"You heard me!" She screamed.

Now I'm thinking, *why did she have to go there?*

My patience meter was over the top and my thermostat had run hot. Did she not know that I was an emotional wreck?

Guess an ass stomp was what she wanted because she already knew I didn't play the overly dramatic crap these days. *So why is she pushing me?* I thought. Guess everybody thinks I'm cotton these days.

"Kyra just calm down. You're showing your guilt." I said with calmness.

"Go ta hell Krisha. You're the only guilty bitch up in here."

Oh really. I thought.

Before I knew it, I'd grabbed her shirt and smacked her across the face with the other hand. I had a good grip on her shirt and had smacked her again before Mia could get between us. I'd hit her so hard and quick she didn't have time to do anything but fall. But the grip I had on her shirt prevented her from hitting the floor.

"Krisha, stop it. Don't do this." Mia screamed. Tussling with me to let go of Kyra's shirt.

I knew Kyra had some serious hands. If I hadn't caught her off guard, it would have been a real brawl up in my house regardless of what Mia was saying. But Kyra already knows she gotta watch me, I got quick hands. Always had em'.

I'm trying to suppress the tantrums and allow sleeping dogs to lie, but these hos keep playing with me.

"No, leave her alone Mia. She knows I'm not that bimbo trick of Todd's."

"Get out of my house. And if I find out you're messing with him, I promise you I'm gonna bring it to you. And you'd better believe that!"

"I'm gettin' out yo' crib, but you better bring it proper when you come! You know I don't play the hands in my face. Jealous ho!"

"Kyra just shut up and go." Mia said, handing her keys to her and pushing her toward the kitchen door.

"I'mma get her dumb ass back for this one Mia."

"You're already gettin' me back. You're doing my husband."

"And your husband is doing half the country including yo stupid ass, so somebody needs to be trynna whip some sense into you. Dumb bitch!" She rolled her eyes, and walked out slamming the door.

I yelled into the kitchen, "Mia, lock my door. You know she's crazy."

Mia rushed back into the family room. "Why'd you have to hit her Krish? You were wrong for that."

"She made me mad Mia. You know she's guilty."

"I don't know anymore Krish. She's our girl. You gotta give her the benefit of the doubt. You treated her like she was someone off the streets."

"You were the main one saying she was guilty."

"But she might be telling the truth. Look into it more."

"I will, but she didn't have to start cursing and getting smart. I was just asking."

"Besides, you can't fight every woman that Todd steps to. You'd be tired as hell, because his ass is foul. Ole' nasty bastard makes me sick."

We burst out laughing.

I couldn't help it on that one. Right about now, I was feeling her. But I had an idea.

I hopped up off the sofa and ran to the computer.

"I'm about to see what's really up. If I'm wrong, I'm running to my girl's house to beg for mercy."

I logged onto the AC&C Wireless website.

Thank goodness Todd hadn't set up an account. It was pretty easy to set up an online account being I had all his personal info. I viewed past and present bills.

It turned out that there was no mistake. Todd had made calls to Kyra for the past six months from what I saw. I couldn't see anything before that so it could have been even longer. Neither of them had mentioned to me that they were even speaking privately to one another let alone staying on the phone almost daily. Go to bed talking, wake up talking. As much as he talked to me, he never talked to me that much.

After about an hour of searching the phone records, my boys came home.

"Are you gonna be okay Krish?" Mia asked.

"I don't know Mia. I gotta think."

Truth was, I was sick. *Hell no I wasn't gonna be okay.*

"I need to go meet Derrick, but if you need me, call."

"I will."

Giving me a hug, she whispered, "Love you girl."

"Love you too Mia."

A tear wanted to fall but I refused. Fought it hard.

Carmen made dinner while I helped the boys with their homework and give them a bath. They ate dinner and were ready for bed around eight p.m.

I thanked Carmen and asked her if she could come the rest of this week. She gladly accepted. She's been saving up for a new car so she didn't mind working extra hours.

Todd came in around eight thirty. Used his key and waltzed in like all was good.

"Why are you here so late Todd?" I asked with an attitude.

"I just got off work. I had meetings all day." Taking a seat at the kitchen table.

"Don't you know how to call first?"

"I haven't *been* calling first. Why do I have to call first now?"

"Things change. You never know, I might have company."

"You can have all the company you want as long as it ain't no hard leg."

"Excuse me."

He quickly got up from the table.

"I just came to see my boys. No drama tonight." Kissing my forehead.

"Well, don't come here talking about who I can have in my house."

"Our house."

"Soon to be settled."

"What's that supposed to mean?"

"It means… I think we need to go ahead with the divorce. It's been almost six months since you've been gone and…."

"Wait, wait, wait. Why are you saying this now? That ain't the song you was singing last night."

"This is a new day. I don't wanna hear about last night." I snapped.

"Look, let me spend some time with my boys. We'll discuss this later."

He barged past me and went into the family room with the kids.

I went upstairs, took a shower, and washed and wrapped my hair. When I was done, I went in to kiss my kids, who Todd had already put to bed.

I assumed Todd had gone so I went downstairs to get a drink and to turn off the lights. I wanted to get back to my bedroom so I could go back online to make some sense of all the calls. To my surprise, he was still there. Watching TV and had helped himself to the leftovers from dinner.

This has got to stop. To say he doesn't want to be here with us, he sure looks mighty comfortable over there. I thought.

"Your woman can't cook?" I sarcastically asked.

"Yeah, you always could burn."

"Real cute, Todd. Hurry up and eat so I can go to bed."

"You can go on to bed."

"Not until you're gone."

He put his fork down to look at me.

"Why are you acting like this?" He stared.

"Why are you acting like this?" I repeated, mimicking him.

He irritated me so bad, I hated to hear his voice.

He stared harder.

"You're being childish, Krish."

"Just go please." I threw out as I turned to go back upstairs.

He jumped up off the couch and ran to grab my arm to stop me. Pulled me to his lean body. Stroked my face with the back of his hand. "What's gotten into you?" He said softly.

"I think you should leave."

"What's wrong baby?" He ran his finger down my neck.

"This whole situation is wrong."

"You've been fine. What's the problem now?"

"You thought I'd stay fine forever?

"No, that's not at all what I thought."

"You and nobody else is going to make me second to another woman. So I think you should go on with your life, so I can go on with mine."

"So, what are you saying Krisha?"

"What I'm saying is, why the hell are you calling Kyra?"

That came out before I knew it. Just rolled off my tongue.

Shock was all over his face.

"Wh..wh..what? Kyra?"

"You heard me."

"Why would I call Kyra?"

"That's what I just asked you."

"I don't talk to Kyra like that."

"You mean you haven't been talking to her on the phone?"

"Hell no. Where'd you get that?"

"Please don't tell me you're sleeping with her too, Todd." Ignoring his denials.

"Krish, let's be real."

"Todd, she's like my sister. I don't have much more than her and Mia."

"Don't you think I know that? Krisha, I would never do that to you. I know how much you guys love each other."

"You're a liar. I see it all over your face. You're doin' my girl!"

The tears welled up in my eyes. I swung at him.

He stopped the blow by taking hold of my forearm. Pulled me to him.

"Get that out of your pretty head."

Kissing my forehead as he spoke, he calmed the situation really quick.

"So, you haven't talked to her lately?"

I looked deep into his eyes for truth.

"I haven't seen her since about two months ago. I saw her at Pebo's having lunch. I waved. She waved. That's it."

I looked up into his eyes still trying to find his truth. I couldn't see it. I only saw his lies. Only found deception.

"Come on upstairs, baby. I want you to sleep on my chest all night so you can be right next to my heart."

He placed a nice kiss on my lips as we retreated to my bedroom.

I awakened around 12:15 a.m. Moved off of Todd's chest and slid out of the bed. Went over to the chaise and searched his jacket for his cell phone. Then, I tiptoed into the guest bedroom and closed the door.

It turned out that he hadn't called Kyra's number all day, but she sure as hell had called him. Five missed calls from her and three from Cassie, total number of missed calls were nineteen.

He hadn't made any calls out today since 11:15 a.m. when he called me. He said he was in meetings all day, until he came over tonight. Guess he told the truth about something.

For some reason, he didn't bother to check his cell though. Guess he really *was* exhausted today. He came here ate, showered, and went to bed. Didn't even want sex. Now that's a first in a long time.

I listened to his messages from Cassie, his baby momma, some Shanice, someone named Bria who claimed to have met him two days ago, Trent, and last but not least, my girl Kyra. My heart stopped when I heard her voice. I replayed it again.

"Todd, call me as soon as you get this message." She said in the message.

I let that marinate for a while and did a little more searching in his address book. Then I dialed Kyra's number from his cell. The phone rang two times. She picked up on the third ring without saying hello.

"Where've you been all day?" She asked in a hurry.

I was speechless for a few seconds. The knot in my throat wouldn't allow me to speak. I knew it in my heart, but what was I gonna say now.

"Hello?" She said.

I opened my mouth, but nothing came out. I kept trying, but I just couldn't say anything. The knife in my back was cutting too deep.

She remained quiet until I hung up the phone in her face.

I lay there and cried for at least an hour. Then I called Mia, who answered on the first ring.

"It's true, Mia. It's true."

"I'm so sorry, Krisha. I didn't want it to be true."

"Mia, why is this happening to me?" I cried.

"I don't know, but rest assure they are both gonna pay."

"Honestly Mia, did you know?"

"No, Krisha. I honestly didn't, but once I thought about some things today, I sensed that it might be true. I just didn't want to believe it."

"How could she do this Mia? I would die for that girl."

"Some men can be dogs Krish. You already know that. And a bitch is just a bitch."

"Why would they cross that line?"

"Your mother told you the answer to that. And she's always been weak for men."

"He's hurt me more now than when he up and left me the first time. This time I'm losing a good friend too."

"If this is the way they love you, you can do without them both. Friends don't do this to friends."

"I'mma get em' both. I told her I was gonna get her ass."

"Krisha, don't be silly. You've got too much at stake than to be going to jail over the two of them. God has them."

Still crying, I said, "I know, but you know I can't let this go. They can get outta my life and leave me the hell alone, but they're gonna know they messed up big time. I was good to both of them." I cried.

"Krisha, do I need to come over there? You just need to calm down."

"You don't have to come here. I'll be okay."

"Okay, some crap! Where's that damn gun?"

"It's locked away in my closet. I'm not gonna get it. I don't wanna kill em' Mia, damn! Regardless of what they're doing to me, I still love both of them."

"Promise me. I don't like this Krisha. Just go to sleep. I'll come over in the morning."

"I can't go to sleep with that bastard in my bed. I hate his ass!"

"He's in your bed? Wow!" She took a deep sigh. "What did I tell you bout that? Didn't I tell you today this was gonna happen? That man is gonna end up killing you. Do you see what I mean?" She screamed.

"Yeah, I see. I see now."

"Clean your house of that slim. If you can't do it, I'm coming to do it myself!" She screamed.

"I can handle this."

I didn't need Mia to fight my battles. I had to do this alone.

"Krish, don't go messing with that girl tonight. It's late. She has a child and you're gonna go your black behind to jail if you go disturbing them folks out there tonight. Start cleaning up *your* house first, deal with her later."

"I know Mia. I will." I said sounding defeated. "And thanks for listening."

"Don't thank me. I don't have a choice but to listen. You better not call anyone else. I love you Krish and try to get some sleep."

"Goodnight Mia."

I thought about what I was gonna do. After another hour of praying, I felt a little better. I was even able to drift off to sleep.

19

Goodbye Love

*T*odd kissing my neck and caressing my back startled me awake. I looked around and tried to remember where I was.

He was sitting next to me as naked as the day he was born. On a normal day that would have brought a smile to my face, but today I wasn't feeling Mr. Taylor in the least bit.

"Where are the kids?" I asked as I wiped sleep from my eyes.

"School."

"What time is it?"

"9:30"

"Why'd you let me sleep that long?"

Raising my short gown to take a peak, he said, "Why'd you get out of the bed with me? You know I like to roll right over into you in the morning."

"I'm not in the mood." I grumbled while pushing him away.

"I can help you get in the mood." He grinned.

"Not interested." I said sharply.

"We'll see about that."

Before I could move to get up, he locked fingers with me, held my hands back by my head on the bed, and straddled me. He began kissing me softly on my lips, and then moved down to my chest.

"Todd, I don't want this." I said with a frown.

"I want you."

He is utterly ridiculous; like walking hormones and I'm *really not for it today.* I thought.

Nevertheless, the touches of his lips on my skin made me change my mind. He already knew what that would do to me. I just kept thinking how much I could not stand Todd Taylor. But, I figured one quick one wouldn't hurt. Had to make this one really count. The way I saw it, this was the last time Todd Taylor would be compromising me in any way.

When he was done with his stellar performance, I was so upset that I could barely conceal my anger.

My body was satisfied. He was magnificent as usual. But after the one minute feeling left, I began to get heated.

I wasn't sure if I was mad at him and the whole situation, or if I was mad that somebody else would be getting his good lovin' for good. Namely my best friend.

Whatever. I thought. It didn't matter. That was something I could not control. She was probably already getting it anyway.

I was extremely upset and ready to clown. I was trying my best to hold it in but truth was, I wanted to kick up some sand this morning.

I got up from the bed to go shower. He went to get dressed.

Several moments later, Todd opened the door to the bathroom as I was stepping out of the shower.

"Have you seen my cell phone?"

"Yes." I replied.

He awaited a further response.

"Could you tell me where it is?"

"Guest bedroom, nightstand drawer."

I continued drying off and began dressing while he went to fetch his phone.

In a matter of seconds, Todd returned to my bedroom with phone in hand.

"Why was it in there?" He asked sternly staring at me hard.

"I put it in there."

"What were you doing with my phone?"

"I made a call on it."

"Why couldn't you use your cell or the house phone?"

"I forgot the number I wanted to call, but you had it stored in your phone."

"Really?" He stared.

"Yep."

He looked at me suspiciously.

I had dressed in a pair of black shorts and leggings, a black hoodie, and black Shox. I unwrapped my hair and pulled it into a high ponytail. I really wanted to act a fool today; I was ready for whatever.

"May I ask whose number you just *had* to find in *my* phone?"

"Yes you can ask."

He waited. Stared me down.

"Who did you call Krisha?" He said sternly and clearly annoyed.

"Take a guess."

He began to look uneasy.

"Look, I don't have time to play games with you." He raised his voice.

"Oh! Now all of sudden you don't!" I screamed emotionally.

"Who did you call?" He said calmly as he moved towards me.

"My best friend! I forgot the bitch's number!" I yelled in his face.

"Mia?" He asked trying to play me to the left.

"Yeah, right. Try again."

"Look, Krisha, you're starting this Kyra bull again?"

"You know what Todd? I'm sorry it took me so long to see that you are nowhere, and I mean nowhere, near the man that I married. But to cheat with my girl, someone I hold in my heart as close as you, is no good. That just tells me you have no decency and you don't give a damn about me."

I held my chest. Had to cut my rant short. I felt sick. The thought alone made me sick.

"Krish, you're overreacting. I don't know how her number was stored in my phone. You must have put it in there."

"Save it Todd. You can take all of that dramatic bull, wrap it up, and stick it up ya' ass!"

I stormed by him and headed to my bedroom.

Went over to the dresser. Pulled his phone bill from my drawer. "Here check this out."

He studied the piece of paper carefully.

"Now do you still say you don't know where the number came from?

I awaited an answer but got nothing, so I answered for him.

"She gave it to you. And you were with her in my house while I was laid up grieving over my mother. Am I wrong?"

I'd thought about it last night until I fell asleep. I thought about her staying in my house day and night taking care of me when I lost my mother. They had all the time in the world to hook up.

The kids were with Mia and I was out of it. He fed me my meds, which put me out like a light. And when I wasn't sleeping, I was too busy grieving.

"Krisha, listen, I....."

I cut him off.

"Did either of you even think about me and my kids at all?"

"It's not like you think."

I knew in my heart he was a liar. He really didn't have to answer.

Ignoring him I asked a simple question, "Why my girl?"

Upset, I plopped down on the bed burying my face in my hands.

He slid down on the bed next to me wrapping his arm around my shoulder. "Baby, I told you, nobody could ever hold a candle to you. Those hos don't mean nothing to me."

It shouldn't have shocked me that he'd just said that, but it did.

I jumped up and shoved his chest with all my strength.

"Hos! If they are good enough to leave me for, why would they be hos? That means I'm nothing. I'm less than a ho. And if Kyra is a ho, you probably made her one."

I don't know why I felt the need to defend her slimy behind.

"Krisha, I know you're upset, but please let's not go there."

"Go there! Go there? Are you serious? All of this time I'm thinking you're trippin' over that stripper broad and it's been Kyra the whole time?"

No response.

"Is that why you're always over here? Is that why you can't take the kids to where you live? Do you live with Kyra, Todd?"

"No I don't..." He started saying.

The question that spewed from my trembling mouth had just dawned on me.

I cut him off. "Todd, no! Tell me you don't live with Kyra. Please tell me you don't."

As if living with her made it any worse. Somehow it did to me. I held my stomach. I thought about the fact that she'd recently bought a new house. He'd probably helped her buy it. She'd always lived in apartments. How could she afford that house in that new neighborhood? I felt sick. Had to lie back on the bed.

"I love you Krisha." He said.

I rolled over on my side in a fetal position holding my stomach.

"You don't love me. I can't take much more of this."

My head was spinning. Chest heaving. Stomach turning flips.

"Then hear me out baby." He said warmly.

"Why her? That girl is my heart. I love that girl." I cried.

I felt so sick.

He walked over to the side of the bed. Picked me up and wrapped his arms around me, tried to console me.

"Please stop before you have an attack baby. Calm down."

I screamed at him and cried simultaneously. I couldn't help it.

"Why Kyra, Todd? Just give me one reason." I kept screaming.

I was overwhelmed. My emotions were out of control.

"I'm sorry but it's not what you think."

"A few minutes ago you said it wasn't anything, now it's not what I think. I'll never forgive her. Never!" I shouted.

"Krisha, don't blame Kyra. I'm telling you it's not what you think."

"Get out!"

"No! Just listen."

"Get out of my house and I never want to see your face again!"

I'd managed to get up from the bed and pointed him the door.

"You don't mean that."

"Like hell I don't. You've gone too far now. I can never forgive you Todd."

"I'm not going anywhere until you hear me."

"I don't wanna hear anything that you have to say. Tell it to my attorney, write a book about it, broadcast it on the evening news, I don't care. Now move!"

I stormed off. Tried to brush past him, but he grabbed my arm.

"Let me go!" I yelled.

"Not until you settle down. I know you're going over to see Kyra."

"So you're defending her too? Go ahead and knock the sense out of me again for your girlfriend."

"That's not fair. You know it wasn't like that."

"Who gives a damn? Move! I need some air." I said as I tried to brush by him again.

Todd took me by the shoulders and turned my body to face him.

"No! Now look at me." He screamed.

"I swear, if you touch me one more time I'm gonna blow another hole in your ass." I huffed.

He surrounded me in a tight bear hug, which halted my erratic movements.

Whispering in my ear he said, "Now, you know you can beat me only if I let you, and if you ever pull that gun on me again you'd better use it. Now, why don't you just settle down before you get sick and listen at what I'm gonna say, okay?"

I gave him the look. He had really changed. My blood was boiling, but my heart was failing. I was going numb.

"What you're talking about...there's nothing to that. Just conversation. It's not what you think. When I couldn't talk to you, I talked to her. I figured since yall were so much alike it was cool. "

I felt myself slipping. Headed toward the floor. He held me up.

He was a damn liar, and a good one.

"I was always there for you." I whispered failing to look at his face.

"Let me finish. What I'm saying is, it never went farther than conversation. I wouldn't do that to you."

With that said, looking into my eyes, he dipped his head to kiss my lips.

I slowly shook my head at his tactics for escaping his infidelities.

Before his lips could touch mine, I decided to give him a little bit of what he was giving me.

This was too much for my little mind and body. He had to feel some of what I was feeling inside.

Wham! I kneed him in his balls. Tried to push 'em clean out of his dirty mouth.

He doubled over in pain.

"Get the last of your things and get out! And don't bring your ass back here until you hear from my attorney!"

I stormed out of the bedroom. Left him standing there balls in hand.

I was tote'n ten loads of profane ammunition. And I'd planned to unload all of it on my pitifully triflin' husband. He just made me wanna cuss and act a fool.

It was difficult for me to understand why the ones you love most, hurt you the most. I wanted to hurt him just as he'd hurt me. It didn't matter that he was my husband; at one time, the sole reason I took a breath. It didn't matter anymore. My heart was crushed beyond anything he could ever say or do. It just didn't matter anymore.

I rushed out of the door to my next destination. I knew that when he stopped hurting, he was gonna warn her that I was on the warpath. Hopefully, I'd catch her before she left for work. If I had my way she wouldn't be able to show up for work for a couple of days.

I drove all the way over to her house, but no one was home. Good thing for her, and I guess me too, because I was really heated and ready to let my best friend feel the brunt of my frustrations. I know I needed to calm down and that I was being extra. But I was riding on emotions that consumed every part of me.

I took a ride over to Mia's to cool down and get my mind right. I knew she was going in late today and I prayed she was still there. I really needed my friend. Truthfully, I just needed a shoulder to cry on.

When I reached Mia's, I hesitantly knocked on the door. Mia opened the door displaying a surprised reaction.

"Come on in Krisha."

We greeted each other with a quick hug and kiss.

I wanted to fall into her arms and scream until the cows came home, but I held myself up as best as I could.

I walked in looking around the living room ready to throw myself down on the couch, but instead my eyes quickly fell on none other than Ms. Goody Two Shoes herself sitting over in a chair by the window.

"What's going on Mia?" I asked as I looked at her in disbelief, then back at Kyra.

"Kyra stopped by to talk Krish."

"Looks like I'm interrupting something, so I'll leave."

"No. Don't be silly. Sit down." Mia offered.

"I don't wanna sit down."

Mia gave me a look of confusion and concern.

"Whatever suits you." She said taking a seat on her couch. "But you guys need to talk."

Silence. Nobody said a thing.

Kyra stared out of the window and I stared upside her head.

I decided to jump in and break the silence.

"Bitch, why you wanna mess with my husband?"

"That's not what I meant Krisha." Mia quickly interjected.

I ignored her. Didn't even look her way.

"Krisha, I told you I'm…."

I cut her off.

"I don't wanna hear your lies or sorries. All I want to know is why? What was it about *my* husband? All of these other brothas you can have, why do you want to do this to *me*?"

"It wasn't much more than conversation, but I guess I was wrong for that."

"You guess, huh?"

"This is so out of character for me. I never would have dreamt in a million years that this would be happening. It was one of my weak moments. Just to have someone to talk to."

"Talk too? Kyra I know you had him in my house while I was grieving over my mother and you talk about only conversation. Both of you knew full well what you were doing."

Her eyes went to the floor. I was probing. But she was busted. Guess he hadn't gotten in touch with her.

"It was only random conversation at first. Todd is a very aggressive man Krish."

I acted like I didn't hear that.

"Then, you help me whip some trick about him, guess you had your own reasons huh? You help me whip his ass, listen to me cry, and tell you all of my business when you knew you were tricking with him the whole time."

"Tricking…how do you figure I…?"

Cutting her off. "I know you. And that's beside the point. You're just as no good as he is."

"It was only that one time. At that time, I was grieving with you. I was dealing with my own problems. I was tired, lonely, hurt, and I just gave in to his advances."

Her conscious must have been really bothering her because she was incriminating herself every time she opened her mouth.

"What you mean tired and lonely? You always talked about your friend after Shannon. How he did this and that. How you two…"

My words were cut short as reality hit me smack dab in the face and knocked me clean off the sofa. I turned to look at Mia, then back at Kyra.

"Please don't tell me you were talking about my husband?"

I could only stare at her in disbelief and shake my head. "Is that what my friendship meant to you?"

"No, no. It wasn't like that." She began saying.

That was the wrong answer; and just like lightning, I was on Kyra giving her a legitimate, well-earned ass whuppin'. She was still sitting on the couch and didn't have a choice but to take what I was giving her.

Mia jumped up and pulled me off her. Then, Kyra got up off the couch and delivered a nice one to my face.

"Good lick homie, now get another one. I promise that'll be your last." I boldly threw out.

I stood still for her to give me another one while Mia urged me to leave.

Kyra didn't move a muscle. She was crying a river, but that wasn't my concern.

"No!" Mia screamed. "Yall gon' tear my house up. You need to settle this in another way Krish. This isn't right. She's our friend."

I wasn't trying to hear that. Friend my ass. With a friend like that, who needs enemies?

Through her cries she managed to instruct Mia to step back.

"Let her go or it will never be over." She said through sniffles.

"You're right. It'll never be over because I'm gonna whip ya ass every time I see you."

Mia quickly released my arm and stepped back. She immediately began trying to move her breakables out of the way.

She knew there was no way Kyra was getting out of there without paying her dues for her betrayal. Nothing and nobody was gonna change my mind. The way I saw it, tapping that ass was well deserved.

For every blow I gave her, she tried to give one back. I always welcome a challenge anyway so that was nothing.

Kyra was a thin one and a cutie, but she had major fight in her. I already knew that. But truth be told, she couldn't compare to me.

Besides, it didn't matter to me because I was hurt and mad, and I found strength that I never knew I had. I had to release it some kind of way.

We fought from the living room to the kitchen. She kept backing up. Had she kept still we wouldn't have had to rearrange Mia's house.

I put my fist in her chest. Knocked the wind out of her. Then I jumped back and kicked her. When she hit the wall and slid to the floor, I started stomping her with all that I had in me. I put my size tens on her and gave it to her real good. I'd forgotten that I once loved the girl.

The next thing I knew, I was sliding under the dining room table on my butt.

I looked around to see what had happened. Discovered that Mia had snatched me up and threw me half way across the room.

I smiled once I realized what she'd done. That Mia was a beast.

I know I can be extra when I'm emotional. That's one reason why I'd left the drama behind me a long time ago. I knew one day my temper brought on by BS would get me into a whole lot of trouble. I didn't bother people and I didn't like them bothering me.

I'd never even noticed that Kyra was bleeding. I got a little scared.

Mia had kneeled down and was helping her to sit up. I could tell she'd gotten a little spooked too. We definitely didn't want an accidental death on our hands.

Blood was coming from somewhere on her face as she held her stomach.

"Go get a towel stupid!" Mia screamed.

I guessed she was talking to me; nobody else was in the room. But why, was beyond me.

"I'm not getting anything for her!" I screamed back.

"Go get something so I can stop this blood girl!"

Mia looked at me like she could whip me good.

Is she really serious? I thought.

I went to get the towel though.

When I returned, I threw it to Mia, hitting her in the chest.

"So you do really want *me* in *your* ass?"

She gave me a serious look and waited for an answer.

I didn't say anything. The way she'd just thrown me, I wasn't about to mess with her. I was tired and out of breath anyway. I wasn't used to that foolishness anymore.

"Why did you go to stomping the girl, Krisha?" Mia asked as she kneeled over Kyra.

"She wanted it to be over Mia."

"You didn't have to mess her up like this." She said holding the towel to Kyra's face.

I wanted to laugh. That sounded so funny looking down at Kyra's pitiful behind.

"Forget her."

Kyra sat there trying to wipe away the streams of blood from her face while holding that eye that was swelling by the second. I felt bad for her. For more reasons than one, I was still hot with her, but she looked a mess.

As I moved my mouth, I could feel my lip swelling. I didn't even feel that lick when it was delivered.

I should get her again for touching my face. She knew better. I thought.

I had a headache, so I sat in Mia's corner and rested my nerves for a while. Buried my face in my hands as they rested on my thighs.

I was surprised that I hadn't had an anxiety attack these days, after experiencing all of the drama from Todd and his mess.

I guess over the years I'd been holding all of my problems inside. Not being able to truly express myself caused me to have those attacks. I always had an inlet but no outlet. Nowadays I've been releasing the built up energy and expressing myself. Even though I knew the release was in the wrong way. Maybe this was me. Maybe I should just be me.

Trying to live and act a certain way to please other people, live up to my husband's, my client's, the whole city for that matter, expectations. That damn award from the city, no doubt tells me that I have a big heart for helping people and I'm good at my profession; however, I feel like people expect me to be perfect. People look at the image I portray throughout the community and the city and expect me to always uphold that image. I asked myself, how would that look, me being over thirty years old, Ms. Citizen of the Year, fighting like I'm fifteen again and swearing like a sailor. That's the kind of pressure that got me sick. I can't be everything to everybody and I'm sure not perfect.

I just want all of this to go away. I thought. I want to be alone. Summer break will be here in a few weeks. I think I will allow the kids to visit Cicily. She says she'll take them for the summer so they won't be here for the divorce and to allow me time to heal. I was against it at first, but then again, I can't be selfish. They are her nephews and I could use the break. I'm also going to appoint someone to take my place in the office or maybe close for two weeks vacation or something. I may just take a trip to Jamaica to see if I can get lucky like Stella. I don't know yet. I just had a whole lot of thinking to do.

I snapped out of my daydream when I heard Mia screaming, "You ain't gonna talk to that bastard while you're in my house. I know that's him."

Kyra was in the kitchen trying to be discrete on her cell phone, but she quickly hung up once Mia walked in and started ranting and raving.

I was really wondering why she was still there. After a good jacking up like that I would be running for the border. But, as I stared up into the ceiling and thought about it, I think we were both still there for the same reasons.

I pulled myself up off the floor and walked into the kitchen where Kyra was sitting at the table with an ice pack on her eye. Looked as if she needed one on the other one too.

I really wanted to knock her clean out of the open window, but I knew if I had touched that girl again I would have caught a charge. Instead, I took a few deep breaths before speaking.

"Kyra, I just want you to know that you really hurt me. But you're not the only one who's hurt me so I'm not gonna take all of my frustrations out on you. I loved you like a sister. I can't believe you would let a man, my husband, come between what we had. You had no right, regardless of what the situation was. You had no right messing with my husband. That's unforgivable. I can no longer call you a friend because true friends just don't bring these issues to one another. That hurts me more than anything. Todd can go screw whomever he desire to, but you're not supposed to be one of them. You were in my life before I even knew who Todd Taylor was. No man was to ever come between us. And you know my story better than I know it, so if you want to allow him to do to you what he's done to me then go right ahead. I can't stop you. But best believe he'll never respect you. I'm his wife and mother of his children, look what I got. So, congratulations to you. I guess the best bitch has won."

I turned to walk away and headed for the door.

As a thought popped into my head, I made an abrupt stop. I turned around, walked back to her, looked at her then did the unexpected.

I let her face meet my palm. In a matter of seconds, she was hitting the floor with a vengeance.

"But there's one thing you gotta remember." I said. "I'm the baddest bitch!"

She knew I didn't play. When you know better and don't do better then you deserve just what you get.

I heard the chair she had been sitting in moving. Apparently, she was trying to get up from the floor.

"Krish, wait." I heard her whimper.

I turned to face her ready for another fight if that's what she wanted. I had a lot more for her, but I knew I'd better leave the girl alone before I began to regret the day.

"I deserve that. I'm sorry." She said softly. "I never asked for this. I didn't mean to hurt you. Forgive me Krish." She cried as she tried to embrace me.

I stepped back out of her reach.

"Don't touch me." I said.

"I'm so sorry Krish."

She broke down. Cried hard. Kept repeating her sorries.

Watching her cry made me shed one tear with her. I loved her too, but right now she was the enemy.

"I'll never forgive myself. I'm so sorry, I'm so sorry." She cried as she confessed.

I looked at her in disbelief. For her to confess after that butt whipping, her conscious was on her and she was really gone.

My husband was definitely as good as I always thought he was, and as smooth as my mama said he was. I just never thought it would be my friend who would co-sign that.

All that could stumble out was, "I'm sorry too. Kiss Paige for me."

I turned and hauled tail out of there. If I could fly, I would have taken flight. Had to get outta there quickly. My heart was exploding.

I jogged down the stairs and didn't stop until I reached my car. Inside my car, my world came down once again. I cried.

Damn, this hurts so bad.

I couldn't find relief from the burning in my chest. Couldn't stop the tears from racing past my cheeks. I cried out loud. I screamed and cried some more. I knew none of it was helping my situation but it was out of my control.

After sitting there a while, I really couldn't believe Mia didn't come behind me. Maybe she decided to stay out of it and not take sides. I didn't know. What I did know was that my head was pounding and I began to feel nauseous. So I opened the door to my car and got rid of last night's dinner.

My stomach hurt badly. I felt sick from head to toe and needed to get home fast. I pulled myself together enough to take a shot at driving home.

After starting the car, I popped in one of my favorite artists, Monica's, CD that Mia had brought me.

As I drove and listened to the words of the songs, I realized that there had to be an underlying message somewhere just for me. The songs seem to fit my life with Todd to a T. Almost as if I'd written the songs myself.

When I got to "Why Her", I broke down and cried again. The song was about my life. Had to be.

Monica was my girl and this was *my* song.

I loved the artist for the beauty in her voice that wrapped securely around words of truth so well. The song was relevant to my life and I could definitely relate to that. Whether it was a song or not, somebody had dealt with some of the same issues as me.

Anyway, I kept playing that song over and over as I drove home, trying to figure out why love was so complicated. If any song could speak what was truly in my heart at this exact moment, this one was doing it for me. Umph, umph, umph. *Why her?* I shook my head and sank a little deeper.

20

Gotta Move On

"What are you doing?" Mia's voice rang out.

"Nothing." I said nonchalantly.

"Where are the boys?"

"With Victor and Nikki Newman."

"Girl you need to stop."

We both laughed.

"They need to stop."

"Anyway, why didn't you show for the Mayor's reception last night? You know you were supposed to be there. I wouldn't have gone if I would have known you weren't coming."

"I didn't fell like getting dressed. I slept from five p.m. until seven this morning. Besides, I had a long week. I was tired."

"Wanna go out tonight?"

"Where? I don't think I want to go to Club 21."

"Why not?"

"I don't know. I think I'm gonna let that crowd go."

"Why? You think you're gonna see Todd and Kyra?"

"Nope. I wouldn't care if I did. They can kiss off. His loss. I didn't lose nothing but a headache."

"Now that's my girl." Mia said holding her hand up for a high five.

"Chill out silly."

"Let's go find you some action tonight."

"Mia, I don't care about a man. If that's what I wanted, I could have had one a long time ago."

"You say that now because you used to not getting any on the regular. Don't be stupid."

"I'm straight…for now."

We laughed.

"For real though, let's go to the Jazz Bar over off Trinity and Highland."

"I heard it was nice. That may be more my speed." I said.

"You driving or me?"

"Mia   you   asked   me   to   go   with   you."

"I know, but let's take your Benz. I feel like stuntin'."

I looked at her side ways. "Heffa, you got a Benz."

"Yeah. Mine ain't new and it ain't no convertible."

"You are truly crazy." I said shaking my head. "Okay but you're driving."

"Fine. Pick me up around five. I want to stop by Macy's then treat you to dinner."

I smiled at that.

"Thanks sweetie." I blew her a kiss. "I'll be there with bells on."

Around ten p.m. we were stepping into the Jazz Club. We'd had dinner and wine at Capital City Grill and caught up on our conversations for the week.

"Mia, this place is nice, but I don't think I wanna be here long."

"Why not? What's wrong?"

"Nothing. I think I may want to hit up Club 21 later."

"What? Thought you didn't wanna go there anymore." Mia said with protruding eyes.

I smiled.

"The wine has mellowed me, and I feel like flirting a little now, and I don't think the kinda man I'm looking for is up in here tonight."

"Ooooooo! You're a trip. Thought you weren't looking for a man."

"And you actually listened to me. Girl, it's been long enough. Time for me to get back out there."

"I feel ya." Giving each other a high five.

"By the way, where's Derrick?" I asked.

"We broke up."

"What? Why? Stop lying." I said in disbelief.

"I'm not lying."

"Why are you so calm then?"

"Because I broke up with him."

"Why would you do that?"

"He wanted to get too serious; talking about marriage. I'm not ready for that right now. I told him I'm too young to be getting tied down."

"Girl please you're thirty-one, and you didn't have to break up with him."

"Thirty-one is still young boo. And he wanted it his way or no way at all, so I chose the 'no way'."

"Something is really wrong with you Mia. He's a good man."

"I know, but he's never been married. I have. I know what it's like. He doesn't. I like things how they are and he's trying to complicate things."

"Every man's not the same Mia."

"I know. I love him; I just need some space."

"If you say so."

I know her. That heffa just wanted the freedom to mess around with other men. Didn't need the stress of getting caught by Derrick. That's what she did when she wanted to do her. I ain't mad at her for that. At least she respected him enough to send him packing first. I can respect that. If my husband had done that at first, then I wouldn't hate him so badly. But no, he wanted to screw me over, then try and leave me after my heart was already damaged.

And speaking of my *ex*-husband, Todd Taylor was still Todd Taylor. He just wasn't my problem anymore. After several months of being divorced, I believe I was finally over him and ready to live my life again.

In my bout with Todd and my marriage, I found out that loving someone doesn't have to hurt. Loving someone should be a good experience. If it's got you in tears and in an uproar more than eighty percent of the time then the true definition and respect of love is not what you have.

After Todd decided to screw over me with my best friend, I just couldn't find it in my heart to forgive him. That was the turning point of our relationship that removed the blinders. And I was finally able to see him for who he was and succeed in letting him go.

I'm happy now and moving in the right direction thanks to my best friend for life, Mia. We were on a mission. And that was to have fun and not give a got damn!

21

I Need a Soldier

Mia

*A*fter arriving at the Jazz Bar, Krisha and I chilled for a couple of hours. We listened, drank, laughed, and conversed. Had a really good time.

We soon got tired of that crowd and decided it was time to go get into something a little more poppin'. So we ended up going to the hood to pick up my cousin, Sharmin, aka Shar.

"Shar, are you ready?" I asked through my cell phone.
"You said you were ready to go thirty minutes ago."

Her slow behind was really aggravating me. We'd been sitting in the car outside of her house far too long for my patience.

"She'll be out in a few minutes." I said to Krisha after closing my phone.

Shar was my girl. She and Krisha never clicked back in the day, but as adults they seemed to be pretty cool with one another. I guess Shar had grown out of some of the triflin' ways that Krisha couldn't stand when we were growing up. But one thing for sure, she was still a paper chaser.

Shar was twenty-eight, four children, four baby daddies, works at Clothes-Mart in the day, works the daddies at night, lives in the hood, and looks like a million bucks every single day. She was definitely a hood princess.

"She said we can come in, but I told her to just come on out when she's ready."

"Let's go in. I need to use the bathroom."

"You sure?"

"Yeah! Just put my top up."

Before we got to the front door, I could hear the music blasting and smelled weed coming from everywhere.

"Damn, somebody's lighting it up out here."

"Probably around back. Come on girl, let's get inside."

I knocked on the door a couple of times before Hakeem, Shar's brother, opened the door.

"What's up peoples?"

We greeted each other with a hug.

"Hey Hakeem, I didn't know you were in here."

"Yeah, we just chillin'; throwing bones. Ain't nothin'."

I introduced him to Krisha.

Hakeem seemed to be taken by Krisha. He was blushing and couldn't seem to take his eyes off her. I grinned at his schoolboy antics.

I showed Krisha where the restroom was and then Hakeem led me to a bedroom in the back that they'd turned into a party room. I guess that's what it was because there wasn't anything in there but two tables, a stereo system, and one sofa. There was no telling what could go down in that back room. He had a room full of guys up in there.

At one table, they were throwing bones, and at the next table there was a spades game going. In a minute, the poker game was gonna start and go on until daylight. I said what's up to everybody and then went to check on Krisha in the bathroom and also to see what was keeping Shar.

Shar yelled she was finishing her make-up and Krisha was coming out of the hall bathroom, so we went back into the back room to wait on Shar.

"Who got downs?" I said to the guys around the spades table.

"We do." I heard someone say.

I looked close and saw that it was JoJo from down the street.

"Who's *we*, Jo?" I asked his fine self.

"Me and C."

"Who?"

"That'll be me." The darkest dude over at the dominoes table spoke. Then he turned around to make himself seen.

When he turned around, I had to admire his cuteness. He was a smooth coal black, with a baby face. Had pearly whites, diamond in the ear, and buff like a motha.

Unh, unh, unh, he'd better be glad I'm taken. I thought. *Wait, hold up. I'm not taken anymore.* I smiled. *In that case, let me get my flirt on.*

I strutted over to where C was sitting. Ran my finger down his neck and arm. "C, do yall mind if we play a hand?"

"Baby, as sexy as you is, you can have anything you want." Searching my body with his eyes.

"Thank you C." I put my cheek up against his for a fake kiss. His aroma was delectable.

"Come on Krisha, these clowns right her trying to get up."

Krisha moved close to my ear. "Girl, these are some good looking brothas in here."

"Yes, indeed."

"I think I like C."

"He's fine huh?"

"Yes mam. Check out the bod. I love muscles on a man."

"He probably just got outta jail, girl."

"You know you might be right. Oh well. Who cares? I can be his rehab." I grinned.

Who don't care is me. I like what I like. I thought.

Krisha and I were kicking butts at the table.

For one, they couldn't get with us. We had some under the table action going on. What they didn't know was that me and Krisha won all the spade games in the hood and college back in the days. We got college rich by gambling and playing spades.

We had already played a few hands before Shar was finally ready to step out. Truth be told, I could remain at Shar's all night gambling and really come up big time off the so-called ballas.

"That's why I don't fool with you ho." I said looking at the time.

"I'm sorry chic. You know I gotta get right. Gotta find me daddy tonight." She sang. "Yall not ready?"

"Hold up Shar. We gotta show these ballas who running thangs up in here." Krisha told her.

"What's up Shar?"

A strong deep voice made me look up from my hand. Another sexy brown coming through the door. Built almost like C, but even finer.

"Hey, Box what's up?" Shar chimed.

Seems as if he caught Krisha's eye also because she kept looking up at him.

"Krisha, watch your hand!" I screamed.

"Hey no talking across the table." JoJo said.

"Man shut up!" I spat.

"I am Mia." Krisha finally replied. Still sneaking peeks at Box.

"No you're not. You're checking out Mr. Box over there." I smirked.

She looked at me like she could die.

I laughed at her reaction.

"That's okay, I'm feeling her too." Box said from across the room.

I threw Krisha a smile as she rolled her eyes at me.

I laughed at the whole scenario. It was so hood-typical, but I loved every bit of it.

Needless to say, we had to raise up because Krisha was no longer concentrating. She was too busy gawking at Mr. Sexy Box of Chocolates.

Thugs just don't look the same no more. These brothas are fine up in here! Yes Lawd! I thought while shaking my head as I left.

When we left Shar's house it was 12:55 a.m. We hopped in the Benz, put the top down, and rolled out.

"Shar, what's up with C and Box?" I asked while driving.

"What you wanna know?"

"They from the block?"

"No, they from around the way, but they both work at the gym down the street. They're personal trainers."

"So they didn't just get outta jail girl?"

"No. They probably ain't never went to jail before. They ain't like these bums around here. They just kick it with 'em cause they used to being around them everyday down at the gym."

"You mean you ain't hollered at them?"

"Girl, the pockets ain't big enough for me. You know I like my money just like I like my man's johnson, long and fat at the same time."

We broke out in laughter.

"You're a trip Shar."

"I'm for real though."

"Any one of the others up in there yo' babies daddy?"

"Nope. Only about four could qualify. They got the cash flow like I like it. I'm working on one and one working on me, but he my girl's man. I don't get down like that."

"Oh! God, please don't go there Shar." Krisha said.

"I'm not girl. I ain't that ruthless. I do have morals and a little respect." She snickered.

"You right a little. Just a little." I said.

"Go to hell Mia."

We laughed again.

"Anyway, the other two kinda tight with their ends I heard, but I gotta focus on one of them at a time cause they all boys, you know."

"Do your thang, girl. Make that money!" I screamed laughing.

"Shut up Mia." Krisha threw out. Looking all upside my head.

I knew she was annoyed by what Shar said, but she knew Shar didn't give a damn. So why should she?

We made it to the club at almost 12:30 a.m; grabbed a table, ordered drinks and as usual, never had to open our purses all night.

Krisha was mingling and enjoying the night. She hadn't been out in a while so I was glad she was having a good time.

Me on the other hand was trying to get a stank breath bastard out my face.

After telling ole boy that I was single, with eight kids and eight baby daddies, he seemed to find a way to ease away from me.

That's when I looked over to the entrance to find trouble with a capital T, walk in the door. The one and only. The man whose chocolate stick could probably get him into heaven.

Seems like every time we're here, he's here. I wondered if he was spying on Krisha or something.

I wasn't sure, but one thing I knew for sure was that his clown ass wasn't about to ruin my girl's night.

I watched him as he took a seat at the bar. Females started flocking to him like flies on fresh shit. He was watching the dance floor from the bar and I saw it on his face when he recognized her. He got up and stood close to the dance floor for a better look. My eyes stayed on him, awaiting his next move. But he just stood back and watched. After a minute or two, he caught a table. He entertained a few women for a while but none stayed too long. He didn't seem too into them. I think he was more interested in keeping any eye on Krisha.

I decided to let him be. Karma was eating him up anyway, so that was good enough for me. I joined Krisha on the dance floor.

22

Thug Love

*T*hough I think the drinks had alot to do with it, I felt really good. My mind was in a good place for a change.

After dancing three songs straight, I moved over to the table to rest my feet. I sat down and chilled while Mia got her dance on then signaled the waitress to bring me another drink. I already knew somebody would be paying for it, but the thought hadn't crossed my mind that it would be my dirty ex-husband.

He waltzed his ass up to my table with my drink in hand. Sat down like I'd invited him.

"Thanks, but I don't need your money." I said taking the drink from his hand.

"You're welcome beautiful and I know you don't need my money. Can I be a gentleman?"

"What do you want Todd and where are my kids?" I stared at him.

He elected to answer the latter. "They're at home."

"So, you have Kyra babysitting your kids while you're out whoring? Why didn't your *main* whore come with you?

"Then who was gonna keep the kids?"

"You're right. She does make a good babysitter." I grinned. I sipped my drink.

"You look lovely tonight."

"I look lovely every night. Did you forget?"

Eyes going from my lips to my breasts.

"Hell no, I didn't forget. I could never forget anything about you."

"What do you want?" I asked with attitude.

"Can we be cordial with one another Krisha?"

"You're lucky I speak to you at all Todd. I think I'm very cordial to you. More than you deserve."

"I miss you." He blurted.

"So! I've told you more than once that I don't want to hear that!"

He was starting to work that overly hyper nerve that has a low tolerance for BS.

He didn't respond; just sat there and stared at me.

"You'll have to excuse me, but you're cramping my style." I said.

I got up and walked away.

He never said another word, but I could feel his eyes watching me as I walked.

I could feel him all night. I didn't always see him, but I knew he was watching me. I knew I should have followed my first mind and not come here. But I refused to let him ruin my night. We run in the same circles, so I was bound to run into him some time or another.

My night was going good though. I didn't let my run in with Todd affect me at all.

The DJ slowed the music down, so I danced with some guy who whispered that his name was Brent, from Cali.

Brent had been sending me drinks all night so I guess he finally decided to approach me when he heard the smooth sounds of my boy, Anthony Hamilton.

He was a cutie, but I had a problem with trusting cuties. So after the dance, I excused myself to go to the restroom. Had to get away from Brent. I had other options. Attracting men just wasn't my problem.

I joined Mia at the table and ordered another drink. I think I was going on drink number three that I actually did drink in its entirety. Around five that I'd sipped on or had in my possession. The three was pushing it for me though. And I knew that I'd better stop while I was ahead, because alcohol does some serious things to me. My head was already beginning to hurt a little so I figured I'd better sip the last drink of Patron before my butt would be my pillow.

"Where's Shar Mia?"

"Girl, Shar snagged a balla a few minutes ago and headed for the door."

"That girl is too much. At least somebody's gonna get them some tonight."

We laughed.

"Krisha, look over at the bar."

I turned slightly to glance in the direction of one of the bars.

"Is that Box?"

"Looks like him."

"I wonder where the other one is."

We scanned the bar, but didn't see him. Took a look over at the other bar; nothing we hadn't seen all night.

"I don't see him in here."

"Well, looks like Box sees us…here he comes."

Before I could primp myself, a tall dark figure was standing next to me.

"Hi again ladies."

"Hey Box." We sang in unison like schoolgirls.

"Please call me Marcus. I like people to know me by my real name."

"Whatever suits you?" said Mia.

"Mind if my boy and I join you?"

"Please, but where is your boy?"

"Outside. He's coming."

"So you guys had enough of the cards, huh?"

"We went on a food run. So we just decided to roll through here for a minute."

I looked up to see lusciousness standing at the table.

"What's up ladies?"

We were both too busy gazing in Box's face that we didn't see C walk up.

He was too fine. The sweetest piece of dark chocolate I'd ever seen.

"Hi C." Mia and I again said in unison.

"Have a seat." I offered.

He sat next to Mia.

For the next hour, we kicked it with Marcus aka Box and Chris aka C; the boys from the hood. Those two kicked it up a notch for us and we ended up having an extraordinary night.

We left the club around two am then followed them to The Seafood Shack where they ordered fried fish, shrimp, and shrimp fried rice for us and the guys back at Shar's. We all went back to Shar's and hung out eating seafood and enjoying each other's company.

The guys were gambling big time with some serious money on the table. After a night of partying, my mind was still good enough to win $600 off the so-called poker players. I got my change and raised up.

I sat outside in my car and talked to Marcus until five o'clock a.m. He shared that he and C had actually come to the club looking for us. He expressed his interest in getting to know me, and I learned a lot about who he really was. The conversation was cool and I was definitely feeling some type of vibe, but it was almost daybreak and time to take my tired behind home. I hadn't carried on like that in ages so my body was extremely exhausted.

I had to pull Mia's hot tail out of Shar's house and from C's lap. It was after five in the morning and she still wasn't ready to leave. Neither of us had thought about looking at our cell phones all night, so when I finally looked at mine, I noticed that I had six missed calls from Todd.

Couldn't be the kids because he was calling from his cell. He'd watched me all night then wanted to talk. I'm sure he saw us leave with C and Box. I was so tipsy, I'd forgotten all about him being there. Not like I gave a shit though.

I bet he's tossing and turning right about now. I smiled at the thought.

Derric had called Mia three times and left messages. She looked concerned. I had no reason to, I don't think.

We made our way on over to Mia's and crashed like we had nothing else to live for.

When I awakened later, it was after four pm on Sunday evening and time for my kids to return.

I remembered getting into bed with Mia when we came in, but couldn't figure out how I ended up on the floor in her bedroom.

I pulled up off the hard floor and sat up holding my neck. The wood had done a number on me.

"Mia, get up." I screamed.

"What?" She snapped.

"How did I get on this floor?"

"You sleep too bad ho."

"How did I get down here though? I don't remember getting up."

"I kicked you down there?"

"Stop lying." I laughed at her words.

"You down there ain't you?"

All I could do was shake my head and laugh. "You are so wrong for that."

"No, you're wrong. Throwing your arms and legs all across me like I'm your man or something. You know I don't play that."

I was cracking up laughing.

"You are truly insane Mia. I need to shower and go meet Todd for 5:00 at Mickey Ds to get my babies. Can I have something to wear? I'd hate for anyone to see me looking like last night."

"Sure, knock yourself out. Do what you gotta do and lock the door behind you. I'm going back to sleep."

"Thanks, boo. I'll call you later."

23

Project Chick

A whole year had passed since my divorce and I still didn't have a steady man in my life. The more I looked at it, I realized that I liked things just how they were. I needed time for myself. I needed time to find out the direction I wanted to follow.

Todd continued to call periodically just to say 'I love you' as he'd put it.

I blocked his office and cell phone numbers from my home and cell phone since that's where he did all his dirt. Then, he began calling late at night from home. I hated to block his home number, because my kids would call me from there sometimes. I guess he had to wait until Kyra was asleep. He was really working on my nerves. I just couldn't get rid of him. If he calls me again waking me up with some foolishness, I promised him and myself I was calling his woman to let her know he was calling me. Killing thing about it, I really don't think he cared.

I dated Marcus and a few other men and just hung out and enjoyed myself. I even accompanied Marcus to Florida for a conference in March and he went with me to San Francisco for my conference in August.

Even though my sex-deprived body was saying one thing, I wasn't mentally ready for sex with him or anyone else. I know that would kick our relationship up to a level I didn't want. I must admit, I was doing really well. I didn't know I could be without for that long.

As for Mia, she was still confused, but Derrick was still hanging in there. They both agreed to chill and see other people, but he was at her apartment at least three days a week. Mia said if he didn't mind, she didn't mind either. She was more afraid of a commitment than I was. She just did her thang.

Every since that night we went to Shar's apartment, we'd been going back to our old stomping grounds just to chill and play cards.

I love my people in the hood, but I am so glad I don't live there anymore. A year ago, I thought I had to "be myself" and display the hood I had in me. I was confused and didn't know if I wanted to live the life of the person I'd become over the years, or live the life that I'd lived growing up as a teenager. I know I could never go back and live there, but I just needed to be there, somewhere where I felt loved; closer to my roots. Mama wanted to move me out and show me a better life. And that's exactly what she did, but there was no reason that I couldn't stay connected.

After chilling from time to time, I realized that you just couldn't get too comfortable; things just didn't change over night in the hood. Everything still goes down the same way, but now people are just plain ole' crazy and don't give a damn about life.

The older women knew of both Mia and me, but the young ones didn't. Truth be told, those are the ones you have to watch closely, with yo' man and with yo' life.

On a Friday night, we were chillin' at Shar's doing the usual. Her apartment was party central every weekend and everybody knew it. Half the time she wouldn't even be there, her brother Hakeem would run the show.

On this particular night she was there, hadn't left yet for the club. Her friend Tracy and two other girls were there too. Shar had made daiquiris, so we were all doing a lot of girl talk and drinking. It was still early so everybody was good. Shar needed some more ice for the drinks, so she asked me to take her to the store. Me, like a fool, told her to go ahead and take my car since none of the other women owned one. The guys sent after some food so Shar and her girl Tracy left. I swear they stayed gone at least two hours. Mia said it was only about thirty minutes, but it seemed that long to me. When they came back, she had another girl with her and they were laughing and talking about how they had stopped at one of Shar's men's house and his girlfriend was there.

Shar and the girl had words, so the girl followed them to the store and got out with a bat going off. She said the storeowner told her he was gonna call the police if she didn't leave. So she left, but said she was going to get her sisters. They went to get their friend then went back by the house blowing the horn.

They were laughing, talking about how they could have fought the girl because she was only twenty years old and messing around with a thirty-seven year old man.

I'm like, now this is some hood drama. Every since we'd been going there, things were fine. Never any drama. I gave Mia a look and told her to step outside.

I eased out the door with my drink in hand.

When I got outside I immediately ditched the drink and began pacing the small yard.

"Please tell me she didn't go to that guy's house in my car." I said getting heated.

"That's what she said and she was wrong for that."

"I thought Shar had stopped all of the petty foolishness."

"Girl, they live for that over here. You know that."

"I hope ole' girl don't come thru here tonight with the drama."

"I hope not but you know how it goes. If she said she's coming with her crew, most likely she's rounding them up now."

"Do you want to leave? I got a feeling its going off ova here tonight."

"Yeah me too. It's whatever you wanna do."

"Let's go tell the guys we're leaving."

Just as we opened the door to go back inside, we heard a screeching crash that made us instantly turn around and duck for cover at the same time.

All the ladies in the front room ran to the door as we managed to stand up.

Looking onto the street, a big black Expedition had rammed the back of my car that was parked on the street in front of Shar's house.

I looked in amazement. I couldn't believe that whoever the driver was didn't seen my nice and shiny silver Benz minding its own damn business.

The music was so loud in the house obviously the guys in the back rooms didn't hear the crash.

We all walked out to the street to see what the hell was going on. As we approached the sidewalk, all of the windows went down in the SUV and a petite girl jumped out.

I spoke first.

"You didn't see my car?" I was livid.

"We don't give a damn about your car!" The driver yelled from the window.

I assumed the girl out of the SUV was the girl who Shar was arguing with. She spoke next pointing at Shar.

"I told you I was gonna get you for coming to my man's house with that bull."

"Lil girl you better take yo' lil behind home before you get your issue." Shar threw out boldly.

"You gon' have to show me what my issue is because I'm finta git in yo' ass."

After she said that, they all fell out of the truck like they'd just come from picking peppers.

Then one of them yelled, "I know that ain't Mia and Krisha. What yall stuck up hos doing over here?"

It was dark so we couldn't see who was talking.

"Who is that?" Mia screamed.

"Them hos thank they all dat." The girl continued.

"What yall come here fo? Either yall gonna do something or get away from my house." Shar screamed.

"Oh the heffa driving gon' get hers before she leaves tonight." I screamed.

I was hot. She'd just rammed my car with no remorse. Like my car was some toy.

"I been had it for you anyway." She yelled back.

For me? I thought. *Was she talking about me?* Now I was really trying to figure out who the voice belonged to. I didn't think I had any enemies. Other than Todd's women.

The next thing I knew I saw someone jump from behind the truck with what looked like a tire iron in hand screaming, "Forget this, we ain't come here to talk!"

About eight of them, young and old, came from around that SUV. I immediately started counting our heads. I'm sure everyone else was too. It was only seven of us, so that meant somebody was really gonna get the business. And didn't look like we could get out of this brawl. *We,* meaning me too. Shar's problem had become mine.

When she approached the streetlight, I recognized the driver as a girl from back in the day who'd hated my guts over a boy. Some old dumb crap that was probably fifteen years ago when we were kids.

Mia and I looked at each other. We recognized them as being the Day family who lived across the way in the next hood over. They lived to fight back in the day. When one would fight, all would fight. Grandmas, mamas, and babies too. Shar had gone and stirred up some drama with the baby sister. Now we weren't getting outta there until we fought all of them. They probably had more on the way. Lord have mercy.

Luckily, Shar's nosy neighbor came out of her apartment. She was down with Shar. Obviously, they were used to this kinda stuff. I wasn't. But at least we were even. I felt a little better. Just a little.

Somebody started talking noise and before I knew it, the hefty driver was swinging on me. Guess she wanted a piece of my ass as much as I wanted a chunk of hers for messing up my car.

Everybody was scrapping. The whole time I'm thinking, *I'm too old for this. And why am I here? What if I die? Where are my kids? How did I get into this? This is so stupid. Damn!*

But yet, there I was again, wilding out, stomping and kicking, and jumping around on that girls' body before being thrown over Marcus' shoulder. From upside down, I could see Mia with a handful of ole' girl's hair dragging her to the street." The guys were trying to pry her hands off the girl but Mia was slinging the girl everywhere.

Marcus put me down but held me as I watched the other guys breaking everything up. The twenty-year old girl was dealing with poor Shar. I wished I could help her, but Marcus' strong self wouldn't let me go for nothing.

When they finally got the girl away from Mia and put her in the truck, Mia rushed over and helped Shar beat the girl out of her clothes. All of them that were in the truck were trying to bail out again. The guys had to man handle the other girls to make them stay in that truck and finally leave.

After that, I took my behind home and I haven't been back over to Shar's place since.

I didn't even worry about my car. Getting the police involved wasn't the way we did things. Besides, if they weren't coming after me, I was straight because I know I cracked some ribs or something on that girl. I have a tendency to flash out and just mess a heffa up quick. They oughta leave me alone!

Nonetheless, that incident was an eye opener and the deciding factor for a lot of things that were going through my head. I decided that I should leave Marcus *aka* Box in the hood where I found him. He was cool, but not exactly what I needed in my life. I just had the feeling that being around him and the crowd he hung out with would only bring more drama. I didn't need that. But before I decided to act like the woman that I knew I was and was used to being and not some crazy hood rat, I had to play one of Shar's tricks.

Asking Todd over and over to stop calling me with the love lies wasn't doing any good. I'd told him that I would inform his girlfriend but he wanted to call my bluff.

He called every single night, seven days a week, around the same time, 11:35 a.m. waking me up out of my sleep talking stupid. I recorded every conversation. Not just for her to hear but also for my safety because he was beginning to act strangely too.

It got so serious that I'd even considered getting a restraining order, but I remembered he still didn't know where I lived, at least I didn't think he did. Besides, our divorce was final a year ago, he did what he did, got who he wanted and for the life of me I could not understand what the problem was now.

After he called the last time, I called her house the next day. I knew she'd be home. She'd quit her job like a dummy. That was strike one against her in Todd's eyes if she didn't know.

She answered on the third ring trying to sound innocent. I know she knew it was me.

"Kyra, this is Krisha." I said boldly.

I hadn't spoke to her since that day in Mia's apartment more than a year ago. For some reason her and Mia had stopped communicating also, so Kyra was like a distant memory to us.

"Todd's not here." She quickly threw out.

"Oh, he's not. Well, can I leave a message?"

"Yeah, I guess." She said after smacking her lips.

"The message is for you. Tell your man to stop blowing up my phone."

"You wish."

I smiled. But continued, unfazed by her ignorance.

"I've already blocked his cell and office numbers. Now he's calling from your house like crazy while you're sleeping. My next step is to get a restraining order."

"Why would he be calling you like that?"

"Oh I think you know why."

I've been trying to tell this girl that Krisha is the truth. She can play stupid if she wants to.

"Krisha, this little trick ain't gonna work. Todd is very much satisfied. Plus, all this time you ought to be over him."

"Funny, I told him that same thing. He ought to be over me after more than a year. Especially since he got the triflin' trick he always wanted."

She sighed heavily. "Let's not even go there."

"You're right. Just give him my message. I didn't call to argue about Todd's no-good behind. You're the only one stupid right now."

I hung up before she could say anything. She was useless.

After that phone call to Kyra, I didn't hear from Todd for about two weeks. I was thankful because he was really beginning to get under my skin.

I had conquered the hardest trial ever. I had succeeded in letting him go. He was now history. There was no way I could allow him to come back into my life. The love would remain, but the hurt and betrayal that I endured behind that man will never allow me to be with him again; no matter how hard he tried.

24

A New Beginning

I met the most handsome and most gentlemanly guy named Ryan through Mia's boyfriend, friend, or whatever he was to her, Derric. Actually, Ryan was a friend of Derric's brother Troy.

Derric introduced us at a dinner party that he held at the Great Hall for his friends and business associates last week. Every since I'd met Ryan he'd called every night. His conversations were interesting and I enjoyed the attention. Just looking at him, my first impression was he was a playa. I couldn't believe that a man that fine was single with no attachments. To tell the truth, I'm still not completely convinced otherwise.

But on the night I met him, he was very polite and nothing less than a gentleman. I really didn't think he'd call me, but was I wrong.

He stood out from any other guy that I'd met since my break up with Todd. Outside of Marcus this was one of a few men that I'd talked to longer than two days. I usually could see right through them. They were usually out for one thing and one thing only. Unless I've run into another smooth talker like Todd, I don't think Ryan is the hit and run type.

Mia came to her senses and chilled out with C and the others. She and Derric became an item again. I think he was more elated than she was to be officially back together. Over the next couple weeks, Ryan and I had been talking everyday and seeing each other every weekend.

I wasn't sure what was going on with Todd, but he hadn't been calling or coming to see his sons. I sure as hell wasn't gonna call after him. I didn't care one way or the other where he was or what he was doing as long as he took time with his children. Suddenly, he was slacking on that. I wondered why. Then again, there's no telling what kind of drama's going on with him and Kyra.

My sons wanted their dad to bring them two video games that he promised them three weeks ago. I told them that we could go buy them, but they insisted that Todd already had them and they wanted to go over and play the games with him.

"Baby, I don't know where your Dad is, but I'm sure he'll bring the games over here when he's free."

"Mom, can we call him?"

"TJ you don't have to ask me to call him. You know his number right?"

"Yes Mom."

"Well, go ahead."

They both raced down the stairs to the phone in the living room.

I went downstairs into the kitchen to prepare a quick dinner. About five minutes later, Malik came into the kitchen crying. "Daddy says he don't have them."

"*Doesn't*, Malik, say *doesn't*. What doesn't he have?"

"Our games."

"Why not? What happened?"

"He says he don't have the money to buy them."

"Doesn't. Doesn't have the money."

He repeated me, correcting himself.

"And what does he mean he doesn't have the money?"

"He said he can't afford them and he'll get them later."

"Is your dad still on the phone?"

"Yes mam. TJ is talking to him."

I wondered what was going on with him. He usually never denies them anything, especially something as inexpensive as video games.

I walked into the living room where TJ was still talking to Todd. "TJ, may I speak to your father please?"

He handed me the phone and stomped off upstairs to his room. Then I heard Malik running up the stairs behind him.

"Hi Todd."

"Hey Krish. How are you?"

"I'm good. Thanks. Todd, what's going on?"

He explained how he'd told the boys he couldn't buy the games because he couldn't afford them. Said his money was tight. With a business like his, he had no business being broke.

"Listen Todd, I'm not trying to get in your business, but if you didn't wanna get the games all you had to do was say so. Don't have them expecting things from you and you don't come through. They've been waiting three weeks now for you."

"I'm sorry. I just couldn't tell them I couldn't buy the games."

"I can buy them the games. That's not a problem. I just don't like my kids being lied to."

"I had intentions on getting them. It wasn't anything deliberate."

"And what's going on with you talking about you can't afford video games that cost no more than one hundred dollars?"

"My money is tight."

"So if you can't afford one hundred dollars, then what are you saying. You can't support your kids?"

"That's something I wanted to talk to you about."

"Go ahead."

"Well, I'm not gonna be able to give you any money this month for them, but I'll make up for it next month."

"What's going on Todd?"

"I just need some time."

"I haven't demanded much from you. You've always provided so that never was an issue. I wanna know why you've been brushing my kids off for the last month."

"You know I love my boys, but I just can't afford to give them anything right now."

"You can always give them your time Todd. That doesn't cost a dime."

"I know. I've been out of town a lot and I've been under a lot of stress lately. I don't want them to see me like this."

"What's going on with you?"

"I don't think I wanna share it Krisha. You don't wanna know."

"You'd better tell me something because that dog ain't barking you huntin' with. My kids are suffering now and I want to know what's up."

He was reluctant but he began to open up.

"Well, you remember my daughter Destiny and her mother? They're in California and have been for a few months."

"And you're taking care of her like she wanted you to, right?"

"Well, Krisha, I really didn't have a choice. She was threatening to ruin my name and put me on court ordered child support. You know I take care of mine. I don't need anybody telling me how much to give my kids."

"That's fine. But you don't have to take care of her, just the child."

"I didn't see any other way."

"So did you ever think you might do better paying the child support rather than taking care of her, paying for a Benz, a condo, and diamonds and all that material crap?"

"Yeah, I thought about it, but that was when one child was involved."

"What?"

Silence.

"Are you telling me you have another child by her?"

Silence. He wouldn't speak.

"Don't get quiet now Todd. Tell me you didn't make another baby."

"I wish I could."

"So you were still sleeping with her the whole time?"

Silence.

"You lied to me! So what she'd said was true. You were still involved with her. But I chose to believe you. Lord help...I can't believe you!"

I had to take a minute to assess the information. Thinking about just how stupid I truly was to believe anything he'd said in the past.

"So what does Kyra have to say about this?"

"She's gone."

"She left you?"

"Yep."

"When?"

"Two days ago."

"She found out about this child, or did she leave you because you're broke?"

"Maybe that too, but she found out Cassie's seven months pregnant."

I laughed. "You're joking right?"

"I wish I were."

"Todd, what is wrong with you?" I asked in disbelief. "When did you get so sex starved? Having sex with all these women at the same time."

"I didn't realize I was."

"I know it's been at least a year since I've been with you, but honestly do I need to get tested for HIV?"

"That's not necessary. I was careful. Plus the baby is fine and so is Sydnee. They've already been tested."

"You call two babies careful?"

Silence. I let out a long sigh.

"Who are you?"

"What?"

"I don't know who I'm talking to. Oh my God! I cannot believe that this man on the phone was once my husband and is the father of my children. I don't know you at all. But let me tell you something, I can't help that you laid your seed everywhere with everybody; that's not my problem. It's yours. I told you once before that my kids were not going to suffer and come in last to nobody and I meant that. If you wanna be stupid and take care of the women too, that's your business, but you ain't gonna miss a beat with mine. I told you this was gonna happen. I told you those tricks wanted a baby to hang onto your pockets. You were just too stupid to see it. I'm sorry Todd, but I've got to do what I have to do before all your baby mamas beat me to the punch. My kids were first and they will forever be first. You will just have to suffer the consequences."

"What consequences?"

"You will be getting served." I spat.

"I aint trippin'. That might even be best Krisha. I'd rather you and my boys get the bulk of what I have anyway. At least I know you're putting it to good use."

"And I'm going to my doctor to have an HIV test. If I'm positive you may as well get your black suit ready because I'm going to bury you."

I slammed the phone down so hard. I believe the foundation moved.

I burst out crying. While I cried downstairs, I guess my kids cried upstairs. I don't know why I was crying. I guess I was scared.

25

Your Smile

I did the best I could to clean my house after dinner. After bathing my boys and myself, I laid across my bed to finish my novel. Just as I was getting engulfed in the book, the phone rang.

"Hello!" I said.

"Hi lovely."

"Hey, Ryan. How are you?"

"I'm wonderful now that I hear your voice."

Out of all the men I'd met over the years, I hadn't seen anybody who appealed to me as much as Todd until I met Ryan.

Ryan had Todd beat in the body department. He was taller, about 6'5" feet, slender, muscular, athletic build. Todd had him with the eyes and that pretty boy look, but Todd couldn't touch that body.

Ryan was very handsome, had a pretty set of white teeth, two dimples, a smile to die for, and wore a small diamond in his ear. His skin was like creamy caramel, and on his head was a low fade that shaped his round head. Ryan was all man. No questions. I blushed. "I bet you tell that to all the girls." I joked.

"No. You're the one and only."

"Ok. What's up?"

"I know it's short notice, but I want to take you out tonight."

"Tonight? You're right that is short notice."

"I'm sorry, but I just gotta see you."

"What's the rush? What happened to our Friday night date?"

"Our Friday date is still on. I just miss you. I haven't seen your beautiful face since Saturday."

"Today is only Tuesday."

"Yeah. That's been three days too long."

I blushed.

"You are so sweet."

"So what do you say?"

"Since you twisted my arm, I guess I can squeeze you into my busy schedule."

" I would very much appreciate that. How about I pick you up at seven?"

"That'll be great."

"And wear something sexy."

"I thought I always wore something sexy."

"Yes you do, but I mean something just for me."

"I think I can manage that."

"Okay, see you then."

"Bye."

I immediately hung up the phone and felt a smile plaster across my face as wide as the Mississippi River is long. I was cheesing up a storm. It had been forever since a man made me blush and grin like that.

Ryan picked me up for dinner at 7:00 pm on the dot. We drove to the next city over to a quiet little restaurant called Aislin's. The food was exceptional and dinner was very romantic. The lighting was soft, and mellow instrumental music played in the background. The atmosphere was very nice. The restaurant sat on a lake, so after dinner we took a walk by the lake and sat and fed the ducks while we talked.

Ryan invited me to his condo for drinks and conversation. I was really feeling him so I readily obliged.

Once at his condo, he poured a glass of wine and joined me on the sofa.

"I'm sorry Ryan, but since tonight is a school and work night, I'm not gonna be able to stay out too late."

"Sure babe. After the drinks, I'll take you home. Is that okay?"

"That's good. I'm not trying to rush. I just didn't want to get too comfortable."

He took my hand. "Krisha, there are some things I need to tell you."

I gave him an "oh goodness" look.

He laughed at my expression.

"It's nothing bad. I just don't know how you'll feel about this. I've been contemplating telling you since day one, but I was afraid."

"Afraid of what?"

"That you wouldn't give me the time of day."

"Just give it to me straight. I'm a big girl."

"Well, the first thing is, I've gotta leave town in another week."

"Why bae? What's going on?"

"I don't have an average everyday job. My lifestyle is a little different."

"What are you talking about Ryan? Please don't tell me you're a drug dealer."

"No." He laughed. "I'm a professional football player and I'll be leaving for training camp next weekend."

"Stop playing."

"I'm not playing Krisha. I'm serious."

I looked at him like he was crazy.

"Get out."

"Seriously." He was smiling. "I would show you all of my paraphernalia, but you'll say I could have gotten that from anywhere. So, I tell you what. I'll let you research me on your own. However you see fit. That way you'll know I'm telling you the truth."

"Okay. Sounds fair."

I looked over to see a laptop on his dining table. Great I thought. Let me Google his ass right now.

I opened up the laptop and Googled his name. To my surprise, there he was, Ryan Mathers, handsome face, perfect smile and all. Number 22, wide receiver, Baltimore Braves.

I moved from the computer back over to the couch where Ryan was still sitting. I looked at him in disbelief. "Why didn't you tell me before?"

"After I saw that you didn't know me, I wanted to get to know you without you knowing what I did for a living."

"So is it fair at this point that you know all about me, but I only know what you wanted me to know?"

"Everything I've ever told you was true. I just wanted to know that you were interested in me for who I am inside, not for what I can give you."

"So you thought I'd be interested in you for your money?"

"There are so many women out there who are."

"That's definitely not me. I can hold my own."

"I know that Krisha. I've been looking for someone like you for a long time." Taking my hands in his, he said, "There are a couple more things I'd like to share with you."

I eyed him suspiciously. "Don't tell me you're married."

He started laughing. "No, baby I haven't gone there." Looking into my eyes. "At least not yet."

He was so sweet.

"Then what is it Ryan? Don't be afraid to talk to me."

"Well, you've mentioned before that you were turning thirty-two this year, right?"

"Yes. But what does that have to do with anything?"

"I guess you didn't notice since you didn't mention it after you got off the computer. I hope it doesn't make a difference to you, but I'm…twenty-six years old."

"Twenty-six. Wow!" I said as I stared at him in amazement. Trying to see the youth in him.

"I hope my age isn't a big distraction. It really doesn't mean anything at all baby."

"Why didn't you tell me your age before?"

"You never asked, so I never brought it up."

I could kick myself for not asking. I thought. *But I was new to this so, it was like learning to date all over again. Besides, he was enough man for me.*

I smiled at him as he nervously watched my face for a reaction.

"There are certain qualities I look for in a man. You have all of those qualities, so the numbers behind you don't matter much to me. There wasn't a need to ask."

Ryan reached over, took my face in his hands and kissed me. I held onto his kiss for a moment as I looked into his eyes.

"There's one more thing I need to say."

"I'm listening." I said as I stroked the side of his face. He was irresistible.

"I've never met a woman like you before Krisha. I want a chance to take away the pain that consumes you. A chance to help you open up so that I can experience all the love that I know you're capable of giving. I don't know if anyone has ever told you, but you're a special woman Krisha. There are more good things that lie in store for you. I want the chance to love you. Will you please give me that chance?"

Huh?

In the middle of his living room floor, he undressed me. Carried me to his bed. Laid me down onto the bed while he shed his clothing. When he took his shirt off, seeing those tight abs and chest, I felt drawn to touch him. So I slid my body to the edge of the bed and kissed his chest stimulating his nipples, then down his navel. I found that his nipples were his weakness. He was irresistibly sexy.

Finally exiting his boxers, I leaned back to take in the sexiness that his body wore like no one else I'd ever seen. Had to admire the masculinity. I was at a loss for words.

I focused on his package as my eyes stood at attention. At that point, I was trying to figure out if making love to him was a good idea. Wasn't sure I could handle massive manhood of this magnitude, especially considering my hiatus of several months.

I backed up a little farther on the bed not sure if I wanted to go through with it. For the first time in many years, I was really afraid. Like I was losing my virginity all over again. But I kept the mood going. Didn't want to get immature on him.

I guess he noticed my apprehension. I'm sure it was evident; I couldn't help it. I have never in my life seen a man that massive in size. And all this time I thought Todd was working with something.

"Didn't I promise to never hurt you?" He whispered.

I'm sure he'd seen that look before.

All I could say was Oh! My! God! in my head.

I was at a loss for words. Both my body and soul has never, ever felt that good in my whole entire life. His entrance was unbelievable.

Ryan touched nerves I never even knew existed. Did things to me I never knew people did. I know I hadn't had sex with a man in over a year but my soul cried.

Talk about addicted. I could slap myself. I'd been addicted to the wrong man all these years. That's what happens when you just don't know any damn better.

And he was trippin' about his age. *Twenty-six.* Please!

Why in the hell had I waited so long with him? I thought. Four whole months. Hell, the way I see, it I got four months worth of catching up to do.

After our second round of unbelievable lovemaking, I finally decided to look at the clock, something I hadn't thought about earlier. It was 2:24 a.m.

He saw my gaze. "Do you still need to get home early?" He joked in a deep masculine tone.

I loved his voice.

"Too late for that huh?" I smiled as I shifted in his arms.

We didn't say anything. Blessed the moment with silence instead. Allowed the sweetness to linger in the room.

As I lay in Ryan's chest, sleep rode my eyelids. I was exhausted and began to doze off as he stroked my arm and caressed my back.

"I love you Krisha."

Wow! Where'd that come from? I thought. *Maybe I'd worked it a little too aggressively.* I thought with a smile. *I knew my ray of sunshine lit up the world and my built-up stash flowed like the Mississippi, yet tastefully satisfying. I was off the top with my skills; so yeah, guess he was in love.* As the arrogant thoughts left my mind, a smile warmed my heart.

I lay in his arms as if I were asleep. Pretending I didn't hear him say a word. I just didn't know how to respond, so I didn't say anything. I felt something. After four months, I was definitely heavily attracted to him. I just didn't know if there was anything else I felt for him.

So I elected not to respond. Instead I slept.

I'd had about three hours of sleep before I pulled myself up to go home. That was so hard to do considering I hadn't been in the arms of a man in what seemed like ages. I really missed being with a man and I wanted to rest my body alongside his for at least another five hours.

Instead I sat on the side of the bed as Ryan's strong fingers touched my skin.

"Where are you going beautiful?

I turned to look at his sweet face, which was covered with exhaustion.

"Gotta get home bae."

I'd drained him. I was fresh off a one-year drought. I could do some damage right now, but I knew I'd better go home now or it would be no time soon before I left.

I told him I would drive myself if that were okay. I didn't mind letting him sleep. He'd put in work.

He hurriedly said sure and told me where to find the keys. I knew that was a way for us to get together later. I didn't mind. I wanted to see him too.

So I raced home to see my kids off to school and to get ready to go into the office, at least for a few hours. I was tired and sore as hell. My muscles weren't used to that kind of action anymore. I needed to sleep.

On the way to the office, I had to call Mia to let her know how my evening went. Of course she was elated. She told me that Derric said Ryan was a good man and I should go for it. I did agree but I just wasn't certain about moving our relationship in a different direction.

As I thought about Ryan all day, I realized that my feelings for him were more intense than I'd let on. It's just that being afraid to open up wouldn't allow me to recognize that. I just wasn't sure if it was *love*.

If someone asked if I still loved Todd, I'd have to say yes. A part of me will always love him. He was my first a lot of things. I just hate him for taking advantage of that. I don't think the pain would be as bad if he hadn't done all those cruel things to me then left me for my best friend. I'll never trust another human being with a split between their legs with my man ever again. But rests assure that relationship was doomed before it ever started. That's what keeps my head up.

I realized today that I could definitely love again. Ryan made me see that.

26

Missing You

*I*t has been two months since Ryan went back to Baltimore. I have missed him so much.

We'd spent every day and night together before he left. Each night was so special and filled with so much passion.

A few days before he left we'd spent the day treating and catering to whatever the kids wanted. The nights were mostly Ryan and I.

We dropped the kids off to Aunt Mae and headed for a romance filled weekend at Lake Essence where Ryan had reserved a beautiful cabin by the lake.

We shared two of the most intense passion-filled nights that I'd ever experienced in all my days on earth. Two nights I will definitely never forget.

After he'd left to return home, he called day and night. He'd invited me to come for the weekend every since he'd been there, but I just couldn't seem to get away. Lately, I'd been working on restructuring my business, so I was extremely busy.

After all our times together and talks on the phone over the past two months, I'd never used those three words on him, though he expressed his love daily. I could tell in our conversations that my reluctance was beginning to bother him.

I felt that I did love him in many ways. I just wasn't ready for those words to escape my lips. I had to be sure.

I missed Ryan dearly so I gave him a call to ease my aching heart.

"Hi sexy." He answered on the first ring.

"Hey baby. How are you?" I asked with a smile.

"Just missing you."

"Awww sweetheart I miss you too."

"Wish you were here right now."

"I know. I wish I were there too."

"It's on you; all you gotta do is say the word."

"That simple huh?"

"Yep, for you."

"And the word is?"

"What?"

"You said all I needed to do is say the word. What's the word?"

He thought for a second and said, "Forever."

"Ah! That's an easy one, my favorite word." I laughed lightly. "Check this out."

Forever you
Forever me
Forever us
Forever we
Forever in love
With you I'll be
Forever tomorrow
It's you I'll see.

He let that marinate for a few seconds.

"Very lovely sweetheart. Didn't know you could flow like that."

"You don't know all my talents. I've only showed you a few."

"Where'd that come from?"

"That's from my heart. For you."

"I love you." He admitted.

"I know."

"Why can't *you* say it?"

I knew that was coming. I thought.

"I feel it."

"Why *won't* you say it?"

"I will."

"I'll call you back." He threw out quickly.

"Okay."

I was eager to hang up, yet I wanted to hear his voice and feel close to him. I don't know why I get choked up when he gets sentimental. I'm so open when we're intimate. I guess if I truly open up and let go, I'll be just that, *wide open*, and that's not safe ground.

Then there's the fact that Ryan is still young. Not even thirty. I'm not sure if he really knows *what* he wants.

Plus, he's like a piece of fresh meat hanging over a fence in a yard full of wild dogs. I don't know if I can deal with a lot of drama from other women again. I'll let him call me.

Why am I still so confused? I thought as I shook my head.

Since Carmen was there with my children, I decided on not going straight home. I called Mia to see if she'd meet me at Chimi's for a late lunch/early dinner and drinks, but mostly for conversation.

Mia agreed to meet me in about thirty minutes. So I took my time getting there.

When I got there I went straight for the bar. My mind was in Baltimore, Maryland. Wondering if I'd messed up.

Not paying attention to what was being said, I looked up at the TVs surrounding the bar. Immediately a big smile of amazement spread across my face.

There was a picture of my boo. Then there he was again being interviewed at his training camp. I was elated to see his face after two months. He was so damn fine in his gear. Although he was sweaty, he was still cute and sexy as hell.

Mia walked up while I was grinning from ear to ear.

"Hey girl." Mia sang as she hugged me from the back and kissed my cheek.

"Hi Mia." I said with a smile.

"What are you smiling so hard about?"

I pointed up at the monitor.

"What?" She said confused.

"Oh well, it's gone off now. My boo was on the news."

"Ryan?"

"Of course, who else would I be calling my boo?"

"I don't ever know with your sneaky ass."

"Excuse me, what do you mean sneaky? I'm not sneaky."

"Whatever ho? Tell that to somebody who don't know you." She smirked.

I guess I looked busted. That's how I felt.

Okay, I failed to mention my boy, Craig who was also my attorney for my business that I'd been seeing every since Ryan left. I've known Craig for the past eight years. We've always been cool. Even when Todd and I were married he would flirt with me but nothing ever went beyond that. Because of course, I was too in love with Todd. But, every since Todd and I divorced, he's been one of the many that has been blowing my phone up at work.

Craig is so sweet, and a very intelligent and handsome brown thang with a lot of skills. But I don't like him like that. I like what we've been doing for the last two months, but that's about it. He's just a little too clean cut for me. I like a man a little rougher around the edges.

I thought about leaving him alone, because in the long run he just may be a problem. But Ryan broke my several months of celibacy and now I just can't see myself going back. I'm still trying to figure out what the hell was wrong with me all those months in the first place.

Besides, Craig has a fetish that I like. And since I likes his fetish, I likes me some Craig.

He's a smooth lover, very gentle but he does seem to be getting a little too attached to my delectable. I might just have to wean him off before my boo comes back.

The real question to it all was, *how does Mia know?* I've never told her about Craig and me. That's one secret I've managed to keep from my BFF.

Or is she talking about Craig? Anyway, who cares? I'm not committing a crime. I'm not married anymore, and I am over 18. Besides, I'm sure Ryan is getting his freak on too with all those groupies they see daily. It's been two months; I'm not totally stupid.

"So what's up?" My best friend asked.

"I just didn't feel like going home. I feel kinda lonely right now."

"Lonely. Yeah right? Why do you have to feel lonely?"

"I miss Ryan I guess."

"You didn't sound like you missed him last night when you forgot to hang up your cell phone after I called."

"What?" I looked at her in disbelief.

"All that purring and moaning…giving commands…"

Cutting her off, I screamed, " Mia!"

She laughed.

"I didn't hang up the phone?" I held my hand over my mouth.

"You didn't say bye and sounded like you just dropped it. I was about to hang up, and then I heard you grunting like somebody was killing yo' ass."

"So you held the phone?"

"Hell yeah! I wanted to hear what was going on. Besides I didn't know if something was wrong or not. After I determined that yo' ass was freakin'. I hung up."

"After you'd heard enough, I'm sure."

"You know it."

We laughed.

"Girl you are wrong."

"And you are too much these days. What about Ryan?"

"What about him?"

"What's up with that?"

"I care about him. I think I love him, but things just began to move a little fast for me."

"He loves you Krisha."

"I know. It's just me. One day I think I'm ready for him. The next day I'm confused. I kinda like things the way they are. Now I see how you felt with Derric."

"You think he'll go for that?"

"I'm not sure. But I doubt it. He wants a commitment."

"Tell me this."

"I'm listening."

"What are you doing to hook these men like that?"

"Girl you know all the tricks." We laughed. "Why are you asking me that?"

"You got them all loving you. Ole boy last night was screaming he loved you."

"Stop lying."

"I promise."

"I didn't hear that."

"I guess not, you were too busy with all that noise."

"Shut up Mia." We laughed together. "Oh my goodness!" I covered my face with my hands. "I knew he was gonna be a problem."

"That's what you get."

"I learned from you ho."

"Obviously you weren't listening because I told you, you can't let every man have a taste test. When you're as sweet as honey, it'll hook em' every time."

"Fo' sho."

We gave each other a high five and laughed.

"Mia, you are truly crazy."

We laughed as we sipped on our drinks.

Thinking about last night with Craig brought about a huge grin. I still can't believe Mia heard us.

As I was reminiscing about Craig, I felt someone approach from behind which startled me.

"Hello ladies."

We turned around on our stools to see something pitiful staring back at us with a stupid grin on his face. Next to him was a numb and anorexic looking heffa. Just enough to ruin my appetite.

Mia gave a dry hello, then jumped into a chatter with Kyra.

I rolled my eyes and turned back around on the stool to face the TV monitor. My heart jumped as soon as I turned. There was my baby on TV again. This time being interviewed on ESPN.

"What's up Krisha?" Todd said in my ear.

"How are you Todd?"

I faced the TV; eyes glued to the screen.

"I'm good."

He leaned closer to whisper in my ear.

"Can't take your eyes off your little celebrity boyfriend huh? I never thought you would be robbing the cradle Krisha."

I turned to my right to look at him. I stared deep into those sexy evil eyes without saying a word. When I finished my stare I turned around to look back up at my boo. He wasn't worthy of a reply, so I remained calm.

"Let's go Todd, I heard Kyra suck her teeth and say from behind."

The Newmans walked away.

"You could have said hello to her." Mia told me.

"I don't have to speak to her if I don't want to. Forget her."

"Did you see her?"

"I tried not to."

"She's small as hell."

"Trouble in paradise, I presume."

"Presume? Please. That man whore is driving her crazy."

"I guess so. He got two babies on her."

"Then I heard he treats her like a punching bag every so often."

That got my attention. "What?" I spun on the stool around to face Mia.

"She's never straight out told me. But she calls every now and then upset, but she won't really say what's wrong. I guess she thinks I'll tell you."

"And you will."

"Yep. You know it. But her friend Teresa told me that Todd whips dat ass, gives her black eyes and everything."

"I don't believe that."

"Why not? He's slime."

"Yeah, but he has never laid a hand on me."

"She's not you."

"Todd has never, ever shown any sign of him being an abuser Mia. He might be a lot of things, but that one is hard to believe."

"Believe Krisha. Why would Teresa lie? She says Kyra comes crying to her all the time? Besides, he respected and really loved you enough to not do that to you. He doesn't really love her. I don't know what that is."

"And I ain't trying to figure it out either. Let's order so we can get out of here. I suddenly don't like the atmosphere."

In all reality, I was fuming inside. I hurt for Kyra. But I was mad as hell at Todd. How could he hit a female hard enough to bruise her? Why would he? Kyra has never been a person who did things to deserve an ass whipping from a man, only from me. If anything, she gave too much to men and always played the fool.

Todd had some serious issues and I would find out what ailed him. Both of them just made me sick all through my body. But what's right is right, and wrong is wrong. And he was dead wrong.

We ordered, ate, and prepared to leave. As we were getting ready to leave, I could see out of the corner of my eye, Todd and Kyra getting up from their table. We ended up going out of the door together. Perfect timing, huh?

We were going to the parking lot, when something told me to say something, so I spoke.

"Todd can I talk to you for a minute? "

"Sure baby."

Mia continued walking to her car, which was parked across from mine. Kyra rolled her eyes and went over to Mia. I wondered when those two started back talking like that. Mia never told me about their little reunion.

Todd came over to my car.

"Yes." He said staring all in my face.

I didn't know what to say. I fiddled with my fingers. Then it dawned on me that this was Todd, my husband of eight years. Why would I be afraid to speak now?

In a whisper to prevent others hearing my words, I said, "Todd all I wanna know is what has gone so wrong in your life now that makes you wanna beat up on a woman?

"Where'd you get that from?"

"Just answer me."

"Consider the source."

"Is it true?"

"What?"

"Are you beating on her?"

"Why is that your business?"

"Because, it's so not you."

"You don't know me anymore, right? Isn't that what you said."

"You're right. I don't know this new Todd. I knew you once. The Todd I fell in love with would never do such a thing."

"She's not you."

"She's a woman. She has family, a child, people who love her. She just doesn't deserve that." Trying to keep my voice down, I said, "I can't stand either of you, but deep down, way deep down, I'll always care for her. Don't do that to her Todd. No woman deserves that."

"You would never understand Krisha."

"Understand what? If you mean how a man could hit a woman then you're right. I will never understand. But she doesn't deserve that kind of treatment. She has a good heart."

"Good heart? Huh. Isn't she with me? Her best friend's husband...she hurt you. What are you talking about?"

"Are you serious? *You* were my husband. You hurt me too. So now you're mad at her for hurting *me*. She didn't do it by herself."

"I'm a man. I ain't shit remember? Isn't that what you said? She wasn't supposed to do that to her best friend."

"You're crazy." I shook my head.

"I'm not crazy." He bit his bottom lip as he spat out his words. "That bitch ain't shit!"

"Why are you saying this about her now? She's the same 'ain't shit bitch' you left me for."

"I didn't leave you for her. Be for real, that whore could never be you. I guess you don't know huh?"

"Know what?"

"She slept with Trent."

"I don't believe that."

"Believe that. She did."

"What goes around comes around right?"

I shook my head. Now he sees how I felt.

I continued. "Then let her go instead of treating her like crap Todd. Don't hold onto her and dog her because of what she's done."

"Can't do that."

"Why not?"

He just looked at me.

"The bitch is pregnant. I may as well keep one of them. At least until I can get a paternity test."

I gasped for air. Held my hand to my mouth.

"Todd, don't do this to her."

I guess he got angrier after he said she was pregnant because his voice got louder.

"Stay out of my business; okay sweetie."

"I'm just trying to help you stupid. I'd hate to see my kids father in jail or dead."

"I wish a bitch would try to call the police or kill me. She'd better make sure I'm dead."

He looked over at Kyra like that was meant for her.

Lord, this man has definitely changed. I shook my head and stared at him in extreme disbelief. Looked over at Kyra and Mia as they waited next to Mia's car. Kyra's face drenched in fear.

"Todd go home and chill out."

"I'm straight."

Calming down like nothing ever happened. "Thanks for the pep talk baby. Glad to know you're still concerned about me. Maybe I still got a chance. Love you."

Before I knew it, he'd stepped to me and planted a quick kiss on my lips.

"Motha...!" I screamed.

I almost tore my lips off I wiped them so hard.

He turned and walked away with a smile.

"Let's go baby." He called to Kyra, who immediately came almost running.

He opened the door for her then bent down to kiss her. Walked around to the driver's side, blew a kiss at me, got in and sailed off.

The man is truly losing his mind. He'd been acting very strange for about the last four months. My kids hardly see him anymore. The every other weekend visitation stopped a long time ago. He said he wasn't getting them so I could lay up with my man. So he picks them up when it's convenient for him. I let them go whenever he feels the need to come. I refuse to be a mother that keeps her kids from their father for her own selfish reasons. Now this drama with Kyra was something new. He's not gonna subject my kids to that crap. No way in hell I'll let them see a man beating a woman if I can help it. I still had plenty to say to that maniac.

When I got into my car, I called to check on the kids and asked Carmen to stay over. I wasn't in the mood to go home. Ryan hadn't called back so I figured I'd make the best of a free night. I followed Mia to her place where we made apple martinis and danced for a couple of hours.

It was a Friday night and I sure as hell didn't want to be alone. I thought I'd be getting ready to go see my man tomorrow, but I guess that was not what he wanted anymore. Oh well, forget it, I'll live.

As the thought escaped my mind, my cell rang. It was Craig inviting me to spend the night with him at his house. Something I'd never done. Always a hit and run.

I promised Craig that I'd be over later. I really wasn't ready to leave Mia yet; we were having too much fun.

We'd gotten tipsy and tired around ten p.m., so we plopped down on the floor.

Within minutes of lying down, I looked over at Mia, who was asleep and drooling all over the pillow. I decided to turn the TV on to BET, my favorite station, to check out the videos. It was just Chingy and those girls in dem jeans; I didn't feel like seeing them shake their tails, so I got up to go to the bathroom.

While in the bathroom, I thought I heard a knock on the front door. I continued to do my business; figured whoever it was would just have to wait.

Lucky for them, I heard Mia call out then open the door.

The next thing I heard was a lot of confusion.

I hurriedly washed my hands and rushed toward the front to see what was up.

When I reached the living room, I couldn't believe my eyes.

Mia was holding Kyra up at the front door. She was screaming and crying hysterically. Blood covered her face and lower body.

"What happened?" I screamed.

"I don't know. Help me get her to the bathroom."

"Should we call 911?"

"No, please no!" Kyra screamed.

"Kyra what happened?" Mia asked.

"It hurts!" Holding her stomach.

That's when it dawned on me what Todd had told me. She was pregnant.

Is she having a miscarriage? I thought to myself. *Then why was her lip and nose bleeding?* The scene was somewhat confusing.

"What happened Kyra? I screamed.

She just cried.

"We're calling an ambulance." Mia yelled out.

"Please don't Mia. Please no."

By the time we reached the bathroom with her, her bottom was soaked.

"Kyra you're hurt, why can't we call an ambulance?"

"He's gonna kill me."

"Who?"

She looked at me. I knew exactly who she was referring to.

"Forget him Kyra, you need some help." I said angrily.

"No Krisha he's crazy."

"He ain't crazy."

"Todd did this to you?" Mia asked. "Krisha help me take off these pants."

They were stuck to her she was so soaked in blood. She kept crying and screaming.

"Kyra you've got to calm down so we can see what we need to do to help you."

"It's too late. I know the baby's gone."

"Just be quiet Kyra while we get you cleaned up."

While she cried we stood up to undress her and to clean her body of all the blood. As soon as we stood her up, something massive fell.

"What the...?" Mia screamed and jumped.

"She's having a miscarriage." I said.

"Why didn't you tell me you were pregnant?" Mia asked.

She couldn't answer for the shock.

Mia continued putting her over in the tub so I could clean up the floor.

Mia washed her off as best as she could, but the blood kept coming.

When I finished cleaning the floor, we were finally able to get Kyra dressed in one of Mia's dresses and underwear with two Super Maxi pads.

She had a busted nose and lip. Plus she'd miscarried her child.

We sat in the bathroom with her as she cried. While she sat on the toilet, I kneeled down to console her. She took to me in a tight hug, crying her heart out.

"I'm sorry Krisha. I'm so sorry. I never meant to hurt you. This is happening to me because of what I did. You loved me so much and I hurt you."

She held me tightly as I cried with her. I did have a heart for the stupid.

"I'm sorry this happened to you."

I kissed her cheek and forehead. We held each other for what seemed like forever.

"Mia she needs to go to the hospital."

"No please."

"He's not gonna hurt you again Kyra. He's trying to get my attention."

"What are you talking about?"

"It's killing him that I've moved on and I have a man. I bet he started the abuse about three or four months ago didn't he?"

Kyra nodded her head, yes.

"When he found out you were with Ryan?" Mia said.

"Yep."

"That's why I can't stand him." Mia screamed.

"Oh God knows best baby, this is in His plan…He'll get his. Trust, he will get his…. Now let's go see a doctor."

The doctors checked Kyra out in the ER. Her blood count was low and she was very weak. We'd been there at least two hours already and I was tired as hell. Mia held Kyra's purse and personal belongings. Not once did Todd ring her cell. Her sister called to allow her daughter to speak to her, as she had taken Paige to California with her on vacation. Thank God the child wasn't home to witness that ordeal.

When they put Kyra in a room, I stepped outside to get a breath of fresh air.

After taking in the calmness of the night, the distinct ring for my boo began humming through my cell phone.

The phone was buried deep in my purse and I couldn't find it for nothing. Just couldn't seem to put my hand on the phone had my life depended on it. *I knew I should have cleaned this bag out this morning.* I thought. *It's after twelve a.m. and I'm not at home or answering my cell. I know he's gonna trip.*

I found my phone when the phone stopped ringing. I was about to dial him back, when the phone rang again. I answered so fast. I didn't notice it wasn't his ring until I said hello.

"Baby what happened?"

Danggit! I thought.

"Craig, I am so sorry."

"I've been waiting on you all night."

"I completely forgot. I'm over at the hospital with Kyra."

"Kyra? What? How did you…?"

Cutting him off. He knew about my situation with Kyra and Todd.

"Long story. I'll have to explain it to you later."

"Is she okay?"

"She will be."

"Hopefully, I'll see you later?"

"We'll see. I'll call you."

"Okay. Take care."

He is so sweet. I don't know what I'm doing, I'm not used to this. I guess I need to call Ryan back. I thought.

My phone rang again, this time it was Mia.

"Girl why haven't you answered your phone?"

"I did. What?"

"Ryan said he called and you didn't answer. He's called your cell, house, the office, and then he called me."

"I couldn't get to the phone when he called."

"I told him the situation and let him know that you walked downstairs to get your phone out of the car. I said that because I wasn't sure what you were doing."

"Thanks Mia 'preciate that chic... Hold a second." Looking at the ID as my phone beeped. "Gotta go girl, it's him."

I clicked over and put on my innocent voice.

"Hey baby."

"Hello sweetheart. Is everything okay?"

"Yeah, she'll be fine."

"Her boyfriend did this to her?" He asked in amazement.

"So she said."

"Wow. Did he ever hurt you?"

"You know I don't play that. That's why, one, I don't understand why he's doing this to her, and two, why she's letting him."

"People change Krisha. Sometimes they hide behind a facade. Never revealing their true inner self."

"He has definitely changed for sure."

"Good he never hit you, cause I was gonna come down there and mess him up real quick."

"If he had, that was before your time."

"So what? Doesn't matter. It's just the idea of him putting his hands on my baby."

"You're so sweet."

"Not sweet. I just love me some you."

"Then why didn't you call me back earlier?"

"I told you I'd call you back, I didn't say when."

"I wanted to hear your voice."

"Then why didn't you call *me*?"

"You know me."

"Regardless of what I'm doing, I'll stop for you."

"I wanna see you." I admitted.

"You will."

"When?"

"Tomorrow."

"How?"

"I was trying to make travel arrangements for you before I called back. I emailed everything to you. So go and check it."

"You're wonderful."

"I just love you. This is how everyday would be with us. If you only let me."

"Babyyyyy. Don't make me cry."

He laughed. "Okay I won't. I don't want my baby shedding tears. Go home and get some rest."

"I will."

"I can't wait to see you." He said softly.

"I'm counting the hours."

"I've never felt this way before nor have I ever done this before, so please know that all my efforts are out of love for you."

"I know that Ryan. I could never think anything less."

"Go get some sleep."

"Good night sweetheart."

I love him. I'll tell him this week. Forget Craig, I'll see him when I get back. I'm saving all my love for my boo.

27

Love All Over Me

$\mathcal{M}$y flight was delayed so I made it to Baltimore around 5:30 p.m. I was exhausted and all I wanted to do was rest. As soon as I stepped off the plane Ryan was there to greet me. He'd been patiently waiting two hours for me to arrive.

When we reached each other. He took me in his arms and held me close. Planted kisses all over my lips and face.

"I've missed you like crazy." He mumbled through kisses.

"I've missed you more."

We stood in the airport and relished in each other while admiring each other's beauty, until we noticed that there were spectators. So I claimed my belongings, hopped into his Benz and got ghost.

"I have a presidential suite with a Jacuzzi and the whole nine ready and waiting for you."

"You got a suite for us?"

"Yeah baby. He reached over and began caressing my leg. I figured we'd go relax a minute before I show you a night on the town."

"I thought I'd be staying at your place?"

"I figured a hotel suite would be more romantic baby, plus we won't have any interruptions."

"Who would interrupt us?"

"Roommate, teammates, family, friends, and anybody who knows I'm there."

"Oh I forgot." I said sarcastically. Not really pleased.

"I just don't wanna be interrupted when I'm with you." His hand had found my inner thighs.

"Go easy daddy."

"Can't."

"Why not?"

"I've missed you woman. All of you." His hands caressed my body.

"Is that why I'm here, a booty call?"

"Yeah."

I playfully punched his arm as we shared a laughed.

"Naw for real, I just wanna be with you pretty lady. I would love to make love to you, but we don't have to if that's not what you want. As long as I can see and hear you breathe, and as long as I can share my days and nights with you I'm satisfied." Still caressing my inner thighs he said, "It's you that I want. It just so happens that this good lovin' comes along with the rest of you."

He drew up in laughter anticipating a lick from me for that comment. I couldn't help laughing with him as I tore a hole in his arm while he drove.

"And you were on a roll you dirty sucker!" I screamed playfully.

At the hotel, I took a long hot bath. Ryan massaged my shoulders and washed my body as I sat almost lifeless in the tub. The warm water surrounded my body as Ryan's hands did wonders for my aches and pains.

I didn't realize how hard I'd been working and how exhausted I was. I guess this weekend was exactly what I needed to recoup. But something was telling me that I'll be putting in a lot of overtime here though.

When I finished my bath, Ryan dried me off, laid me down and massaged my entire body. At least that was his intention. I guess he massaged my whole body. I fell asleep halfway through the back massage.

As I slept, I entered into a peaceful dream. I dreamt about my mother. I could see her face as clear as day.

We were at home going about our daily routine as we used to do when I was a teenager, nothing special in particular. She told me that she wanted me to be happy. "Live your life to the fullest baby, but don't sleep on anything. Keep your eyes open and your head up, that's the only way for you to see." I could hear her voice so clearly, but as she spoke her face began to fade away.

I called out to her. Yearned to hear her voice again. My desire was to be close to her again.

"Baby." I heard her say.

I smiled, as I knew I'd found her again.

When I reached her voice, I fell into her arms and cried. Heard myself saying, " I love you momma, don't leave me, please don't leave me."

I opened my eyes to find myself in the arms of Ryan who had cradled me and was rocking me back and forth as he caressed my face and back. I looked up at him; he looked as if he had tears in his eyes. I fell into a deep state of depression and cried for my mother. I felt so alone. Though I was in the arms of a man who claimed to love me, I felt like I had nothing, nobody. I thought about my life and began to think that it had gone all wrong. I couldn't stop the tears.

"Are you alright baby?"

Took me a minute to speak. But he waited.

"I'm sorry. Sometimes my dreams are so real."

"It's okay, I understand."

Ryan had lost his father to cancer three years ago. I guess he did understand.

"I'm sorry you had to see me like this. It hasn't happened in a while."

"You have absolutely nothing to be sorry for."

Silence.

I laid in his strength. Surrounded by security.

"You hungry?" He asked.

"Starving."

"Feel like going out?"

"I thought you had this special evening planned for me."

"Well you slept three hours. It's after nine o'clock."

"Why didn't you wake me? I wasn't trying to go to sleep."

"If you fell asleep like that, I figured you were tired. So I let my baby rest. You're gonna need all the strength you can gather."

"Is that a promise?"

"Fo' sho'."

"Well let's get this dinner out of the way, so we can get to the dessert."

After dinner, we picked up a bottle of champagne and rushed back to our suite. I was full of energy at this point. Those three hours of sleep had rejuvenated me.

When we reached the hotel, the overly affectionate caresses started. In the elevator the kissing and exploring began and continued until we reached the suite.

"Give me a second baby. " I said after entering the room.

I slipped into the bathroom with my Louis bag. Showered quickly and changed into a sexy red thong with matching bra and a pair of red stilettos. I pinned my hair up and dabbed a little perfume between my breasts.

When I stepped out of the bathroom, KC and JoJo were singing and the room was led by candlelight.

Ryan sat on the edge of the bed in his boxers, feet planted on the floor.

As I exited the bathroom, he leaned back on his elbows. Watched me take a slow and seductive stroll toward him. Making sure he took in every curve through the candlelight.

I stopped halfway and made a few moves to the music making sure I turned around enough to give him a view from every angle. His eyes pierced my sexiness.

"My God you're beautiful."

He was in awe. As if he'd never seen me before.

"So I take it you like?"

Licking his lips and rubbing his chest, he uttered. "Uh huh...I like."

I turned around, swayed and twirled my hips to the music.

Easing my body down using my legs as my strength, I moved into a squatting position. Slowly came back up swaying my hips to the rhythm of the music.

Dancing a little. Provocatively. For his eyes only. I was feeling the music.

When I turned around, my baby was in a glorified trance. Lust in his eyes. Love in his heart.

"Where'd you learn to do that baby?"

No words.

Instead I put on a seductive grin and moved toward my lover. Crawled onto the bed between his legs, up his body to his broad and steel hairless chest. Planted soft kisses. Stimulated his nipples with my tongue. Made them recognize who I was. Gave love to his lean neck. Down to his abs. Made circles with my tongue down to his thighs.

I seductively moved my body back up to his tight and sexy abs; loved every piece of flesh my lips came in contact with. He gasped for air.

Being with Ryan Mathers made me want to travel undiscovered lands. I used better judgment and moved my body along his, until we were face to face.

He took my face in his hands and kissed my eager lips. The softest lips I'd ever felt. And his tongue, so plump and soft, expertly loved my inner mouth.

Kisses then went to my amazingly flat after two kids stomach. Then to the throbbing between my thighs.

He sampled my pleasure, then parted me with his fingers and took all of me in his mouth. Suckled softly.

My toes curled as I let out a long awe of satisfaction.

Created was an endless flow of juices that escaped my warm and inviting body.

Ryan was doing a hell of a job loving me. I hadn't been turned on to that degree in a minute and was really feeling the moment.

"Baby please." I begged.

He wasn't listening.

"Make love to me." I whispered.

He moved up to face me. My love glistening on his face.

I brought my two long legs together and positioned them high above my head. Eased my bottom up a little off the bed. Then slowly placed it back on the bed while spreading my legs wide. Legs long and straight. Wide and inviting.

"Tell me what you want." He whispered while sliding into me.

"Make love to me...slowly."

I kissed him as he entered me slowly.

Incredible.

Slow long strokes allowed me to get my grind on. I moved my hips under him. Rotated them as I worked my muscles to perfection.

With each thrust, I brought him deeper into my web of pleasure. He was just where I wanted him.

Legs snuggled tightly around his frame. Loving him so good. I was in control.

After several moments of an amazing display of our desire for one another, I began to release. My body took to the sensations of a magnificent, toe curling orgasm. Sweet fire pierced my loins as sweat dripped from my warm skin.

In a matter of seconds, I heard my name being sent into a screeching octave. Then a mound of trembling flesh onto the bed beside me.

"This is serious." He said trying his best to catch his breath. "Damn I love you girl!"

"You are a magnificent man Mr. Mathers." I said with a satisfied smile.

"I promise you are the original, the best, the one and only Sunshine baby." He kissed me.

We laughed together.

"I love you Krisha. I'm serious." He panted.

"Are you sure it's not lust that you feel? You know sometimes it's hard to tell the difference."

"I loved you before we ever made love for the first time."

"But you didn't tell me until after we did."

"Look woman, I like you, I love you, I lust you, I adore you, and I want to be with you. I don't ever want to leave you... Yeah! I lust you too, but I most definitely love your hot ass..."

We laughed.

"Krisha, if you're not ready for what I'm ready for, because I know things may be complicated with the distance between us, then I'll have to respect that. I know you've been through a lot. I'm a patient man. I just don't wanna lose you."

"You won't lose me love."

I slid my body up along his wet body and kissed his lips. We made love again.

After we'd shared with each other, Ryan held me in his arms. I felt at peace with him. I was safe. My heart was in a good place.

I stared at the ceiling and called his name.

"Yes baby." He answered in a masculine whisper.

"I love you."

He slid down to face me. Looked deeply into my eyes. I smiled and kissed him.

"You got my heart on lock." He kissed the tip of my nose. "I love you too."

When I left Baltimore on Tuesday morning, I was definitely sprung. In love like a college girl again. Ryan had truly swept me off my feet.

The weekend experience was more than I'd imagined it would be. The unforgettably romantic experiences that were shared between the two of us had strengthened our connection. What I felt with Ryan ran from the top of my head to the tips of my toes.

If I didn't think I was in love when I came. I was definitely in love when I left. I really didn't mean for this thing called love to invade my life again so soon.

I believed his love for me was genuine, but the fact that we never went to his condo still didn't sit right with me. Yet, I didn't ask any questions; I rode my high on home.

28

Can't Get Enough

*T*wo days later I was putting my sons on a plane to spend the remainder of the summer with their aunt Cicily in Virginia. Sad to say, I was kinda happy for the time to myself. I needed to get a lot of work done and do a lot of thinking. So I was grateful that Cicily wanted to spend time with them.

Craig and Todd had been calling but I wasn't answering. Todd had left several messages while I was gone, but I didn't try returning his calls. I just wasn't in the mood for old drama. And what Craig didn't understand was that he couldn't even get with Ryan. We were on such a different level than the meaningless romps with Craig.

By the next week, I was feigning for my boo again. My desire to be close to Ryan put my mind in a state of a love guided reaction. I made an impromptu decision to fly back to Baltimore to surprise Ryan on Wednesday evening.

I'd talked to him the night before until around 1:00 a.m. He told me he was going to practice in the a.m. and wouldn't be in until the p.m. I thought I'd already be there once he finished his day.

So I made the necessary arrangements and off I was.

When I arrived I rented a car, researched his address and did a little shopping. After all was said and done, I called Ryan.

"Hey baby." He answered.

"Hey boo. What's up?"

"Missing you."

"Really?"

"Yes."

"Are you having a party?" I asked.

I could hear music blaring in the background.

"No that's just Jace. He's entertaining a little company."

"What are you doing while he's entertaining?"

"Thinking of you."

"Well, why didn't you call?"

"I just finished showering and I was grabbing a bite to eat before I called you."

"Have dinner with me."

"I wish I could."

"You can."

"What are you talking about girl?"

"Look outside."

After a few seconds of hesitation, I saw a crack in the blinds on the lower level.

"Do you see a black Tahoe?"

"Yeah!"

"Then open the door."

I hung up the phone and got out of the truck, walked up to his door. Had to wait at the door a minute or two before he opened and took me in his arms. Gave me a quick kiss.

"Woman, what in the world are you doing here?" He asked while holding me in the doorway.

"I missed you so I thought I'd surprise you." I said looking up at his handsome face.

"You're too much."

He brought me closer to his body. Kissed me again.

"Man let the woman come in." I heard a male voice say.

"Oh! I'm sorry. I was just so surprised. Come on in baby. Where are your bags?"

"In the car."

"Do you have a hotel room?"

"No…not yet."

I moved into the living room.

"Krisha, this is Jace." He said looking at another very attractive brotha.

"Nice to finally meet you." I said extending my hand.

"I've heard so much about you. I feel like I already know you."

He took my hand in a short embrace.

"C'mon man, Ryan interjected."

I could hear the music playing in another room.

"Where's the party?" I asked.

"Come on in Ms. Krisha. Make yourself at home. We're back here on the patio. You're welcome to join us."

Jace was nice. I thought.

I looked at Ryan. He said," Go ahead let me put my shirt and shoes on. I'll be right out."

He started up stairs. Jace and I started to the patio.

There were two young ladies out on the patio, barely dressed sipping on champagne. I spoke to them. Jace did the introduction.

"Would you like a drink?" Jace offered.

"That would be nice."

Jace went over to the bar on the patio and poured me a glass of whatever they were drinking.

"Here you are pretty lady."

He placed the flute in my hand.

"Ryan told me about your business savvy and intelligence but he never told me that you were so beautiful."

"Really? Well thanks Jace. I can't believe he left that part out." I said playfully.

Like was he really supposed to brag and give details to his boys about his woman? Is that how they did things around here? Sounds little boyish to me. I thought.

I didn't reveal my thoughts.   Instead, I grinned while I watched him undress me with his eyes. He was respectful but I could tell that if I weren't with Ryan he would be trying to come at me.

I sipped on the champagne and watched Jace mingle with his friends. Neither of the girls had said anything other than hello to me. Which was fine; I wasn't interested in talking at the moment anyway.

Jace walked back over to me, champagne bottle in hand.

"Would you like a refill Ms. Krisha?"

"No, not right now. I just remembered I left my purse in the car."

"I can go get it for you."

"Oh no, entertain your guests, I'll get it."

He went back to his guests.

I didn't head for the front door; I headed for the stairs. I had no intentions of going to the car. I wanted to see where my baby had run off to. It shouldn't have taken him that long to put on a t-shirt and shoes.

When I reached the top of the stairs, I didn't know which room was Ryan's or which room he was in, so I chose the room I heard the voices coming from.

Before knocking, I listened outside the door.

"Look I'll call you later. I got something to take care of." He said.

"You ain't got nothing to take care of but me. Tell that bitch to leave, I was here first."

"Why are you trippin'? You know it ain't even like that between us."

"Like that? What you mean *like that?* Seems like to me its 'like that' or did you forget already?"

"Come on now T. This is my lady. Don't do this."

"Do what Ryan? I'm here with you all the time, now some triflin' ass bitch comes here from who knows where and you wanna put me to steppin'. Whatever! I ain't going nowhere!"

"Don't make me act a fool girl."

"Go ahead and act a fool. I bet yo' girl gone know the real deal. Matter a fact let me go get the bitch right now."

I heard footsteps moving toward the door.

I saved her a few steps, opened the bedroom door, and calmly stepped inside. "The bitch right here boo boo." I said with patience.

She was stunned. Ryan could have soiled his britches.

I was bold, dangerous and always ready for the next level of drama to pop off, so what?

She was a little chocolate petite chick with a tapered cut. Manufactured breast that peeked out of the little girls' halter she had on. And...I was fly, body banging, hot, and what?

He looked like he was gonna pee his pants.

"Is there something you wanna say to me princess?" I said with a grin.

She rolled her eyes, folded her arms across her chest, but didn't open her mouth.

"Funny how you did a whole lot of talking about a woman you don't even know a few seconds ago. Now you don't have anything to say."

Silence. Nobody said a word.

"Just like a scary bitch." I added, getting ghetto. Then turned my attention to Ryan.

"Ryan." I said as politely as possible. "My bad for coming unexpectedly. I should have called first. Baby all you had to do was be honest with me and say you had company, I would have understood." I smiled.

I walked over to him, who was still speechless. Wrapped one arm around his neck. Caressed the back of his head with the other. Gave him a nice seductive kiss on the lips.

I looked into his eyes before walking off, and smiled at the girl before leaving the bedroom.

Confidence. It's called confidence. Something I didn't have with Todd.

I walked down the stairs and out the front door not bothering to say goodbye to Jace or his company. When I reached my rental car, I noticed Ryan coming behind me like I knew he would.

Whatever he was saying, I wasn't hearing. He grabbed my arm to keep me from getting into the car. I threw him a "don't mess with me stare" and he quickly released my arm. I got in the car and left him standing in the driveway.

I didn't need to hear the explanation. It really didn't matter. I was thinking like Mary J. No more drama.

I got a room, stayed the night and left on an early morning flight. I was back in my home in Louisiana at 10:00 a.m. the next morning.

Ryan blew my phone up all night. On top of that, Todd and Craig were calling. My mailbox was full and I had several missed calls on my cell. All three had called my house numerous times.

But it was something in Todd's voice that told me something wasn't right with him. He sounded tired and confused. I just didn't know what he wanted with me. I hadn't spoken to him in several weeks. He probably didn't even know his boys were with his sister.

I decided to go against all judgment and call Todd back, and then I'd call Craig, to hell with Ryan. All the men in the world, I wasn't gonna waste my time with one triflin' man ever again. Todd had left my nerves so bad I'd probably kill another no good man.

I went ahead and called Todd before I changed my mind.

"Hi Todd."
"Krisha?"
"Yes."
"Finally. Now where the hell have you been?"
"Excuse me? Is something wrong?"
"I've been trying to reach you for days now."

"What is it Todd?" He was scaring me. Made me think something was wrong with the kids.

"I really needed to speak with you."

"For what?"

"Had to let you in on some things."

"What is it Todd? I don't have time for games."

"You've been with your little playmate huh?"

"That's none of your business."

"Oh! Like hell. As long as you have my kids it's my business."

"I guess you're all in them other tricks business too, oh! Or are you still banging all your baby mommas?"

"I told you a long time ago, I didn't love them."

"Look I'm hanging up."

"Wait Krisha. I wanna make it up to you." He was talking fast.

"Make what up?" I screamed.

"We need to talk seriously. I wanna come back home."

"Home? You told me your home was in Virginia, so I suggest you go back there."

"I miss you. I don't know why it took me so long to see that it's you that I really need. I realized that I can't live without you."

"Todd you made your decision a long time ago, now let me get on with my life."

"A life with that ball playing playa huh! Well my kids won't be a part of it."

"So that's what this is about? Don't ever try that with me again. As long as you did *you*, everything was fine. Besides you haven't done anything for my kids in months. But am I stressing it?"

"You can't trust people these days."

"I trusted your little girlfriend with my kids."

"You knew her, that was different."

"And by the way, you're dead wrong for doing that to her."

"For doing what?"

"I believe you *tried* to kill that baby. Didn't want another one in your pockets huh?"

"She probably did that to herself. Yeah we fought, but I didn't make her lose that baby. She knew it wasn't mine. Besides, I don't wanna talk about that silly broad."

"What makes you think I want you back after you left me for a stripper and my best friend? Then impregnated the stripper ho and another broad all within days of each other?"

"That's all in the past." Was all he had to say.

"Look I gotta go. Your kids are fine, just in case you wanna know since you didn't ask."

"I told you, you were never gonna be with anyone else and I meant that."

"Is that a threat Todd?"

"Take it how you want to. I love you girl."

"Get a life Todd." I hung up the phone furious. I knew I shouldn't have called his psychotic behind.

To clear my head, I called my girl Mia to see what was on and poppin'. I told her about Todd's call. She warned me to be careful. Said he'd been calling her to find me. He knew Kyra was staying with her and never even asked about her.

"How's Kyra?" I asked.

"She's doing okay. She's gonna start her old job back next week and she enrolled in college to finished her degree."

"Really? That is wonderful."

"You're not gonna stop by."

"Mia…don't start. I'll say hello to her. With that I'm being good. But holding a conversation is totally different. I really have no conversation for her right now. And I'm not about to start pretending. Our relationship will never be the same."

"I feel ya. Please don't feel like I'm choosing her over you. She just needs some help right now."

"I know. If Paige needs anything let me know, but I just can't pick up where we left off like nothing ever happened. Because if

Todd wouldn't be dogging her, she would still be there with him."

"I understand boo. Hey, wanna chill with me this weekend? We haven't been out in a while."

"That's cool. But I don't think I can go out Friday night. I gotta drive to North Louisiana to take care of some things at my new office. But Saturday is okay."

"Good, well you can go with me to the ladies party on Saturday night."

"Ladies party? I don't know Mia. I got pretty much all I need."

"You never know you might find something new."

"Take Kyra she might need to buy her something new."

We laughed.

"Oh! She's going alright."

"Then I know I'm not going."

"C'mon Krisha." Begging me.

"Look you know how those parties can get and I don't want to hear her referring to being with my husband."

"Ex-husband."

"Whatever. You know what I mean. I might have a flashback and lay her out."

"Krisha you know what your problem is?"

"I'm sure you're gonna tell me."

"You know the real reason why you can't whole-heartedly commit to Ryan or anyone else?"

"Go ahead let me have it Mia."

"You need to forgive Kyra and Todd for what they did and move on. You will never go on with your life as long as you hold hatred and animosity in your heart. You're holding on to something you cannot change, no matter what you do or say. What's done is done. Do you still want Todd?"

"Mia, don't make me reach thru this phone and slap you."

"Then what's the problem?"

"Is she there with you?"

"No, I gave her some money to go shopping for her and Paige. Todd wouldn't let her get any of her things."

"Well let me say this, Todd is the father of my children. I can't change that. He was my first love. He was the first real man in my life. I can't change that. I grew into adulthood with him. I learned with him. He took care of me. I loved this man more than I loved my own life. I don't wanna change that. You already know all of this and so did Kyra. I don't want to be with Todd now and some of it is because of Kyra's deception. I despise him, but I do have love for him because we've shared so much including two precious little boys. On the same token, I have the same kinda love for Kyra, but it's so deep I can barely feel it anymore."

"Stop. Forgive them so you can be happy. I wanna see you happy again. This thing can't plague you forever."

"I've moved on Mia."

"No you haven't. Not totally."

"How the hell you gon' tell me?" I said in a high pitch. She was working my nerve.

"Tell them you forgive them. Embrace her. Talk to her without cursing and fighting. Stop letting it bother you and stop letting him see that it bothers you. You're letting him know he still holds the key to your heart. Besides you already know there are plenty fish in the sea."

"The fish in the sea ain't a problem. You know how I do it." We laughed.

"See that's what I'm talking about." Mia screamed. "Just let it go."

After speaking with Mia, I thought long and hard about her words. It *was* time for a new attitude. I had moved on over the months but not completely. Mia was right. I'd carried this baggage long enough. It was time to get rid of it all. It was time for some soul cleansing.

I got on my knees and prayed long and hard. I definitely needed some answers. I knew there was only one way to get the right answers. After I prayed, I slept. My body was exhausted. I awakened to the sound of the phone ringing. It startled me, so I quickly answered.

"Yes."

"Krisha?

"Yes."

Silence.

"May I help you?"

"Baby this is Ryan."

I knew who it was.

"What do you want?"

"I want you to listen to me."

"I'm listening."

"First of all, I love you."

"Huh…look, I don't care to hear that. I'm so tired of all the "love" lies."

"It's not a lie. This was all a big misunderstanding."

"Looked pretty clear to me. You half naked – Girl half naked, up in your bedroom together, talking reckless about me."

"It's not what you think."

"Then what is it? You mean to tell me you're not in a relationship with her. Let's remember, I'm over thirty, and I'm not one of those airheads you're used to. I know a woman's attitude when she's having sex with a man. And I know a man when he's been busted."

Silence.

"Oh! Now you can't speak" What do you want with me Ryan? I'm a woman with two kids and a decent life. I'm not interested in petty childish games. I need a grown man to compliment me, because I'm a *full*-grown woman. I need someone who's over the drama and knows what he wants in life."

"I know what I want."

"Oh! Do you? What is that?"

"You."

"You gotta do better than that baby. Everybody that want me can't have me."

"Can I come see you?"

"At first you couldn't get away, now you can up and leave. No, hell no!"

"Why are you being so mean Krisha? I never knew you to be like this."

"Think about it Ryan. If the situation were reversed would you be smiling right now? Plus, that just goes to show, you don't know me."

"What does that mean?"

"It means, your girlfriend better be glad *she* didn't know me to be calling me all those bitches and you better be glad you need all your body parts to make your money."

He let out a quiet chuckle. "Girl you're a trip. I never saw this side of you."

"Trust, you ain't seen nothing yet."

"Seriously, I wanna see you. We need to talk face to face."

"You trying to down play what I'm saying, but I don't wanna see you right now. And to think I had a wonderful week planned for us. "

"I'm sorry baby. Krisha, please." He begged.

"No Ryan!"

"So what it do baby?"

"I'm saying…Just let me rest."

"Let you rest? I'm not letting you go, so you can forget that, if that's what you're trying to say."

"How the hell you got a choice? If I don't want yo' ass, you're history brotha!"

I know I was being mean, but he made me go there.

"Don't say that baby, just let me see you." He begged some more.

"Bye Ryan. I may call you later."

"Are you sure?"

"I said I might. I gotta go."

I hung up the phone.

Now he's acting like he's kinda slow. Lord have mercy. What have I gotten myself into? I knew I shouldn't have said those three little words.

I picked up the phone to call my babies before I called it a night. I took a bath and went to bed early to get an early start on tomorrow.

The next morning, I left home around 4:30. I worked in Monroe until 3:00 pm., conducted two interviews, kept appointments with three local bank executives and had lunch with Cheryl and other staff members. I also took pictures for a billboard advertisement, did a radio ad, and then left everything in the hands of my wingman, Cheryl.

I'd sent Cheryl to work in that office for three months until operations were running smoothly. She was my right hand and I knew if anybody could do it, she could.   So, I left north Louisiana with the confidence that my new project was off to a great start.

When I arrived home around 8:30 pm, I found at my front door the biggest bouquet of roses. They were my favorite color: purple. Purple roses meant someone desired my love and attention. The card read "Let me make it up to you. Love you with all my heart."

Ryan wasn't giving up. I must admit the gesture was so sweet. I thought about calling him, but I guess that's what he expected. So I put the roses in water, called Mia to let her know I'd made it in. I showered, called my babies and went to bed.

29

Ain't Leavin' Without You

I decided not to go out with Mia on Saturday. I was still tired from my trip on Friday. On top of that, I was awakened around 3:00 am to some noise behind my house. I stayed up peeking out of every window and crack until around 6:30 am. I just couldn't go back to sleep until daylight.

When I did finally get up, I worked in my home office and listened to Keyshia Cole's, Monica's, and Tamia's CDs all day. Gosh I love those girls.

When night came, I poured me a few drinks and danced all night by myself. Todd and Ryan had called all day. I refused their calls. I didn't feel like being bothered with their drama.

When I checked my email earlier, I saw that they both had sent messages claiming their "love" for me. Which to me at this point didn't mean a thing. Because right now I was hypnotized and that's the way I wanted to remain. That is until my buzz started wearing off around 10:00 pm. I was tired of drinking, tired of dancing and was now ready for some real action.

My phone rang in the middle of that thought. It was Craig.

"Hey baby." I said seductively.

"Hello sexy. How's it going?"

"Thinking about you." I lied.

"Funny, I was thinking of you too."

"Really, what were you thinking about?"

"The way you feel, the way you smell, and the way you taste."

I blushed from ear to ear.

"Don't do that to me, please."

"A beautiful, sexy, and most talented woman like you has no business being home alone. Especially when I got all you need."

"Well what good is it when I'm over here and you're over there."

"We can solve that problem very quickly."

"What you got in mind?"

"Can I come see you tonight?"

"Lucky for you, my children aren't here, so yeah. I'd love to have you."

"I'm on my way."

"I'll be waiting."

"Krisha." I heard him call out before hanging up the phone.

"Yes."

"Open the door in those edible panties I sent you a few weeks ago; that's all you need. I'll bring everything else."

"I got that... you just hurry up."

I knew it wouldn't take Craig long to get here. So I ran upstairs to shower and shave.

I guess Craig had forgotten about my rejecting him the last couple of weeks. He was just glad to be finally getting to see me. I loved the attention and the sex with him, though he was no Todd or Ryan. But he *was* a stone freak. Almost a bigger freak than Todd.

He had his own way and it was good, no doubt. No I take that back it was grrrreat! But, I know deep down I shouldn't be getting it in with Craig. He wasn't the one I really wanted. It was only about the curve in his highway that rode right on into home, perfectly.

About thirty minutes later, my doorbell rang. I strutted down the stairs wearing what I was instructed, accented with a pair of stilettos.

I opened the door to see a very happy Craig looking as fine as the bottle of wine he was holding in his hand.

Before I could speak, he took me around the waist and pulled me into him while kissing my lips and backing me up inside the house and out of the doorway.

"I've never seen anything more perfect." He grinned while looking down at my body.

I spun around on my heels. "So you like what you see?"

"Girl, you'll make a blind man see."

"That's too lame." I laughed. "Stop it and come on in." I closed the door, then led the way to the family room. Making sure I strutted a little extra, putting on a show.

"Would you like a glass of wine?"

"Yes, I would. But I'll take mine all over that ass." He licked his lips.

I pointed to the bar. "Come this way baby we ain't got nothing but time. You can have this ass anyway you like it." I said seductively with a locked gaze.

Craig poured. We stood at the bar and sipped. I threw my arms around his neck. His hands surrounded my waist and pulled me close. He was definitely ready for me.

"Krisha, before tonight progresses I'd like to tell you something."

"Yes baby." I stroked the side of his face with the back of my hand. Not really caring what he had to say.

"I want you." He said softly looking deep into my eyes.

"I already know that. Isn't that why you're here?"

"No, I mean I want you as my lady. I want you all to myself."

I thought to myself. *Here we go.*

"Craig, why do you want to complicate things?"

"What's complicated about that? I'm just stating my feelings. I really care about you."

"I care about you too, but can we talk about this later?" I pressed my lips to his to shut him up. Gave him a soft kiss.

Then slowly licked his lips with my warm tongue. Felt him rising to the occasion.

"Follow me." I said taking his hand in mine.

He knew what time it was.

He reached for the bottle of wine and quietly followed me up the stairs to my bedroom.

After eating the thong off me, and a whole lot of other stuff, Craig and I came up for air about two hours later. I was exhausted. I would have probably fallen asleep right there on the bed, but the last condom broke. So I jumped up sky high off the bed to go shower.

I had a feeling tonight was gonna be trouble. Something kept telling me not to do it. Hopefully those new oral contraceptives I started taking three weeks ago were already in my system.

Craig joined me in the shower then helped me change my sheets and make the bed. By the time we were done, my nerves were bad. I tried not to show it though. Tried to remain cool thinking I was protected and everything would be okay.

Lying awake thinking about how stupid I was, Craig interrupted my thoughts.

"Krisha."

"Yes."

"I'm serious. I want to be with you."

"You are with me Craig."

"You know what I mean. I want to take care of you. I want you in my life everyday."

"You're so sweet."

I gave him a peck on the lips.

"I'm not enough for you or something?"

I rose up to look at him. He had the look of defeat on his face.

"Don't be silly, Craig. Anybody would be happy to have a man like you."

"Anybody but you huh?"

"No. That's not what I'm saying."

"Let me show you the real Craig. I want you for more than for sex every now and then."

"What makes you so sure you want me?"

"I've known you all my life. I love what you represent."

"You haven't known me all…" I began to say before he cut me off.

"Well, not technically, but I used to see you around the hood back in the day."

"You were always so beautiful to me."

"If you used to see me around the hood then you know I got some stuff with me. I come with issues. I'm not Ms. Perfect."

"I understand that. We all have faults. Where do you think I'm from? I carry baggage too. Besides, I know you a hood rat." He said laughing playfully.

"Don't trip." I laughed as I lay in his arms.

"Just playing girl." He said in laughter. "What I'm saying is, I respect you. You came out, you moved on just like I did. Now look at you. You are a beautiful and very successful entrepreneur. Your name is next to God around this city. People look up to you."

He ran his thumb down to the tip of my nose.

"I understand your struggle Krisha. I understand your life. I understand all of the pain you've gone through. I love you for all that. You're a soldier, girl. All woman and all I wanna do is show you that I'm the man for you. I'm in love with you. I have been since our first date. I've been infatuated with you for eight years."

"Eight years…When Todd and I were together?"

"Of course. You've been with him all your life."

No I hadn't. I thought. But I ignored that comment.

"You never led on."

"I could never come between a man and his wife. I wished you were mine. I often said if you were mine I wouldn't be tripping. You'd be enough."

"So you knew."

"Well, sometimes, men let other men see things."

"Why is the woman the last one to know?"

"You wouldn't have believed it if someone had told you. You loved his pretty ass."

I didn't respond to that either. Yes I did love my husband. Wasn't I suppose to?

And yes, he is a pretty boy, that's his whole problem. He ain't a suit boy like Craig, hood like Marcus or rough around the edges like Ryan. He played baseball in college but never really got his hands dirty while working. He never had to want for nothing. His parents, from what I'm told, spoiled him to death and his sister took over when they died. He's all brains and good looks. But I loved all of that about him. I learned the hard way that all that looks good to you, ain't good for you.

"You're probably right."

"I know I am." You were always in the Todd zone."

"I was faithful."

"I know." He kissed my forehead. "I respect that. You're a good woman who needs a good man, and you got him, right here." He poked his chest. "No women drama or baby mama drama. When I love, I love hard. Just think about us okay."

"I will. Now get some sleep." I said.

I snuggled closer to Craig and threw my arms across his chest.

This felt strange. Strange, but good. It dawned on me that I'd never actually *slept* with Craig.

"Krisha you realize this is our first time actually spending the whole night together."

"Funny, I was just thinking the same thing."

"See we *are* made for each other. We even think alike."

"Go to sleep Craig."

We laughed.

"Good night love." He pulled in closer.

Before I could say goodnight, I was asleep and dreaming about my favorite rapper, Luda. He was at my house and we were cuddled in front of my fireplace and he was professing his undying love for me. Then next thing you know we were being married on a beach somewhere. We were just about to get busy on our honeymoon when I heard knocking at the suite door.

Wait a minute. Or is that in my house? Realistically, I jumped up from the bed and sat straight up. I sat and listened to see if I was really dreaming. Just when I was about to dismiss the thought, I thought I heard talking.

"Craig…Craig wake up." I shook him hard.

With eyes still closed he said, "Yeah Babe."

"Craig I hear something."

"Like what."

"Like something outside." That got his attention and he sat up in the bed.

"I don't hear any…"

"Shhh! Listen."

We waited to hear.

Then there was something that sounded like wind blowing. Craig got up and went over to his clothes on the floor. He retrieved what looked like a .45 auto caliber handgun. Looked exactly like mine.

"You got a gun?" He asked.

"Yeah, but I left it in my car from my trip yesterday…Why?"

"Because I'm going downstairs to look around."

"Go ahead I'll be okay."

Craig went downstairs with gun in hand seeking protection for his woman. While he searched the house, I peeked out the window to see if I could see anybody or anything.

How in the world could I leave my gun in the car in this big ole house in the woods? I thought. I believe I'm getting more stupid by the minute.

I sat still on the bed and waited for Craig to return.

After a few minutes, he returned to the bedroom and put his gun back up.

"I didn't see anything."

"Neither did I."

"Guess it was a dog or something." He suggested.

"I haven't seen any dogs all the way back here in these woods. Maybe deer, a coyote or something."

"Yeah could be."

"I've been hearing that same sound lately though."

"Don't tell me you've got all the animals in the woods riled up too." He laughed.

"Cute Craig, real cute." I rolled my eyes.

Hell, I was scared and he was playing.

Craig held me close to his heart and we managed to fall asleep again. I swear I could feel someone starring at me while I slept. Maybe it was an angel; my mother watching over me, protecting me. I'd hate for her to see me laid up like this though.

Sometime later, after finally falling asleep, I had the urge to use the restroom. So, I shook myself up out of the deep sleep I was in and pulled out of the tight hold Craig had around me.

When I rolled over and opened my eyes briefly, I caught a glimpse of what seemed to be a figure standing at the end of my bed. As I wiped my eyes and focused, things became clearer.

I instantly sprang up from the bed. Heart beating a mile a minute. Eyes as big as saucers.

"What the hell are you doing here?" I screamed.

Silence.

"How did you get in here…what do you want?" I screamed some more.

Craig stirred. "What baby? Who are you talking to?" He said sleepily.

"Craig, get up."

I elbowed him in the side.

"Yeah Craig, get up."

Craig immediately sat upright in the bed.

"Wh...What's going on? He stammered.

The only thing I could see was the shiniest gun I'd ever laid eyes on. It was a very big gun. Looked like a .357 revolver. I don't know, but that barrel was a foot long. I was shocked speechless.

"What are you doing with my woman man?"

"Your woman? C'mon man stop trippin'."

Shocked beyond scared, I managed to say, "What are you doing?"

-

"Shut up, you're just like all the others, doing any and everybody. I thought you were better than that."

"Hey man, you don't have to go there."

"Shut up before I put six holes in yo' ass."

Silence.

"So has this been happening behind my back?"

"No, I wouldn't do that to you."

"Yeah that's what all yall bitches say."

I heard my voice cracking. "What's wrong with you?"

I don't know if I was beginning to cry because I was really scared or because the words really hurt coming from him.

He'd never talked to me like that before. He always adored me and chose his words carefully. That hurt. And that big gun didn't make it a bit better.

"Tell me this friend, was it good? Was it worth dying for?" He asked Craig.

"C'mon man just calm down."

"I ought to really mess you up for touching what's mine. And for you to be with somebody that was close to both of us. That's foul Krisha."

I know damn well he didn't say that. Now I know he is really crazy. I thought.

"It's not what you think." I said instead.

"Oh! It's what I think alright. I heard everything. You were enjoying this little make shift honeymoon. What the hell else am I supposed to think?"

"Look, what do you want man?" Craig interjected.

" I told you to shut up, lil bitch."

"Bitch? Put that gun down and I'll show you the bitch."

"Craig just be quiet please." I whispered.

"Naw. He ain't nothing without that gun. I'll whip his pretty ass all around this room."

"Craig please." I pleaded.

"Get you're man Krisha. Then again, is he really you're man? Or are you just playing him too. Did you tell him you were robbing the cradle? Does your boyfriend know you're sleeping with him?"

Craig looked at me stupid. I looked down at the covers on the bed.

He knew there was somebody else so he'd better not trip. Or he shoulda known at least. Not now Craig. Not now. I thought.

"Krisha. I love you so much... and if I can't have you this punk right here won't. He ain't no better than me."

"What do you mean by that?" I asked shaking in the sheets.

"It means that you're going wit me. Now put on your clothes and come on."

"Say man, you're not taking her anywhere."

"Look man, I really don't wanna hurt you so just stay out of family business."

"Don't do this. Just go back home, please. I'll come see you later." I begged.

"I am home."

The next thing I knew, I was being jerked off the bed by my arm. Nakedness exposed.

"Get dressed!"

I cried as I dressed in a pair of jeans, a T-shirt, sneakers, and a cap. Both of them were watching me. Craig watching from him to his pile of clothes, where his gun was. I prayed he didn't go for it.

"I thought you really loved me?" I said softly.

"I do."

"You just wanna control me. We can talk about whatever it is. Just don't do anything crazy."

"I won't stand for you sleeping with half the city."

"You know that's not me."

"I can't tell. Just shut up and come on maybe you still got enough for me."

Craig hopped up.

"So you gonna rape her?" He screamed. "You some man, huh?"

He moved closer to Craig aiming the gun at his head.

I threw up my hand in a motion for Craig to be still.

"No I'm not gon' rape her. This bitch is mine anyway. Let's go!" Grabbing at my arm.

"Okay I'm going. Just put that gun away please."

"Hell no!"

"Please. You know I hate guns, baby please."

I thought about it as soon as the words left my mouth. *Damn that wasn't a good lie.*

"Girl, stop with the dramatics."

"They still make me nervous. Please I'll go if you just put it away."

"You're going regardless. I didn't give yo' ass a choice."

I stood pleading with him looking him directly into his eyes. I guess my eyes must have said something my mouth couldn't say. Because he finally stuck the gun down the front of the jeans he was wearing.

Taking my arm squeezing the blood from it. "Let's go."

He had a serious death grip on me.

Craig jumped up. "Don't touch her like that man! What's your problem?"

At this point I was wondering what Craig was thinking. He should just let me go. This had the potential to turn and get really ugly. I could feel it.

"Say man, I told you to mind your own business. This is between me and my wife."

"I don't think the lady wants to go with you playa and I just can't let you hurt her."

"Look man, I told you this ain't got much to do with you. So chill."

"When did you get all those balls man?" Craig challenged him.

"Look bruh, if you wanna clown let's get at it. If not, me and my woman got something to take care of."

"Craig, just let it go, I'll be okay." I said softly with defeat in my voice.

I just didn't want anyone hurt. He had come for *me*. I was willing to go with him.

"Krisha, you know I can't do that."

"What are you gonna do? Just let me go!" I screamed.

I was really pleading for him to stop and think about how this could turn out.

"Hell no!" Craig moved toward us. Looking at his clothes trying to determine what it would take for him to reach his gun.

I read his mind. "Be for real Craig." I said cutting his thoughts. "This isn't about you!" I screamed as he halted.

"Krisha, you know I can't do that." He looked at me. "I can't let this psychotic fool take you like this."

"If I was crazy I woulda killed you when I heard you having sex with my wife."

"Would you please stop calling me your wife?"

"Let me kick his ass." Craig huffed.

"Tell you what, I'mma put this gun away and give you your chance since you wanna play hero." He said then placed the gun on my dresser.

Bold move. I couldn't believe he'd said that. And I definitely couldn't believe that they were in my bedroom fighting like crazy people.

I ran from one to the other trying to stop blows and convince them to let it go. But I guess each one had something to prove to the other.

I was in a stuck. I cared deeply for Craig and didn't want to see him hurt, but I loved the other. Would die if anything happened to him, though his behavior was totally out of character and very surprising to me. He had a place in my heart and I couldn't bear the thought of him hurting because of me.

I had to do something. I could have joined in and helped Craig take him and then I wouldn't be taken against my will. But could I do that to him? Craig would try his best to kill him, I already know. Would my heart allow me to do such a thing?

Before I could object again, I caught a glimpse of another small but shiny gun strapped to his ankle.

Craig would never win. This man was strapped. He came for business. He came for me.

"Stop. Please!" I screamed while crying." Please stop hitting him."

I ran to Craig trying to pull him away from the blows and stop them with my hands at the same time. Craig was still handling his, but blood covered his face. Looked as if it were coming from his nose.

"Please just leave him alone. I'll go with you, just stop!" I screamed hysterically.

At this point my bedroom looked like a hundred people were in that baby tearing it to pieces.

"Nawww he asked for this." Todd huffed as he gave Craig a crucial blow to the head that sent him sprawled out on the floor.

"I'm asking you to stop Todd. Just leave him alone." I begged and pleaded. "Let's go please!"

As Todd stood looking down at Craig's body on the floor, I grabbed a piece of a cloth, a shirt or something and put it on his face to stop the bleeding.

I patted his head with the cloth before being snatched up by the front of my shirt. I dangled in the air a second before being dragged to a standing position.

"Let's go." Todd demanded.

"Craig." I looked down at him on the floor. "I'm sorry."

I thought I saw him nod his head. I wasn't sure.

Todd picked up all of Craig's clothes not touching the gun. I'm sure he felt the weight though.

Todd told Craig, "Stay right here playa unless you want me to hurt your lil beauty queen here. When we're gone, look downstairs somewhere for you clothes. Told you to just stay out of it. I don't know why you wanted to underestimate me."

"Let's roll." Todd threw out to me.

He nudged me in the back with the gun.

I took a quick look back at Craig as I was forced out of my bedroom and down the stairs. He was still laid out on the floor.

"Todd." I started.

"Shut up!"

He was behind me. I didn't see the gun anymore.

I was beginning to feel a little weak. Nerves were extra bad. Jumping all over my chest.

"Todd. I don't feel so good." I said.

Walking toward the door, he said, "You'll be fine. Keep moving."

"No I think I'm gonna be sick."

As soon as I turned to make a dash for the downstairs bathroom, I thought I heard a knock at the kitchen door.

I closed the bathroom door and emptied my lunch and dinner into the toilet. I hurt from the bottom of my stomach as

I purged myself. I could hear Todd saying something. Then I heard another voice. I felt even worse. Like my strength was being pulled from me.

That voice. It seemed to be coming at me. My head hurt. Fierce pounding. I didn't know whether to run or hide. But I do know there was no way I could pull myself up and off the floor at that point. My head was spinning and I saw stars. I saw three men in white suits. Arms stretched wide. Telling me to come be with them there was no place to hide. I didn't know what path to follow. I didn't know what chance to take. I couldn't tell what road to go down, or what decision to make. I felt in my heart love for all three, but couldn't determine my destiny. I heard his voice. I imagined his face. I knew in my heart it was him, but I dared show *my* face. Stress took over as I closed my eyes, I could feel the pressure from my gut arise. Seeing all black was how I rode this one out. On the cold floor, as I tried to move about. My fight was unless as I stretched my arms wide, I waited for the wave, waited on the tide. I rode with my savior, and as we came near. I asked myself, where do I go from here?

I opened my eyes to a pitched black road. *How did I get in this car?* I thought. *And whose car is this? Where am I?* My head hurt really badly.

I could tell I was still on the road that led from my home. Not another house for at least a quarter of a mile. Right now I was wondering why the heck had I moved all the way out here.

Todd was really on that dumb. This whole night was so out of character for him. It was evident that he was definitely on something good.

My stomach ached badly. I held my stomach and head and cried like a kid.

"If I tell you one more time to shut up, I swear I'm gonna hurt you."

He was nervous. Hands shaking. Evil in his eyes. I believed him.

But after a couple minutes, I began to get upset at the fact that this dude was getting mad. Who the hell was he? He broke into my house, beat the crap out of my man, and stole me from my home *and* the arms of my man; handling me while holding a gun to my body.

The more I thought about it, the more upset I got. Not only was I mad, I was plain ole hurt. This man claims to love me, but continues to put me through crap like this. Why won't he just leave me alone? I thought.

"Why are you doing this to me? What gives you the right to try to own me?" I cried.

He ignored me. Not taking his eyes off the road.

"Answer me! You made your bed now lay in it! I don't want you no more…. you fucking make me ss…."

Before I could get it all out.

Bam!

I saw stars from my left side.

Todd had popped me up side my head. The blow was so hard that the right side of my head hit the passenger side window with a vengeance.

"Why'd you do that?" I screamed.

"I told you to shut up."

I was overtaken by rage. I wasn't thinking about anything else other than him hitting me.

With nothing else said, I jumped across the seat over on his head and started pounding the hell out of him. With one hand, he pushed me back into my seat but I came back stronger. I got a good one in to the side of his nose. I popped it.

When I saw the red blood, I then saw the red in his eyes. Todd threw the car in park. Almost threw us both through the windshield.

He took the keys out of the ignition and threw them at my head. I ducked. He was furious and it showed. But what the hell! So was I. I started hitting harder.

With one hand he grabbed my neck and squeezed, pushing me up against the door.

"I catch you having sex with another man and you want to trip. I'll show you who to play with. Don't ever get it twisted, I'm a man!"

He pounded his chest at the last statement.

He never let my neck go with one hand, and I never stopped swinging on him. He was across the console leaning into me, my back up against the window.

When he did release my neck, he obviously thought it was over. I started punching and kicking. I had to do something to get away from him. I had never in my life seen Todd that irate.

Then he just sat there taking my licks and hitting the steering wheel while he spoke, "You wanna see what happens to hos that try to mess over me? You're no better than your friends."

He hopped out of the car, jumped across the hood to get to the passenger side, but I had already locked the door.

"Open the door! You ain't so bad now since you don't have your friends or your gun."

I looked at the ignition for the keys to start the car but forgot he'd thrown them at me. I searched the floor for the keys while Todd screamed for me to unlock the door. I wasn't crazy, I didn't dare. I was seeing a different Todd and was beginning to get extremely scared.

Next thing I knew, glass was coming at me from my right side. I let out an alarming scream.

He'd broken the window with one single punch.

I was hiding my face from the glass, when the door was swung opened and I was snatched out of the car.

When I hit the ground, I kicked and screamed at Todd to leave me alone.

"Dude don't want you Krisha. You're just a piece of ass for him." He screamed as he stood over me.

He snatched me up to my feet by my shirt and ripped it open. I jumped back and started throwing punches. I connected a few times but it wasn't a match for what he had.

I got a slap that made me stumble against the hood of the car. I raised my leg and kicked at his crotch. I missed and he went for my throat again.

This time I wasn't crazy. In situations like this, you gotta be smart.

I hauled ass down the dark road.

The only lights were from the headlights on the car Todd was driving. It was dark and I was off balance and couldn't run fast. So he quickly caught up to me.

We wrestled with each other. I know I was overpowered but I wasn't gonna just let him hurt me.

"Krisha stop it and get in the car." He screamed while trying to get a grip on my body and pick me up from the ground.

"I'm not going nowhere with your crazy ass." I was crying and screaming like death was on me.

"Oh hell yeah you're going. Now get in the car!"

"Just leave me alone. I don't want you. Why can't you accept that?"

I regretted saying that as soon as the words left my lips. I saw an uncontrollable rage.

"You're sexing everybody else, so why don't you want me Krisha? Huh? We're even now baby." He spat.

Bam. He slapped me.

Hurt wasn't even the word to describe that lick to the face. It was absolutely unbearable. I was dazed.

"I told you that you were mine. I'll kill your ass before I let anybody else have you."

"Todd no." I cried.

Now I was officially scared as hell at this point. This just wasn't worth it.

"It doesn't matter to me Krisha. If I don't have you, I don't have a life. I don't have anything else to live for."

What is he saying? I thought. *Oh my God. He's gonna kill me. I went about this all wrong. He's really gonna kill me.*

The only thing I could think of was to fight for my life. Talking to him had done no good. So I fought like a crazy person. I found sticks, rocks, and everything I could find to hit him with. We were several feet away from the car in a ditch rolling like two insane people.

I found a short, sharp stick in the ditch and used it to stab his arm. I came down twice really fast with all the strength I could gather. Must have hit a vein because blood shot up and out of his forearm.

"Awww shit!" He screamed.

But that didn't stop him. Next thing I knew I saw the back of his hand come down across my face. Then another to the side of my head, and another to the same side of my head.

I screamed for him to stop. But the pain kept coming.

I saw another thick hand coming down on my face. Felt the pain it left behind. Then both hands surrounded my neck.

As I looked into the eyes of my love, I knew then that my fight was over. I was blinded by love for so long that I refused to see the jealousy and anger hidden so deep within.

My passageway to life was being cut off. The blows to my head only allowed me to see black and white as my vision went in and out. Found it difficult to breathe. My strength was leaving me. I couldn't fight him anymore.

I closed my eyes and saw my babies. Opened them and saw darkness. I closed my eyes and saw my mother. Opened them again and saw rage. I chose to close them and leave them still. Didn't like the sight I saw through the blood and tears. I wanted to remember him loving me with a smile. I wanted him to know that I understood his tribulations and trials. Stillness came over me, and darkness prevailed. The love of my life, in his hands my life he hailed. With all I had for him, with all that we'd shared, how could love turn deadly, how could love be despair. It hurt me more to know that it was him that I feared, that it was him that brought harm, him that brought the tears. It hurt me more to see that he was in control of my life, leading my destiny. I had no choice but to follow his path; in the direction he was leading me. Had it been a stranger, I wouldn't have shed a tear, but for it to be my soul mate, I knew the end was here. Before the darkness overtook me, I heard whimpering, I heard sounds of love, I felt a touch from above that told me its okay, you're surrounded by love. Be still my darling, life is just a test. You've run a long race, now it's time for you to rest.

Epilogue

At the end of Krisha's trials and tribulations with her husband, she realized that love was what she felt in her heart for Todd as well as what he felt for her, but he lacked a certain respect for who she was and what she meant to him which in turn brought about many undesirable actions on his part. One thing that we must understand is that love and respect go hand in hand. If you don't have one, you can't have the other.

Can't Leave Him Alone is a tool for empowerment in women in that it is a good example of the obstacles some women endure in life with men and relationships, and it serves as a reminder of the strength that we as women sometimes forget we have. God gives us everything we need to armor ourselves from woes as Krisha endured, but sometimes we leave those things behind and follow our hearts instead of our minds.

The story of Krisha and Todd is not meant to disrespect women in any way or discredit men on any level. But it is one of many avenues designed to get women to take a look at how we succumb to and tolerate BS all in the name of love. It is a piece that is designed to open the eyes of the blind and strengthen the weak, and remind us that degradation of spirit, health, and self-esteem happens without even realizing its happening as we subconsciously allow.

As I mentioned in the book, when someone is on the outside looking in, things seem so clear. But when that same person is on the inside, sometimes things get a little blurred and the same advice that he or she gave is a hard pill for they themselves to swallow. Every reader saw where Krisha went wrong and some even called her stupid for following her heart. Wasn't that easy to see? But love can most definitely be blind. And everyone has been a Krisha at some point, or has known someone who has. I've traveled that same road myself. But you've got to understand that when your so-called love relationship gets to the point where you are no longer happy, maybe you should look a little deeper into self and redefine what you call love.

The key: Believe in yourself and know who you are. I am a firm believer in the fact that knowing who you are is what you need to build character, set standards and demand respect from not just men but everyone in general. We all know that anyone will do as much as you allow him or her to do. So, being strong, knowing who you are, and having morals will lead you to making good life choices which in turn mean good relationship decisions.

I urge all women to find happiness in a mate. But don't allow incidents like Krisha's struggles to play a part in your relationship. The mindset of Krisha was to stand by her man; and she was right to do so as her man was her husband. That makes another interesting point...make sure the man is **your** husband. Sometimes we carry baggage from men who call themselves our men, but have no intentions of ever being our husbands. I honestly don't believe it takes a man several years to decide whether he wants you as his wife or not. And if you're good enough to do everything else with why not marry. Again that's where self-respect and knowing your worth comes in.

Bottom line: You've got to know who you are to know where you're going. Take Krisha's trials as a lesson to love you first.

Discussion Questions

1. Do you think Todd really loved Krisha as much as she loved him? Why do you think he could not be faithful?
2. Was Krisha right for going to Todd's baby mama's house?
3. Who do you think was in the car with Todd when he had the wreck?
4. Do you believe love and respect go hand in hand?
5. Was Mia wrong for texting her to tell her Todd was in the club with his mistress? When should friends get involved?
6. What do you think made Krisha continue to forgive Todd and hang in there with their marriage?
7. How much did sex play a part in their relationship? Was it based on sex?
8. What do you think makes a spouse cheat? Is anything at anytime justified for cheating?
9. Was Krisha wrong for not accepting Todd's child? For not telling her kids about their sister? How would you have handled that?
10. In real life, do you think a man really wants someone like Krisha in a relationship? Do you think she was too passive?
11. How would you describe Mia? Who would you rather be a *Krisha* or a *Mia*, in character?
12. Do you think Kyra and Todd's relationship was strictly conversation? Are conversations off limits with your friend's spouse? Did Krisha overact with Kyra or were her actions justified?
13. Is it possible to make a man love you/be faithful?
14. What are some things a woman must be equipped with when in a relationship like Krisha's?

Acknowledgements

I thank God for my journey through this amazing race. The struggle from 2006 to this very day has truly made me stronger. There have been so many things that have happened in my life since I began writing this book, good as well as unfavorable. I look upon them all as encouragement for growth and determination for success. I just want to thank everyone who pushed me through, even when the thought arose to just leave it alone. Thank you for seeing things in me that at the time I could not see.

A special thanks to my three little girls, for bothering me every time I picked up my laptop. Had it not been for you I would have finished this project a long time ago. But God had a plan and it was right on time. So thank you girls for the love-filled delay.

And to my husband for not quite always understanding why I was up til the sun came up, but allowing me to do it anyway. Your patience and support meant a whole lot.

To my mother, from whom I learned the meaning of the 3Ds, direction, determination, and dedication. Thanks for the installation of strength and perseverance that surrounds who I am today.

When I say I owe everything to Katabitha Parker (Tab) and Yolanda Frazier (Dody), I definitely mean what I say. Words can't even express my gratitude. Much love ladies!

For my ride or die crew, my sister/bestest cousin in the world, Dana Topps, Katabitha Parker, my other bestest cousin and sidekick for life, Yolanda Frazier, Karneka Courtney George, and Delisha Wilson, the ladies of Divas In Motion Readers Group, Amite, Louisiana, you guys were with me from start to finish and were the first to share your thoughts. Your encouragement gave me just what I needed to make this happen. Thanks for the love, margaritas, laughter, and fun.

My heart, BFF, Ericka Zanders, although we don't see each other as often as we used to. I can never forget the times we shared and the experiences we conquered together. Let me just say, thanks for the inspiration.

To my special friend Lawanda Irving, thank you for your words. Your speedy reading and dedication to assisting me with this project was outstanding and meant everything to me. Thanks chic. BFF.

To my sister, Chancelee Rose Galmon, thank you for your immaculate skills. You're a model of perfection. I love you so much girl, you don't even know!

To all my FaceBook friends whose comments mean so much, thanks guys for the support.

And to the greatest HBCU in the whole world. SSSSSSU....Southern University, Baton Rouge, Louisiana. Where my inspiration began. From my mother who insisted that I attend no other university, to all the instructors who gave me what I needed to be successful in all my endeavors. And to the memories of life on the yard that I will carry with me forever. There's no other experience like the SU experience...JAG til the end baby!

And last but certainly not least, to the Devastating Divas of Delta Sigma Theta, Incorporated. Hammond Area Alumnae Chapter.....Muuuuaah!!! Thanks for all the love and support.

MickiMichelle

For more Hot titles from the author visit

www.mickimichelle.com

For information on booking the author for book signings, interviews, and other speaking events, contact:

MickiMichelle at mickimichel@live.com

www.ingramcontent.com/pod-product-compliance
Lightning Source LLC
Chambersburg PA
CBHW030403030726
47497CB00002B/455